LIKE THEY DO
IN THE MOVIES

Praise for Nan Campbell

The No Kiss Contract

"I absolutely adored *The No Kiss Contract* by Nan Campbell! From the moment I started reading, I was hooked. The writing is witty, the characters are relatable, and the story is filled with delightful surprises...Nan Campbell's storytelling is flawless, weaving together humor, heart, and found family moments in a way that kept me turning the pages long into the night. I just couldn't get enough. It's a must-read for anyone who loves a lighthearted, charming, and swoon-worthy second-chance romance."—*Station12Reads*

"This is an unputdownable fake dating meets second chance romance. It's a smooth, beautifully told love story with great chemistry, and a wonderful example of what family can and should be...The best part about Nan's work is her writing. There are fun facts sprinkled throughout, clever puns, and I especially love that she uses elevated language and themes, and trusts the reader to stick with it. I'm definitely along for the ride."—*QueerMediaReview*

"I was utterly swept into Davy and Anna's story. A beautiful second chance at love, battling through angst, unexpected family members, trampoline bouncing, and work drama. It's a brilliant masterpiece of a book and made me fall in love with second chance at love romances."—*ScottishLassBookReviewer*

"This book was slow-burn, filled with sexual tension and had really wonderful characters. I loved the way Davy and Anna's relationship played out, the instant family vibes with Louis, and the teenage dramatics of Tally. This book was written beautifully, and it had me not wanting to put it down."—*JessReadsWithPride*

Lambda Literary Award winner
The Rules of Forever

"This is one of those books where silence fills the air when you put it down because your brain is saturated with the characters' voices while reading. I loved it. Beautifully written with tons of interesting tidbits about art, literature, New York, and life. The characters were so well developed and I loved following both of their journeys. The tension that typically comes wasn't overly dramatic though it was gut-wrenching. I was totally rooting for these too and would be so happy to have just kept on reading about them."—*Queer Media Review*

"I needed this book. I won't say I have been in a slump, but it's been a while since I really liked and related to the main characters. Nan Campbell's debut book gives us two complex, well developed women. In a terrific balance of romantic chemistry, angst, and humor. I can't wait to read whatever she writes next."—*Odd Girls Media*

"I bought into *The Rules of Forever* hook, line and sinker. This is mainly because the characters are so likable…Besides well-developed characters, Campbell uses sound literary devices that give readers a romance they can count on but not find overly predictable. She charms readers with her delightful dialogue, entertaining subplots and engaging secondary characters. In addition to that, her use of conflict and sexual tension is masterfully done. Readers quickly become engrossed as well as captivated. The romance flourishes because of it." —*Women Using Words*

"This was such a fun story to read. Aside from the whole second chance arc, there's also the rich girl/poor girl storyline and while you think you know where the narrative is heading you'll be in for an interesting ride that seriously keeps the pages turning…This is an amazing debut for new author Nan Campbell and I can't wait to read her next."—*Bookista*

By the Author

The Rules of Forever

The No Kiss Contract

Like They Do in the Movies

Visit us at www.boldstrokesbooks.com

LIKE THEY DO IN THE MOVIES

by

Nan Campbell

2023

LIKE THEY DO IN THE MOVIES

ISBN 13: 978-1-63679-525-6

This Trade Paperback Original Is Published By
Bold Strokes Books, Inc.
P.O. Box 249
Valley Falls, NY 12185

First Edition: December 2023

CREDITS
Editor: Jenny Harmon
Production Design: Stacia Seaman
Cover Design by Inkspiral Design

Acknowledgments

One of my most beloved tropes is a Hollywood romance. Who doesn't love a story that includes the magic and moxie of the entertainment business? When I fully embraced writing Sapphic romance, I knew I had to try my hand at setting a sweeping tale against the backdrop of sound stages, movie studios, and luxury Los Angeles real estate. For my first story that isn't set in the NYC tri-state area, I did a ton of research and really enjoyed portraying a place that was unfamiliar to me. I just may have to conjure another tale set in the Southern California sun!

I owe many thanks to Radclyffe, Sandy, and everyone at Bold Strokes Books. Thank you to Ruth for the marketing help, Toni for her ebook magic, and Inkspiral Design for this fantastic cover. My editor, Jenny, puts up with all my grammatical foibles with grace and humor, and makes my writing exponentially better. I truly feel like she has my back. Thanks to the Writing Sprints crew, who are the best with camaraderie, advice, and motivation.

My beta readers, Michele Brower, Rita Potter, and Cade Haddock Strong, graciously read and commented on a rough, incomplete version of this novel, and—as always—their unvarnished input has improved this book in many ways. I appreciate you three so much! Location experts Beth Atkins and Jane Ragasa answered all my questions about the intricacies of living in Los Angeles and helped me decide which neighborhoods were appropriate for my characters.

I am indebted to my family for all their support. My three sisters are always up for distracting me when I need a break but are also quick to tell me to get back to the writing. Thanks also to two Janes: Jane Austen and my niece, Janie. Her *Pride and Prejudice* summer reading assignment reminded me just how long I've been a fan of romance (since I was her age).

My extraordinarily busy wife is more supportive than I deserve, and even took a week's vacation to join me on a research trip to Los Angeles. June, you're awesome for being so willing to accompany me on all the new adventures my writing has brought into our lives, like driving pretty much the entire length of Mulholland Drive in order to find the perfect view for my characters! I am so lucky to have you!

And finally, thanks to everyone who has read one of my books and reached out with a review or some words of encouragement. I'm very grateful to be a part of such a supportive reading and writing community, and your kind words help me meet my writing goals and fuel my inspiration!

For June
The only person I want to be stuck in Los Angeles traffic with

CHAPTER ONE

Fran Underhill refreshed all her social media accounts and scrolled. Friday afternoon was typically a slow celebrity news day, but there had to be something she could turn into a post that would garner a few clicks. A snappy headline, some suggestive images, and five hundred words were all she needed to round out a miserable week churning out garbage for intravenousgossip.com.

This is what she had been reduced to. Two hundred bucks a post freelancing for a *news* website that did not remotely fit the definition of news. What constituted news on this website was definitely not fit to print, and if somebody wanted to waste the paper, better it be used to wrap fish or line birdcages. This was not news. It didn't matter that the posts attributed to her avatar, F. Ulysses, regularly attracted many thousands of views. Regurgitating some publicist's press release into a clickbaity vehicle for online ads was not journalism. And that was fine by Fran because she wasn't a journalist. She was a writer.

And what pissed her off the most about the way she currently earned her living was that it benefited a class of people she had come to despise—celebrities.

It hadn't always been this way. She had been as starry-eyed as any other young hopeful arriving at LAX with a little bit of money and a dream, convinced she would make her fortune by spinning words into moving images projected onscreen. Now, eight years later, the realities of trying to make it as a screenwriter had ground her foolish dreams into a fine powder. But as her phone buzzed in her hand, she conceded there were still a few nuggets of hope lodged within the dust.

It was her agent—finally. She tapped connect before the second ring. She'd only gotten to this stage once before with any of her previous screenplays, and the contract for this one was contingent on the rewrite she had handed in three days ago. "Kevin, tell me something good." When he didn't immediately launch into a verbal list of bullet points without stopping for breath, Fran knew it was bad news. But then, it was always bad news.

"They're not moving forward with your script." Kevin's voice was heavy, his usually upbeat attitude not present today.

She clenched the phone tighter. "Why?"

"Why? You know why." He sounded like he was trying to keep his exasperation in check. "It's the same reason as all the others. Nobody's making romantic comedies for the big screen, and they sure as hell aren't making them with two female leads."

"But they were interested! You said they were."

"Yeah, they were. You're a helluva writer. It's a solid script. They thought they could get one of the streamers interested, but you refused to be flexible about a few minor details, so they're walking away."

"Changing one of my lead characters from Marcia to Mark is not minor!" Fran began to pace the narrow channel between her bed and her desk.

"Your rewrite ignored the one note they gave you. That was a deal breaker."

"It's not my fault if you led them to believe I was willing to turn my story into some heteronormative drivel that's just like every other romantic comedy out there. There are a million films where the woman falls in love with a dude, but mine is not going to be one of them!"

"And I'm walking away too."

"This is bullshit. Hollywood claims it's all about representation, but—what did you say?" She stopped pacing.

Kevin's voice was quiet. "I can't do it, Fran. I could sell any one of your scripts if you'd make them more mainstream. I'm not going to waste my time on this anymore."

"Waste your—you're dropping me?" Fran swallowed the lump that arose in her throat. "I thought you believed in me." She hated how her voice went all high and plaintive.

"I do. You know I do. I want more queer representation just as much as you do, but the gatekeepers at the studios are not willing to invest in stories like yours right now. I'm sorry. Give me a call if you write anything that'll appeal to a wider audience, and I'll take a look. Promise. Take care of yourself."

A wider audience? Fran threw her phone down on the bed and stalked to the kitchen. Her screenplay was good. And love stories were universal. Add in the comedy and who wasn't going to like it? This story *would* appeal to a wider audience if it could ever appear before one. She'd been so hopeful when Kevin had distributed this latest script to all the production companies in town and immediately got back a few nibbles. But every last one of them wanted the same change, and Fran simply couldn't do it. She had sold her soul once before, had done the rewrites and changed the genders as requested, immediately regretted it, and the deal had fallen apart anyway. The celebrity asshole who had promised the moon lost interest and the project had languished in turnaround. It had ultimately been a good thing. She wouldn't have been able to live with herself if the picture had been made. And now she was resolved to never alter the genders in any of her scripts in order to cash in.

She sank onto a stool at the breakfast bar with her cold cup of coffee to consider her plight. Back to square one again, no prospects and now no agent, no different than when she had arrived in Los Angeles years ago. Only this time, she had less money than what she had arrived with. The upkeep on a Los Angeles life didn't come cheap.

The door slammed. "Anybody home?"

Fran's often-absent roommate Trina stood about fifteen feet away, and Fran was clearly visible to her in their tiny open concept apartment.

"In the kitchen," Fran called out. They both giggled at their idiotic inside joke. Trina could cheer Fran up without even trying. She was the personal assistant for a mega-celebrity. Maybe she had some good stories that would distract Fran from her shitty news. "Did you just get back?"

"Yep. Straight from the airport." Trina put her dark curls into a ponytail.

"How was Croatia?" Fran grabbed another mug from the cupboard and waggled it at Trina.

"Yes, please." She sat at the breakfast bar. "It was great, right up until I got fired."

"Not again."

"Yeah, the entitled prick. He waited until we were ten minutes from landing in Van Nuys to do it, too."

"What was it this time?" Fran set the mug in front of her.

"He changed the password on his laptop and got mad at me for not knowing it." Trina grimaced after she took a sip and pushed it away.

"What? Not hot enough?"

"Bleh." Trina stuck her tongue out. "I don't like to chew my coffee before swallowing."

Fran dumped it in the sink and started a fresh pot. "I don't get it. Why do you put up with him? He's got this saintly image where he's talking up the endangered migration patterns of sea turtles between multimillion-dollar paychecks. At the same time, he's a complete dick to you. Not to mention, he's a talentless hack."

Trina's smile was a picture of patience and perception. "Let me guess, F. Ulysses posted about his sea turtle initiative."

"Of course I did. He's guaranteed clicks. It's hard to bring the snark when you're talking about a cute sea turtle, though. By the way, you should tell him to get someone to spellcheck those press releases before they get sent out."

"Not my job anymore—at least for the time being."

"You think he'll come crawling back?"

Trina shrugged. "It'll take him too much effort to break in someone new."

"It's that phrase *break in* that concerns me." Fran put her own mug in the sink. "Would you even want to continue working for him? He's terrible to you."

"The money's great. You know my mom and dad depend on me to send a good chunk of my paycheck home. And at this point I know how to deal with him. Why wouldn't I?"

"But wouldn't you like the world to know what an arrogant ass he is? His public persona is a gigantic fraud. And they're all like that."

"Who's all like that?"

"All these celebrities I waste my life writing about. They all show one face to the public while behaving in a completely opposite way in private. Don't you want to tell the world what he's really like?"

"Even if I did, which I don't, there's a little thing called an NDA that I've signed."

"Damn. I forgot about the NDA." Fran thought about it

for a moment. "I haven't signed one. I could write about it for intravenousgossip. My editor would probably name all their children after me if I did."

"While I enjoy the image of a bunch of tiny F. Ulysseses biting at the ankles of your scary boss, if you did that, I'd be sued six ways to Sunday. And I really won't get my job back."

Fran took the stool beside her and nudged her with her shoulder. "You know I won't. Maybe I should start investigating some other celebrity. They're all fake as hell. I could really tear the mask off one of them and boot them off whatever pedestal they've taken residence on."

"Doesn't sound like you. Some of the funnest nights in this apartment are when you invite a bunch of actors over to read scenes from whatever screenplay you're working on. You love actors. You have a ton of actor friends."

Fran nodded. "My friends are actors. They help me bring my stories to life. My day job is writing about *celebrities*."

"I don't really see a difference. And isn't it their job to be fake?"

"Anybody can be fake, but celebrities raise it to an art form."

"Fran." Trina looked her dead in the eye. "When one of your screenplays gets optioned, you're going to want the biggest celebrity you can get to act in it."

"That has yet to happen." And Fran now feared it never would. "The only thing that's paying my bills are my gossip posts, and it's not nearly enough. I'm sick of making a pittance by amplifying the talking points of celebrities who have a fragrance to sell or a collab to promote. I need to figure out a way to make my editor sit up and take notice—and raise my per word rate."

Trina frowned. "I thought the gossip gig was temporary. Wasn't there some interest in your last script?"

"Not happening." Fran's shoulders slumped. "Same old story. There's no money in two women falling in love and living long enough to be happy about it. And I just lost my agent, so this temporary gig is my only source of income." Fran didn't mention she had never earned any money from her real writing, which was a thought that drove her closer to despair every time she was forced to confront it.

"Kevin dropped you? That really, really sucks, Fran. I'm sorry. What are you going to do?"

"Drink. It's just about happy hour, isn't it? Care to join me?

There's some vodka in the freezer, or we could crack open that bottle of Clase Azul you got from the entitled prick for Christmas? Drown our sorrows together?"

"Sure, I've got no one to stay sober for right now. Let me just take a quick shower. I smell like airplane."

"I thought private planes had showers."

"They do. The one I just flew in had two." Trina stood.

"Let me guess…"

"Yeah. He wouldn't let anyone else use them."

Fran shook her head.

"The money is worth it." Trina seemed to say it more to herself than to Fran. "Hey, if my phone rings, would you answer it? I don't want to miss his call when it comes. And it's going to come. The guy can't survive without me. Just tell him I'll call him right back." She put her phone on the counter and rolled her luggage toward her bedroom.

"You got it." Fran checked to see if they had any limes in the fridge. A couple of shriveled-up old ones, but they'd do. The water began to run in the shower, and it was a testament to how small their apartment was that Fran could hear Trina's groan of relief when she stepped under the spray. Trina's phone rang, and Fran scooped it up without looking to see who it was. "Trina Carson's phone. How may I direct your call?"

There was a pause, and then a woman's voice. "Is this Trina?"

"No, this is Fran. Trina is indisposed at the moment but I'm authorized to speak on her behalf." She grabbed a pen and wrote the number down on the back of an envelope, then kept the pen poised to take notes. It was a habit she'd acquired when she started writing gossip.

Another pause. "All right. My name is Joyce Adler and I'm a talent manager. I heard Trina is currently without employment and I wanted to know if she's interested in a personal assistant position with one of my clients."

"Wow. That news traveled fast." The tone for an incoming text sounded. And then again. Trina's phone was beginning to blow up.

"You know how they say *good help is hard to find?* Well, it's true. Her reputation precedes her," Joyce Adler said over the buzz of constant text alerts.

"She's the best." Another call beeped in Fran's ear. "I have your number. I'll have her call you ASAP."

"Time is of the essence—"

"Got it, Joyce. She'll get back to you." Fran ignored the texts and connected the incoming call.

It was a harsh male voice. "Trina, I need you back here. Why aren't you answering my texts? Where the fuck are you?" The entitled prick himself.

"Trina's phone, who's calling please?"

"Who the fuck is this? Where's Trina?"

"Do you mean Trina Carson, who is currently unemployed but already fielding calls for new opportunities?"

"Fielding calls?"

"She's in demand, bro. The word is out that she's available."

That shut him up—momentarily. "Shit."

"You might have to cough up a skosh more dough if you want her back." Fran was starting to enjoy this.

"Who is this?"

"And a polite apology wouldn't go amiss, now would it?"

"Okay." Much more subdued. "Message received. Would you put her on, please?"

"Listen to that! *Please!* Your mother would be so proud. I will have Trina call you right back, but I'll know if you start forgetting your manners again. So you'd better straighten your ass up, you hear me?" Suddenly the phone disappeared from Fran's hand, plucked by Trina, still wet and wrapped in a towel.

"Hey. What's up?" Trina's death glare at Fran transformed into the round eyes of astonishment as she listened to her ex-boss. "I-I accept your apology…Yes, three years next month…I agree. It is about time for a raise…that sounds fair…Okay. I'm on my way."

Fran tried to make her grin not too shit-eating as Trina stared at her phone in disbelief.

"You got me a raise, Fran."

"You deserve it."

"And he apologized. He's never done that—ever."

"Well, that's just wrong." Fran wondered if she should ask her next question. "I know it's a bit indelicate, but how much does he pay you?"

When Trina told her, she almost slid off her stool. And then she had an idea. And then another idea on top of that one. The wheels started to turn so fast she didn't pause to consider the ramifications of any of it. "Somebody else called right before your newly restored boss."

"Yeah? Who?"

Fran filled Trina in on Joyce Adler's predicament. "Have you heard of her?"

"Yeah. She's Beau Dunlap's manager, I think."

"Since you're back with Entitled Prick, would you mind if I called her and put my name forward for the position?"

Trina darted a surprised look her way. "You want to be a personal assistant?"

"Maybe it's time for a change. Screenwriting's not working out, obviously." Fran directed her gaze over Trina's shoulder as her brows lowered in suspicion. "So, you know, maybe I could make some money doing this."

"What about your freelance gossip stuff?"

"Hmm, yeah. I don't know. Time for a break?" Fran tried to project the innocence of puppies, kittens, and white middle-aged tax evaders.

"My job is hard," Trina warned her.

"I have a college degree, just like you do. If you can do it, I can too. I have a brain in my head and a working familiarity with common sense."

"Pfft. Right. You have no idea what you're in for. If you wanted to be a personal assistant, I could have helped you years ago. Why now?"

"I hadn't been dropped by my agent years ago." She looked anywhere but at Trina.

"No." Trina was definitely not buying it. "You're doing that shifty-eyed business. Something else is going on here, Franny. What are you up to?"

Fran had to level with her. "Look, I came out to LA because no one loves the movies more than me. I used to really love this town. It's where dreams come true and stories become real, but my enthusiasm has"—with her finger, she mimed a missile nosediving into the kitchen counter with accompanying explosion sound effects—"cratered. Nothing has gone my way, and I don't want to be on the outside looking in anymore. You can't deny that there is an appetite for celebrity backlash, and Dunlap seems like a good candidate. If I can't sell a screenplay at least I can make some money exposing him."

Trina's mouth dropped open. "You don't even know that he's done anything wrong!"

"He doesn't have to do anything wrong. He's already all over celebrity media. Pics of him—and that ex-wife of his—are a near constant. It's clear he welcomes the attention. And he's profiting from a system that props up unreasonable standards of…just about everything. It's time to sacrifice one of the herd so the rest can thrive."

"That makes absolutely no sense. What if he isn't the client she was talking about?"

Fran shrugged. "Doesn't matter. This is the way the game is played, isn't it? People who make their living in this industry know that going in. They need the entertainment media just as much as the entertainment media needs them, and there's no such thing as bad publicity— "

"That's not strictly true," Trina muttered.

"Think about how easy it'll be." Fran barely heard her objection. "I get in there, I assemble a few stories about how they're out of touch with reality, they treat their staff like shit, they're addicted to…whatever. Boom. Page views will go through the roof, as will my advertised rate. My editor will eat it up."

"The posts you write as F. Ulysses are funny and heavy on the irony, but they're never really malicious—and they're based in truth. I feel like you're turning on the thing you love."

Fran tried to control her indignation. "I don't love celebrity gossip!"

"But you do love the movie industry. Why would you throw someone who's a part of it to the gossip wolves?"

Fran avoided her gaze. All she knew was if she couldn't satisfy her creative goals in this town, she should at least make some money from it, like everyone else. "Do I have your permission to call Joyce Adler?"

"Knock yourself out. I doubt you'll get past the first interview."

"We'll see."

CHAPTER TWO

Chelsea Cartwright peered at her phone and watched what had to be the worst job interview in history.

"So, yeah, I'd really like this job? But I do have a few non-negs." The young woman's eyes were glued to her own phone as she spoke.

"Non-negs?" Joyce's voice prompted her. Chelsea could see the interviewee through Joyce's FaceTime window. The young woman's interview outfit consisted of Gucci sweatpants, a tank top, and plastic slides that looked appropriate for a communal shower.

"Yeah, that means non-negotiables." Finally, she looked up from her phone and announced, "Hang on, I need my nicotine gum. I'm feeling a little L.E." She scrabbled in her designer handbag and popped four shiny square tablets from their blister pack. "That's low energy. It happens to me a lot," she added as all four went into her mouth. "It's a medical condition."

"I see." The picture wobbled and a second later a text appeared at the top of Chelsea's phone screen. *Do we need to see any more of this?*

I kind of want to know what her non-negs are, she texted back. It was scary-fascinating in the way that watching baboons mate was. This young woman seemed like a different species altogether, but in actual fact, she was a Bel Air college dropout with a father who had connections—an exec at TriStar, if Chelsea remembered correctly.

Joyce's sigh was audible. "What are your non-negs?"

As the young woman launched into a list of prior commitments and tasks she simply could not do, Chelsea sat in Joyce's office chair and wondered how she had arrived at this particular moment in her life. She resented that she had to be here choosing a new assistant. How could her old one have let her down so badly? How could Lorraine have been capable of such duplicity? And she also was a little dumbfounded at how much she had relied on her. It had been four days since Lorraine had admitted to informing photographers of Chelsea's schedule, and Chelsea's life had been a fecal typhoon ever since.

How did she replace someone who had been her right arm for going on six years? How did she get past the betrayal she felt? And how did she begin to trust the next person who took the job?

Chelsea's screen was dark. Joyce must have laid her phone down on the table. She could hear her escorting Nicotine Gum out of the conference room and a moment later, returning with the next candidate. "You're a friend of Trina Carson's, right?"

"That's right. Fran Underhill."

The laconic, low voice—devoid of Nicotine Gum's vocal fry— sounded much more businesslike and mature, and was instantly intriguing to Chelsea.

"Nice to meet you. We spoke yesterday when I called Trina, didn't we?" Joyce's phone swung wildly about for a few seconds before settling into the crook of her arm. Chelsea could see the blue silk of her sleeve at the bottom of the video chat window. Above that was a woman wearing a gray fitted T-shirt with *The Future Is Female* emblazoned on it. Didn't anyone dress up for interviews anymore?

"Yes." Fran Underhill gave Joyce an easy smile. She had a terrific smile. "You called during the extremely brief window of time when Trina was unemployed."

"Can't blame me for trying. I thought she might be ready for a change. I hear her boss does that often."

Fran lost the smile. "Too often, if you ask me." She had shoulder-length, shaggy dark hair and penetrating dark eyes. She seemed older than the other interviewees, maybe thirty or thereabouts, and expressed a quiet confidence. It showed in the way she sat back in her chair and crossed one dark denim-clad leg over the other, unwilling to fill the silence with nervous chatter as she waited for Joyce to say something. Chelsea leaned forward in Joyce's chair as if she could get closer to her.

"That shouldn't be a problem with this position. The last person in the role held on to it for five or six years," Joyce said.

Fran raised her eyebrows. "That certainly speaks well of your client. What happened to that last person?" She seemed comfortable asking the questions.

"That's a confidential matter. Speaking of…" Joyce wrested control of the interview back. "You would have to sign an ironclad NDA in order to work for my client. Any objection?"

"None at all. I'm the soul of discretion. I also have no issue with working nights, being around alcohol and people who imbibe, or working with powerful men, though my T-shirt might suggest otherwise."

The hell? What was this woman trying to say?

But Joyce had caught on. "I know my client roster is short, and easily google-able, but this job is not for the person you're probably thinking of."

Chelsea frowned. What's-her-name thought it was an interview for a job with Beau?

"No? Beau Dunlap is a talented guy. Mister My-muscles-are-enormous-and-my-brain-is-just-as-big." The woman in question sat up straighter in her chair. "My strengths are organization and time management. I would be an asset to someone as busy as he is." Something seemed false—canned—about this response. Chelsea held her phone closer.

"What if my client was not Beau Dunlap? What if it was Trevor Hasselblad?"

"I didn't know you represented him."

Joyce did not, in fact, represent him.

"He hasn't worked in a while, has he?" she continued. "He's a legend. He was around when they started making talkies, right? I thought he retired. If he needs assistance I would be happy to help."

Joyce queried her about two other actors she didn't represent before she said, "What if it was Chelsea Cartwright?"

She seemed to grow tired of the guessing game, and her smile became thin. "The patron saint of mom and girlfriend roles? She's very talented. Whoever it is, I can handle it."

Chelsea's hands clutched her phone tighter in annoyance. So what if she'd booked a few mom roles lately. It was still work, for God's sake. And it paid well.

Joyce picked up a piece of paper. "But you don't have any experience as a PA, Frances."

"Please call me Fran. That's true."

Yes, that was her name. Chelsea could see the corner of Fran's résumé in Joyce's hand.

"You seem to have held a variety of short-term jobs over the last several years—customer service, wait staff, retail—"

"I'm a screenwriter—well, was a screenwriter. Those are my day jobs. And before you ask, I don't have any credits."

"I wasn't going to ask."

Fran nodded. "If you need references, I can give you names and numbers. And if whoever is watching our interview on your phone wants to join us, by all means, let's get them in here." She looked right into the phone's camera when she said it. It was as if she had caught Chelsea doing something naughty, and her skin grew hot. "Maybe it'll speed things along."

Chelsea got up and left Joyce's office. She threw the conference room door open, and both Joyce and Fran turned to watch as she sat down. "Here I am. Saint Chelsea of the moms and girlfriends. In the flesh."

"Wow. Chelsea Cartwright. Your hair really is that color. Auburn doesn't really describe it. Not quite Titian either. Dark autumn flames maybe?" Fran closed her mouth with a click, as if she were trying to bite the words back into her mouth. "You're the client?"

"Yes." Chelsea smoothed her hair with one hand and waited for this woman to say something.

Fran leaned forward and put both elbows on the table. "I'm going to level with you. I've never done this kind of job before, but I think I can do it. I'll work hard for you. If you give me a chance to prove myself, I don't think you'll be disappointed." The woman's eyes bored into Chelsea like she could see right into her guts, but then a sly grin overtook her features. "And I just want to say that wives and girlfriends are some of my favorite fictional characters."

"You said moms a minute ago, not wives."

"I'll take all of them over a superhero any day. Give the juicy parts to the moms, wives, and girlfriends. Love to see them on any type of screen." The smile turned wolfish, and Chelsea could only stare into her dark eyes in return, at a loss for words.

"All right"—Joyce looked down at the résumé again—"Frances. We'll let you know."

"It's Fran. Frances is for official documents like résumés and tax returns." She stood and shook Chelsea's hand. Fran's grip was warm and strong and Chelsea found herself not wanting to let go. "I look forward to hearing from you."

She and Joyce watched Fran stroll from the room.

"That's all I could find on short notice," Joyce said. "Do you want to hold off until I can rustle up a few more candidates?"

Chelsea thought about it for a moment. She and Joyce both knew she was due on a new set soon and would need help. It wouldn't be Lorraine-caliber help, but she needed somebody.

From out in the hallway, someone shrieked, "Joyce! Joyce! Come quick!"

"That's my receptionist." Joyce lunged for the door.

They hurried into the waiting area and saw several people standing over Fran, who was kneeling and gently patting the cheek of the previous interviewee, the young woman with the non-negotiables. She was a crumpled heap on the floor, unresponsive, and with her mouth wide open.

The receptionist wrung her hands. "She didn't leave after her interview. She sat down and took a phone call. When she stood up, she fell right down."

Fran dragged a chair over and propped the girl's ankles onto it. "Let's get the blood to her head. Can someone get some water and possibly something to eat?"

The receptionist ran to the water cooler. Chelsea hurried to Joyce's office and brought back an apple and an orange from the fruit basket on the credenza. Fran was back at the girl's head, pulling up her eyelids and examining her eyes. She fished in her bag for some tissues and made a cold compress. It seemed like as soon as the cool tissue made contact with the girl's forehead, her eyelids began to flutter.

"What's her name?" Fran asked.

Chelsea had no idea. Joyce opened her mouth and closed it again.

"My name is Ashley," the girl moaned. Fran helped her sit up. The receptionist brought more water. All Chelsea could think to do was peel the orange.

"Take it easy, Ashley." Fran took the water and offered it to her. "How about taking a sip of water? When did you last eat?"

"Wednesday." Ashley drank from the plastic cup. She looked up at all the people who surrounded her. Her eyes widened when she saw Chelsea. "Oh my God. Chelsea Cartwright."

"You must be hungry if you haven't eaten in two days." Chelsea knelt and separated two segments from the orange and handed them to her. Out of the corner of her eye, she saw Fran nod approvingly at the exchange.

"I'm going to a premiere tomorrow," Ashley said, as if that explained everything. She ate one of the orange segments.

"Does she need an ambulance?" Joyce asked Fran.

"I don't know. Everything I know about first aid comes from TV and the movies," Fran answered. "Do you think you can sit in a chair? Do you want to go to the hospital?" She helped Ashley up. "I think you should at least eat some more." She nodded at Chelsea, and she gave her the rest of the orange.

When Chelsea tried to give her the apple, Ashley pushed it away. "I hate apples. I want to call my mom."

"Good idea," Fran said, and stood. Joyce handed Ashley her bag.

"Did I get the job?" Ashley asked as she rummaged for her phone.

Chelsea would let Joyce handle that question. Fran backed away from the crowd and pressed the elevator call button. Chelsea followed her. "You were very calm. I'm glad you were here for her. You should stay. I bet her mom would like to thank you."

"Can't. Got another interview to get to." The sly smile she gave Chelsea made her wonder if this was true. "I think she'll be fine. I heard her talking on the phone earlier. She's on some kind of ridiculous fast." She pointed at the apple Chelsea still held in her hands. "I don't hate apples. Can I have it?"

After Chelsea handed it over, she took a big bite, her dark eyes confident and amused. "Thanks." The elevator doors opened and she stepped in. "See you around."

Joyce joined Chelsea by the bank of elevators. The young girl was typing one-handed on her phone with half an orange in her other hand as they walked past on their way to Joyce's office. "The mom is on her way," Joyce said. "My receptionist will keep her company until then."

Chelsea flopped onto Joyce's sofa. "Good. When can she start?" She burst out laughing at Joyce's appalled expression.

"Poor Ashley. She's not yet acquainted with the real world. And you'd end up assisting her, I'll bet." Joyce sat beside her. "I think

The Future Is Female really is the standout today, but the lack of experience…What do you think?"

Chelsea considered Fran Underhill. Could she see herself spending a ton of time with her on a daily basis? The rest of her team had been with her a long time, and it had been years since she had to adjust to someone new. Fran was certainly the best option they had seen today, but how could Chelsea know if they would mesh, or whether she would grow to trust her? Chelsea couldn't even trust her own judgment of character right now. Still, she needed someone to help run her schedule, and she needed her quickly. "Make her an offer."

CHAPTER THREE

Fran looked at the clock on her dashboard and sucked her teeth. She was supposed to be in Pacific Palisades at Chelsea Cartwright's home at six a.m., but it was ten past and she was stuck in traffic on the 405. She texted Joyce's number but didn't get a response, and had the sneaking suspicion it was her office landline anyway. At least she could use this time while she was at a standstill to text her editor and let them know what was happening.

She scrolled through her contacts and found Carmina Piranha. Everyone at intravenousgossip.com used a pseudonym. Fran didn't know her editor's real name, and didn't know their gender. She typed, *Just wanted to let you know I won't be posting regularly for a while.*

They answered almost instantly even though celebrity journalists weren't known to be early risers. *WTF! Why?*

Got a job as a personal assistant.

For who? Someone in the industry?

Yes. She put her phone down and inched her car forward about two feet.

When she picked it up again, her boss had texted one word: *Who?*

Not going to say. NDA, she replied.

You're still going to post. We can do it blind.

Fran's lip curled at the presumption. Still… *Maybe. It would have to be worth it.*

Carmina Piranha knew exactly what she was talking about. If it would pay off in clicks, Fran deserved a better per word rate.

The ellipsis bounced for a few seconds before Carmina's response appeared. *We can talk about it when you show me what you've got. How long will you need before you can post something?*

She nudged the accelerator again for a half second. *Not sure. A week or two?*

OK. Keep me informed.

Fran shoved her phone into the cup holder. Not one word about how they would miss her daily posts or anything like that. It was a cutthroat business and there would always be someone to fill the void she left. Truth be told, she was glad for the break, glad to be earning a decent wage instead of always hustling for the next post. But she was in a unique position right now and she could definitely capitalize on the access she would get as an employee of Chelsea Cartwright. Unbeknownst to her new boss, of course.

She smiled when she thought of their encounter on Friday. Chelsea Cartwright was hot. She was the biggest celebrity Fran had ever met—of course she was hot—but it went further than that. It was almost like her beauty was unreal. And that hair. How could a person even look like that? So perfect? Chelsea Cartwright had been an omnipresent fixture in entertainment for years—looming over Sunset Boulevard on billboards, plastered all over magazine covers, the works. But Fran hadn't seen one of her movies in a long time. Lately, the only place Fran had seen her was in the paparazzi pics posted by intravenousgossip.com on the regular.

She always appeared so harried and stressed in those posts. Fran knew that many paparazzi ambushes were the result of careful orchestration, usually by a celebrity's publicist, and that was probably true with Chelsea Cartwright. Just went to show how good an actor she was when almost all the pap shots showed her looking all pinched and pissed off.

Fran shook her head. That look on Chelsea's face as she got on the elevator. Was that a spark of interest in those famous green eyes? Had they shared a *moment*? Fran could swear they had. But that couldn't be, could it? She'd never heard even a rumor that Chelsea was queer, and she shouldn't be thinking like that anyway. No moments allowed with the new boss. *Focus on getting there as quickly as you can! The early bird catches the worm!*

She craned her neck in the hope of seeing some movement ahead. She was definitely not the early bird today. But worms had to be available at all times of day. Birds didn't only eat in the morning, right? What was the rush? And who the hell wanted a damn worm anyway?

Finally, traffic started moving again. Even if her reasons for taking the job were spurious, she didn't want to get fired on the first day for being late.

Stupid worms.

❖

The winding road Fran had followed for the past ten minutes had been gaining in altitude and featured lots of privacy hedges. At Chelsea's address, there was a solid iron gate that was enshrouded in professionally unkempt greenery, almost obscuring the intercom she had to buzz to gain entry. When she pulled onto the sprawling property, Joyce Adler was standing in the circular drive in front of an enormous Spanish mission revival-style home, which was surrounded by sumptuous landscaping and a high stone wall. There was something about it that reminded Fran of a sunny, Southern California version of the Corleone compound from *The Godfather*. Joyce pointed to a narrow space next to a multi-car garage and Fran maneuvered her ten-year-old Sentra into it.

"You're late."

Tell me something I don't know. Starting on the back foot. Not exactly making a good impression. "It was the 405. An overturned trac—"

"There's always traffic. Figure it out." Joyce handed her an iPhone in a bright orange case and charged into the house. Fran had to jog to keep up. "That has all the numbers you'll need and the calendar that we all have access to. Do not forget to keep it updated. Even the smallest thing goes into the calendar. Got it?"

"Yes." Fran took a closer look at the phone. The bright orange case could probably be seen from miles away, and there was a small sticker of a ladybug right below the camera lenses. Cute.

"There are several files in the notes app with Chelsea's preferences and also the personnel she has regular contact with. Study it. Memorize it. You'll have a few light days before Chelsea is expected on set. You're going to have to pick things up quickly."

"Okay."

"You are the last line of defense. You handle absolutely everything you can before it gets to her. Your job is to make sure she's always able to do *her* job. You remove every distraction, every disturbance, any interruption or interference. You take all the noise out of the way so she can function to her highest level."

"Wait. Chelsea Cartwright didn't all of a sudden become a brain surgeon or president of the United States, did she? She's still just an actor, right?" Fran knew she shouldn't have said it the moment it left her mouth.

Joyce turned suddenly and Fran stopped short. She gave her a look so icy, Fran wished she had brought a sweater. "I'm not sure what that comment was supposed to convey. Your ability to deliver low quality sarcasm? Disrespect for your new employer? A general unpleasantness you'd like me to be aware you possess?" Joyce sniffed as she gave Fran a head-to-toe inspection. "Whatever it was, you should think twice before biting the hand that feeds you, hmm?"

"You're right. Sorry." *Dumb! You're showing your hand already.* It would be utterly stupid for Fran to reveal her bias against celebrities like Chelsea this soon into her covert operation.

"I have some documents for you to sign. Then I'll be on my way." She laid out two copies each of the employment contract and the NDA on the kitchen counter. "Any questions?"

"About what?" Fran bent and signed without reading them. She'd go over them later.

Joyce rolled her eyes. "The job. Now that you're here, I can get on with the trillion things on my calendar." She handed Fran one of each and stuffed the others in her briefcase.

"You're leaving?"

"Job starts now, sunshine." Joyce checked her watch. "It's 7:20. You're expected to be here by six a.m. It's all in the calendar."

Fran looked at the phone in her hand. "What's the passcode?"

Joyce shrugged. "Try one two three four or whatever."

It didn't work. She tried pressing one a bunch of times. That worked. "I'm in."

"Good. I'm sure I'll be talking to you soon." Ten seconds later, Fran was by herself in the enormous kitchen. It was your standard rich person's kitchen. The morning light coming through the wall of windows was golden and gorgeous. Fran slid the glass door open and walked out into Eden, the focal point of which was a cool sapphire-blue pool. Off to the left side was a structure in the same mission style—possibly a guest house—and to the right was lush greenery that dissolved into the steep, heavily wooded hills of what was probably Topanga State Park. Right in front of her, beyond the pool and down a gently sloped lawn, was a panoramic view of the Pacific Ocean. Fran was pulled toward it in a way that was almost involuntary. At the edge of the property there was a low wall that didn't impede the view, and once she got past the guest house, she could see the Santa Monica Pier and all the way to downtown, glinting hazily in the distance. At this height, there were a few houses below Chelsea's property, but nothing above. It was just about perfect as far as high-end Los Angeles real estate went.

She turned and gazed at the Cartwright home from the back. It was distinctly different from the luxury real estate Fran had seen in glossy shelter magazines over the years. It wasn't one of those stereotypically modern showplaces that lined the shore with wide-open access to the beach and the ever-present sound of the roaring surf. The house was like Don Corleone himself—ever alert to possible danger and situated with its shoulder to the wall, or in this case, tree-covered hillside. This property—while as beautiful as anything Fran had ever seen—was all about protection.

After a last lingering gaze at the view, Fran returned inside. She opened the calendar app and saw fifteen-minute segments shaded in pale green for the first two hours of the day. She'd already missed five—whoops, now six segments, so far. She clicked on 7:30 a.m. Breakfast—two shots espresso with warmed oat milk, one soft boiled egg, Lorraine smoothie. *Do I do this? That's not what an assistant does, is it?* She put the orange phone down and grabbed her own phone.

Hey, she texted Trina. *Am I supposed to make her breakfast?*
Trina texted back right away. *Did she ask you to?*
I haven't seen her. Do you make EP breakfast?
EP? Trina followed that with a shruggy emoji.
Entitled Prick. She exhaled. Jesus. Keep up, Trina.
If he wants me to. I do whatever he wants. THAT'S MY JOB!
"Okay, okay. You don't have to yell," Fran mumbled.

"Who are you talking to?"

Fran turned to see a boy of around eight years old. He was either one of the kids or a very short security guard.

"Myself. I'm Fran. Who're you?"

"I'm Forge."

"Forge?" As in, where hot metal gets turned into sharp pointy things? What kind of name...

"Yeah."

"Nice to meet you, Forge."

"What are you doing in my house?" He opened a floor to ceiling cabinet next to the fridge and pulled out an enormous rainbow-colored lollipop. It was nearly as big as his head.

"I work for your mother. It's my first day. Hey, you don't by any chance represent the lollipop guild, do you?"

Forge tilted his head in confusion. "The what?"

"Never mind. Do you know where your mom is?"

"Upstairs."

A girl of maybe thirteen or fourteen stepped into the kitchen. "Mom said we aren't allowed to eat anything Dad sent us yet, Forge. She'll be mad."

"I'm not going to eat it. I want to show it to everybody." He gazed at the candy as if it were his new best friend.

The girl gave Fran the hairiest of eyeballs and asked, "Are you the new Lorraine?"

"I'm Fran. Not new. Been around thirty-one years. And you are?"

The girl didn't answer, just continued to stare in that sullen teenage way.

A young woman carrying two backpacks entered the kitchen. "You're not taking that to school, Forge. Put it back." She turned to Fran. "Hi, I'm Bernice. I'm here four days a week. Colleen is here the other three." *Two nannies?* Bernice put a hand on the girl's shoulder. "She's Petal. A little grumpy in the mornings." Bernice offered a welcoming smile and grabbed two bags out of the fridge. "We're off to school. Good luck."

All three were out the door in two shakes.

Fran poked around the spotless kitchen, found a small saucepan, and dropped an egg into it. There was a complicated coffee station that came with a laminated instruction sheet, so she did her best with

Chelsea's coffee order. She gazed at the cup, steam rising from it. *Better go bring it to her.*

She mounted the stairs, treading heavily so she wouldn't surprise her new boss. It felt absolutely wrong to be wandering around in Chelsea Cartwright's home. She turned right at the top of the stairs and looked into the open doors of children's rooms and guest rooms, what looked like an office—all unoccupied. She backtracked to what had to be the primary suite and knocked. No answer. Fran stood there, undecided. Was she supposed to enter Chelsea Cartwright's bedroom?

The door swung open and Chelsea Cartwright stood there. The sun streaming in the windows behind her haloed her auburn hair so that it seemed tipped with fire. The coffee cup rattled in its saucer as Fran took in the faded T-shirt, the yoga pants, and the absence of makeup. Chelsea Cartwright fresh out of bed still looked better than ninety-nine point seven percent of humanity.

"Good morning. Sorry I'm late." She held out the cup and saucer.

Chelsea's eyebrows dipped in what might have been distrust and was definitely displeasure.

"I'm Fran, your new assistant. Remember?"

"I'll take that in the kitchen."

"Right." Fran stood aside and followed Chelsea. As she settled into a chair at the table, placing a well-thumbed manuscript off to the side, Fran set the coffee down and went to see to the egg. She found a cute little tulip-shaped eggcup in the cupboard above the stove and set it on a plate with a spoon. She was psyched that she was able to fish the egg out of the boiling water and slide it into the cup like she was on a cooking show and hoped Chelsea was watching, but she wasn't. When she brought it to the table, Chelsea looked up from her phone.

"Sit down, please."

Fran sat. "Like I said, I'm sorry I was late on the first day. It won't happen again. There's something called a Lorraine smoothie on your breakfast order, but I don't know what that is. If you tell me the ingredients, I'll try to make it."

"Spinach, kale, usually berries of some kind…there'll be a list of fruits and vegetables that my nutritionist gave me, probably in the desk drawer in the kitchen if it's not on your phone." Chelsea's expression turned mournful. "I don't know how she made it. I just know it was the perfect way to start the day."

"Oh. Maybe I can ask Lorraine. Does she cook your food or something?" She picked up the orange phone and scrolled through the contacts. "She'd be able to tell me."

"If you tried to call Lorraine, you'd be calling that phone." Chelsea pointed to the phone in Fran's hand. "She's my former assistant. And you are not to contact her. Just look up a recipe online and make that— for tomorrow. Make sure it has more greens than fruit. No bananas. And no added sugar in any form. Don't deviate from the approved list. The egg will be enough for today."

Fran took notes on the orange phone but stopped when the tone of Chelsea's voice went from dictating facts to a softer, more wistful quality.

"I was with my former assistant a long time. It might take a while for you and me to get a rhythm going, and if I call you Lorraine, I sincerely apologize." She stood and retrieved a steak knife from the drawer, using it to slice the top of the egg, shell and all. Steam rose from the pate of the severed egg, and Chelsea dashed it with a saltshaker before scooping out some of the white and the yolk, which was hard-cooked and chalky-looking. She made a face and set it on the plate.

"Whoops. Is it overdone?"

"It's not your fault. Lorraine's cooking skill was a side benefit I got used to. Anyway, I don't expect you to know everything on day one."

"Are you sure I can't talk to her? Maybe just get a day or two of tips and training?"

Chelsea shook her head, her expression closed off. "That's not a good idea."

Fran leaned in closer. There was a potential story here; she could smell it. Chelsea wouldn't be so opposed to it if there weren't. "If you want me to do my job properly, I should know this. Don't you think?" She decided to push a little. "Why did your former assistant leave?"

Chelsea shut her eyes for a moment, in annoyance, or irritation, Fran couldn't tell which. When she opened them, melancholy seemed the most pronounced emotion. Fran wondered if Chelsea was acting right now, but her manner appeared to be entirely genuine. Whether the sadness she was projecting was put on or not, it made Fran feel bad, but Chelsea spoke before she could retract the question.

"Despite my profession, I'm a very private person. But my privacy disappeared when circumstances in my life changed a few years ago and the entertainment press became very interested in my family and me."

She had to be talking about the end of her marriage to Beau Dunlap. It had been all over every entertainment news outlet for months. It still was, but to a lesser degree.

"We had round-the-clock security for some time, but that's no way to live for anyone. Eventually, some other story came along and my ex-husband and I were no longer the absolute main focus of the entertainment news cycle, and things got better. And then got worse again. Swarms of photographers everywhere I went, every time I went out, even with my *children*. It got to be dangerous. And it was Lorraine who was informing the press of my movements."

Fran frowned. "Really? Didn't you just say she was your employee for a long time? Why would she suddenly start doing that?"

"I don't know. I have to assume money became more important than our relationship." For a second, her face twisted in pain before it became opaque again.

There had to be a reason. Did Chelsea really not know or was she concealing the reason from Fran? "But—"

Chelsea touched her arm. Her eyes were an intense emerald. "My family and I haven't yet recovered from this, and I'm still hounded by photographers in my private life. And I'm telling you now—I will not allow this to happen again. I'm not a vengeful person, but if you betray my trust, my lawyers will come after you."

Message received. Chelsea seemed deadly serious, but her words felt like lines from a soap opera script. There was more to this story, and Fran was going to find out what it was.

Chelsea withdrew her hand and folded her arms across her chest. "Usually one of the first things we'll do is go over the day's schedule. We're a little behind today."

Fran took the hint and recited the day's appointments on the calendar. To her, it looked like there were only two real things Chelsea had to do today. Lunch at La Scala at noon with her agent and a few other people, and then a meeting at one of the studios at three. But every moment was scheduled with tasks—workouts, script prep, breathing mindfulness, which Fran surmised was as woo-woo as it sounded.

"What time will we leave for lunch?" Chelsea asked.

"Oh, I'm coming with you?" Fran felt foolish when she saw Chelsea's face.

"Of course. And you'll drive."

Fran guesstimated how long it would take to go from Pacific Palisades to Beverly Hills. "How about eleven forty-five?"

"Fifteen minutes, says the woman who was over an hour late today." Chelsea raised an eyebrow. "I'm known for my punctuality."

"Okay. Eleven thirty, then."

"That seems more reasonable. Plot it out in Google Maps just to be sure." Chelsea picked up her manuscript, and left the room. She hadn't touched anything Fran had prepared for her.

❖

Fran followed Chelsea outside when it was time for them to leave for the restaurant. She walked to her car but then adjusted her trajectory when she saw Chelsea headed toward the garage. *Duh.* Chelsea stepped up into the passenger side of a black Land Rover Defender, so Fran took the driver's seat. It was enormous, a little more rugged than she expected, and built like a tank.

"I hope you don't mind driving." Chelsea flipped the visor down and inspected her face in the tiny mirror. She looked spectacular. Not red carpet glamorous, but an everyday loveliness that was bright, friendly, and alluring. A girl-next-door who could also handily win beauty contests. Chelsea darted a glance her way and pointed to a fob sitting in the cup holder on the console.

Fran took a moment to get accustomed to the massive vehicle, and then backed out of the garage. "I don't mind driving. I might be the only person in LA who likes sitting in traffic. I welcome being alone with my thoughts."

Chelsea wasn't paying attention. She had grasped the door handle and the console with a white-knuckled grip. Fran glanced her way and saw that her jaw was clenched. She slowed the car to a stop as the automated gate that separated Chelsea's property from the street began to open.

"Are you okay?"

"Yes." Chelsea gave a forced laugh. "I don't drive much anymore, and I've become sort of a nervous passenger, too."

"I'll be careful. If it helps, I've never gotten a ticket." She didn't take her foot from the brake.

"It does help, thank you." Chelsea gave a small smile. "I haven't had to explain my driving anxiety in a while. I'm afraid you're going to have to get used to my quirks and strange habits." Her expression was rueful and shy almost.

Fran felt immediate empathy for her. "I guess that'll be a two-way street. I have quirks too."

Chelsea blew out a breath and placed her hands on her knees, making a visible effort to relax. "Let's go."

Fran proceeded slowly through the gate. She observed every speed limit and rule of the road on the way to the restaurant. When they arrived, they surrendered the car to the valet, and Fran watched as Chelsea legged it into the restaurant, ignoring the three or four photographers who stood near the entrance. La Scala was a known industry haunt, and these people probably hung around on the off chance that a celebrity would arrive and make it worth their while, but Chelsea had behaved like she was trying to escape a barrage of enemy fire.

Fran wasn't sure what she was supposed to do. An assistant wasn't expected to eat lunch with Chelsea and her companions, right? She stood awkwardly to the side of the entrance and checked the orange phone for messages that had come in while she drove. One was from the agent whom Chelsea was meeting, confirming his arrival. As she gazed at the screen, a text appeared from CC—Chelsea Cartwright.

Where are you?

I'm outside, Fran replied.

We've already been seated. Hurry up.

Okay. She was eating lunch with these people.

❖

Hours later, Chelsea tossed the fajita veggies in their sauté pan and covertly watched Fran at the kitchen table. Her new assistant stuck a tiny sword in the hand of an action figure and battled Forge's figure until his whacked her sword away with a light saber. She made the figure writhe on the table, dramatizing its painful-sounding death throes. Then the orange phone buzzed and she stood and wandered into the butler's pantry. "Be right back, Forge. Duty calls."

Fran had seemed to relax a bit over the course of the day, after her late arrival. Chelsea could tell she had been embarrassed, and her energy had been anxious and a bit pushy at breakfast. There was no need to master everything in the first minutes of the job, and Chelsea doubted Fran could learn much from Lorraine anyway. It was simply going to take some time. Fran would learn. And Forge seemed to like her. Petal didn't. But Petal didn't like anyone lately. *Including me.*

The day had gone relatively smoothly. Fran went MIA at the restaurant, but came immediately when Chelsea texted her. Later, back in the car, she said she didn't know she was supposed to sit and actually have lunch with Chelsea. Chelsea had explained that sometimes she wouldn't, but she'd let Fran know in advance if she wasn't needed and would often have a driver for those occasions. A working lunch like today's required Fran to take notes. Plus, Chelsea always felt a little more secure if she had someone she trusted sitting beside her. Not that she trusted Fran, but she was better than nothing.

That wasn't fair. She needed to be more charitable. Fran had been kind when Chelsea had her little freakout out in the car. And here she was, engaging with Forge when she really didn't have to.

Fran approached, her eyes on her phone. "Your agent received those two scripts you discussed. He's going to read them tonight and messenger them over tomorrow." She shoved the phone in her pocket and leaned against the counter.

"Thank you." She cleared her throat. "In the future, with places that have a valet, could you please make sure the car is right out front before we leave? I wasn't comfortable waiting for them to bring the car with those photographers there."

"Yeah, I'm sorry about that. I get how it wasn't ideal."

"There are websites that'll buy anything—even me going to a work lunch on an ordinary Monday. I'm sure they've already been posted."

"You're pretty interesting. I bet they'd love to know you ordered the chopped salad."

Chelsea focused on the sauté pan, pushing its contents around with a wooden spoon. "I'm really not, but bottom feeding websites like intravenousgossip.com go with the territory." She noticed Fran stiffen, her shoulders tense and arms rigid. What had Chelsea said?

"I'll do better next time. Promise." Fran pushed herself off the counter. "Do you need any help with dinner?"

She gazed at Fran in surprise. "That's not part of your job. And anyway, I like to cook."

"Good, because I hate it. I don't mind the eating part, though." Fran froze for a second. "Not that I want to eat your dinner. It smells great, but I wasn't inviting myself to your meal. I don't mind eating as a concept, but—I guess that would be pretty peculiar if I didn't like eating. I'd probably die."

"Yeah, you'd probably die." Forge snickered.

"Forge," Chelsea warned him.

"But she started acting like a fan. Babbling and all," he protested.

Fran reddened, but her smile was completely disarming. "Sorry about that. I almost made it the whole day without revealing the fact that I'm a little bit starstruck."

"You're fine. We'll see you tomorrow. Six sharp." She sent a quick text to the orange phone. "Those codes will open the gate and the front door. See you tomorrow."

❖

Fran opened two beers and handed one to Trina.

"How'd your first day go?" Trina asked.

"I learned I don't know how to boil an egg."

"Oh, no. Is she one of those three minutes and twelve seconds kind of people?" Trina took a sip from her bottle.

"Remains to be seen. I'll try and get some more details about how she likes it tomorrow, I guess."

"Is that going to be the subject of your first exposé? *Chelsea Cartwright insists on a jammy yolk.*" She held up her hands like she was picturing a newspaper headline.

"We'll see." Fran hadn't had much time to think about her gossip gig until Chelsea had mentioned it in the kitchen. At that moment, the cognitive dissonance of working for Chelsea while also being one of the *bottom feeders* she had mentioned had given her a little jolt.

In Chelsea's eyes, Fran was one of the bad guys. In Fran's other line of work, Chelsea was the bad guy—a mega-celebrity deserving of scorn. But was she? Well, not exactly. No, Chelsea wasn't a bad guy. But as the subject of so much media attention, she was a little unreal, or at least, she had been until today.

It made Fran's head hurt to think about the paradoxical component to her new job. She dropped onto the opposite end of the couch and gazed at Trina's cereal bowl, trying to decide if she should get some for herself. "She also smells unbelievably good—like nothing I've ever smelled before. I don't think it's a normal people smell."

"Probably a bespoke scent. Lots of celebs do that. Have you seen the Oscar yet?"

"Nope, and I'm not exactly snooping around for it." She was pretty sick of thinking about and talking about Chelsea Cartwright. "How was your day?"

"I hate when he's between jobs. He's got so much more time to think of ridiculous things for me to do."

"Like what?"

"I went through his closet, holding up one article of clothing after another, so he could decide what he wanted to keep—"

"And what he wants to give to charity?"

"Charity?" Trina scoffed. "He wants to auction it all off. Another thing I'll be put in charge of."

"He's not going to donate the proceeds to the sea turtles?"

"As you say, remains to be seen. What's Chelsea Cartwright up to these days?" Trina picked up the TV remote and navigated to one of the streaming platforms.

"She starts filming a role in a Netflix movie in a few days. It's called *The Chromium Conundrum*. She plays a mom, natch."

"Why is she doing all those moms? She's so hot. She should be, like, a sexy assassin or something. She's still got it."

"You don't have to tell me. I'm seeing it up close and in person."

Trina typed Chelsea's name into the search engine and the television show *Landon's Way* appeared first. "Ooh, let's watch that."

"Oh wow," Fran said. "All my friends from high school loved this show. They tried to get me into it."

"And Chelsea's so young in it. It had to be her first big role. But it didn't get good until later." Trina clicked on the first episode of the second season, and then forwarded to a scene that featured a youthful Chelsea, engaged in a blistering argument with her onscreen mother.

"She was awesome as Sabrina Butler. So fiery and rebellious. My first crush. I discovered it on cable like ten years after it was first on. How old do you think she is there?"

"I don't know, maybe eighteen, nineteen?" Fran leaned in to get a better look. "I remember this. Sophomore year, my friends and I would all go over someone's house and watch those weekend marathons. Two days straight of *Landon's Way*. All these little baby dykes living vicariously through her. They wanted Sabrina Butler to end up with her best friend. What was her name again?"

"Melody. Their ship name was Melbrina." Trina snorted. "Sabrina Butler had heaps more chemistry with Melody than she ever did with the love interest—that beefy, blond lunkhead."

Fran hadn't thought about *Landon's Way* in years. Her friends had been super into it; she was only interested in old movies. All the screwball comedies from the thirties and forties she could find. Irene Dunne, Carole Lombard, Myrna Loy—those were the women she looked up to, aspired to be like, dreamed of make-out sessions with—in her teens. Sometimes she even managed to convince her friends to watch one of those classic old movies, but they never appreciated them the way Fran did.

She watched as a young, agitated Chelsea Cartwright furiously tore down the road on a beat-up mountain bike, dropped it on her friend Melody's lawn, and ran into her house without even knocking on the door, interrupting her friend's dinner. She and Trina watched in rapt silence as the two girls climbed the stairs to Melody's room and cuddled together on her bed as Sabrina poured her troubles out.

Trina giggled. "This is so gay."

"In the best way possible," Fran added. The scene had more than a touch of Sapphism to it. Pent-up desire seemed to be written all over Chelsea's face, and it looked like her scene partner was just as caught up in youthful, wayward attraction. Had Chelsea been directed to play the scene that way?

"No wonder they killed off Melody at the end of season two. Can't have Chelsea, their breakout ingénue, lusting after her female costar now, can you?"

Fran took a long drink from her beer, suddenly thirsty. "So that's why all my friends wanted Chelsea Cartwright to be queer." She hadn't paid all that much attention back then.

"Maybe she is."

Fran didn't want to admit how exciting that would be. "Hollywood's paragon of wifeliness and motherhood? It seems a stretch."

"We all know how this town works. And wives and mothers can still be queer." Trina stood. "I'm going to bed, perchance to dream of my teenage self, gently cradling Sabrina Butler in my arms while she cries upon my bosom."

Fran frowned at Trina's retreating back, but then stayed up way too late fast-forwarding through a bunch more episodes of *Landon's Way*, pausing only when Chelsea Cartwright appeared on the screen.

CHAPTER FOUR

Chelsea sat on the sofa in the formal living room, a cashmere throw tucked around her legs to ward off the predawn chill. She'd had a restless night and had finally given up trying to sleep in favor of studying her upcoming role. Her script was on her lap, but she hadn't read a word.

It had been a week since Fran had started assisting, and the results had been decidedly mixed. In many aspects, Fran was doing all right. She was a careful driver, pleasant to be around, and friendly with household staff. There had been one or two problems with correspondence. She had emailed some documents to Chelsea's publicist instead of her lawyer, but had the error fixed as soon as she realized it. A couple of phone message mix-ups. Chelsea thought it was simply a matter of Fran not being familiar enough with the team of people Chelsea surrounded herself with, and that would right itself with time, because Fran certainly was not stupid. She had made a few incisive comments over the past few days, but mostly she stayed quiet and listened.

Chelsea could cope with these mistakes, but she could not cope with Fran's attempts at breakfast anymore. She hadn't realized how much she had taken advantage of Lorraine's penchant for cooking, or how talented her former assistant had been in the kitchen. Lorraine had enjoyed catering to her dietary needs far more than the administrative side of the job. It remained to be seen which parts of the job Fran would excel at, but the results of her food prep had been uniformly dismal.

A simple soft-boiled egg had not been prepared the same way twice, and the smoothies—Chelsea couldn't quite believe how bad they had been. None of the permutations of fruit and veg Fran had tried had been edible. The last one had tasted like wet chalk with tiny little buds of broccoli floating throughout that gave it a crunchy texture. She shuddered at the memory. The breakfast routine was definitely not working.

Still, she liked Fran, believed she was trying her best. And she felt safe with her, which was the most important thing.

Fran had an old-fashioned courtliness about her, which showed up in little gestures like a brief hand on the elbow as she guided Chelsea through a busy lobby. She always opened Chelsea's car door for her and darted a glance at Chelsea's seat belt before putting the car in gear. She was never without that charming smile, which Chelsea was growing to like very much. The fact that she was very easy on the eyes, and had Chelsea noticing her—a woman—in a sensual way was something she had tried to avoid thinking about.

And by trying to avoid objectifying Fran, it was now all that occupied Chelsea's brain. She had noticed Fran's hands at various moments over the course of the week. Once during a particularly tedious meeting, she had studied Fran's fingers as they cradled her phone, her thumbs flying over the keyboard as she seemed to record every word that was said. Slim and dexterous, with blunt, polish-free nails. Chelsea detested the word *shapely*, but it came to mind. How could fingers be shapely?

And her eyebrows. They were dark and thick and not plucked and shaped within an inch of their lives, as Chelsea's were and had been since the nineties. They looked natural and framed Fran's face in an attractive way, a complement to her keen dark eyes. *What in God's name…?* She couldn't be caught ogling. She had never noticed Lorraine's hands or eyebrows before. Fran was an employee, for Pete's sake. Still, she hadn't taken notice of a woman—or anyone really—in the way she was noticing Fran's various body parts in a very long time. It was sort of surprising to know that part of her brain was still in working order.

At 5:55 a.m., the front door opened, and Fran entered. She stood in the foyer and looked at her phone, then started to walk toward the kitchen.

"Fran."

She halted and peered into the living room. "Chelsea? I'm not late, am I?"

"No, you're not late. Right on time. Come sit." Chelsea watched her come closer. A brown crewneck sweater accompanied her T-shirt and jeans today, and she wore no makeup, which could've covered up the deep shadows under her eyes. Why wasn't she getting enough sleep?

Fran sat in the Barcelona chair across from the sofa and hiked her shapely thumb toward the kitchen. "I thought I was supposed to—"

"Yes, in a bit." She ran a self-conscious hand over her face and hair. She probably had some pretty substantial bags under her own eyes. "I thought we might have a state of the state conversation. You've been here a week."

She placed the orange phone on her knee in preparation for taking notes.

"You won't need that."

Fran gave her an uncertain look and swept the phone against her stomach.

"In my anxiousness to get back into my regular routine, I haven't been fair to you. I don't think we're playing to your strengths. I think we need to figure out something different for the mornings now that you're here."

Fran's expression turned absolutely sheepish. "Is this about breakfast? I looked up a new smoothie recipe. I think this one's a winner. And I think I've almost got your boiled egg nailed."

"I like to cook. I think I told you that the other day. You've met Magda, who cooks part time, but I really only rely on her for the kids, for when I'm regularly going to the set and out of the house all day. Don't you think it's odd that a person like me, who says she enjoys cooking, doesn't make her own breakfast?"

Fran looked at the floor. "I know I'm not great at it yet—"

"My last assistant was a wiz in the kitchen, and she loved whipping things up for us. I'm now realizing that things had gotten a little unhealthy there. She'd been with me for years, and she saw me through a pretty rough patch. These past few years have been difficult, and she began to take on tasks that, I guess, were supposed to make me feel taken care of? She would come in and wake me so I wouldn't have to hear an annoying alarm. She sometimes laid out my clothes. She would prepare me for the day, so I could prepare my children for their days. And she made me breakfast, as if I were a child."

"It must have been a real betrayal when you found out what she was doing."

"It was. She is—was—wonderful. Mary Poppins, Mike Ditka, and *His Girl Friday* all rolled into one."

Fran gave her that easy smile. "I love that movie. Now I'm picturing Rosalind Russell, all competence and capability. How am I ever going to live up to that?"

"I want to be clear—I don't expect that from you. And you are officially relieved of breakfast duty."

Fran made an exaggerated wiping-the-sweat-from-her-brow gesture.

"This is the moment to establish some boundaries." Keeping it professional went without saying, but this was a new working relationship, and she could create something healthy and lasting with Fran. What that looked like, Chelsea was not sure of. "I leaned on Lorraine far too much. But she's gone, and you're here. I'd like to figure out between us how that will work. It's something we can both have input on."

Fran nodded.

"Any ideas?"

"This is your show, Chelsea. I'm brand new at this. I guess I just want to be treated like a human being."

"I hope I can manage that." It seemed like extremely low expectations to her. At least it was a starting point. "Let's make this an ongoing dialogue. If you're happy, that probably means I'll be happy. We should talk about the schedule. It's Thursday. That means it's legs and abs day. My trainer will be here soon."

"That sounds absolutely horrible."

Chelsea cast her eye over Fran's trim frame. "I bet you can eat anything and not gain an ounce. When you get to be old like me, you'll be doing all you can to keep the cellulite at bay."

Fran opened her mouth and then closed it.

It made Chelsea curious. "What?"

She shook her head. "I wouldn't want to violate the boundaries that were put in place"—Fran looked at her wrist and the invisible watch there—"four seconds ago."

"Now you've got to tell me."

"I was going to say"—she grimaced and spread her hands wide—

"you're the most beautiful person I've ever seen. But I thought it might embarrass you. It sure as hell is embarrassing me."

Chelsea couldn't help but laugh. She'd heard every type of flattery, so she wasn't taken in, but Fran certainly knew how to employ the charm. "One thing you're going to learn from being around actors—we love being told we look good. I'll never get tired of it."

"If it makes you laugh, I'll tell you every day. I wasn't being funny, though."

Chelsea stood and squeezed Fran's shoulder as she passed. "You're sweet. Let's have some coffee and talk about the day."

❖

Fran hefted the dry cleaning and brought it upstairs to Chelsea's closet, a spare bedroom that had been fitted with built-in hanging space and shelving. A good-sized portion of the space was empty, and Fran guessed that was where Beau had kept his clothes. She debated putting the dry cleaning there, but made room among Chelsea's things instead. She heard voices coming from the open door of Chelsea's bedroom.

"Is that The Future Is Female? Let's ask her." That was Joyce.

"Her name is Fran." Chelsea's voice. "Come here, Fran, please."

This was the first time Fran had entered Chelsea's bedroom, and she shouldn't have been surprised at how large it was. It was like a generous studio apartment with breathtaking views of the ocean. A king-size bed dominated one part of the room, and a settee and two easy chairs surrounded a large fireplace. Chelsea stood on an ottoman in a deep purple gown. Joyce gazed at Chelsea, a hand on her chin, while a blond woman, presumably a stylist, adjusted the full skirt. Petal sat on the window seat staring mulishly at her phone and Forge perched on one of the easy chairs with an orange tabby in his lap. Chelsea had a cat?

"What do you need?" Fran asked.

Petal turned baleful eyes to her, but then whined at her mother. "Why are we here? Why do I have to watch you try on stupid dresses?"

"I'm starting a new job soon. I know this isn't exactly fun, but I wanted to spend time with you, and as soon as we're done, we're going to make cookies." Chelsea spoke in a tone that Fran hadn't heard before, both gentle and firm at the same time. Her mom voice.

"Lemon meltaways?" Forge asked.

"Whatever kind you want."

"Yay! When we eat them, can we give Cheeto some milk?"

"Sure." Chelsea plucked at the side seam and tilted her head at her reflection. Forge cuddled with the cat, who seemed more than happy to accept his love. Petal muttered darkly and went back to her phone.

"Was there something you needed?" Fran asked again.

Chelsea turned her eyes to her. "Right. What do you think of this color? Petal and Hannah are nays. Joyce and Forge are yeas. You're the tiebreaker."

Fran allowed herself to really look at Chelsea. She struggled to calibrate her brain between the real Chelsea towering above them on the ottoman and the one who'd been the plucky and resourceful protagonist trying to outwit her stalker ex-husband in the early 2000s movie she had watched last night.

Ever since that night she had stayed up watching Chelsea as a teenager emoting with all her might in *Landon's Way*, she had begun a full-bore investigation into Chelsea's filmography. It was something she had often done in her younger days, when she obsessed over certain genres of film, or a director's oeuvre, or a particular actor. Each evening, after spending the day with Chelsea, Fran would go home and watch her on her laptop screen, absorbing the different characters she had played over the years.

Looking at her now, Fran felt off balance. She had been relieved to get out of Chelsea's house and run errands this morning, to focus on something other than this irresistible pull she felt toward her new boss. She had a job to do, yes, but she was also supposed to be gathering intel to use in her exposé, not fixating on her performances like a stalkery fan.

She focused on the Chelsea who was currently standing before her. The gown was beautiful, but she believed it was Chelsea *in* the gown that made it all the more striking. Her auburn hair, pulled away from her face in a simple ponytail, complemented the deep jewel tones of the fabric—what might have been silk to Fran's untrained eye. "Stunning. Royalty, power, heliotrope." She said the first words that came into her head, and almost didn't recognize the low, breathy sound of her own voice.

All three women turned to look at her.

"Well, that sums it up pretty well. She's swayed my vote," the stylist—Hannah, Fran surmised—said.

Joyce put her hands on her hips. "What's heliotrope?"

"It's a plant," Chelsea said. "With purple flowers. It's really pretty."

Fran felt her face get hot as Chelsea gazed at her.

"Sounds like a contagious disease. Perfect for you, Mom." Petal said it quietly, without looking up from her phone. Fran saw the cheeriness fade from Chelsea's eyes.

"Shut up, Petal," Forge shouted. "She's not a contagious disease. You're just mad because we're not going to Dad's this weekend." His agitation seemed a bridge too far for the cat, which bounded off his lap. Forge ran after it.

Chelsea stepped down from the ottoman and sat beside her daughter. "Don't shoot the messenger, Pet. I'm sorry, and I'm sure your dad is sorry. He only let me know he's going out of town this morning. Did you text him? What did he say?"

"He said he'd be back next week and he'd take us to dinner. He didn't even say what he was doing, or that he was sorry." Petal gave her eyes an angry swipe. "It's all your fault."

"How is this—" It was clear Chelsea was trying to tamp down her frustration. "How is this my fault?" she asked in a calmer voice.

Fran didn't want to be here for this. She wanted to shoo everyone from the room, but Joyce was busy on her phone and Hannah was taking another gown out of a garment bag—both ignored the private family moment happening just a few feet away. As she was backing out of the room, Chelsea stopped her.

"Fran, can you get in touch with Beau and see if he can meet me for lunch tomorrow? Or any time really he can spare. Tell him our first place."

Petal sat up ramrod straight. "Can I come?"

"You have school, honey."

"I don't care about school! We haven't seen Dad in two months. Please, Mom."

Fran nodded at Chelsea and left the room, glad it wasn't her who had to disappoint a young girl who wanted to see her father.

CHAPTER FIVE

Chelsea got into the idling Defender. She'd have the length of the car ride to mentally prepare for the meeting with Beau.

"Where are we going?" Fran put the car in gear.

"The valley." She fumbled for her phone. "Ventura Boulevard in Encino. I'm looking up the address."

"That's my neck of the woods."

"You live in Encino?"

"Reseda," was Fran's breezy reply.

"I lived in Canoga Park a long, long time ago. I consider myself a valley girl, still."

"Are you from Los Angeles?"

"Is anyone? No, I'm from New York. Upstate."

"Me too. Downstate, though. Queens, home of the amazin' Mets." The pride in Fran's voice was unmistakable.

"A city girl. I grew up in the stickiest of the sticks. On a farm."

"There are farms in New York?"

"Watch it, city slicker." Chelsea said around a smile. "Yeah, New York has farms."

"What was the name of your town?"

"I'm sure you've never heard of my hometown. Ah, here it is. Marchetti's Ristorante and Pizzeria on Ventura. I'll put the address in the GPS for you."

"Thanks." Fran fiddled with the climate control. "Is Canoga Park where you lived when you were Sabrina Butler in *Landon's Way*?"

"Now that's a blast from the past. And you were far too young for that show when it was on."

"I watched it when it was in reruns. My friends totally wanted Melbrina to get together." Fran took her eyes off the road to gaze at Chelsea for a moment. "You know about Melbrina, don't you?"

"Yes." Chelsea made her tone absolutely neutral and didn't elaborate. *Where is this going?*

"They were head over heels for Sabrina Butler."

"But you weren't?" Why did Chelsea have to ask that?

"No, I am—er, was. I was part of a posse of teen gays who latched onto any kind of representation whether it was real or imagined. We all wanted Melbrina to be true."

Chelsea now had confirmation that Fran was not straight. It sent a quiver down her spine, which immediately made her feel uneasy. How long had it been since she had felt a visceral reaction to words simply spoken aloud? Her assistant's sexuality was immaterial.

"I was watching it recently again with my roommate. You were fantastic in that show."

"That implies I was less than fantastic in other moments of my career."

Fran was silent for a moment. "I don't think it implies that at all. I've only known you a short time, but I've noticed you do that a lot. Put yourself down. It also makes it seem like you think I'm being insincere, but I'm not. Sorry if I'm speaking out of turn, but it bothers me. I would've thought you'd have learned how to accept a compliment by now."

Now Chelsea was quiet while she wrestled with Fran's assessment. "I'm sorry. I shouldn't have said that—"

"No, you're right." Her self-confidence was not what it once was. She felt like she was doing everything wrong, and her life had veered off course, and no matter what she tried, it seemed impossible to get it back on track. "Thank you. It's very kind of you to say so." It was what she usually said when stopped by strangers who praised her for one performance or another, but her canned response only seemed to annoy Fran further.

"I won't claim I've seen everything on your IMDb page, but the stuff I have seen? You've been super-memorable in it. Which is great for some of the projects you've done because they are *not* memorable. Your talent is far above what you've been in lately. You raise mediocre stuff to your level. You exude intelligence and passion. It's all in your eyes—" Fran abruptly stopped talking. "I should really shut up now."

Chelsea was speechless. Fran had never been quite this forthright before. It was a mix of criticism and compliments, but it felt genuine, like someone was finally telling her the truth. She had been in one shitty project after another, but nobody was offering her anything good. Silence accompanied them for a few minutes and her voice sounded stiff when she finally said, "What do you suggest I do about it?"

"No. I'm definitely shutting up. It's really not my place."

"I asked. I want to know what you think."

Fran appeared to be considering a response as she navigated the on-ramp of the 405. Then she shrugged. "I have no idea. I love film, but I'm only an audience member, a consumer. Nobody's coming to me for advice. I mean, what does your team say? Joyce? Your agent? Aren't they supposed to help shape your career? Assist with your decisions?"

Chelsea had opened the door. Now she had to walk through it even though it made her slightly uncomfortable to talk about Beau with Fran. "Even before my breakup, I wasn't booking much. I wanted to be home with Petal and Forge." She paused there. No. She wasn't going to confess to Fran all her fears about Beau's inability to support his children. "When it became clear that I needed to make work a priority, I took whatever was offered. We—the team and I—have been operating by that guiding principle ever since."

"And once you start doing a certain kind of role, that's all you'll get offered."

"Exactly." She was relieved she wouldn't have to explain anymore.

Fran tapped the steering wheel in a contemplative way. "If you could be in any movie that's ever been made, and make the role your own, what would it be?"

"I don't think that's a helpful—"

"What? You haven't thought about it?"

Of course she had. She had even been close to starting a production company about five years ago in order to have a firmer hand in steering her career and developing roles for herself, but then her family had imploded and all that had been put on the back burner.

"Come on, there has to be something or someone you're inspired by, or that you admire."

"There is, but you probably haven't seen it. It's old."

"I love old movies." Fran's energy seemed to shoot up toward the sunroof. "Try me. I've seen a ton. And I have an encyclopedic memory."

"*Cool Hand Luke.*"

"Oh, yeah. Paul Newman. Of course I've seen it." She nodded thoughtfully. "A classic—but if I remember correctly, it only had two female roles—one was male-gazy eye candy, the other Luke's dying mom. That was a good scene but it was more a showcase for Newman, not the mom."

"Yeah. I'd want the Newman role."

Fran seemed impressed, and nodded with enthusiasm. "Good choice. Tell me why."

"Well, I'm not putting myself in Paul Newman's category—"

"Why shouldn't you? He won an Oscar and so have you."

"He won Best Actor. I won Best Supporting. He was nominated something like ten times. I've only been nominated once."

"So far."

"Plus, he's an icon."

"So? You're an icon in the making."

"You're sweet."

"Whatever. I'm not blowing smoke. Why do you want to be Cool Hand Luke?"

Chelsea was getting excited talking about the business, and she couldn't remember the last time that had happened. She turned in her seat so she could look at Fran. "How many female roles are there that embody all the humanity, the ambiguity, the contradictions of Luke? The fire? The depth? He's so flawed, yet so virtuous. That character isn't just a meal—it's a banquet. And Newman ate every bite and licked all ten fingers afterward."

"I've seen you do that, you know. Express layers—ambiguity, desire, fear, hope—all those. Not long ago, in fact, when I was watching *Landon's Way*. Every scene between Sabrina and Melody has that."

She scoffed. "How can you even compare the two—a major, award-winning motion picture from practically the golden age of cinema with a shoestring television family drama on a second-tier broadcast network?"

"It's not the medium that's important, it's the performances. Both you and Newman have that ability to make people feel something—audiences empathize with you."

"I had no idea what I was doing in *Landon's Way*. That wasn't acting." Chelsea faced forward. *All these enormous feelings between the two of us, and nobody had the decency to tell us it was written all over our faces.*

"You mean…" Fran shot her a sidelong glance. "Those emotions between you and Melody were real?"

Chelsea couldn't believe she'd let that slip. She was completely comfortable in her bisexuality, but it was private. It wasn't a secret to her family and close friends, and Fran fit into neither category. Maybe there was a tiny part of her that wanted Fran to know they shared something in common besides New York State. But it was unwise.

"I can see you're uncomfortable." Fran's grip on the steering wheel tightened. "It's none of my business." Silence descended in the car for a mile or so. "Sorry. I can't help it," Fran burst out. "I just want to say—a million Melbrina stans would be freaking out if they knew those feelings were real." The exhilaration in Fran's smile and her clearly repressed excitement utterly disarmed Chelsea. "I mean, imagine if they had written it into the show. What that would have done for queer kids at the time? Sorry, sorry. I'm gonna zip it, lock it, and throw away the key." She mimed those actions over her lips and tossed an invisible key behind her.

Chelsea couldn't help but laugh. What was it about Fran? She somehow had the knack of putting Chelsea at ease. "I was so naive. I thought we could just be quiet about it. That it was nobody's business but Katie's and mine—Katie played Melody."

"Are you still in touch with her?"

"No." Chelsea groaned and put a hand over her face. "There was this big meeting with the show, the network, both of our management teams. It was deemed best that we quietly end our relationship before the press got wind of it. If it came up, we were supposed to tell the media we were simply work colleagues and the best of friends."

"Deemed best for who?" Fran's indignation sent a curl of warmth through Chelsea.

"Everyone. Then they ended Katie's contract and she blamed me, never forgave me for it."

"I can't believe they forced you into the closet. Made you be straight."

"Whoever said I was straight? You're not about to pin me down with a label, okay?" Instantly, Chelsea felt like she had rolled over and shown her pink, soft underbelly, and was just begging Fran to give her a hard, sharp poke. The sharing was nice, but monumentally stupid. Had she taken leave of her senses? There were about seven questions locked and loaded in the horizontal lines that furrowed Fran's forehead, and Chelsea didn't want to answer any of them. "And I want to remind you of the NDA you signed. Any mention of this would be actionable."

That shut Fran up, and despite herself Chelsea felt bad about how those questions were now trapped behind her downturned lips. It couldn't be helped. "Now, I'm not sure how this meeting with my ex-husband is going to go."

"Um, do you want me to take notes?" Fran darted a glance at her.

"Not necessary."

"Should I stay with the car?"

"No. I don't think they're officially open yet, but get a slice if you can. The pizza is fantastic. Just be nearby, in case I need you."

"Got it," Fran said.

"This place was somewhere Beau and I went in the early days, when we had just started seeing each other. I was jobless, and sort of at loose ends after five seasons on *Landon's Way*. Beau used to deliver pizzas here. This was before he broke out. People don't remember that I was the more established actor back then."

Fran nodded, back in assistant mode.

They pulled into a strip mall that had seen better days. It was early for lunch, but this was when Beau said he could meet. His yellow Maserati was parked right in front of the restaurant—she'd always hated that car. They parked next to it and stepped inside. The air was humid with the fragrant aroma of marinara sauce.

Fran stopped in the restaurant's shabby vestibule and pulled out her phone. Chelsea moved beyond the vacant hostess stand and into the dimly lit dining room, letting her eyes adjust from bright daylight.

Beau was the lone occupant, sitting in the last booth facing the door. "Hey," he said loudly. "I already got us a pitcher and a pie."

She almost turned around and walked out. Even from this distance she could tell he was loaded. Anger surged through her.

"Half cheese, half pepperoni, just like the old days." He met her where she stood, motionless, where linoleum met the sticky carpet of the dining room. As he hugged her, she was enveloped in the familiar woody notes of his aftershave, but beneath that was the sour smell of whiskey and beer. "Come on, sit. I'm glad you wanted to meet. Surprised, but glad." She followed him to his table, where the beer pitcher was already half empty.

Jesus Christ. It's eleven in the morning. She got right to the point. "What's so important that you have to bail on your kids after being away for two months?"

The charismatic smile that Beau was known for, that earned him millions, froze on his face. "I texted with Petal about that, didn't I?" His eyebrows dipped like he was trying to remember.

"You canceled, but you didn't give a reason. I want to know the reason."

"C'mon, Chels. I just got back from two months in the frozen tundra of Toronto. I needed a breather, and Tommy's having a bachelor party in Vegas this weekend." Beau had been a loving partner in their early days, but his behavior had been devolving into selfish, juvenile hedonism for many years and had accelerated toward recklessness since the divorce had become final.

"For his fourth marriage! You seriously want to party instead of seeing Petal and Forge?" Chelsea couldn't believe it. *This. This right here is the reason we're no longer together. I tried to get you help, but you didn't want it.*

"I work hard." The stubborn set of his jaw was a familiar sight. "Don't guilt me for wanting to let loose now that the shoot is over and I can release the pressure valve a little."

She waited while their pizza was brought to the table. Beau grabbed a slice before the server could put down their plates and cutlery. As soon as he was out of earshot, Chelsea leaned in. "Petal isn't doing well. She needs her dad. And Forge has taken it upon himself to be the man of the house. I don't even know where he heard that phrase, but he believes it. He thinks he has to be silent and strong, but he's still our little boy."

"I told him that. It's what my father told me when he got sick."

"You're not sick. You are completely capable of fathering your children."

"And I will! As soon as I get back from Vegas."

Chelsea regarded him, at a loss for what to say. He had promised he wouldn't let their separation affect his relationship with Petal and Forge. What had happened? Was it a case of out of sight, out of mind? And here he was cramming pizza into his face without a care. "I'm worried, Beau."

"You're always worried." He was all bravado, but shame lurked in his eyes when he finally looked at her. "Will you let them come next weekend instead?"

She sighed. "Yes."

"And I already told Petal we'd get together for dinner during the week. She wants to go to Pink's. Why don't you come? We'll have a nice family meal."

"We can't do that. That place is always mobbed with tourists. Every cell phone will be trained on us."

"So what?"

"Look, if you want to invite that kind of scrutiny, that's up to you. But being seen together will only stoke the popular but erroneous belief that I'm pining away and itching to get back together with you."

Beau's pint glass halted on the way to his mouth. "And you're not?"

Chelsea shut her eyes in frustration. Why was she the only one moving on with her life? Sure, she hadn't moved very far, and she could admit after two years that being alone was tremendously difficult, but she and Beau were never going to recouple. Even if she had yet to reenter the dating world, she knew Beau had not been a monk. Far from it. "You should know better than to ask."

Fran appeared at their table, her face pale. "I'm sorry to interrupt—"

Beau held up a hand. "No selfies right now, sweetie. We're having a private conversation."

"Beau, this is my new assistant, Fran."

"Oh, right. Sorry, Fran." Beau gave her the movie star grin. "So you're the new Lorraine? Jerry told me he talked to somebody new."

Chelsea shot him a glance. Where was Jerry? Beau's PA was usually never very far away. And why was Beau out alone, especially if he was drinking?

Fran ignored Beau and squatted beside her. "There are seriously about fifty photographers outside the front door right now."

Chelsea's blood froze. "What?"

"They all arrived at once, descended like a plague of locusts."

Fran glanced toward the front of the restaurant. "One minute I'm texting your facialist, the next they're all over the parking lot. They haven't come in yet."

"They won't. They'll wait for us to come out," Beau said.

Chelsea resisted looking toward the door. "They will. It's only a matter of time before one of them decides to get a pizza and a quick photo." She eyed Beau. "What did you do?"

He raised his hands in a gesture of innocence. "You know this was not me. This is Lorraine's MO. I don't care enough about my image to organize a pap ambush." He began to laugh.

She kicked out at him, but missed. "What is so fucking funny?"

"Didn't you fire Lorraine because she was leaking your movements? Looks like it wasn't her."

Now was not the time to think about that. "I absolutely cannot go out there. They can't get pictures of us together." Her breaths started to come more quickly, and she searched wildly for an escape. The gossip about her wanting to get back together with Beau was ever-present background tabloid speculation. This would bring it to the forefront again. Fran got her attention with those deep brown eyes.

"Sit tight, Chelsea. I'm going to figure something out. There has to be some way to sneak out of here."

"The delivery operation is through there, in the rear of the kitchen. You can leave through the back door." Beau chomped on another slice, appearing completely unbothered by Chelsea's distress.

Fran stood. "Thanks. Be right back."

❖

The kitchen was a hive of activity, but everyone looked up as Fran burst through the swinging door. Besides several people dressed in kitchen whites attending to various cooking tasks, there were two men in street clothes folding pizza boxes in a little alcove near the back of the kitchen. And there was a wooden-framed screen door that led to the back of the strip mall. She made a beeline for it.

"Hey lady, you can't be back here," one of the pizza box folders said to her.

"I know." She exited through the screen door and surveyed her surroundings. There were several scooters, presumably for delivery orders. It was where the restaurant's dumpsters were kept, along with drums of what was probably used cooking oil. The area was big enough for garbage trucks to come through, so she could potentially get the Defender back here.

She stood and thought. The swarm of photographers had created a mob around the front door, and they surrounded both Chelsea and Beau's vehicles. If she went out there to bring the car back here, they could all easily follow her and get evidence of Chelsea sneaking out the back door. Not ideal. She gazed at the pizza delivery scooters.

One of the street clothes-wearing dudes came outside and lit a cigarette. "You with Chelsea and Beau?"

"Yeah. Listen, how much to borrow a couple of scooters?"

He grinned. "Trying to escape the paparazzi? This kind of shit never happens here. Celebrities don't usually come to Encino."

"How much?"

He shrugged. "Not my circus, not my elephants. Talk to Dominic."

Dominic shoveled ice into a large white bucket while they talked. He was amenable to a deal. Next problem—he wouldn't take Venmo. She returned to the table. Chelsea looked like she was about to undergo a root canal, she looked so miserable. Fran found herself desperate to make the situation better for her.

Chelsea's eyes reflected trepidation and hope at once. "Well?"

"Do you have any cash? I need five hundred dollars to borrow two pizza scooters and buy the silence of everyone in here."

"Look at the newbie." Beau sounded impressed as he took out a wad of bills and peeled off a bunch of hundreds. He gave five to Fran and left several more on the table. "A sound investment. I was only going to lose it at the poker table tonight anyway."

Instead of the relief Fran expected, Chelsea's frown deepened. "Pizza scooters?"

"Like a Vespa. You know, they have those boxes on the back so the pizza stays warm?"

"I'm not getting on one of those things. I don't know how to drive it."

Fran had not thought of this, but it made sense. If Chelsea was nervous in a car, there was no way she'd want to operate a scooter.

"It's not that hard," Beau condescended. "Remember, we did it that time in Bermuda."

"I rode on the back, and I don't care if it's hard or not. What are we supposed to do? Drive it on the freeway?"

"I don't see another way." Fran looked toward the restaurant's entrance and saw one of the photographers come in. He talked to the hostess, but his ginormous lens casually rested in the crook of his arm and was pointed right at them. The tall booth hid Chelsea from view, but Beau was on display, and they all heard the quiet whirr and snick of the shutter opening and closing. "We have to go. Now."

A large man entered and approached the photographer. He used his bulk to persuade him back toward the door and outside again.

"Oh, good. There's Jerry. Perfect timing. You'll have to ride on the back, Chels. Just like in Bermuda." Beau slid from the bench. "Go. I'll distract them while you make your getaway."

Chelsea grasped Beau's hand. "Be careful. You're not driving, are you?"

"Of course not. Jerry loves to drive the yellow beast. See you next week." And with a roguish grin, he was gone.

Fran walked behind Chelsea to shield her from potential photographs. They entered the kitchen and everyone stared, but not one of them had a phone out. Dominic stood by the back door, a helmet in each hand.

Chelsea gave the kitchen staff a little wave. Her posture straightened and the worry disappeared from her face, replaced with cool confidence. There was carefree laughter in her voice when she said, "Sorry to disrupt your workday, everyone. Your pizza is the best." And the movie star smile was the same one Fran had seen on magazine covers. It could knock a person over. One of the dishwashers started clapping.

"We're only going to need one scooter." Fran exchanged the cash and fastened the strap of her helmet.

He shrugged. "You've got it for an hour. We'll need it for the lunch rush."

Chelsea tucked her hair under the helmet and donned a pair of sunglasses—another form of disguise. Fran took Chelsea's bag and stowed it in the pizza delivery box. Now that she looked at it, the box overhung the back part of the saddle. It was going to be a tight squeeze. She started the engine and gestured for Chelsea to come out.

She threw her leg over the seat, and Fran immediately felt the warmth of her thighs flanking her ass. "You said you live in Reseda, right?" Chelsea said over the whine of the idling scooter.

Fran nodded.

"Go there. We're not taking this thing on the freeway."

Shit. She saw the sense in it, but she absolutely didn't want to take Chelsea to her place—for many reasons. The scooter bucked as she put it into gear, and Chelsea's hands grasped her waist and sent heat up Fran's spine. It was going to be a long ride.

❖

Chelsea's heart beat a mile a minute as they lurched forward, and it was only now that she bothered to wonder how much experience Fran had with driving this thing. They slowly made their way down the alley behind the strip mall, but then Fran increased their speed when she pulled out onto a side street and made a right onto another street that ran parallel to Ventura. Smart. They didn't need to take the main road, and they could get far away from Marchetti's without the media knowing.

She relaxed slightly. The side street had stop signs at every intersection, and it took effort for Chelsea to control her torso so her chest didn't bump against Fran's back every time she slowed to a stop. Chelsea kept her hands low, gripping Fran by the denim belt loops just above her hips. The helmet smelled musty, like old sweat, and she was grateful there was no face shield to impede her access to fresh air.

At the next stop sign, Fran said, "I'm going to turn onto Ventura. I'll have to go faster. Will you be okay?"

"Yes." It was kind of her to ask. After she made the turn and they seemed to be flying down Encino's main artery, Chelsea gave in and wrapped her arms around her, pressing her body against Fran's back and resting her chin on her shoulder. Fran stiffened momentarily, but then her body relaxed and she leaned back, as if giving permission for Chelsea to use her for support, to borrow her strength. Chelsea felt ridiculously pleased by that release of tension.

Now their bodies were touching from knees to shoulders, and Chelsea was hyperaware of the warm, snug fit of Fran's bum wedged against her thighs, at the stomach muscles that flexed beneath her fingertips with only a thin layer of cotton T-shirt between. Added to all this was the low-key vibration of the motor radiating from beneath and between her legs. She pressed her mouth to Fran's shoulder and the stink of stale sweat dissipated as she breathed in the clean scent of laundry detergent.

Chelsea couldn't remember the last time she had been this aware of someone else's body so close to hers. Even while buffeted by the cool wind, she felt hot, and it was a heat whose source was deep within her, below her belly, at the base of her being. It was as if she were a furnace that had ignited from being so near to Fran. It felt molten—dangerous, but exhilarating too.

Before she knew it, Fran had pulled into a stuccoed low-rise building that had open-air parking underneath. She steered the scooter into an empty spot and killed the engine. She dismounted quickly, took her helmet off, and whipped out her phone. "I'll get you a Lyft. I can return this to the restaurant and pick up the car."

Chelsea sat there, trying to make her bones reassert themselves from their current jellified state. She suddenly had a powerful thirst. "Could I get some water?"

Fran lowered her phone. "I just ordered your car. Want me to run up—"

"Cancel it. Let's go to your place. I need a moment. And a bathroom."

The flat line of Fran's mouth told Chelsea she wasn't happy about this, but she led the way up to the second floor and into her small unit. The front door opened into a modest sitting area with a sofa and a recliner. A peninsula-style counter separated the room from the kitchen, also small, with cheap Formica countertops and old appliances.

Fran busied herself clearing empty beer bottles from the coffee table and tidying the kitchen. When she unfolded a dish towel and placed it over the piled-up dirty dishes in the sink, Chelsea let out a laugh.

"I didn't know I'd be having company today." Fran's defensiveness was cute. She opened the fridge. "Would you like anything? I have… beer or strawberry Jell-O. Sorry. Those two pathetic items are all I can offer."

Chelsea couldn't stop grinning. "Just some water, please."

She poured Chelsea a glass of water. "Have a seat while I check the state of the bathroom."

From the sofa, Chelsea saw that Fran went past the bathroom

into a bedroom and closed the door. The sounds of tidying—drawers opening and closing, rustling papers—followed. What in the world—did Fran think Chelsea would want to see her bedroom?

When she came out, she closed the door behind her and went into the bathroom, quickly exiting with an armful of towels. She reopened the bedroom door and threw the towels in and closed the door again. All the door business reminded Chelsea of a play she had been in years ago. A British farce right here in Reseda, she thought as she bemusedly watched Fran's antics. There was another room across the hall, but Fran didn't go in there at all.

"Bathroom's usable." Fran flopped into the recliner.

Chelsea didn't move. "Is that TV stand from Ikea? I think I had the same one years ago."

"I have no idea. It belongs to my roommate. This chair is mine." Fran stroked the threadbare arms of the chair with affection. "A chair like this could never be accused of being fashionable, but it sure is comfortable."

Chelsea gave the chair a haughty once-over. "It'll be a dark day indeed when maroon pleather comes back into fashion." Despite the scruffy furnishings, she felt comfortable in Fran's small living room. It reminded her of her first place in Canoga Park. "Here's what I think we should do. You return the two-wheeled pizza deathtrap and come back with the car. I'll wait here. Maybe take a nap in your very ugly chair. Test these claims of comfort you're asserting."

Fran clapped her hands on either side of the headrest, as if they were the recliner's ears. "Don't you listen to her," she said to the chair. "You're beautiful to me."

Chelsea laughed again. It was incredible that she felt so at ease after the stress of less than an hour ago.

"You shouldn't have to hang around my janky apartment. An Uber can be here in minutes."

"I'm getting the feeling you don't want me here."

"No." Fran's eyes looked everywhere but at Chelsea. "I'm just a little embarrassed by my place. It's no mansion in Pacific Palisades."

This gave Chelsea pause. Fran didn't strike her as someone who cared about keeping up appearances, but then she didn't know her very well either.

Fran cracked her knuckles and twisted her fingers into what

looked like a painful configuration. "It's fine if you want to stay here."
It didn't look fine. "I just ask that you stay out of the bedrooms. Trina,
my roommate, is obsessed with privacy, and…I guess I am too."

"So we have that in common."

Fran still refused to look at her, but she nodded and looked down
at the nubby brown carpet.

Chelsea couldn't fathom Fran's changed mood. She wracked her
brain as to what might have made her so somber. "Hey, I know it wasn't
you who engineered all the paparazzi showing up."

Fran gazed at her in confusion.

"It couldn't have been you. You didn't even know where we were
going until I told you in the car."

"It wasn't me. I wouldn't even know how to contact a member
of the gossip media." Fran went from confused to ultradefensive in an
instant.

"I know. That's what I just said. Lighten up, Francis."

"Please don't call me—oh." Fran flashed her a sheepish grin.
"*Stripes*. Lighten up, Francis."

Chelsea smiled. Nobody ever got her movie references. She'd
have to further test Fran's movie trivia knowledge at some point. "I'll
stay out of your bedroom." Chelsea couldn't help teasing her a little
more. "Don't worry. Your addiction to medieval battle armor is safe
with me. I won't go looking under your bed for your collection of chain
mail pajama bottoms."

"The only thing you'll find under the bed is the jar of toenail
clippings I've been collecting since childhood."

Chelsea hesitated. She couldn't glean whether this was a joke
from Fran's serious expression, which was pointed at the floor again.
But then she raised eyes filled with mischief and Chelsea giggled. "You
had me worried there for a second."

"And teeth. I have a jar of teeth as well." It was so cute how she
tried to suppress her smile, but it was a losing battle.

"You didn't want to trade them for cash from the tooth fairy? I'm
assuming you're talking about your own baby teeth?"

"Yeah, and wisdom, from when I had those out when I was sixteen.
A few that got knocked out during my world-class kickboxing career.
And my grandmother's. Hers aren't baby teeth, though. I have her full
upper palate."

"That is alarmingly grotesque, and this has been one of the strangest conversations. I know you're joking about the kickboxing. I remember you telling me how much you loathe exercise. I'm ninety-five percent sure you're joking about the rest of it, but all those details have me wondering if there really is a jar of teeth under your bed."

Fran waggled her eyebrows in a totally dorky way. "I'll never tell."

A key sounded in the lock. A moment later a tall, curly-haired woman stood blinking at them. "Hi, Franny," she said. "I've heard of bringing your work home with you, but this is ridiculous."

Fran stood. "Chelsea, this is my roommate, Trina."

"Hi, Trina. I'm awfully sorry to be here violating your privacy." Chelsea levered herself off the couch and shook her hand.

Trina looked completely unbothered. "No worries at all."

Fran scratched the back of her neck. "Hey, are you doing anything right now? We had a little mishap with the press and I have to return a pizza scooter to Encino and get Chelsea back home. Can you give her a ride so I can do the transfer to get her car back?"

Trina, not fazed by the inclusion of a pizza scooter in Fran's summary, was the epitome of laid back. "No problem."

"Does that sound okay to you, Chelsea? I know you just met Trina, but she's super trustworthy and has a ton of experience being a PA. She taught me everything I know. It'll only be a few minutes back to the restaurant."

Chelsea smiled politely at Trina but directed her words to Fran. "I would rather not go back to where there might still be photographers hanging around."

Fran grabbed a hat from the coat rack by the door. "How about you go incognito? You can borrow this." It was a black baseball cap with the royal blue and orange insignia for the New York Mets, a little faded and obviously well-loved.

"You're going to give her your lucky hat?" Trina sounded surprised.

"It'll protect her." She gave Chelsea a severe look as she handed it over. "It's just a loaner. Not for keeps."

Chelsea put it on. "It's a lovely hat, but I don't think it's going to render me invisible. We need a better plan."

Fran opened the map on her phone. "We can designate a place to meet, then. You can wait in Trina's car. There's an El Pollo Loco right down the street. How about I meet you in their parking lot?"

"That's perfect. I'm starving," Trina said.

That was when Chelsea realized she was hungry too. She hadn't eaten any pizza with Beau. "Sounds good. Let's go." As they exited the apartment, she couldn't help noticing how much happier Fran looked when she shut the door behind them.

CHAPTER SIX

Fran sat at the desk in her room, the blank screen of her laptop staring at her accusingly. Why wasn't she writing? It was Saturday, and even though she was technically on call right now, Chelsea said she would be spending the day with her kids, so Fran had a big chunk of time to devote to her gossip gig. It was the first such chunk since beginning her new job, and her editor Carmina Piranha had emailed a thinly veiled demand that Fran post something soon, not to mention Chelsea had handed her a scoop of astronomic proportions.

Chelsea was queer, and had been in a relationship with a costar. Melbrina was real. It was a huge story. It was exactly why she had taken the job in the first place. So why wasn't she bashing out a thousand words as quickly as she could?

There was the NDA, for one thing. And as soon as something was published, even if it was done as a blind item, Chelsea would know Fran had a hand in it, and she would be fired. Aside from that, outing someone went against her personal code of ethics. There was not a doubt in her mind that Carmina Piranha would have absolutely no qualms about publishing the story, but just contemplating it made Fran feel almost physically ill. This was a matter of literally listening to her gut. It went against every instinct she had. She couldn't do that to Chelsea.

So that was out.

All she had to do was sit tight. The longer she worked for Chelsea, the more information she could gather, and the number of potential stories would increase. The only other lead she had right now was

Lorraine, the vanished former assistant. If she could find her and get her side of the story, there might be something worth posting there. Was she missing something? What else could she possibly write about?

Chelsea was usually on her guard. Fran guessed her revelation in the car had surprised Chelsea herself, with the way she had clammed right back up. Fran would probably have to wait a very long time for Chelsea to relax her defenses again, and she doubted any stories she wrote that revealed Chelsea as a shallow, grasping, vapid boss would be anything other than fiction. Chelsea was none of those things. She understandably guarded her privacy like the sphinx protecting the pyramids, but she also seemed to be a decent person, a caring mom, and underneath the caution and hesitation, a complete straight shooter with Fran.

No matter what Fran did, her mind kept drifting back to that scooter ride yesterday. It was funny that Chelsea had made that reference to chain mail underpants or whatever, because Fran had felt like a knight in shining armor rescuing her fair damsel as they made their escape from a pack of camera-wielding ogres. And the pleasant shock from Chelsea's arms stealing around her waist as they sped down Ventura Boulevard had been the highlight pretty much of her entire existence. Okay, that was overdoing it maybe a little, but Fran honestly couldn't remember the last time she had felt that thrill from being touched, or from the comfort of Chelsea pressed against her shoulder blade. It made her feel like she was bowing before her lady on the tourney ground, asking for her favor.

Yikes. What was wrong with her? She usually only slipped into romance clichés when she was drafting a screenplay, and when that happened she crushed them beneath the merciless boot of revisions. The same thing had to happen now. Any ridiculous thoughts about being Chelsea Cartwright's champion had to be crushed. If anything, she was the opposite of her champion, secretly working against her interests. Knowing Chelsea as she sort of did now, there was nothing worse that Fran could do than what she was thinking about right now.

She picked up her squishy stress ball and tossed it from hand to hand, and then stood and prowled the open area around the bed. It helped her think.

There was a knock on the door and Trina poked her head in. "Hey. I heard you pacing. Am I interrupting? Are you writing?"

"Trying to. I didn't know you were here." Fran opened the door wider and Trina came in and flopped onto Fran's unmade bed.

"Just got home. Night shoots suck." She blew away the curls that fell into her eyes. "Screenwriting or gossip writing?"

"Neither at the moment. Hey, thanks again for helping me out with Chelsea yesterday. I hope I didn't mess up your sleep schedule."

"Do you think I minded chauffeuring Sabrina Butler around for half an hour? I tell you, I did not. She's so pleasant. Not anything like my boss. Plus, she paid for my Pollo Loco."

Fran nodded. Chelsea had bought a ton of food to bring home to her family for later and had invited Fran to eat lunch with her once they had returned to Pacific Palisades. It really had been a sweet gesture. "What did you two talk about?"

"I didn't get a chance to tell her how awesome she was in *Landon's Way*. She mostly asked questions about you."

"Me?" Fran was surprised.

"And me. And how we met and how long we had been roommates and that kind of thing."

"What did you tell her about me?"

"Don't worry, F. Ulysses," Trina drawled. "Your gossip-writing secret is safe with me."

Fran felt relief, but was still curious to know what was said.

Trina roused herself. "I'm gonna go crash in my own bed."

"I'll be quiet." She sat back down in her desk chair and glowered at the blank screen again.

Sharing Chelsea's world and interacting with people Chelsea knew, people in the business, could yield some good stuff for intravenousgossip. Maybe she wouldn't have to write about Chelsea at all.

And there was another angle to consider. The comfortable number on her paycheck meant Fran could now contemplate *not* writing gossip since she would be making more as a personal assistant. But that would mean she would have to embrace this job for real. It wasn't a difficult gig so far, and the administrative tasks were a bit boring but manageable. The gofer-ing was less fun, but her ego could take it. The best part of the job by far was being around Chelsea and getting to know her. Not that Chelsea would ever see her as an equal, but the more time Fran spent with her, the more she liked her.

Fran enjoyed talking about movies in pretty much any capacity, but their conversation about *Cool Hand Luke* had been a real insight into what Chelsea valued in a role. That movie had been memorable for many reasons, and Fran now thought of its famous hard-boiled-egg-eating scene. Boiled eggs. Even though the job was supposed to be meaningless—a means to an end—there was a part of Fran that wanted to perform it well. Failing in the egg and smoothie department was something that made her feel like she had let Chelsea down.

Fran transferred her laptop to the bed, firing up one of her many streaming services. Any kind of writing was simply not happening right now. Instead she'd get back to her study of Chelsea's filmography. There were plenty of her movies she hadn't seen yet, and what better time was there to acquaint herself with more of Chelsea's work? The appealing idea of getting to stare at Chelsea for a while from the comfort of her bed didn't factor in at all. At all.

CHAPTER SEVEN

The production sent a car for Chelsea at five a.m., so Fran made her own way to the lot early Monday morning. It was her first time witnessing a working film set, and she was practically jumping out of her skin with excitement. No caffeine required today. Getting through security was a breeze, but she had to park in Siberia. It was well after six when, after asking about fifty different people, she finally found Chelsea in makeup.

She was sitting in the farthest chair from the door, lighted mirror before her but unattended. Her script was open on her lap. A young boy in the next chair over bopped his head to whatever was coming out of his ear buds as he had his hair styled. Fran got a little jolt when she recognized Jack Westerly sitting two feet in front of her, leisurely perusing his phone while the makeup artist did her thing on his famous cheekbones. She paused, a pink, egg-shaped sponge poised over Jack's face, and gazed at Fran, standing in the doorway. "Can I help you?"

Jack inspected her through the mirror.

"Good morning, Fran." Chelsea smiled and waved her over. "Everybody, this is Fran, my assistant."

A mumbled chorus of *Hi, Frans* greeted her. She maneuvered her way around all the bodies crammed into this small space and stood behind Chelsea's chair. She wore no makeup and her hair was scraped back in a ponytail, but she was radiant—even under those bright, unforgiving makeup lights. The wide smile she gave Fran was cheerier than it had any right to be at this early hour.

"Sorry I'm late—again." Fran shook her head in consternation.

"It's okay. I figured you would be. Getting through all the rigmarole at the gate takes a while the first day."

"I passed by craft services. Do you need anything? A coffee? A smoothie?"

"A coffee would be great. Then could you go to wardrobe and pick up my costume? Just bring it to my trailer and wait for me there, okay?"

"You got it." Fran quickly returned with Chelsea's coffee and then wandered around looking for wardrobe. The set was bustling with activity, with people moving equipment around and perching on ladders, fiddling with lights. Everyone had a purpose, and Fran was glad to have an opportunity to see filmmaking in action, to finally be on the other side of the industry. She was a tiny cog in the creative process instead of being a consumer of it, and it was thrilling.

She introduced herself to anyone who made eye contact, exuberantly telling strangers that it was her first time on a movie set. Most were kind in return, but even if they rolled their eyes or were short with her, it didn't dent Fran's platinum-plated enthusiasm.

Instead of waiting for Chelsea inside her trailer, Fran sat outside on its steel mesh steps to watch all the activity. It was mostly people rushing by, talking into headsets or typing on phones, but she couldn't get enough of it. Chelsea returned almost an hour later, chauffeured by a production assistant in a golf cart. She seemed pleased as punch to see Fran sitting there.

"You look like you're waiting for the bus on the first day of school, and you're one of those kids who really likes school."

"I can't help it. It's all so exciting."

"It's a lot of hurry up and wait. Wanna run lines with me? They aren't going to need me just yet, and I think I've got the scene, but it never hurts to be sure."

Fran didn't say it would be an honor. She attempted to contain her eagerness with a casual, "Okay." As she followed Chelsea into the trailer, she wondered where the Fran who had been so blasé about Chelsea went, where the judgy, presumptuous person who had derided Chelsea's choices had gone. Because she was now fully on board the Chelsea train. Over the weekend, after she had given up trying to write, she had watched the movie Chelsea had won an Oscar for, *A Dynasty Less Than Sublime*. Chelsea's career might be in a valley at the moment, but this was a woman who had once hit the highest peaks of performance, and possessed the chops to ascend again, Fran was sure.

The trailer was luxe. The sitting area was large and comfortable and led to a fully kitted-out kitchen. Beyond that was a closed door where Fran imagined a bedroom and bath would be.

"Here's what we're doing today." Chelsea opened her well-thumbed script to an early scene. Her character's lines had been highlighted in pink and there were penciled notes all over the margins. It looked like she had come prepared. Fran barely had time to read the stage directions before Chelsea had launched into the scene. "What time did you come to bed, honey?"

Fran was no actor, so she began reading the lines without inflection. It became clear that the purpose of the scene was to flesh out the male protagonist's character as a maverick and a rebel, and to establish Chelsea, the wife, as one of the obstacles holding him back from achieving his goal. It was lazy, ham-fisted writing, and Fran tried to disguise her distaste for it, but it was a losing battle. As the scene went on, and Fran continued to recite Jack Westerly's part, her line readings took on the petulance of a sniveling boy who's railing against his parents. She had to admit, she got a little dramatic at the end. "Why can't you ever just support me, Gayle?"

There was a moment of silence before Chelsea chuckled. "Tell me how you feel about this scene without telling me how you feel about this scene."

Fran covered her face with the script. "Oh, God. I'm sorry."

"No, it's true. It's dog shit."

"Still..."

"It's my own fault. They did a rewrite. Everything I liked about it disappeared, and my role was reduced to a handful of scenes. I could've walked away, but my salary was locked in." She shrugged. "Same money, less work."

"If it's any consolation, I think the way you're playing it is perfect. Understated, calm. Makes him look like an asshole."

"I'm sure I'll be directed differently."

"Yeah, probably." Fran flipped through the rest of the script and saw Chelsea's character had scenes with the young boy character. "But you can still make something of it. You'll probably have a little more freedom in the scenes with the kid. You'll be the boss there."

"Here's hoping." Chelsea moved to the fridge and pulled two bottles of water out. "Do you have any training? You seem pretty comfortable rehearsing with me." She handed one of the bottles to Fran and sat on the opposite end of the sofa.

"Acting training? No." Fran had read scenes with actors a million times, starting back in college for class assignments right up until as recently as a few months ago, when she enlisted a bunch of friends to help her workshop her last screenplay in return for pizza and beer. Her screenwriting had been mentioned in the job interview, but Chelsea probably didn't remember, and Fran was reluctant to bring it up now. "I just love the movies."

"Is that why you tried screenwriting?"

So she did remember. Still, Fran didn't want to talk about her failures. "Yeah, I guess. My grandma took care of me a lot while my parents worked, and I would do my homework while she cooked or whatever, always with Turner Classic Movies on in the background."

"She of the upper palate in a jar under your bed?"

Fran grinned. "The very same. It's because of her that movies became my friends. They kept me company. They taught me so much about life and the world."

"What's your favorite movie?"

"An impossible question. You'll have to narrow it down some."

"Narrow it down how?"

"Let's see. By genre? By decade? By country? By director? By all of the above?"

"Okay. How about favorite horror film from the 1970s?"

"That's easy. *The Velvet Vampire.*"

"I've never heard of it. Must have been really scary if you don't even have to think about it."

"It was low budget and zero special effects. Totally not scary. Even though I was only eleven when I saw it, I knew it was actually pretty schlocky."

"Why is it so memorable then?"

Fran tapped the script on her knee. "You don't want to hear about how movies shaped my formative experiences. Are there any other scenes you want to rehearse?"

Chelsea leaned in with her elbows on her knees. "Your reluctance has me curious. Now you've got to tell me."

"It's not that big a deal. It was the first time I ever saw two women kiss on screen—or off screen, for that matter."

"Ah."

"It's about a female vampire who seduces a couple. It came out during a wave of lesbian vampire movies—exploitation stuff—in the early seventies. A woman directed it too. Stephanie Rothman. I wrote a paper on her in college."

"And you saw it when you were eleven? Not with Grandma, I hope."

Fran chuckled. "No, she was not present."

"How did you even find something like that?"

"It was the middle of the night during a Halloween marathon on some cable channel. And she would've killed me if she had known I was up. This was definitely not a movie I should've been watching, but it totally opened my eyes. Suddenly the crush I had on my saxophone teacher made a lot more sense."

"We'll get back to the saxophone. I hope you have pictures." Chelsea laughed. "So that movie made you a horror fan?"

"I'm not a horror fan. I did go through a lesbian vampire phase in college—you wouldn't believe how many of those they churned out. But watching that movie did begin my lifelong pursuit of any film that had women who love women in them. I watch them all, no matter how dire the production values or unhappy the ending—and there are a lot of unhappy endings. Case in point—the lesbian vampire did not ride off into the darkness with her new girlfriend."

"Bummer, but finding all those other movies—that's dedication." Chelsea tucked a foot under her leg.

"No, that's a desire to see myself represented in my favorite medium."

"And your favorite movies are any that feature queer women?"

"No." Fran laughed. "Boy, you really want to pin me down, don't you?"

"I'm interested. You seem to have pretty decided opinions."

"I do. But they're not popular ones. Or mainstream ones," she added derisively.

Chelsea gave her a shrewd look. "I have a feeling the genre you write in is the one you care about most."

Fran didn't say anything.

"Stop dancing around the topic and tell me what it is. I think you want to."

"You do, huh?" She took a sip of water. It was ridiculous to feel protective about something from which she wanted to make her living. She should be proud to tell Chelsea all about it. To even sell her on the idea. Who knew what a connection like Chelsea could lead to?

But there were several problems with coming out—no pun intended—and telling her. First of all, she'd be leaving herself open to Chelsea's disdain. She didn't think Chelsea would wipe her feet on Fran's dream, but you just never knew. Also, she didn't want Chelsea to think she was using her for a leg up in the industry. Even though it was exactly the way this town worked, the idea of it left a bad taste in her mouth. And lastly, there was a certain amount of guilt that had suddenly welled up in her. Chelsea was asking her to come clean about something, but little did she know it was the wrong thing.

Chelsea sat back in her chair. "Tell me."

Fran took a breath. "Romantic comedies."

She leaned forward. "Really? That's what you write?"

Fran nodded. "They're the movies my grandma loved, and I loved watching them with her. Screwball comedies from the thirties and forties. We watched them all, and when we ran out, we watched the rom-coms of the eighties and nineties."

"Didn't take you for a pie-in-the-sky romantic type."

"I guess you don't know me very well, then." She raised both hands in a gesture of surrender. "I'm a bona fide fan, currently waiting out a very long dry spell."

"It's true. They're not very fashionable right now, and they're hard to do well. I wish I had been in one."

"Never too late."

"But..." Chelsea stared at her, as if she were trying to figure something out. "Oh. You write two women?"

Fran nodded. "I'd like to think that's the only reason I haven't had one made. It couldn't possibly be a lack of talent," she said with a smile.

"Do you have a favorite rom-com?"

"Again, impossible to name only one. Now, enough about me. What about you? What's your favorite movie?"

Before Chelsea could answer, there was a knock on the door. "Saved by the knock. Come in."

A production assistant poked his head in. "Ten minutes, Chelsea."

"Okay, thanks." Chelsea grabbed her costume from where it was draped over a stool. Before she headed to the bedroom to change, she said, "I'm going to need you to go to Joyce's to pick up mail for me. That's a Monday task. But why don't you wait until lunch so you can watch some of the filming?"

"I'd absolutely love that. Thank you." She waited, and practically leapt off the couch when Chelsea returned and handed Fran her phone.

"Another job for you. Hold on to this. Check the notifications, but don't bother telling me about anything unless it's from Petal or either of the nannies—Bernice or Colleen."

"You got it."

❖

Chelsea found her mark again and stood still while makeup futzed with her face. The director was the type who stayed hunkered down in video village, more concerned with shot setups and lighting than eliciting any kind of authentic emotional resonance from the actors. Chelsea had worked with his kind before. During their brief rehearsal, his feedback had been that her delivery was too placid, too muted, and he wanted her to dial up the hysteria and the hectoring, as she had predicted. This didn't mesh with the version of the character she had developed—a rational, encouraging, supportive partner to her brilliant but frustrated astrophysicist husband, but she was nothing if not adaptable.

Jack seemed to be having trouble accessing the emotion needed for this scene. They had barely rehearsed, and he had rebuffed Chelsea earlier in makeup when she asked if he wanted to discuss intent and motivation. Granted, it was her first day on a production that had already been underway for a month. He might have done all this work already and didn't see the benefit of a quick conversation with her, but didn't they all want this to be a success? Chelsea reminded herself that there was a limit to what she could control, and focused on the things she could.

She took a settling breath as the first AD spoke with the director over his headset. Just past the complicated lighting setup, Fran stood behind a thicket of director's chairs and gave her a smile. She seemed to be having a great time. When was the last time Chelsea had felt such enthusiasm? Not just for her job, but for anything? The panels of LED lights were suddenly illuminated and Chelsea's environment was reduced to the upscale kitchen set her character was preparing breakfast in. It was her cue to start focusing on her performance in the upcoming scene, but her mind was still stuck on Fran.

One thing Chelsea appreciated about her was that she was honest. Fran made no secret of disliking the scene Chelsea was performing right now, but she didn't feel judged by her. It felt—and she could be wrong about this—that Fran was in her corner. Yes, they both knew this was a tepid, by-the-numbers action vehicle for a former MMA star, and she was there to prop it up with her fading Oscar credibility. It was refreshing to face her circumstances with such honesty for once.

She had to find better projects than this. But if she wanted to do better, she was going to have to start saying no to these easy paychecks and be a helluva lot more choosy. Of course, this was complicated by the fact that these paychecks were what kept Petal and Forge in private school, and funded their college accounts, and kept the wheels of her life and the lives of everyone who depended on her rotating. She didn't have the luxury of depending on Beau to take care of his children, not when he sometimes failed to take care of himself.

The AD called last looks, and makeup replied, "Yeah," and scurried off the set. Now began the refrain of call and response between the AD and the departments, and voices sounded beyond the glare of the lights. *Roll sound. Sound speed. Roll camera. Camera speed. Marker.* It was in the comforting reliability of these seconds when the set went from chaotic to quiet that Chelsea discarded all thoughts but those of the character she was about to inhabit, and the emotional space she needed for the scene. She barely registered the camera assistant who stepped in front of her with the slate and said, "Scene fourteen, take six."

As the director called *action* over the walkie, Chelsea looked inward and tried to find the exact right note of pre-hysteria for her character, and a little bit of joy for herself.

CHAPTER EIGHT

There was a room in Chelsea's home, off the kitchen but separate from the mudroom, that Fran had quickly adopted as hers. It might have been a laundry room once, but there was an extravagant space for that purpose upstairs now, right next door to Chelsea's closet-room.

Fran's room was clad in built-in cabinets and shelving and a desk. The cabinets held overflow kitchen equipment, and the shelving was packed with mostly cookbooks, along with the detritus of family life—a flowerpot with paper flowers, folders of old schoolwork, and a Happy Mother's Day handmade pasta noodle frame with photos of a grinning, front tooth–less Petal and toddler Forge.

Fran had commandeered the desk and was opening boxes and cataloging their contents. Businesses of every description sent their products to Chelsea in the hopes that she would wear them in public or show herself using them in an Instagram post. Joyce had a large room in her suite of offices just to hold all the unsolicited packages her clients received. It was Fran's job to list and describe all this stuff for Chelsea, and she guessed she would be writing thank you notes for some, if not all, in the not-too-distant future. After that came the fan mail. Fran didn't know how she felt about reading Chelsea's mail, but it was part of the job, and she'd have to do it.

"It's almost eight o'clock. When's Mom going to be home?"

Fran turned to see Petal hunched against the doorframe, looking like she smelled something bad, as usual. "Not sure. Why? You've had dinner, right?" Forge and Petal wouldn't wait to eat, would they? Fran had no idea how their schedule worked.

"Yes." Petal was peevish. "What does that have to do with anything?"

"I don't know. Do you want to text her?" Fran had returned Chelsea's phone to her when they broke for lunch. She didn't know who was monitoring it now.

"I did already. Jeez, do you think I'm an idiot?"

"I do not think you're an idiot." *Just super annoying.*

"Did we get anything good?" Petal nosed around in a box that Fran hadn't gone through yet.

"Define good. There are a lot of clothes." Fran took the box from Petal and exchanged it with another one filled with socks.

"I was looking at that one," Petal complained.

"Give me a chance to process it first, then you can look. Does your mom usually allow you to have any of this stuff?"

Petal paused a moment too long. "Yeah."

That would be a no. "Why don't we get her permission first?"

"I just said she lets me. God, you're the worst. Lorraine was so much better than you."

"Lorraine isn't here anymore."

"She was cool."

Unlike me, I suppose. "Sorry, I've never been cool. I'm a total rule follower." Not exactly true, but true enough when it came to Chelsea's kids. "Where's Bernice?"

"Probably at home? It's her day off."

"Oh. Where's Colleen, then?" *Why aren't you getting the message, kid? It's not my job to watch you.*

"How the fuck should I know? Bernice and Colleen are here for Forge, not me. I don't need a babysitter."

Fran gave her a little extended eyeball just to let her know that the cursing was out of line, but Petal didn't take the opportunity to apologize. She jutted out her chin in defiance instead.

"Right," Fran said. "Well, I'm a little busy, so…"

Petal flounced past her and flopped into the desk chair—the only chair in the room—and twirled. "You were at the set with my mom today, weren't you. Did you see Jack Westerly?"

Fran got back to package processing. "Yes."

"Is he just as handsome in person?"

"I guess. If you're into that sort of thing."

"What's that supposed to mean? What sort of thing?"

"I don't know. Dude beauty. Square jaw, shaved chest, lots of muscles, not many brains."

"Just because he's fit doesn't mean he's stupid."

"If you say so." Maybe he had turned his brain off today. All Fran knew was Chelsea acted circles around him. Who the hell was going to buy that guy as an astrophysicist?

"My dad has muscles *and* brains." Petal's tone dared Fran to disagree.

"That he does." She wasn't going to shake Petal anytime soon. Maybe she should try to get some information out of her, if she was such a fan of Lorraine. Before pausing to consider the ethics of gathering intel from a child, she said, "Hey. Do you know what Lorraine put in your mom's breakfast smoothie?"

"No." Petal looked disconcerted by the change in topic. "Why?"

"She didn't leave a recipe, and your mom liked them. What's Lorraine's last name?" Might as well use those moldering amateur journalism skills to track her down.

"I don't know."

Really, Petal? You don't know the last name of your best friend Lorraine?

She took out her phone. "Maybe it's in her Insta bio."

That could be useful. She peeked over Petal's shoulder and made a note of Lorraine's handle. It would certainly help Fran find her.

Petal twirled in the chair and pushed herself away. "It's not. But I'm DMing her right now and telling her how much I miss her and how awful you are."

"Knock yourself out." The orange phone buzzed with a text from Chelsea.

Help. Coerced into dinner with Jack, director, and producers. At Chateau Marmont. Need a ride.

"Who is that? Is it Mom?"

"Yeah, I have to go pick her up." Fran shot off a text to say she was on her way. "So to answer your initial question—she'll be home soon."

"Can I come?"

"Nah." Fran looked up from her phone. "Next time you want something, think about how you treat the person you have to ask for it." She started to walk out of the room.

"Please? I'll be good." Petal's begging was an instant turnaround from the haughty teenager she pretended to be. She sounded like a little girl.

Ugh. Now Fran was going to have to disappoint her. "Sorry, Petal. She's at this froufrou place called the Chateau Marmont, and I'm going to have to go into a restaurant or maybe a bar to find her and I don't think she'd like you to come."

Petal's eyebrows dipped. "What's froufrou?"

Besides an excellent band from the early aughts? "It means fancy. Not a place for kids. There might be photographers there, and they seem to make your mom kind of nervous."

"I know." She rolled her eyes. "They're only taking pictures. There's nothing to be afraid of."

"Maybe not, but we have to respect your mom's fear, you know? Just like I'm sure she respects whatever makes you fearful."

"I'm not afraid of anything."

"Good. I hope that will always be the case. I have to go."

❖

Chelsea breathed an involuntary sigh of relief when she saw Fran stride across the patio toward her. Their entrees had just arrived after two rounds of drinks and a starter course, but it had been a long day, and she was done socializing. She swallowed what was left in her wine glass. That gorgeous Barolo was the only redeeming thing about the evening.

Fran came around the table to her side and whispered in her ear. "You can tell them any emergency you like. I'll walk you out when you're ready." Then she took two steps back and waited behind Chelsea's chair.

"Oh no," Chelsea said in a loud voice so she could be heard over the producer's nonstop prattle. "My assistant has just informed me that one of my children has become ill. Please excuse me, gentlemen."

They departed before the men had finished offering their sympathies. Fran's pace across the lobby was rapid, and none of the bright young things draped all over the decadent décor stopped them. She handed Chelsea her black Mets ball cap right before they stepped outside, and she pulled it low on her forehead. The number of photographers outside seemed to have multiplied by a factor of ten since Chelsea had arrived, but the car was close to the entrance and Fran passed the valet some money as they made their getaway. They were in the car so quickly there had barely been time for anyone to so much as lift a camera in their general direction.

"You're learning." Chelsea clicked her seat belt home as Fran made a right onto Sunset Boulevard.

"Just settling into the job, ma'am."

She nudged Fran's shoulder. "Don't call me ma'am. Makes me feel a hundred years old."

"Sorry. If it helps, you sure don't look that old." Fran took her eyes off the road to give her a quick smile, but then her expression changed to one of concern.

"What's wrong?"

"The paparazzi were tipped off, I think. Possibly right around the same time you called me."

Chelsea froze. "What makes you say that?"

"When I made the turn off Sunset, a whole bunch of cars followed me in. And did you see how many photographers were out there?"

She had—far more than when she entered the hotel an hour before. "Shit."

"It wasn't me, Chelsea. I wouldn't do that."

"Of course it wasn't you. But how do they know? Who's telling them?" She took Fran's hat off and slapped it against her knee. "I guess it could be one of the producers this time, trying to drum up some free publicity…"

"I don't know."

The car was quiet as they settled in for the journey home—safe now and away from the prying of the cameras. It had been a long day and she finally felt able to regain a little bit of peace in the quiet interior of the car. "Thank you for coming. You must think it's ludicrous of me to be so leery of the press when it's an obvious occupational hazard."

"I don't."

"I didn't used to be. In the early days, I craved their attention. And once I started to get it, I welcomed it. Even when it became outrageous when Beau and I first got together, and I realized that my notoriety was beginning to stem from my private life instead of my career, I took it in stride." Chelsea didn't know why she was telling Fran. Maybe she wanted her to understand. "Then something changed when my marriage started to break down. It was as if they could smell blood in the water, and we were all of us—me, Beau, the children—surrounded by this heaving, swarming entity whenever we went out. It became dangerous."

Fran's jaw clenched. Chelsea could see it as they passed under a streetlight.

"I hit one, you know," she revealed. "He just wouldn't get out of the way, and I kept nudging the car forward, but he didn't move. Forge was with me. It was madness."

"I'm sorry that happened to you." Fran looked pained. "Is that why you don't like to drive?"

She nodded. "The photographer wasn't hurt but he still tried to sue. Whenever I got behind the wheel after that, my brain would return to that moment. The crush. The constant flashes. All the yelling." Even now it made her throat tighten with dread. "It was disturbing to the point of debilitation, almost. I can still hear that thud against the front fender. So I just stopped driving." Chelsea took notice of her surroundings. "Hey. You missed the turnoff for the freeway."

"I know. I thought we could take Sunset the whole way. Sure, we'll meander a bit on our way home, but it should be quieter this time of night."

"I'm surprised. You don't seem to be someone who meanders. You're more of a straight shot between two points."

"I am?" Fran raised her eyebrows in surprise.

"Aren't you?" Was that too presumptuous to say?

Fran shrugged. "When offered the choice, I'll take the more scenic route. And don't worry, it won't take longer than the freeway."

"Whatever you think. I trust you." She realized it was true. After only a couple of weeks, she was relying on Fran. And she liked her. Something about her made Chelsea want to open up.

She leaned back against the headrest, soothed by the silence. For the first time since that morning, she felt herself relax. But as soon as she did, a dart of pain shot from her neck down her spine. She tried to rub it, but it was just out of reach.

"What's wrong?" They had stopped at a light and Fran was openly watching her contort her body so that her fingers could ease her aching muscle.

"Nothing. Just a twinge."

"Where? Can I help?"

Chelsea turned her back toward her. "Right below my fingertips. Can you press there for me, please?"

Fran's fingers ghosted over Chelsea's linen blazer and prodded her, to the right of her shoulder blade, and it felt good to have that pressure against where the muscle had stiffened into a rock-hard bundle. The knot there under her skin began to give way almost instantly, and she groaned with relief. "Yes, that's it. Thank you. Keep doing that." Two fingers pressed hard into her muscles in a regular soothing rhythm until a horn sounded behind them.

Chelsea missed the pressure of those fingers keenly when Fran put her hand back on the steering wheel and focused on driving.

"Long day, huh?"

"Yes." Hours upon hours of holding herself rigid, of building up the rile in her character, of centering that tension, always utterly drained her. By the end of a day of shooting, no matter the project, she was as worn out and feeble as a used strip of gaffer tape—devoid of all adhesion. The additional performance of socializing with execs this evening had pushed her right up to the edge of exhaustion. And she had eight more days of this.

She couldn't say that out loud. How churlish would it be to complain about this job that she loved? And she did love it, or she used to—exhaustion or not. Creating a character, collaborating on the construction of a story, whether it was the peak of the form or one step up from background noise, was something she used to feel so much pride for, take so much delight in.

They had stopped at another light, and Fran's hand slid across her shoulder and dug into the skin where her neck met her back, gripping the indurate muscles that were seized with tension. "Is this okay?"

Chelsea let out a hiss. "It's wondrous." She dropped her head forward as Fran's fingers continued to knead the area at the top of her spine. Besides the relief to her muscles, Fran's touch was a comfort. How long had it been since she'd been touched by anyone other than her children? Too soon, the light changed and those fingers disappeared.

Over the next few miles, she anticipated the red traffic lights, when Fran would take a hand from the wheel and place it on her, and silently cursed the ones that remained green. Then the road progressed into dark twisty curves that hugged the canyons. Traffic lights were few and far between, and Fran needed both hands for driving. But something had changed inside the car, and there was an intimacy between them now that didn't need words or Fran's gentle touch. Maybe it was completely in Chelsea's head, but she felt cared for by Fran. Understood. Protected. This woman whom she hadn't known a month ago was now a source of sympathy and strength, standing behind her, ready to help keep her steady and upright, and Chelsea only wanted to ease into her and let her be the strong one for a while.

Much as she refused to admit it at the time, she had always been strong for Beau. People might not believe that her big, strong husband had been privately needy and insecure, that she had always been the one to pep-talk him into the day. She imagined Fran would be a supportive partner, someone to be counted on in difficult times, a source of compassion and loyalty. *Whoa. Wait just a second.* How was she even thinking of Fran in the same category as Beau? A romantic partner? Fran was her employee, and she needed to shut down the direction of these thoughts immediately. She would only ever be Chelsea's assistant.

But even as assistants went, Fran seemed incredibly different from Lorraine. Lorraine was a clucker, expressing her sympathy for Chelsea's woes but leaving Chelsea to figure out a solution to them. Fran had been a problem solver from day one. And Chelsea couldn't remember Lorraine ever touching her like this, or at all, really. And now Lorraine's actions had put every single encounter in a different light. *Argh.* She didn't want to think about Lorraine. Was it wrong to want to focus on what was currently good in her life? And what felt good was how secure she felt with Fran.

They were nearing home when Fran said, "Petal wanted to come with me to pick you up. I hope it was okay that I told her no."

"She did? I'm surprised. I'm not her favorite person these days. I haven't been for a long time." It was more than teenage capriciousness or impatience for one's parents. Petal blamed her for the divorce. Chelsea had blown up their lives, and Petal's longstanding anger showed no signs of abating. "You were right to refuse her. If she ever puts you in that position again, or if Forge does, call me. I'll be the bad guy."

"It sucks that moms so often have to be that."

Chelsea nodded. "Yeah, but it's necessary. Beau used to understand that. He certainly won't be the bad guy anymore." She didn't want to talk about Beau. "How did you like your first day on set?"

"So cool," Fran said right away, and gave her a quick smile. "Beats picking up the mail."

"I'm sure it does." Chelsea regretted dispatching Fran to mail duty. Lorraine had rarely left her side. Their conversation in her trailer that morning revealed to Chelsea how deeply Fran appreciated the movie business, and her outsider's perspective was interesting, insightful even. More than that, it had been fun, kind of electric. What did it say that a casual chat with her assistant had been the highlight of Chelsea's day? *I had to send her away.* It had felt unprofessional to push for personal revelations. But here she was wishing Fran would put her hands on her again—what could be more unprofessional than that?

At any rate, she wanted Fran with her. "It was a bit harder in the afternoon without you. They gave me a production assistant, but I didn't trust her with my phone. You'll be with me all day on set, all right? I hate to ask, but can you be at my place by four forty-five? We'll take the car together."

"No problem."

Thank God they were finally home. There was no reason to be without Fran at the set. She needed her there doing her job. She was her assistant, and she would assist. Chelsea would just have to keep things professional. But stimulating conversation was one thing. Fran's lovely hands rejuvenating Chelsea's back muscles at the end of a long shooting day was something else entirely, and it absolutely couldn't become a thing. She wouldn't be availing herself of Fran's touch again. "Oh, and would you make an appointment with my masseuse?"

"Sure." Fran gave her a rueful glance as they waited for the gate to open. "Didn't get much relief from my amateur poking?"

Chelsea gave a short laugh but didn't answer. The truth was she'd liked it a little too much.

CHAPTER NINE

E *agerly awaiting a bombshell.*
  When am I going to see what you're working on?
What's happening? Care to share?
It's been four months! When are you going to submit something?
Hello?? Are you alive? Get back to me ASAP!

Fran turned her personal phone off and shoved it back into her bag. Her orange phone was charged, and anyone who needed to get in touch knew to contact her on her work number. Answering weeks-old texts from Carmina Piranha was not the priority right now. The orange phone buzzed with a message from Trina.

We still going to that bar tonight?

Yes, Fran replied. *Meet you there? Eight-ish?*

OK! So excited! Haven't been out in ages!

Fran was excited too, but for a reason she hadn't disclosed to Trina. After Instagram-stalking Lorraine for weeks, she had a pretty good idea of the woman's schedule and knew exactly where she would be this evening. Tonight she was finally going to get some answers.

"Everything okay?"

"Great." Fran turned her attention to Chelsea, who sat beside her at the conference room table. The mossy green blouse she wore did amazing things for her eyes and hair, and she looked comfortable but a little restless. She was so beautiful today—let's face it, Chelsea could be lying in a ditch covered in sewage and she'd still be dazzling—and Fran was having a hard time not saying so.

The thing was, she was deriving a ton of satisfaction from doing her job. It felt really good to fulfill Chelsea's needs—to make her happy. Her boss's existence was comfortable, luxurious even, but not easy, and Chelsea was doing her best with the life she had made and the responsibilities that came with it. And Fran was doing her best to help her meet those responsibilities, by anticipating her needs and just generally helping. She had no idea if she was a good assistant, but Chelsea had so far voiced no complaints. There were moments when Fran thought she had definitely drunk the Kool-Aid. There was very little she would refuse if Chelsea asked her.

She opened the messenger bag she had begun stocking with things Chelsea might want. She pushed aside the assortment of caps and sunglasses she now carried everywhere in case several people needed to keep a low profile. "Lip balm?" Chelsea reapplied multiple times a day.

"No. Thank you."

"What do you need? Hand sanitizer? Water? Are you hungry?" She held up a protein bar.

"None of the above. Relax."

It was a bit ironic for Chelsea to tell her to relax. Keyed up was one way of describing Chelsea over the past few days, ever since her agent had informed them that a production company wanted to pitch something to her. Even Joyce didn't know what it was regarding, but it was with a busy and vibrant organization that had irons in many different fires within the entertainment industry. They were boutique-ish—no superhero tent poles to be found on their production slate, which Fran wholeheartedly approved of, not that anyone cared what she thought. This company regularly produced films in many genres that seemed to catch the attention of influencers and the media, and they also made popular narrative and reality television. Fran was also dying to know why they wanted to meet with Chelsea.

A group of people entered the conference room and sat down, filling all the chairs at the table but one. Joyce and Chelsea's agent, Tommy, were the last ones in, so Fran quickly got up and sat in one of the less-comfortable chairs lining the wall. Chelsea didn't notice. Fran could tell by the way she was fiddling with the pen in front of her that she was distracted, and maybe nervous.

The biggest wig in the room began talking, clearly buttering up Chelsea before getting to the point of the meeting. They were offering her a host spot on a new daytime talk show. After a long explanation as to why they thought she would be a good fit—including discussing her unparalleled ability to connect with audiences, her popularity with the thirty-to-sixty-year-old female demographic, and her following among white moms across a range of income levels—he finally ran out of steam.

Chelsea didn't say anything, and Fran couldn't discern from her view of Chelsea's back what she thought of the offer. Chelsea's agent talked with the lawyer types there about terms and contract clauses and some other things that went over Fran's head. Then at a break in the conversation, Chelsea said, "I really appreciate your thinking of me for this opportunity. It could certainly take my career in a new direction, one I hadn't thought of before. Joyce, Tommy, do you have any more questions?"

Chelsea's agent and Joyce shook their heads.

"You'll allow me to take a little time to think about it, won't you?" It was a question, but Chelsea wasn't asking. After a little more ass kissing from the execs, Chelsea stood. The meeting was over.

As they walked to the car, Joyce tried to catch Chelsea's eye. "Well?"

Chelsea said, "I can't be the first person they've asked."

"I think you are. I'm guessing they see it as a coup, to get you. Nobody has you as talk show host on their radar."

"Can you find out?"

"Yeah, I'll make some calls." Joyce veered away from them toward her own car, already talking to someone through her AirPods.

Chelsea was silent the whole way home. Fran had learned to pay attention to these moods, and was quiet too. When they arrived back at Chelsea's home, she dropped Chelsea at the front door before continuing to the garage. This early morning meeting was the only one Chelsea had today, and they wouldn't need the car again. That was good because Fran had a long to-do list, starting with replying to several of Chelsea's emails.

❖

Chelsea found Fran in the old laundry room later that day.

She hurriedly slapped the space bar on her laptop before turning her attention to her. "Hey. What do you need?" Fran asked around a bite from the half sandwich that sat on a napkin in front of her.

"I'm sorry to interrupt your lunch. You don't have to eat in here, you know." Chelsea took a step closer, spying the Ziploc baggie that held the other half of the sandwich and a paper bag nearby. Fran brought her lunch? She didn't want to eat Chelsea's food?

"I know. What can I do for you?"

"I made some notes on this contract—"

"The talk show contract?"

"No. I haven't seen that one yet. This is for a Japanese face cream ad campaign."

Fran raised her eyebrows. "You're going to Japan?"

"Maybe. We'll see." She moved behind Fran and put the contract on the other side of the desk. "Can you scan it and send it to Joyce and Tommy?"

Fran brushed her hands together. "I'll do it right now."

"There's no rush." She could now see that Fran had been watching a video, something in black and white.

"And that?" Fran nodded to the dress Chelsea held in her other hand by a padded hanger. "Do you want me to add it to the dry cleaning?"

"This? No." Chelsea had almost forgotten she'd been carrying it. She hooked it to one of the bookshelves and gazed at it. It was color-blocked in neutral tones and suitable for day or night—a go-to from the old days. Was it right? She stood back and looked at it from another angle.

"It's pretty." Fran wasn't looking at the dress. She was looking at Chelsea.

"I'm thinking about it for the press junket next week."

"It's classy. I like it." Then Fran frowned. "Don't you have a meeting with the stylist about that on Monday?"

"Will you cancel it? Tell her I'll figure something out. I don't want to spend three hours trying on clothes for one day of press." Chelsea didn't take her eyes from the dress. "I like this, but it's old. I've had it for a long time. I don't even want to try it on. What if it doesn't fit anymore?" She gave Fran a dramatic frightened look.

"You could wear a different dress from your closet," Fran said. "I'm sure you'd look great in this one too, though."

"I'm undecided." Chelsea snuck a look at Fran, who was obviously trying hard to say the right thing. She still wasn't looking at the dress, but at Chelsea herself. Judging from Fran's taste in clothes, she probably couldn't be less interested in Chelsea's fashion choices. Suddenly, she wasn't very interested in what she would wear to a function that was still six days away either. She smiled playfully. "I'm just a girl. Standing in front of a dress. Asking it to fit her."

Fran slapped her knee and cackled. Making Fran laugh was the best. Her enjoyment of the joke made Chelsea feel like she'd won something, and she couldn't contain her own giggles.

"You aren't watching *Notting Hill* by any chance?"

"No, but I do love that movie." Fran swung her leg in her desk chair.

"Put your show back on. Relax. Finish your lunch. You've earned your break. What are you watching?"

"Ah, an old favorite of mine. I can put it on for ten minutes or so and it's like catching up with a friend."

"Well don't let me stop you. I just have to find this recipe I need." Chelsea reached over and tapped the space bar, then turned to the cookbooks behind her on the shelves. She browsed a cookbook or two, but there was no recipe she was in need of. Magda had already prepared everything required for their dinner tonight. The truth was, she was curious about Fran's movie. It starred Cary Grant and another actor, a woman Chelsea didn't recognize. She could tell by the way Fran hadn't touched her sandwich that she was waiting for Chelsea to leave. After grabbing a random cookbook, she exited the room but came back a minute later with a kitchen chair. "Move over. What movie is this?"

Fran pressed the space bar, scooted her chair over, and adjusted the laptop so Chelsea could see it better. "*The Awful Truth*. Cary Grant and Irene Dunne."

"Will you start it from the beginning? Before you do that, though, is there something wrong with my food? Why did you bring your lunch?"

"Oh, no, nothing's wrong. I went food shopping last night for the first time in a while. I have a full fridge right now." Fran sounded extra proud of herself. "You know when you go to the supermarket and buy a whole cartload? You kind of want to use it all up right away? I bought bread and all this sandwich stuff, so I made my lunch."

"I haven't been in a supermarket in probably fifteen years."

"They're the same. Probably more kale since the last time you entered one—and kombucha. That's totally a thing now. You're not missing anything. If I could avoid it I would, but even though I hate to cook, it's sometimes nice to make a sandwich just the way I like it. Here, have this half." She gave Chelsea a napkin and put a triangular slab in her hand.

"I can't eat your food."

"Sure you can. If I get hungry again, I'll just eat some of yours." Fran grinned and took a bite. Then she started the movie from the beginning.

Chelsea ate Fran's lunch. Turkey and American cheese with mustard on whole wheat. Very ordinary, but made with love. Soon she was so absorbed in the movie she didn't realize Fran had gotten up and returned with two spoons. She handed Chelsea a plastic container of red Jell-O. Chelsea took the offered spoon. "You brought dessert too?"

"It doesn't hang around long in my house, but I'm willing to share."

"You like Jell-O?"

"Love it. So comforting. My grandma would let me drop grapes into a bowl of cooling Jell-O at just the right moment so they would be suspended like little bombs that never reached the ground." She laughed a little self-consciously.

"I honestly can't remember the last time I had Jell-O. Maybe in the hospital when Forge was born?" Chelsea ripped the foil off as she watched the actor on the screen. "She is mesmerizing."

"I know, right?" Fran said it as she exhaled, and she almost sounded lovelorn or something. "Irene Dunne is one of my absolute faves. She was such a talent—she could sing, dance, do comedy, drama. Tremendously versatile. But the roles dried up pretty early for her and she didn't work much after that."

"She's sure giving Cary Grant a run for his money here." She dug her spoon into her Jell-O. Chelsea liked Irene Dunne, but she didn't want to talk with Fran about her anymore, and she tried to stifle the ridiculous pricks of jealousy she felt over a woman long dead. She wondered what it would take to get on Fran's list of absolute faves.

❖

Chelsea stayed for the entire movie, chortling at Cary and Irene's antics while Fran got back to work. She'd seen the film so many times she could practically recite the dialog along with the actors. Toward the end, when the characters were rushing headlong back into each other's arms—figuratively speaking, of course—Chelsea had leaned against Fran, her upper arm and shoulder almost snuggling into her for… companionship? Camaraderie? Fran didn't know.

She had forgotten how intimate watching a movie with someone could be, even if they were sitting in two mismatched chairs in a glorified laundry room. They had shared the experience, and maybe because it was a romantic comedy, or screwball comedy if you wanted to get technical about it, it left Fran feeling such warm and fuzzy affection for Chelsea she hoped it wasn't written all over her face. When it was over, Chelsea had turned to Fran with a smile that seemed both complacent and dazed at the same time. "That was the best movie I've seen in a long, long time," she had said. Then the front door opened and Forge and Petal were home and Chelsea left without another word, taking her undecided dress with her.

Fran stayed busy until quitting time. She found Chelsea outside, in the pool with Forge. She stood in the shallow end and threw a series of diving rings across the pool for Forge to retrieve. He seemed to love it. "Hey. Sorry to interrupt."

Chelsea turned. She wore a sleek black one-piece bathing suit, and Fran forced her eyes away. If she was feeling warm and fuzzy for Chelsea before, allowing herself to look at her in a bathing suit produced feelings of a much higher temperature.

Forge broke through the water's surface with three rings in one hand. "Fran, want to come in the pool?"

"It sure looks inviting. You're having fun with your mom?"

He tossed the rings in his mother's direction. "Yup. Wanna play Marco Polo?"

"You're welcome to join us." Chelsea squinted up at her, a hand shading her face.

Fran hesitated. Was this a work requirement? She did not want to be in the water with Chelsea and Forge, for several reasons, but she had learned not to say no in the presence of her employer and her family. Avoidance was better. "I wouldn't want to intrude."

Chelsea seemed to get it. "Will you pour me a drink? And get one for yourself." She pointed at the poolside table where a pitcher of iced tea, drenched in condensation, sat on a tray with some plastic glasses. It didn't seem like Fran could refuse, so she did as asked. After she handed the tea to Chelsea, she poured a half glass for herself and sipped awkwardly.

"Will you sit for a minute?" Chelsea placed her glass on the lip of the pool. "I wanted to ask you before, but I got distracted by that movie, which was terrific, by the way."

Fran sat cross-legged on a dry, warm spot of concrete. Ask her what? What was this about? Chelsea threw the rings to Forge, who treaded water in the deep end, and then she moved closer to Fran, gripping the pool's edge with both hands.

"What did you think? Of the meeting today?"

"The talk show offer?"

Chelsea wanted her opinion? This was new.

She took a moment to weigh what she should say. "Yeah. Sounds like something that could be…something. Ellen, Rosie O'Donnell. They had talk shows. Pretty successful ones." Had she injected enough enthusiasm into her voice?

"Is there a reason why you only mentioned the lesbian talk show hosts?" There was amusement in Chelsea's voice. "What about the most successful one of all? Oprah?"

"Right. Oprah. Forgot about her." Fran nodded.

"Couldn't I be the next Oprah?"

Fran tried to decipher Chelsea's tone—a musing, trying-it-on kind of voice. "Do you want to be Oprah?"

"Well." Chelsea chuckled. "Who doesn't want to be Oprah? Her home in Santa Barbara alone—"

"Have you been there?" Fran demanded.

"Once. For a luncheon. However amazing you think it might be, think bigger."

"Damn. You really are a big star. But you didn't answer the question."

"Neither did you."

Fran flicked a glance at her. "You want to know if I want to be Oprah?"

"Not really. I don't see that for you. But I asked you what you thought and you deflected with Rosie and Ellen. In our brief working relationship, you've always been honest with me."

Four months. Fran guessed that was brief, but it felt like a lot longer to her. She liked Chelsea, and this opportunity was big. But if she was continuing with the whole honesty thing... "Oprah was a fantastic talk show host."

Chelsea sighed with impatience.

"I'm not deflecting. I'm just taking a meandering route to the point." She flashed a knowing smile at Chelsea.

She acknowledged it with a nod. "Go on."

"Oprah is the indisputable queen of daytime talk shows, probably always will be, but she was less successful as an actor."

"She was nominated for an Oscar for *The Color Purple*!" Chelsea objected.

"True. But in my opinion, that performance was an anomaly in her acting career. When I think of all the other actors who could've really done justice to the role of Sethe in *Beloved*, it makes my heart hurt a little. Oprah was not up to the challenge."

Chelsea looked a little stunned. "So what you're saying is that Oprah should have stayed in her lane."

She shrugged. "Probably not the most popular opinion, but that's all it is—my opinion. Maybe it's because I pictured Angela Bassett in my head when I read the book." Fran paused. What was she really trying to say to Chelsea right now? "If you excel in something, you should share that excellence with the world if you can. And keep being excellent at it. I think for you, a talk show would be a mistake."

Chelsea let out a long breath. "I'm following your reasoning, but tell me why anyway."

"It's a waste of your talent."

"Aren't you the one who called me the goddess of mom and girlfriend roles? Those parts only need somebody with ovaries—they're utterly interchangeable. Newsflash—I'm not using my talent. Anyone with half a brain could turn in a credible performance. Less than half a brain."

Fran nodded but didn't say anything.

"A talk show could be a real pivot for my career—give me some longevity. Might as well take a giant payday talking to people who have projects to sell. And the schedule? I'd be keeping regular hours, which would benefit Petal and Forge."

"All that is true." Fran stopped. She didn't want to overstep.

"But?" Chelsea waited. When Fran stayed quiet, she said, "Out with it."

"You're too good for a talk show. And it's something you'll never come back from. Once you become a host, the public will see you differently."

"Is that a bad thing?"

"Maybe not. Those execs are absolutely right about your ability to connect with audiences. You're warm, approachable, compassionate. People really love you. I hate to admit it, but even I, someone who detests daytime TV, would watch a show with you as host."

"Do I really want to chitchat mindlessly with people all day long? Help other actors sell their movies instead of the other way around?" The question seemed rhetorical. Chelsea gazed at Forge as he came up for air and then duck dove again for ring retrieval. "It would be something different than the less-than-challenging stuff I'm booking now."

Fran had to speak up. This wasn't a good idea. "If you take this offer, it's like you're admitting defeat. You're giving up."

There was real dismay in Chelsea's expression before she masked it with that opacity Fran remembered from the early days with her boss. It was only when she saw its return that she realized Chelsea never looked at her that way anymore.

"It's true that you're in a bit of a slump right now," Fran said hastily, "but that can change."

"How?" Chelsea slapped her palm against the surface of the water. "I read every single thing my agent gets sent. It's all the same crap. Beau attracts top-level writing and direction, and I have to wallow in the great pit of second-rate, indistinguishable content. I'm three times the actor he is."

"I know."

"I was riding pretty high there for a while. And all on my own, I stepped back." Chelsea was on a tear now. "I only took short-term and local jobs so I could be home more for Petal and Forge. Beau never did that," she spat. "It wouldn't even cross his selfish mind."

"I don't doubt it."

Her anger seemed to deflate into despair. "He never asked me to do that, though. We could've gotten more help. Who knows how that would've turned out? I sacrificed my career for my kids, and my daughter hates me anyway."

Fran wasn't sure Chelsea was talking to her now.

"So what am I supposed to do, Fran? How do I get out of this rut that I put myself in?"

"You have to find better projects. You could develop them yourself."

"I tried that."

"You did?"

"Kind of. Not really. I almost had a production company."

"I didn't know that."

"This was a while ago—after *A Dynasty Less Than Sublime*. I was in the process of negotiating a deal with Universal."

Fran nodded. A vanity production company. Many celebrities had them. It was a way for studios to lock in their involvement with talent that could draw eyeballs to screens. But Chelsea's clout in Hollywood wasn't what it had been following her Oscar win.

"It was really exciting to think about my future like that, you know?" Chelsea's voice sounded wistful. "I can't act forever. I don't *want* to act forever. I honestly thought my career would transition to behind the camera—producing, developing interesting projects, maybe even...directing? God, am I a total cliché or what."

"You could do it." Fran thought Chelsea had the perfect temperament for directing. "But the deal didn't go through?"

Chelsea shook her head. "My marriage ended and I got busy holding everything together, so it kind of withered. It was terrible timing. And my producing partner has moved on. We touch base every six months or so, but I feel like that ship has sailed."

"What are they doing now?"

"Her name is Helen Cho. She was a script supervisor for a long time. She's genius at it, and knows every detail of moviemaking. Directors totally trust her. We got to know each other on *A Dynasty Less Than Sublime*. She also has lots of fundraising connections. Now she's an exec at Universal. She really believed in me."

"I believe in you too. Will she work with you again?"

"I don't know. I could find out."

"Let me know if you want me to set something up," Fran said. "Now. Question—what's the first step to choosing better roles? Answer—it's finding better scripts. Leave that to me."

"Oh." Chelsea suddenly looked embarrassed. "I know you're a writer, but—"

"Not my scripts," Fran said immediately, her face in flames. "I'm not trying to sell you something. Besides, you're not right for my stuff."

She tilted her head. "I think I'm a little bit offended. What's wrong with me?"

"Nothing! I'm just trying to avoid a totally cringey moment here." Who was she kidding? Chelsea Cartwright would be dream casting for any of her romantic comedies. But she had to concede that a Sapphic love story wasn't what Chelsea's career needed right now. "I have a lot of screenwriting friends. They'll be able to help locate some good stuff. It might be a little risky, a little outside the usual channels, but it might be good. I'll see what I can do. But in the meantime, how long can you hold them off?"

Chelsea frowned. "Who?"

"The talk show people."

"Oh." She stared past Fran, her expression sobering. "You got me so excited, I almost forgot. But I can't ignore an offer like this. I have to think about what's best for my family."

. "I totally get that." *But please don't deprive yourself and audiences of your ability either.*

"I'll have to talk to Joyce about it."

"You could at least loop her in on this. Even if you're considering the talk show, your team should put the word out that you're not looking for any more characters that prop up the male lead. No more wives, girlfriends, or moms unless there's something else that makes the character compelling." Was she too pushy?

"You're being so forceful and strategizey right now." Chelsea's smile seemed impressed. "I'll do that. I could even look for smaller character parts. Sometimes there's real gold in featured roles." She seemed a little bit lighter somehow. "Sure you don't want to swim? There are plenty of bathing suits in the pool house you could borrow."

"I'm sure." She stood. The absolute last thing she should be doing was staying to swim. It would be so easy to think of Chelsea as a friend, or someone she could have feelings for, so it behooved her to keep this professional. It would only muddy the waters, no pun intended. If their conversation made her feel like they were equals, that was Fran's mistake. She was only the hired help.

"How about dinner? Want to stay? It's homemade pizza night." Chelsea nodded with her chin toward the pizza oven—the centerpiece of the outdoor kitchen. "Forge's favorite."

"I can't. I have plans."

"Of course." Chelsea looked as if she'd been chastised. "Something fun, I hope?"

"Just drinks with my roommate." She would not be divulging the reason for hitting up this bar in particular.

Chelsea nodded. "Trina, right? Tell her I said hi."

"Will do."

CHAPTER TEN

Fran entered a bar in Silver Lake at a little past eight. It was a laid-back place, with laughter and conversation overlaid on nineties rock. There were a few empty barstools, and two of the booths that ran along the right wall were vacant. She ordered two draft beers and slid into one of the booths. Trina followed a few minutes later, plopped down in the booth, and downed half of her pint glass.

"I got here by Uber, so you're driving home, 'kay?"

Fran nodded.

"So what's so special about this place that we have to schlep all the way to Silver Lake for what appears to be an ordinary neighborhood bar?"

"It's also a pop-up, plant-based burger joint, and I heard they were good." There were a few people along the bar enjoying burgers, and a woman whose hair was hidden under a green bandana breezed past with an armful of plates.

"Since when do you like plant-based burgers?" Trina asked, but was distracted from her own question by someone across the room. Her eyes had locked onto the blond bartender in a sleeveless shirt shaking a cocktail tin with each hand. "Whoa. Would you look at her."

"Yeah. Do you want a burger? I'll go get them." Fran followed the green bandana to the back room, where there was an order window. After the two people in front of her were finished, she took a quick look inside the tiny kitchen, where three people were cranking out burgers. A woman stood at the broiler, her back to Fran. She was almost certain it was Lorraine.

The woman turned and stood at the window. "What can I get you?"

"Are you Lorraine?"

"That's me. Have we met?" Her smile seemed genuine. She was probably a few years older than Fran but had an aura of good cheer and healthfulness even under the unflattering fluorescent lights in her tiny kitchen.

"No. I follow your Instagram. I'm looking forward to these burgers. I'll take two with"—Fran checked the board—"cashew queso, please."

"You got it. Glad to see my minimal promotional efforts are paying off." Lorraine gave her a wink and took her money. She handed her one of those metal stands with a number on it. "It'll be about ten minutes."

Several people had lined up behind her, so she couldn't start a conversation. She reluctantly returned to her table and found it vacant, except for two half-drunk pint glasses. Then she heard Trina's flirty laugh. She was leaning against the bar, hanging on every word the hot blond bartender said as she poured the contents of her shaker into a tall Collins glass.

Fran let her be and sat down in the booth. Trina should be having fun. She worked really hard for a thankless boss. Fran sometimes felt a little guilty that she had lucked out with Chelsea, who always said thanks, who valued Fran enough to ask her opinion on her career.

She wanted to talk to Lorraine, hear what she had to say, but there was a giant part of her that felt extremely disloyal. She shifted uncomfortably on the bench. Chelsea had asked her not to get in touch. Why was she even pursuing this? What was to be gained from it?

It wasn't too late. She could simply eat a burger made from mushrooms and mung beans, have a few drinks, and watch Trina chat up the bartender.

The way she saw it, there were two reasons to initiate contact with Lorraine. The first one was obvious—find out the story behind her departure. Why had Lorraine leaked information to the paparazzi? This was what Chelsea had told her, and Fran felt indignant on her behalf. But what if it wasn't true? Photographers continued to plague Chelsea, and to a lesser degree her ex-husband. If Lorraine was responsible, why was it still happening? Yes, post-divorce Chelsea was still a victim of the creepy leer of sustained public interest, so Fran could understand how paparazzi images garnered lots of clicks. But Chelsea was actively minimizing her exposure. Something was not adding up.

Instead of the green bandana-wearing woman, Lorraine came toward her with a plate in each hand. Fran reached into her pocket for her orange phone just as Lorraine arrived at her table. She set the phone down on its surface, making sure the ladybug sticker was on full display.

Lorraine stared at the phone. "Where did you get that?"

"Where do you think?"

"Are you Chelsea's new assistant?" The plates clattered onto the table.

"Yes." Fran watched her expression carefully. To her surprise, Lorraine gripped her forearm, and then glanced toward the kitchen.

She backed away from Fran. "I'll be right back. Stay right there."

After Lorraine dashed off, Fran inspected the burger. It smelled really good. She was savoring the first surprisingly delicious bite when Lorraine came back and slid into the booth. She swallowed quickly and said, "I can't believe how good this is. This is a tasty burger!" She took another bite.

Lorraine's smile took up just about her entire face. "Thank you! I told the rest of my crew that I'm on a break now." She glanced at the phone again. "How is Chelsea doing? How are Petal and Forge? And Magda? Bernice and Colleen? What's Cheeto been up to?"

"Who's Cheeto?"

Lorraine looked incredulous. "Forge's cat."

"Oh, right. He's fine, I think. I've only seen him once."

Now she looked appalled. "You're not feeding him? Who's feeding him?"

"I don't know. Forge, maybe? Nobody told me that was my job." Now Fran was on the defensive. Wasn't she the one supposed to be asking the questions?

Lorraine studied her for a moment. "How long have you been working with Chelsea?"

"About four months. I started a few days after you left."

"And Chelsea? She's doing okay?"

Time to take control back. "What do you care? You sold her out."

Lorraine sat back and put her hands in her lap. "I took the blame. That doesn't mean I don't still care about her," she said with quiet dignity, and the way she gazed unapologetically into Fran's eyes was a little disconcerting.

"Why did you do it?"

"How is Forge? Is anyone making his favorite lemon cookies for him?"

Fran wouldn't be deterred. "Why did you do it?" she asked again. "You worked for her for years, didn't you? Why do this now?"

"Six years." Lorraine's voice was sharp. "Chelsea was a good boss, and I considered her a friend. I was very sorry to go. How is Petal? Is she still…the way she is?"

Fran ignored that. "What kind of person does that to someone they consider a friend?" As she was saying the words, her own hypocrisy arose in her, and the delicious burger she was eating almost came right back up. She forced the thought away as Lorraine glared at her.

"Look, I'm not going to talk about it. It's between Chelsea and me. I have a clean conscience. Is that the only reason you came here? To try and dig up some dirt? If that's the case, I'm not going to waste any more of my time." She started to get up.

"No, wait. Please." Even though Lorraine had admitted to doing wrong, Fran still had questions. Maybe a different approach was required. They sat for a moment and regarded each other in silence. Fran said, "You know, everyone called me the new Lorraine. You're a tough act to follow."

Her smile was sad. "That's nice to hear."

"Chelsea has rejected all my breakfasts. She tried to be kind about it, but she takes one sip of a smoothie I've made and puts it down like it's laced with arsenic. And let's not talk about the boiled eggs."

"She's so great." Lorraine smiled as if reliving pleasant memories. "I like to cook"—she gestured at the food on the table—"obviously. And she encouraged me. She'd willingly try all the new dishes I'd make at home and bring in."

"I can testify. You're a great cook." Fran pulled her plate closer and took another bite. "This burger is fucking delicious," she said with her mouth full.

"Even though my relationship with Chelsea and her family and staff ended badly, it turned out to be a good thing. It pushed me out of that comfortable, but—let's face it—limiting job and into this. Making veggie burgers in the back of a bar isn't the pot of gold at the end of the rainbow, but it could be the start of something."

It was a limiting job. It didn't matter that Fran was starting to get good at it, or that she enjoyed spending time with Chelsea. Assisting someone else accomplish their goals was never going to be satisfying long term. At the risk of pushing Lorraine away, she had to ask. "Is that why you did it? To force yourself to chase a dream? And to earn some seed money? You must have made bank from tipping off the press."

Lorraine was immediately heated. "I didn't make any money besides the salary I earned."

"Okay." She lifted her fingers off the table in a placating gesture. "Look at it from my perspective. I'm just trying to get some answers here. You lost your job because Chelsea believes you informed the press of her whereabouts, but the paparazzi is still showing up about half the time when she goes out."

Lorraine looked surprised by this. "They are?"

"Yes."

"Fuck." She looked down at the table and up again. "That's not me."

"And it's not me either. But who else knows her schedule with that amount of detail and can tip off the cameras?" Now Fran started to think out loud. "Is Chelsea doing this herself? Does she actually want the press's attention? Is she that good an actor that she can make me think this isn't what she wants? But why would she even bother with the subterfuge?"

"Chelsea isn't doing this."

Something in Lorraine's voice got Fran's attention. "How do you know?"

She crossed her arms over her chest. "I just do."

"So you know who's doing it?"

"I didn't say that."

"Is that burger for me?" Trina appeared at the table and sat on Fran's side, bumping her with her hip to get her to move over. "Hi, I'm Trina." She grinned at Lorraine as she reached past Fran for the untouched plate beside hers.

"I'm Lorraine. I made your dinner." She seemed utterly relieved for the interruption.

"Oh, snap. You did? Wait—" Trina took a big bite. "It's so good!" she said before swallowing. "Who knew plants could taste so much like meat? Whaddya think, Fran?"

"It's awesome."

"You work here?" Trina asked Lorraine. "I just met the bartender. She's Norwegian. She seems like really good people."

"I kind of work here, but not really. I don't know her."

"Ooh, a seat just opened up at the bar. Sorry, y'all. I'm gonna go spectate while she works. She's dreamy." Trina grabbed her plate and her now warm beer, but she paused before she stood. "You okay, Franny?"

"I'm fine. Go have fun."

After the whirlwind that was Trina was out of earshot, Lorraine said, "She's not your girlfriend, is she?"

Fran shook her head. "Roommate."

"I was gonna say…" Lorraine turned the orange phone over to check the time. "I have to go. It's tough for only two people to handle things. It wasn't exactly nice talking to you, but I'm glad Chelsea has someone who cares."

Fran was reluctant to let Lorraine leave, but she doubted she would be able to pry anything else out of her. "Before you go, can you tell me your smoothie recipe?"

"I just use whatever's on hand from the list of approved fruits and veggies. You know about that, don't you?"

"Yeah, but—"

"Have you tried adding sweet potato?"

Fran pulled a face. "She really hated it that day."

"Let me guess, you added it raw, and then you had to run the blender for, like, twenty minutes."

"Yeah, I did. And it was still chunky."

"The trick is to roast them in the oven for about an hour before-hand. Then they live up to the name—sweeten right up. You only need about a quarter of a potato—less, even. She definitely liked her morning smoothies more when I started doing that. Chelsea may deny it, but she has a fearsome sweet tooth. Oh, and don't forget at least half a fresh-squeezed lemon."

"Thanks. And her eggs?"

"Steam. Only use about an inch of water and let the egg steam for six minutes. It'll be perfect."

"Thanks, Lorraine. And thanks for talking to me."

She picked up the phone again and pressed a few buttons. "Haven't changed the passcode, I see. I'm giving you my number in case you have any more questions. But don't tell Chelsea, okay?"

"I won't."

"Things were really rough for her before she made the break from Beau. I still care about her and her family and wish nothing but good things for all of them. I hope she's doing well."

Fran watched her walk back to the kitchen, resolving to stop for some sweet potatoes on her way home. She was more confused now than when she walked in. She had come for answers, but only had more questions.

One thing had become absolutely clear to Fran. She was never going to make Chelsea's life harder than it already was, and that included publishing gossip about her. From that moment on, Fran's only job was assisting Chelsea. And now that decision was made, Fran knew she needed to unburden herself completely and tell Chelsea about her former line of work. And Fran didn't know how she would ever work up the courage to do that.

CHAPTER ELEVEN

Chelsea was almost done with her workout when Fran came out on the deck with smoothies and ice water. It was pleasing to focus on Fran's lean figure while her body struggled to do what her mind commanded. This was no time to poop out. Troy had come early this morning since there was so much to do today, and she and Fran hadn't had their morning meeting. Was that what had her mildly unsettled? No morning dose of Fran? Was she suffering a withdrawal of her attentiveness, her willingness to please, her thoughtfulness? Chelsea had ruminated over their conversation the previous evening. Fran seemed to believe in her ability more than Chelsea herself had lately. It was flattering to be sure, but she also trusted that Fran was being honest.

Fran set the drinks down on the table by the pool and looked to where Chelsea and her trainer had set up on the lawn, halfway through her reps of Sumo squats. Really not the most elegant movement in her body circuit repertoire, Chelsea thought, as she lifted her left knee high after rising out of the squat. "Want to join us for some cardio?" she called between puffs of air, ignoring the tremor in her quadriceps.

"I don't need cardio." One side of Fran's mouth lifted. "I don't have a heart." She looked absolutely delicious with that self-satisfied look on her face. The sun was already making itself known but she looked cool as a day on the water in her white button-down shirt and jeans. The exact opposite of Chelsea in her overheated black workout wear.

"If only it were that simple," Chelsea's trainer Troy panted. "Three more."

A minute later she was done. She wiped her sweaty face with a towel as Fran approached with water.

"Besides, being heartless probably saves me a couple of pounds, right? Bye to all those unnecessary workouts."

"Less than a pound," Troy said. "The heart is not that heavy."

"Even though mine's caused me pain in the past, it's a weight I easily bear." Chelsea chugged the water. "Better to have loved and lost and all that."

"It was just a joke. Please don't turn all existential on me." Fran passed her a smoothie and tried to give one to Troy, but he refused.

"Thanks anyway, but I'm out. Gotta beat the traffic. See you tomorrow, Chelsea. Bye, Fran."

"Did Magda make this?" Chelsea asked.

Fran shook her head. "I did."

She tried to tamp down her puzzlement. "I thought I relieved you of smoothie duty."

"You did, but I thought I'd inflict this new recipe on you. See what you think. If it's no good, you can go back to a smoothie-less existence."

She sniffed it with suspicion.

"This smoothie comes in peace, as do I." Fran laughed. "Just try it."

"I seem to recall you saying you'd tried every combination from the approved list and there was never going to be anything that tasted better than berry-flavored dirt."

"I got a few tips from a pro. Give it a chance. Here, I'll drink this one. Your royal taster." Fran took a sip and smacked her lips with gusto. "Perfecto. Chef's kiss."

She took a tentative sip. It was delicious. Fresh and light with a bit of tang—and there was a sweetness that she remembered from the Lorraine era, but had been absent from any of Fran's previous attempts. "No sugar?"

"Everything from the approved list, and nothing extra."

"It's good. I like it." She resisted gulping it down. *Morning smoothie, I've missed you.* "You've cracked the code. I hope you can replicate it."

The look of pride that flashed over Fran's features was adorable. "Every day from now on if you want."

"No, this isn't a part of your job. Why don't you share your method and I'll do it myself or have Magda do it."

"I don't know if I want to give up my trade secret so easily. This kind of information is my only currency."

"And just what are you trying to buy?" Chelsea was coming dangerously close to flirting. She needed to shut that down. "Never mind. I don't need to know. Promise that if you ever plan on leaving me, you'll share the recipe. I wish Lorraine had done that." Yikes. That statement was loaded on several levels. She shouldn't have said it.

Fran gazed out at the view. "Maybe she didn't get a chance. She did leave in a bit of a hurry, didn't she?" She didn't wait for Chelsea to answer. "Hey, who feeds Forge's cat?"

"Cheeto?" Glad for the subject change but nonplussed nevertheless, Chelsea said, "I do. I also clean his litter. Why?" Forge was supposed to do it himself, but Chelsea didn't want the poor guy to starve. Forge loved Cheeto, but he was still a self-absorbed, forgetful eight-year-old boy.

Fran seemed to heave a sigh of relief. "Just wondering. He and I were never formally introduced."

"Apologies. We got him after Beau and I separated. He mostly stays upstairs, but he likes to make a run for it every now and again. Just keep an eye out." Why were they talking about the cat? "Can we meet now?"

"Of course." Fran sat down and pulled out her phone, ready to go over the day's calendar. "Big day."

"Is it?" She wrinkled her nose.

"Maybe not for you, but it is for me. *A Triceratops in Tarzana* premiere." Fran's tone was light. "I've never been to a premiere before. A lot of firsts today for me. First time assisting at a red carpet event. First time wrangling not only my boss but her two children as well. First time in a limo."

"Never been in a limo?"

"Nope."

Not even for your prom? Chelsea didn't ask, but she wanted to. She was starting to want to know all she could about Fran. "I stand corrected. Limousines are a rite of passage. It is a big day for you."

"And for you."

"No, I've ridden in a limo before. Many times, actually." She waggled her eyebrows but didn't get the reaction she sought.

"Come on," Fran chided. "You should be proud. Plus from what I've heard, Forge and Petal are going to have a blast tonight."

"What have you heard?"

Fran took a moment to pull something up on her phone. "A rollicking and rip-roaring adventure…fun family entertainment reminiscent of the first *Jumanji*. Intravenousgossip.com has an advance review."

"Those assholes." Chelsea sniffed.

Fran's eyes seemed to cloud over. She gazed at her phone's screen but didn't comment.

Chelsea put the tabloid website out of her mind. "The kids have been to a few premieres. This will be the first one without Beau. But Bernice will be there to help with them."

"Great. Hair and makeup will arrive here at three. I picked up Forge's suit yesterday, and your stylist is bringing yours and Petal's outfits." She continued to read the schedule, but Chelsea let the words wash over her while she examined her assistant and her beautiful brows. She didn't want to talk logistics.

"I'm curious to know what you'll think of this movie," she said, when Fran paused in her recitation.

"You are? Why?"

She shrugged. She barely knew herself. "It's going to be big, I think. The writing is better than average, and definitely better than what I've done lately. I couldn't make the cast screening so I haven't seen the final cut yet, but I feel lucky to be a part of it. It's still a mom role, but at least she's a three-dimensional woman, and she gets some excellent lines. She's a bit of a snark-fest. I think I would enjoy knowing her if she were a real person."

"I'm totally intrigued." Fran rested her elbows on the table. "You have a great sense of comic timing."

"And how would you know? I haven't done comedy in years."

Fran turned noticeably red. "Well—"

"Shh." Chelsea cut her off and leaned in close. "Do you hear that?"

"What?" Fran's gaze darted all around.

"It's your heart." In an impulsive move, she put her hand on Fran's chest. It rested in a really awkward spot above her breasts but below her neck. Fran looked down at it, and Chelsea withdrew it as if it were on fire. What the hell was she doing? Her laugh came out more like a self-conscious chirp. "I can hear it pumping blood up to your face, turning it that delightful shade of pink. What brought that on?"

Fran sat back, her expression rueful. "There you go, proving my point. You're hilarious."

"You do have a heart." She nudged her arm. Why did she feel the constant need to touch her? "Now, tell me why you were blushing so hard."

Fran cleared her throat. "In order to be a better assistant to you, I've been studying your filmography. I thought it would help me understand you better, so I recently watched a bunch of stuff you've been in—"

"Now that's what I call going above and beyond. There are some real duds in my past."

"Some real winners too. And in this role, you were magnificent. I laughed my ass off. And that rarely happens for me anymore. I'm way too critical."

Chelsea frowned. "I honestly can't think of any movie I've been in that would have you rolling on the floor."

"It wasn't a movie. It was *Noises Off* at the Geffen Playhouse. I found a bootleg on YouTube. Your Brooke Ashton was inspired." Fran giggled, clearly remembering something from the play.

"There's a bootleg online of a play I did fifteen years ago?"

"I know the internet can be an evil place, but I will eternally be grateful to the person who broke the law and uploaded that file to YouTube. You were the funniest, in a play filled with funny people. You kind of reminded me of Judy Holliday."

"I don't know who that is. Was she in one of your old-timey movies?"

"Yeah. *Born Yesterday*. Oh my God, you have to watch it some time. But you know…you're great at comedy. I'm really looking forward to tonight." Fran lifted her eyes to her, and Chelsea couldn't look away. It seemed like both self-assurance and shyness existed in Fran's expression. It was incredibly alluring. "I love watching you perform."

Something lifted in Chelsea, making her feel light and warm and wanted, even though she was sitting in her sweaty workout clothes. And on the heels of that, she felt danger. She grabbed her smoothie. "Thank you," she said, before making her escape.

CHAPTER TWELVE

L imousines were fancy, but nobody ever talked about how awkward they were to get into and—presumably—out of. Fran had yet to unlock that level in the journey.

She and Bernice sat right behind the driver and faced Chelsea, a child on either side of her. Seated as she was, it was hard for Fran to not stare. Her boss sat serenely watching a cat video with Forge, and the glam squad had outdone themselves on her hair and makeup. Her auburn tresses were elegantly swept upward, and the vivid makeup, designed to captivate on the red carpet, made Chelsea's beauty look almost otherworldly. Her full skirt was an amaranthine waterfall of fabric overflowing the back seat and eddying over Forge and Petal.

Petal gazed out the window while the limo stopped and started its way to the drop off area. She looked older than her fourteen years with professional hair and makeup treatment, and for once, didn't look like she had bitten into a lemon.

Fran craned her neck to see out the window as well, looking for Chelsea's publicist even though they were still far from their destination. She double-checked her contact list for the press Chelsea was going to speak with and then rummaged through the tote on her lap, ensuring it contained anything Chelsea might need throughout the night. Bernice sat calmly with her hands in her lap. She had done this before and knew what she was supposed to do with Petal and Forge. Out of everyone in the car, Fran was probably the most nervous.

Before she knew it, they had arrived, and she let Bernice and Forge go first before scuttling out onto the bright sidewalk. There were lots of people with headsets and clipboards milling around, and fans were lining the entry behind movable barriers. The horde of cameras Fran had expected was not present. Petal got out next. Fran held out a hand to help her, but was ignored.

Chelsea's gown was like another being to be wrangled, and Fran bent back into the car to lift it while Chelsea maneuvered to the door. Then she stood to the side and offered her hand again. Chelsea smiled up at her, directly at her, and Fran's heart leapt into her throat. She had never been on the receiving end of a smile from someone who looked so perfect, so magnificent. Chelsea took her hand, her grip warm and firm, and Fran—overcome by how right that hand felt in hers—pulled slightly too hard. Chelsea was instantly upright and a hair's breadth away from her. Her grin widened and she laughed. "My heroic assistant," she murmured.

"Whoops. Sorry," Fran said, and backed away. She attempted to calm the hell down while devoting her attention to Chelsea's voluminous skirt. She straightened and fluffed while the racing of her heart slowed to beats per minute within normal range.

When she stood again, Chelsea caught her eye. "You look lovely. I've never seen you so dressed up."

Fran had taken advice from Trina about what to wear and had borrowed the black sleeveless top and pencil skirt she wore from her. Chelsea, looking like she had stepped from the pages of *Vogue*, was complimenting her?

"Chelsea!"

Her publicist arrived and ushered them forward. A bottleneck of celebrities appeared before them, waiting to face the phalanx of photographers. Forge jumped up to get a better look at what was ahead. Petal was doing her best to seem nonchalant. Chelsea squatted in front of her children. "You two and Bernice are going to bypass the cameras and the press, okay? I'll meet you in the lobby."

Petal looked like she was about to argue until she saw the implacable look on her mother's face. Forge hugged her waist and waved, and the three of them disappeared in the crowd.

Chelsea handed Fran her clutch. "Can you hold this for me until I'm on the other side?"

"Sure. Are you nervous? All these cameras pointed at you?"

"Not even a little bit. This is part of the job, and I'm used to it. I'm good at it, even."

"But—" Fran bit her lip. Probably not the best time to express her confusion.

"What?" Chelsea put a hand on her arm. She'd been doing that a lot lately. Touching her. And there was not one part of Fran that was bothered by it. "Oh. Because of how much I want to avoid photographers usually? This is different. They're in their appropriate place, and I'm in mine. Look." She gestured to the fenced-in risers where probably one hundred photographers had set up their tripods and were shouting and snapping images of Chelsea's costar. "It's all controlled. And there's security to make sure it stays that way. I know how to turn it out for publicity's sake. I do my part to sell a project. It's when they disrupt my private life that I can't abide." She darted a look at Fran before she stepped forward. "See you on the other side."

Fran scurried behind her, out of camera range, as the photographers started yelling—the hum of a hundred cameras continuously shooting was deafening, and a hundred flashes flashing created a blinding strobe effect. From her position outside the frame, Fran watched Chelsea put on that winning smile, that confident air. She really was a superstar, and this was another kind of performance. One of the photographers called out, and Chelsea answered him with something that made everyone laugh, but Fran was too caught up in watching how easy and laid-back Chelsea made it look to pay attention to what she actually said. And it was only in that moment, when Fran realized she would be happy to gaze at Chelsea pretty much forever, that she knew she was in trouble.

❖

The after-party was beginning to give Chelsea a headache. It was hard to dance while dragging around seventeen yards of heavy purple fabric—only a slight exaggeration—and her feet were killing her. Petal and Forge had been allowed to stay for a half hour before Bernice took them home. Petal had enjoyed herself, Chelsea thought. It had been nice to see her smiling and excited for once—a pleasant change from her habitual moodiness. Forge, of course, had delighted in the myriad desserts that had been arrayed along one wall.

She'd been here long enough, right? She'd danced with three producers and the up-and-coming young costar who played her teenage son. She was sure pics of that would end up in the tabloid press tomorrow, but that wouldn't be such a bad thing. Maybe it would make the world move on from speculating over her and Beau.

Yes, it was time to get out of here. Now, where was— No sooner had she thought it than Fran appeared at her side.

"Need something? You haven't eaten. Would you like me to get you a plate from the buffet?"

Chelsea linked arms with her and lowered her voice to a conspiratorial whisper. "A tip—never eat where you could be photographed. An invitation to unflattering images that will live forever online."

"Got it."

"Call the car? I'll start saying my goodbyes."

"Absolutely. Give me ten minutes."

Chelsea made the rounds. The party was only just getting started, but it was time to go. She had begun the night with such high hopes for this film. She should've known better. But the smile never left her face, and she had to make an exit before her mouth muscles completely gave out on her. And she was starving.

Fran found her minutes later. "Ready?"

"God, yes."

As if they hadn't already taken enough pictures of her tonight, photographers were waiting outside the venue, but Fran whisked her into the limo, and they sprawled side by side on the back seat as they sped away. Chelsea took her shoes off and called through the lowered partition. "Driver? What's your name?"

"Larry, Ms. Cartwright."

"Larry, can you take us to the closest In-N-Out Burger, please?"

"My pleasure, ma'am."

"Ugh. Ma'am." She flexed her toes and let out a long sigh. Why in God's name had she worn heels? Nobody could see her legs in this purple monstrosity. She pressed the button that raised the privacy partition.

"Want some water?" Fran offered her a bottle.

"Thanks. Well, what did you think?" Chelsea braced herself. Fran wouldn't pull any punches. *Here it comes.*

"What a thrill! Movie premieres really are as exciting as they look on TV." Fran's eyes reflected enthusiasm and fatigue. "You're such a pro. You had that woman from E! News eating out of the palm of your hand. And you talked longer with *Entertainment Tonight* than anyone else on the red carpet."

"Well, good for me." She had spent so much time effusively gushing over the movie so nobody had a chance to mention Beau. That had been a mistake. Note to self: reserve praise for after you've seen the final cut. "I meant the film."

Fran didn't—or chose not to—hear her. "And just like I told you, Forge and Petal really seemed to love it."

"Yeah. I think they had a good time." Chelsea decided to let Fran's unrestrained zeal wash over her. It was pleasant to wallow in positives instead of dissecting all the ways the film had gone wrong for her.

"A *great* time. Forge laughed so much. The bit with the pterodactyl boogers was pitched right at him. And Petal liked it too, and she didn't seem so b—" Fran shut her mouth abruptly.

There was a pregnant pause in the back of the limo. Chelsea wasn't in the mood to mince words. "What? What were you going to say? Bratty? Bitchy? Beastly?" She rubbed the ball of her foot. "It's okay. You can say it. It's not like we're not all thinking it."

"I was going to say belligerent."

Chelsea exhaled. "We're struggling with how to be a family— Petal especially. Sure, it's been two years, but it's still hard. I honestly don't know how to help her."

"Nights like tonight are probably a step in the right direction. The three of you together. I bet she liked it."

Larry pulled into In-N-Out. It was a zoo, and the drive-thru line snaked back into the street. "Looks like we'll have to go in, but I really don't want to put on those shoes again."

"I brought you flip-flops in case you wanted to change. They're in my bag. But you stay here." Fran gazed out the window. "Can you park somewhere, Larry? I'll go and get the food."

She took Chelsea's order and asked Larry what he wanted too. Chelsea watched her cross the parking lot and get in line behind what seemed like half the population of Los Angeles. This was going to take forever. She pawed through Fran's bag and pushed aside leggings and a casual top that she had thoughtfully brought along, and found a pair of flip-flops enclosed in a Ziploc bag. She scooped up Fran's black Mets hat that had appeared from the bottom of the bag and plopped it on top of the bedraggled remains of her hairdo. Then she hotfooted it into the In-N-Out. It was time to save the day.

❖

Fran stood in line and watched a teenager try and flip his skateboard with his foot. He wasn't successful, and the people around him were annoyed by it. It got away from him and he laughed, but he looked to the door and the laughter died on his face. The whole restaurant got quiet and Fran turned to see Chelsea, the people's princess in a purple gown and baseball cap, walking toward her.

She swished by Fran, giving her a little smirk, and the crowd parted. Nobody stopped her as she passed by all the people waiting to order and stood at the head of the line, immediately gaining the attention of the person behind the cash register. Fran followed.

"Fran, this is Mariana. Mariana, Fran." Chelsea introduced her to the cashier as if they were attending a cocktail party. "Her mom is a big fan of mine. Tell her what you want. What did Larry want?" She gazed at the people around her, who were starting to recover from their surprise. A few had their phones out. "I'm hungry! What should I get?"

"You gotta get your fries animal style, Chelsea," someone called from the crowd.

"Do I? Okay." She nodded at Fran, who added it to the order. Then she leaned in close and murmured, "Have Mariana add a couple thousand on the credit card so we can pay for all the people we just cut in front of."

Fran did as she was told, and included some extra for Mariana and the rest of the staff too. It was only fair. While they waited for the food, people approached for selfies and to talk and ask questions, and Chelsea was terrific with every last one of them. Each got a smile and a moment, a short conversation, a little bit of Chelsea to take home and tell their friends and loved ones about. There were lots of people recording and taking pictures, but Chelsea didn't seem bothered by it. This was the girl-next-door amiability people associated with Chelsea Cartwright. Smiles, jokes, and kindness.

Their order looked like enough food for three times their number. Fran collected several paper sacks of food, and the crowd began to press in as she and Chelsea turned to go. Chelsea grabbed one of the bags and handed out burgers as they made their way to the door. She seemed to be In-N-Out's goodwill ambassador for the evening, and Fran rode the wave of benevolence with her across the parking lot.

Once they were back in the limo, Chelsea tossed the baseball cap aside and said, "Larry, we got you plenty of food. Can you drive us up Mulholland to that scenic overlook? You know the one I'm talking about? That looks over the Hollywood Bowl?"

"Yes, ma'am, but I don't believe we'll be able to stop there."

"Let's give it a shot anyway, okay?" Chelsea grabbed Fran's tote and removed the clothes she had packed for her.

"Yes, ma'am."

"And please, Larry, stop calling me ma'am. I'm Chelsea."

"Okay, Chelsea."

"Yes, Miz Daisy," Fran muttered.

Chelsea laughed and smacked her in the arm. "Shut up."

"Yes'm." Fran shot back, cracking up.

After Chelsea raised the partition behind Larry's head, she raised her left arm over her head. "Unzip me? I can't quite reach."

Fran did as she asked, and then her mouth dropped open as Chelsea shucked the dress completely off. "Um, what are you…Do you want us to pull over so I can get out and give you some privacy?"

"Don't be silly. You brought the clothes for this very reason, right?" She tossed the dress forward onto the facing seat. "Look away if you have to. This shapewear is coming off. Why the hell a family film needed a formal premiere, I'll never know." Chelsea's ivory thigh-length foundation garment was more chaste than the bathing suit Fran had seen her in recently. The way her skin contrasted with the silky ivory, though, and the way the bustier displayed lots of creamy cleavage activated Fran's salivary glands. When Chelsea started to peel it off, Fran put her eyeballs back in her head and turned her whole body toward the window. There was rustling, a few grunts, and then Chelsea said, "Okay. I'm decent again." She flung the body suit on top of the dress and sat back. "Let's wait until we get there to eat, okay?" Her fingers reached into her hair and began removing bobby pins.

"You don't want to go home? You're not tired?"

"Getting a second wind."

When they arrived at the turnout, Chelsea grabbed the sacks of food and said, "Bring the dress." She waited for Larry to lower his window and passed him one of the bags. "Here you go. Can you come back in half an hour?"

And that's how Fran found herself standing at the top of Mulholland Drive with Chelsea's gown in her arms. A giant lock and a sturdy length of chain secured the gate that led to a small parking area and the viewing platform. The sight of the spiky iron bars, at least eight feet in height, had her imagining a painful end should Chelsea suggest they attempt to climb them.

"Come on." Chelsea didn't even look at the gate. She led Fran farther up the road, beyond the fencing, to a well-worn dirt path that wound around the official scenic overlook and over a barrier clearly put there for their safety. An after-hours workaround for people in the know. The view was indeed spectacular—it overlooked the lit-up grid of downtown and the entire Los Angeles basin. Chelsea's dress became the world's most expensive picnic blanket the moment she took it from Fran, spread its voluminous skirt, and sat down on it.

"Wait! Don't put the food on that." Fran set her tote bag down and propped the paper sacks inside it. "You really want to sit on this? Your stylist is going to murder you."

"It'll be fine. Come on, sit." Chelsea grabbed a burger and crammed it in her mouth. "Damn, that is delicious."

Fran passed her plenty of napkins. Not that Chelsea would intentionally wipe her greasy fingers on the dress, but it would be best to avoid that if possible. Chelsea made quick work of the burger, kicked off her flip-flops, and sat back. Fran offered her some fries.

She put a couple in her mouth and gazed out at the view. "I'm really disappointed."

Fran knew she had to be talking about her role in the movie they had just watched. "I'm guessing they cut it down more than you were expecting?"

"Butchered it," Chelsea spat. "Removed all the things that gave her dimension—a personality. I'm just the humorless shrew, once again."

"I'm sorry."

"I can't keep doing this, Fran. Something has to change. Maybe those executives are right. I should just bail out of acting and host a talk show."

Fran thought this was a mistake, but she'd already told Chelsea that. "What about developing your own stuff? Getting in touch with that woman you were going to produce with? What was her name?"

"Helen Cho. God, I hope she doesn't see that shit heap of a performance. She has even less of a poker face than you do." Her chuckle was dry and wholly unamused. "I can just picture her trying to say something nice about it. It would be funny if it wasn't so depressing."

"There was nothing wrong with your performance. It was the plot that began to make less sense. The special effects took over and coherent storytelling went out the window."

"Three months of cowering at a tennis ball in front of a green screen. I'm getting too old for this shit," Chelsea muttered. "Is there anything to drink?"

Fran handed her a soft drink. "You're not too old. You don't turn forty-two until next month."

She blew a raspberry. "And then I'll be too old?"

"That's not what I meant—"

"It's not fair that you can easily find out anything you want about me, like my birthday, and I can't do the same."

"Sorry, boss, but that's the business you chose." Fran smiled at her, but Chelsea wasn't looking. She was engrossed in the view. "I turned thirty-one last October."

Chelsea shot her a glance. "Happy belated."

"You must not have seen what I saw back at In-N-Out. The way you had instantly made a hundred new friends. How everyone you talked to felt special and seen, and didn't even notice when you cut the line."

Chelsea laughed, seemingly in spite of the sour mood that had quickly descended over her. "It's my superpower."

"It definitely is."

"And I don't mind people and their cameras if it's my choice. I chose to walk in there knowing full well that I was going to draw attention."

"And boy did you draw attention. You have a gift, Chelsea. There are very few people who can do what you do."

"What?" Chelsea snorted. "Move to the head of the line at a fast food joint? Get paid for being dinosaur food?"

"Connect!" Fran moved closer and took Chelsea's hand. It got her attention. "Since I started working for you, I've spent a lot of time watching you."

"Yeah, that's kind of your job."

"No." Fran was a little embarrassed, but she kept on. "I mean your performances. At this point, I've seen most of your filmography." She let go of Chelsea's hand and grabbed her phone, "Wait, I'll show you." She opened YouTube.

"You don't have to show me anything. I was there. I know what I've done." Chelsea's voice was quiet.

"I don't think you know how good you are." Fran searched up the clip she wanted. "Or maybe you've just forgotten."

"I can guess what you're teeing up. The dinner scene from *A Dynasty Less Than Sublime*, right? All the tears and snot and carrying on won me the Oscar."

"Wrong. A performance filled with emotional excess is always going to be showered with praise. Of course you were excellent, but there's something else I want to show you. Here, look." Fran played a short clip from *Frankie's Fortune*, an indie from several years earlier. It was from the point of view of an autistic eleven-year-old boy, and the scene showed Chelsea sitting beside the young actor who played Frankie in the principal's office, when he was about to be expelled.

"My first mom role. I can't believe you watched this. It sank like a stone at the box office and went straight to cable." Chelsea's voice was rueful.

"Where everyone has seen it." Fran shuffled closer and held the phone so Chelsea could watch. "It's the kind of movie you put on when you're folding laundry or cooking dinner or whatever, but then you become entranced by the story and forget everything around you. And that's mostly because of your performance."

Chelsea's snort was the definition of dubious.

"I'm serious. The kid is good, but you just blow me away here." Fran started the clip. "The director was super smart. He must have done a close-up on this kid as he receives the news that he's getting the boot, but he went with the two-shot of you and him from across the principal's desk instead." She shut up and watched when the clip started. Both actors were silent; the scene was all about reacting. The kid didn't register much emotion as the principal droned on, but

Chelsea's face revealed everything about this mother. It looked as if she was trying to keep her features frozen—the tough, defiant mom masking her feelings—but then came the anger, then frustration, grief, and finally despair rippling across her face. Chelsea showed so much while barely moving a muscle. The restraint. It was breathtaking. When Fran first saw it, she went back and watched the scene about ten times. It was truly masterful. Even now, she couldn't take her eyes from the tiny screen.

When she finally raised her head, she saw that Chelsea wasn't watching. She was staring at Fran, her eyes stormy. Before she knew what was happening, Chelsea invaded her personal space and kissed her on the lips—fast and hard and urgent, and then withdrew just as quickly.

"Thank you for seeing so much in me." Her voice betrayed an intense emotion that Fran couldn't identify. All she knew was that kiss had only been a sip, and she wanted the whole bottle of wine.

She dropped the phone and reached for Chelsea, needing to feel those lips again. This time, Fran noticed things that had happened too quickly moments before. Chelsea's lips were soft and sweet-tasting, and welcoming as Fran pressed hers against them. She pulled Chelsea close at the waist, then let her hands drift upward along her back over the cotton of her shirt. Fran could hardly believe they were doing this.

Chelsea had a hand on Fran's shoulder, and when they separated for an instant, she let out a harsh breath of what might have been impatience before drawing near again. "What are you doing to me?" she muttered, and kissed her once more. Chelsea deepened the kiss, and Fran welcomed her in when she felt Chelsea's tongue on her lower lip. Everything felt hot—her, Chelsea, the entire world—and Fran couldn't tell how long it had lasted when Chelsea grasped her face and nudged her back. She searched Fran's eyes with something that looked like desperation, and then they heard the light tap of a horn from above.

"That's Larry," Chelsea said. She scrabbled away from her and headed up the path without looking back.

❖

Chelsea waited in the limo for Fran. She had walked away and left Fran to clean up their impromptu moonlit picnic. It had been rude of her, but she had to get away before she lost any more control of herself than she already had. The first kiss had been an impulsive thank you of sorts. Fran had been so endearing, so unswervingly in Chelsea's corner—it had made something burst within her. But those feelings of gratitude had turned into something a lot more carnal when Fran had responded in kind. No, not in kind, because Fran had set Chelsea's world on fire. It had been all-consuming—a hot, dense inferno that had snaked through every molecule of her body and threatened to overwhelm her. Putting physical distance between them had been the only way Chelsea could stop herself.

A thousand thoughts careened around her head at once, most of them telling her what a bad idea this was. It didn't matter that those forty or so seconds she had just had with Fran were the most alive she had felt in years.

Chelsea wanted to wallow in its possibility, but there was no way she could let herself do that. Things were different now. There were other factors to consider. The last affair she'd had with a woman was decades ago, when she was barely out of her teens. She'd been a nobody. Now she had a career, children, and the scrutiny of what felt like the entire world to worry about.

The door abruptly opened and Fran's arm tossed the now-dusty purple dress to the front of the interior space. She poked her head in and arranged her shoulder bag and the remains from their meal on the floor away from Chelsea. "There's no garbage can here. We'll have to find somewhere to dispose of this stuff. Or we can bring it ho—back to your place."

Chelsea nodded and moved all the way over until her body pressed against the upholstery on the other side of the car, leaving as much space between her and Fran as possible. Fran noticed and hesitated before settling in her seat.

"Do you want me to sit over there?" She pointed to where Chelsea's dress had landed.

"Don't be silly. Just get in so we can go." She had tried for light-hearted, but knew she had come off snippy and curt. Fran clicked her seat belt home and sat silently with her hands on her knees. Chelsea reached out and placed her hand over Fran's for just a second before removing it. "It's not you, it's me."

Fran gazed at her, her expression solemn, but didn't say anything.

"Take us home, Larry, please." Chelsea pressed the button that raised the partition. She was silent for a moment and then said in a rush. "We can't do that again, Fran. It's not that I didn't enjoy it—I did. Believe me. But you're my employee. I don't want to confuse things, or put you in a position where you're doing something you don't want to do—"

"I do want to—"

"No." Chelsea cut her off. "It can't happen." She touched Fran's hand again for a second. "We can't complicate this. I want to keep you around. We work well together, don't you think?" She waited, and Fran nodded. "Do you want to continue working with me, knowing that I just abused my position as your boss? Because I trust you, and I would hate it if you lost your trust in me."

"Maybe you shouldn't trust me," Fran muttered, looking at her lap.

"Nonsense. We can get past this. Can't we, Fran?"

"Yes." When Fran raised her eyes, Chelsea thought she saw guilt in them.

She had to fix this. "You did nothing wrong. This was my mistake." She grasped Fran's hand again where it sat on the seat between them. She gripped it hard and didn't let go. Their fingers twined together as if they were a singular entity, stronger together than apart. Holding Fran's hand felt like support and companionship. Someone she desired and who seemed to desire her back. But she had blown past the boundary she had tried so hard to keep in place. She felt too much, was out of control, and it scared her. She let go of Fran's hand and gazed out the window, and they rode the rest of the way home in silence.

CHAPTER THIRTEEN

Fran had escaped to her hidey-hole next to the kitchen. It was late on a Friday afternoon, and they had just returned from a day of fittings for a job Chelsea would start in a few weeks. Fran hadn't really been needed for anything except ferrying coffee and water and snacks to Chelsea and the costume team. Not hard work, but exhausting just the same.

Chelsea had disappeared to see what the kids were up to and hadn't come back. And Fran wasn't especially keen to look for her. Ever since their kiss at the top of Mulholland Drive, things had been a bit delicate between them. She understood where Chelsea was coming from, and appreciated that Chelsea was unwilling to take advantage of her position of power, but what if Fran absolutely wanted Chelsea to take advantage of her? To kiss her senseless, and whatever came next after kisses? She'd spent the whole week trying not to succumb to dejection, and also trying not to stare at Chelsea's lips and think about when they had been pressed up against her own. Chelsea either hadn't noticed or was ignoring her, and Fran couldn't decide which was worse. The thread between them had once been twangy with easy friendliness, but now it was pulled taut—the give-and-take between them now vibrated with tension.

Voices in the kitchen pulled her from her thoughts, Forge's excited high pitch and Chelsea's lower murmur. Fran paused but didn't hear anyone calling for her. Colleen the nanny passed by, shouting a goodbye as she headed for the side door.

Fran pulled out her laptop. Between interruptions today, she had been working on an email to Helen Cho from the account Chelsea used for business. When Chelsea mentioned her name, Fran did some investigating, and thought it might be to Chelsea's benefit to renew that relationship. Chelsea hadn't given Fran permission to reach out to Helen Cho, but the woman's email address was right there in Chelsea's contacts, and since Fran saw all emails before forwarding the necessary ones to Chelsea's personal account, it was a manageable risk. She could take credit if Helen responded positively; if the response was negative or nothing came of it, then Chelsea didn't even have to know.

As her machine booted up, the icon for Final Draft, her screenwriting program, caught her eye. She hadn't touched it in months and didn't have even the spark of an idea that could tempt her to fire it up. She really needed to stop devoting every single thought to Chelsea and get back to her true purpose for being in this goddamn city in the first place—writing one of the best romantic comedies in history that just so happened to feature two women. A story *she* could relate to.

Hey. A girl could dream, right?

However she had spent her days in the time before Chelsea, there had always been a stew of ideas, the seeds of a plot, snatches of dialogue between imaginary people taking up space in her brain. Now? There was nothing. Thoughts of Chelsea had completely taken over. It was a fact, and Fran didn't know how to feel about it.

She finished up the message to Helen Cho and sent it. After logging out of Chelsea's email, she checked her own. It had been ages, and she might as well see if there was anything important she'd missed. Mail from all her email addresses, including the one for F. Ulysses, was funneled into the same inbox, and she felt a glint of unease when she saw eight or nine emails from Carmina Piranha. She opened the first one, sent six days ago on the morning after Chelsea's movie premiere and the incident that had happened high on Mulholland Drive. The incident that Fran was doing her best to not think about. The subject line read *Busted* and all it contained was a grainy JPEG of Chelsea handing a burger to a smiling young man at In-N-Out. Fran was clearly visible over her shoulder.

She grimaced. Probably ninety people had their phone pointed at Chelsea that night. Of course it would've been all over social media. But how did Carmina Piranha know what Fran looked like? They had never met in person. That question was answered in the next email, subject line: *Did you think I didn't know who you are?* The body of that message was two sentences. *I'm a journalist. I know how to do research.*

She clicked through the other messages, all variations on the theme of getting in touch or else.

The last message, sent the day before, read:

Okay, I'm done playing nice. Intravenousgossip.com has been good to you, and this is the way you pay me back? Chelsea Cartwright's distaste for celebrity journalism is well documented. Obviously, she doesn't know about your past life. If you don't reply within seventy-two hours with something click-worthy, I will expose you. That is a story that will definitely yield a million clicks.
Fondest regards, C. Piranha

Fran read the text four times, but it didn't change. She was fucked.

She sat back in her chair and tried to think the problem through. What would actually happen if she was exposed? Chelsea would look like an idiot who didn't do her due diligence in hiring Fran. She would be front and center in all the gossip blogs again. She would fire Fran, which, fair. And Fran would never again share space with her.

That last one really felt like a punch in the gut.

There was no way Fran was letting this happen. She stood and began to pace the small room, from the open doorway to the window that looked out onto the terrace and pool. Back and forth, only about four steps, but it worked. It started to shake a few things loose. Unfortunately, they were the wrong things. Thoughts of the events of Saturday night once again arose to distract her from this very real predicament before her.

That kiss. Cutting that face-melting moment short felt like when the match touches the fuse of a firecracker, but then someone with quick fingers—Chelsea—pinches out the flame. Chelsea hadn't let them go boom. But if she had, Fran had absolutely no doubt that they had enough combustible material between them to light up the night sky a hundred times over.

Enough! *Get back to the matter at hand, Fran.* If Chelsea found out, Fran was finished. Her stomach felt like a roiling pit of snakes at the thought of hurting Chelsea. But confronting the disappointment and injury in Chelsea's eyes— Fran exhaled violently and quickened her pacing. It couldn't happen. How had she painted herself into this corner?

Fran had already decided she was never going to publish anything about Chelsea or her family. So why hadn't she formally quit before any of this could happen? Carmina Piranha wouldn't let her squirm out of this now, and time was ticking. Her pacing brought her to the window, and she stood there with her fingers laced behind her head, feeling the minutes tick by while she considered a host of terrible options. She vaguely registered Forge calling out from somewhere outside, but she didn't see him anywhere—she wasn't seeing anything at the moment. By her estimation, she had until tomorrow night to resolve this—or tell Chelsea to prepare for the worst.

"What are you doing?"

Fran spun around to see Petal standing by the desk chair, her head tilted as she gazed at Fran with suspicion.

Damn. Petal was as stealthy as a ninja. Fran hadn't heard her come in. "Nothing. Thinking. What are you doing?"

Petal twirled the chair and sat in it, her eyes still trained on Fran. Her foot rested on the power cable for Fran's laptop, which Fran followed up to the desk to the laptop itself.

The screen was open and still showed the email from Carmina Piranha. Fran lunged for it and slapped the computer shut.

"God. What's wrong with you?" Petal glared at her.

She exhaled in relief. Petal hadn't seen the screen or what was written on it. "I don't know, Petal. Why don't you tell me? I'm sure you have an opinion." She wasn't in the mood for Petal's surliness.

"Petal? Fran? Anyone? We need help out here." Chelsea's voice teetered on the edge of alarm, and it was coming from close by.

Petal rushed from the room, and Fran followed her after shoving her laptop back into her bag. Out on the deck, Forge stood with a distressed Cheeto in his arms. The cat was calm-ish, but clearly unhappy, and he was moaning piteously. Chelsea kept her distance, about ten feet, with a hand over her mouth and nose.

"Oh my God," Petal cried. "What is that smell?"

"It's skunk," Chelsea said.

"I left the door open, and Cheeto got out, and when I found him out by the trees back there, he smelled real bad. I had to help him." Forge was defensive, and also on the verge of tears.

"It's okay, honey. How close did you and Cheeto get to the skunk?" Chelsea asked.

"I didn't see any skunk. I think he was gone by the time I got there."

"So you weren't sprayed, Forgey?"

"No, Mama."

Fran whipped her phone out and searched for a solution. "Maybe we should deal with the cat first. Then Forge."

"Right," Chelsea said. "Petal, go get the hose."

"Gladly. Anything to get away from the stench." Petal started down the steps to the lawn.

"No! Just a second." Fran kept reading. "Water will only make it worse. We need a bucket, hydrogen peroxide, baking soda, and dish soap. Do you have all of those?"

"I think so," Chelsea said.

She looked up from her phone. "But I think we should do it in a contained environment, in the tub."

"We have to bring him in the house?" Petal made retching sounds. "There's no way you're using my bathroom."

"Use mine," Forge said.

Nobody moved for a second. Fran exhaled and took charge. She slowly approached Forge, the skunky odor of sulfur and burnt tires making her eyes water. She removed the cat from Forge's arms, ignoring Cheeto's howl of protest, and gingerly held him away from her body. "I think you should stay out here until we're done. Cheeto's worse, but you don't smell that great either."

"She's right," Petal said to Forge as she retreated back to the sliding door. "I'll go get your Switch so you're not bored out here."

"I'll find those other things. Meet you up in Forge's bathroom." Chelsea took a step closer to Forge, but then swiftly moved back and covered her nose again. "Will you be all right out here, sweetie? Fran'll take good care of him. Won't you, Fran?"

Fran gazed into Cheeto's skittish eyes and wondered how she had become the cat cleaner. "Yep. Let's do this."

Up in Forge's bathroom, a nautical-themed room that Fran had never entered until this moment, she put the lid down and sat on the commode. Cheeto's heart was still beating rapidly, but she guessed he was feeling safe because when she loosened her grip on him, he didn't try to bolt. She had no doubt he would once she tried to clean him. Unbelievably, he started to purr and knead her legs with his claws, and she mourned her favorite pair of jeans. Would the smell ever come out?

Chelsea knocked and entered with the items needed for the skunk smell remedy. Fran held her phone in one hand and dictated the recipe, and Chelsea mixed up a slurry in the bucket. "Do you have a washcloth you're willing to sacrifice?" Fran asked as she transferred Cheeto into the tub and knelt beside him. Chelsea reached under the sink and tossed one to her. Fran kept her hand on Cheeto and dipped the cloth in the solution, but he started to wriggle and she had to grab him. His heart rate shot up again, and the poor guy started to tremble.

"What can I do?" Suddenly, Chelsea was beside her, her upper arm and shoulder pressing into Fran as she put a reassuring hand on Cheeto.

"Do you want to hold or clean?"

Chelsea took the washcloth and draped it over Cheeto's head, careful not to get any of the solution in his eyes as she massaged it into his fur. Cheeto started scrabbling and caterwauling, and Fran incongruously wondered if the word caterwauling had anything to do with cats. She did her best to hold him while Chelsea scrubbed. By the time he was all lathered up, he had crawled up Fran's chest and she was barely holding on to him. Her entire front was now soaked in sudsy peroxide.

"I'm sorry," Chelsea said, darting a look into her eyes as she worked the cloth over the soft pads of Cheeto's back paws. "Are you getting ripped to shreds by his claws?"

Fran adjusted her hands so she had a stronger hold on him. "A little, but it's okay." Cheeto had got her good a couple of times, and she already felt the sting of it. But it was bearable, especially with Chelsea so close to her. They were almost as close as they had been the night they had kissed, and Fran couldn't stop the memory of that night from flooding her senses. She had to get a grip—on her emotions as well as on Cheeto. "Do you want to turn the water on? I think we can rinse him now."

Chelsea took the hand shower from its holder and turned the knob, then tested the spray with her hand for temperature. Fran pulled Cheeto's claws from her T-shirt and placed him in the tub again, but as soon as the water hit him he sprang toward her again, this time raking his claws against her forearms. "Ow, Cheeto, you fucker. Knock it off."

"Franny, I'm so sorry." Chelsea's apology sounded sincere but there was a giggle behind it.

"I think I deserve a raise." Fran muttered, but gave Chelsea a grudging smile. There was no way she could be angry with this woman. She took the handset and pretty much turned it on herself and Cheeto together. "Why don't you get Forge? I'll finish this guy."

A few minutes later, Forge and Chelsea appeared at the door. Fran was back on the commode, gently towel-drying Cheeto, who only looked mildly miffed at this point.

Forge came close and tried to give Cheeto scritches under his chin, but he was not having it. "He looks so different when he's wet."

"Let's go, Forge," Chelsea said. "Take off your clothes and put them in here." She shook open a plastic garbage bag. "Get in the tub. I'm going to wash you with this stuff before you get wet."

Petal stood in the doorway. "Is Cheeto going to be okay?"

"Yeah." Fran fluffed the fur behind his ears. "You want to take over drying him? Go sit on Forge's bed and I'll bring him to you." She wrapped him up in the towel and deposited him on Petal's lap. "He's pretty comfortable right now. Just keep working the towel over his fur."

Petal held him reverently. "It's going to be okay, Cheeto."

Fran stood and watched with her hands on her hips. Petal took the job seriously and cooed nonsense at Cheeto. For once, she looked at peace, and a lot younger than her fourteen years.

She rooted around in Forge's drawers and brought a selection of his clothes into the bathroom. Chelsea rinsed the suds from Forge, pressing the handset against his belly and making him giggle.

"Shorts and a T-shirt or PJs?" Fran asked.

"PJs," Forge cried.

"Pajamas it is." Chelsea turned off the spray and wrapped him in a towel. She briskly rubbed his body. "Haven't done this in a while for my big boy. Please be careful, Forge. I never want to see you get hurt."

"I didn't get hurt. Just smelly."

"Ain't that the truth." She rubbed the towel over his head. "Thank you, Fran. You've been"—Chelsea turned to her and the smile left her face—"oh, you're bleeding."

Fran lifted her palms upward. A multitude of scratches along her inner forearms were nasty-looking and seeping. And a few blurry red spots had bloomed across the chest of her soaked baby blue T-shirt, and her dark bra was now showing through. "Yeah, he was not a happy kitty."

"I'll be back in a second, okay?" Chelsea ushered a half-dressed Forge from the room.

Fran surveyed the carnage around her. A whitish crust was drying in the tub, and the floor tiles and bath mat were saturated. She opened the cupboard next to the vanity, hoping to find some cleaning products and rags, and did a double take at what she saw. There among stacks of towels and a motley assortment of bath toys, light gleamed off the golden curves and grooves of an Oscar statuette sitting at the back of the shelf in front of her. A string was tied around the neck of the trophy and attached to a plastic boat, the kind a child would play with in the bath.

She wrapped her fingers around its stylized legs, marveling at the weight of the thing, and brought it into the light. *Academy Award to Chelsea Cartwright—Performance by an Actress in a Supporting Role—A Dynasty Less Than Sublime*, Fran read on the engraved base. Holy shit. She turned toward the mirror and stared at herself holding a genuine Academy Award and cradled it like it was a precious, bottom-heavy, gold-plated infant. All the adolescent dreams she'd had of succeeding as a screenwriter cycled through her brain, and for a moment she vividly hallucinated standing in front of an audience made up of the crème-de-la-crème of Hollywood, accepting the award for best original screenplay to the sound of deafening applause. *I'd like to thank the Academy…*

"A toy boat is a rarely seen accessory on the awards circuit." Chelsea leaned against the doorjamb with a white plastic first aid box under her arm, a tiny smile on her face. God only knew how long she'd been standing there, bearing witness to Fran's totally cringy behavior.

"I'm sorry." The statuette landed next to the sink with a thud, and Fran stepped away from it. "I saw it and couldn't help myself."

"No one can. It annoyed the shit out of Beau. It used to sit on the piano downstairs, and everyone who came over picked it up and had their fantasy moment."

"Like me," Fran said, feeling like her face was on fire. "You don't mind everyone being all grabby and covetous of something you worked really hard to get?"

"I'm happy to share him." Chelsea closed the door and took a step closer. Her smile turned wry. "It's hard to break off pieces of him, but everybody deserves to be Spring Fling Queen."

"Right." Fran relaxed slightly. "If that's true, why is it hidden away in the bathroom closet?"

"Well, Forge took a liking to this guy. He would make a grab for it whenever we walked by the piano with him in our arms. Poor Oscar has taken a tumble more than a few times." Chelsea patted the figurine on the head. "Then when Forge was old enough to lift him, he ended up in his bedroom. Then the bathroom, and then in the bath itself, where Forge would plunk him down on the bottom of the tub and use him as a mooring for his toy boats." She took the string between two fingers. "As you can see."

"That didn't bother you? Hiding this staggering achievement away?" Fran leaned against the sink and watched as Chelsea pushed the statue aside and opened the first aid kit.

"Nah." Chelsea didn't look at her as she said it, but that could've been because she was busy ripping open an antiseptic towelette. Still, there was something in the tone of that denial that said there was more to the story.

Fran decided not to push. "You know, I've been pretty much doused in peroxide. That little wipe probably isn't going to add much in the way of sanitizing my battle wounds."

"Better safe than sorry." Chelsea moved closer and gently tended to the scratches on Fran's forearms.

At Chelsea's nearness, Fran's blood turned thick and hot as it slowly pushed through veins that felt too tiny to contain the gush of heat. The millions of cells that made up her body were highly attuned to the light touch of Chelsea's fingers, and Fran tried mightily to keep her hands to herself. She stayed silent while Chelsea groped for another towelette and pressed it against a tiny laceration on Fran's neck that she hadn't even been aware of until the sting of antiseptic registered. But it was nothing compared to the ache she felt for Chelsea. She drew in a breath and tried to exhale as quietly as possible.

Chelsea raised her eyes to Fran's and paused, two fingers pressed right beside Fran's carotid artery. What she saw Fran could only guess, but it was enough for Chelsea to bite her lip in a confused sort of way, and it made something within Fran shift, like Chelsea was a lever that easily pried Fran's heart open. The need to be closer, to feel more, was overwhelming. She placed her hands on Chelsea's hips and brought her a half inch closer. If Chelsea was going to back away, here was the moment she was going to do it.

But Chelsea remained where she was and dabbed at the nastiest of Cheeto's visible damage, a small but deep cut on Fran's jaw. Her eyes darted up at Fran again, and the undeniable desire in them made it seem like all the moisture in Fran's body had evaporated. She licked her parched lips.

"Don't do that," Chelsea murmured.

"Do what?" Fran's voice was husky and low.

"You know." Chelsea tossed the wipe into the sink and dragged her hands from Fran's shoulders a short distance to her chest, her fingers grazing the two reddish blots there. "I can't see how bad these are."

Fran pulled off her damp T-shirt and dropped it, and her hands gripped Chelsea at the waist. "How is the view now?"

"Perfect," Chelsea breathed, her eyes glued to the pale curving skin just above Fran's black bra. She turned her face away and took a tiny step back, but not far enough to be outside Fran's reach. "You're making this really hard."

She grabbed another antiseptic wipe and tore it open, focusing all her attention on that small white square as she carefully unfolded it. Her cool hand was a balm as she rested it over the two scratches, the thin fibers of the towelette the only barrier to Fran's scorching skin. Fran clamped onto Chelsea's wrist and dragged her hand downward, leaving the towelette in place. Chelsea cupped Fran's flesh, her palm nudging against silk and the outline of her erect nipple. Her other hand reached up and both thumbs swiped across the achingly sensitive tips of Fran's breasts. Her breathing became labored, and she couldn't bear it another second. "Chelsea. I need to kiss you."

It was the wrong thing to say. Chelsea lifted her head and gazed into Fran's eyes, and Fran could see the exact moment when the cloudy haze of sexual need was replaced by caution. Chelsea retreated, putting a few feet of space between them.

Fran's brain struggled to catch up with reality. How were they not still in each other's arms? The turn of events was wrenching.

Chelsea came close again for one second and plucked the wipe that was stuck to Fran's chest. "We shouldn't be doing this. The fact that my kids are both sitting in the next room is one of a million reasons why not."

"Can we at least talk about it?" Talking about it was not what Fran wanted to do right now, but a discussion might alleviate Chelsea's unease, and it was better than nothing.

Chelsea didn't seem to hear the question. "Nothing good can happen here in this smelly bathroom. The last thing the media needs is another story of someone taking sexual advantage. No. Nope. That's not going to be me."

"Chelsea, I would never—"

"Of course not, Fran. I know that. But if we were to continue, and someone noticed, it would come out. Times have changed since it happened to me."

"What?" Fran froze.

Chelsea shut her eyes as if she couldn't believe she had let that slip. "Nothing. Never mind." She crossed her arms over her chest. "Look, if things were different, I could see…"

"What?" Fran prompted. "What could you see?"

Chelsea's lips pressed into a hard line. She was as closed off as Fran had ever seen her. "Nothing," she finally said. "There is no upside to this. It's not going to happen. Somehow some unscrupulous person would find out and use it as currency in this shitty town."

That brought Fran up short. Someone was trying to do exactly that, and they were hours away from doing it. Never mind how she herself was culpable in that brewing mess.

"This really can't happen again. Do you understand that?" Chelsea seemed to choose her words with care. "If you can't accept it, we may not be able to work together any longer."

"No, I understand." She wasn't willing to give up on whatever this was with Chelsea, but little claws of guilt punctured her conscience. Besides, nothing would be gained by arguing her point now. Plus, she needed to take care of the looming threat Carmina Piranha posed. Once her former boss was dealt with, Fran could own up to her gossip job and she and Chelsea could start fresh. She picked up her gross, wet shirt from the floor and put it on. "I should go. I have a few things to take care of tomorrow. Do you think you'll be needing me?"

"No." Chelsea didn't meet her eyes as she exited the bathroom. "Enjoy your day off."

CHAPTER FOURTEEN

In the end, it didn't take much effort to track down Carmina Piranha. Fran simply texted a fellow intravenousgossip freelancer—who was happy to talk smack about their coworkers, imagine that—and got the skinny on where her editor spent most of his days and nights. Yes, Carmina Piranha was a man, and he pretty much lived out of a coffee shop in Van Nuys.

She now had his legal name. Her colleague had actually worked with him years ago at a Cleveland daily, and shared a pic of him at a holiday party with a Santa hat on his head. With his name and that image, she began her research, and unearthed a number of promising nuggets in various online repositories of public records that might be useful.

After that, she called a former roommate who worked for LAPD. Patty's personal life was a mess, but she was a star on the rise in law enforcement. Fran asked her to check out her former editor, but that kind of intel took time, and Fran didn't have it. The ammunition she currently had would have to be enough—for now.

It was Saturday, and the coffee shop was busy when Fran arrived at around one in the afternoon. She spotted him instantly. He looked the same, only a few years older, a few pounds heavier, and minus the Santa hat. He sat hunched over a laptop, expensive-looking headphones over his ears and black-rimmed readers sliding down his ski slope of a nose. Nothing about him suggested greasy, parasitic bottom feeder, but that's what he was. How had Fran let herself get sucked into this line of work?

As she stood in line for coffee, her phone buzzed with a text. It was Lorraine, Chelsea's ex-assistant.

Hi Fran! Hope you're well. Can you come by the pop-up for a chat sometime? There's something I need to know.

Sure, she typed and shoved her phone back in her pocket. She didn't have time for Lorraine right now.

Carmina hadn't moved a muscle since the last time she snuck a glance at him. It seemed the only time his eyes shifted from his screen was when he glanced at the phone lying next to it. How sad for someone to be so engrossed in the lives of strangers that he had no situational awareness of his own.

Once she picked up her latte, she didn't hesitate, even though her plan was half-baked at best. All she knew was appealing to his sense of decency and the standards of ethical journalism were going to cut exactly zero soap.

"Carmina." She sat down across from him.

He looked up and the surprise leached from his face as he realized who she was. He pulled his headphones from his ears and let them dangle around his neck. The strains of some bombastic piece of classical music seeped from them until he slapped a key on the keyboard. "F. Ulysses, as I live and breathe." His smile looked smug and sinister at the same time. "Ultimatums work, I see, at least on you. Excellent to know."

"I'd say I'm pleased to meet you, but I'd be lying."

He let out a high-pitched giggle. "F. You wound me." He looked her up and down, or as much as he could from the top of her head to the top of the table. "But bygones and all that. Glad to have you back in the fold. What do you have for me?"

The utter gall of him. "Nothing. Chelsea Cartwright is completely unremarkable in every way, and everything published about her has been fabricated." Lies, but she'd meet his confident bluster with some of her own. "That is what I have learned in the five months I've worked for her."

"Bullshit."

"It's been the most boring job of my life." Nothing could be further from the truth, and he obviously wasn't buying it. It had been worth a try.

"Well, there you go. Write about that. With the F. Ulysses touch, I foresee a million clicks." He leaned in and gave her a shrewd look.

"Time was, you could take the most mundane fact and spin it into something loaded with snark and sarcasm all while standing on your head." He pointed at her. "You, my dear, have turned to the dark side."

Have not, she wanted to say. But if getting close to Chelsea and making her life better with the thousand little tasks she did for her was the dark side, she definitely had. Maybe she should start communicating via sonar, like a bat. Because she liked it here in the dark. "I'm not going to write about Chelsea." She wouldn't do it. And he couldn't make her.

"Then we're back where we started. You forcing me to turn lemons into lemonade with a story about how Chelsea Cartwright doesn't know a celebrity muckraker is living in her back pocket."

"I really wish you wouldn't do that."

"And if wishes were horses…we'd be back to the old west or some crap. I never understood that saying."

"Don't you think it's worth it to leave me there? What if I stumble across something really juicy? You blowing my cover ends any possibility of the inside track. Think about it. I'm in contact with celebrities on the daily now. Working as an assistant gives me access." Fran was disgusted with herself. She didn't plan on ever using her position to expose any aspect of Chelsea's life, public or private. The guilt chickens were coming home to roost, and if she didn't come clean to Chelsea soon, Fran thought she might be pecked to death with shame and remorse.

His eyes flashed with irritation. "But you haven't published anything in five months."

"Well, I have to be careful, don't I? Once I publish anything that can be traced back to me, it's over. I'm fired and in violation of my NDA. A huge story could be right around the corner."

"And meanwhile, I'm out the income your posts generate while we wait for this huge story that may never materialize. I need you back in the saddle, Ulysses."

Had her measly two-hundred-dollar posts brought in that much coin? If Fran had known how valuable she apparently was to Carmina's website before she took this job, would she have done anything differently? It didn't matter now. Here was her moment to let him know exactly how many cards she held.

She looked him dead in the eye. "I will never be back in the saddle. I will never write gossip again. But I can provide information when it arises and if it doesn't jeopardize my situation." Best to keep him stringing along. She took a sip from her nearly forgotten latte before delivering the kill shot. "And if that's not enough for you, I'll be contacting the Employment Development Department and your ex-wife." She shook her head and tsked at him. "A fraudulent unemployment claim and unpaid child support is not a good look for a titan of gossip, Carmina."

He gazed at her with something like grudging respect. "Mutually assured destruction. You did come to play."

"Leave me alone. If I have anything for you, I'll get in touch." She picked up her coffee and left.

CHAPTER FIFTEEN

After only two days, Chelsea already knew she would miss the *Tolstoy Was Right* set when she finished shooting. It was the first role she had accepted after handing down the new brief to her team. The priority now was substantive, meaty roles, even if they were smaller than her usual second or third billing.

Grace Commerford was shooting a family drama that the studio planned to release in an awards-baiting theatrical run first before hopefully garnering big numbers on one of the streamers. She was a young director who had made a name for herself with a cheap but artful production that had been a darling on the festival circuit a few years ago.

An actor had dropped out suddenly and Chelsea's agent had swooped in and suggested her. Grace Commerford had been thrilled that an actor of Chelsea's caliber was now on the call sheet for her first major studio release. Chelsea's role was the visiting alcoholic sister who arrives like a tornado and leaves just as much destruction in her wake. It was a showy role with only a handful of scenes, and it was instrumental to the plot, so no danger of it being cut down.

So far, Grace's direction had been stellar. She wanted to hear Chelsea's ideas about her character and was open to collaboration. The set was respectful and productive—ahead of schedule, even—an anomaly in Chelsea's experience. There was great camaraderie among everyone, both cast and crew.

The AD called lunch, and Chelsea looked around for Fran. In the seven days since their tête-à-tête in Forge's bathroom, there had been moments of tension, but they had mostly brought their working relationship back on track. Both of them were now pretending their two moments of intimacy had never happened. Containing those actions and feelings was for the absolute best. She knew this.

Now Fran was quieter, a little more reticent, but sometimes Fran gazed at her with a naked hunger that lit Chelsea up with arousal. And sometimes Chelsea couldn't tear her eyes away from the smooth planes of Fran's cheeks, or her hands, or her shoulders, as she sat at her laptop and composed emails on Chelsea's behalf. The wild but inconvenient attraction notwithstanding, she really liked Fran, enjoyed her company, got along well with her.

Chelsea wandered in the direction of her trailer. For a moment, she allowed an image of herself stripping Fran of her clothes to flit across her mind, of finally getting a look at her body. What would it feel like to lose herself in Fran's kiss? To surrender to these swirling feelings that were getting harder and harder to contain?

Would it really be so bad if she and Fran expanded the dimensions of their relationship? They were two consenting adults, and there was no corporate policy or HR department expressly forbidding a dalliance between them. It wouldn't be illegal, just bordering on inappropriate. The optics were…not good. But was that what she even wanted? A dalliance?

As she passed the little open area adjacent to craft services where the crew ate lunch, she saw her. Fran sat there, paying fierce attention to one of the grips who was speaking. A camera assistant pulled on Fran's sleeve, directing her attention to a piece of paper that looked like it had a lighting set up sketched on it.

Had Fran just recently developed an interest in the technical side of filmmaking, or had it been there all along? How much did Chelsea really know about Fran anyway? She had quickly developed into a competent assistant, but she was also a writer, Chelsea knew. What were her aspirations? Being an assistant wasn't an end goal, not for someone as intelligent as Fran. How much longer could she expect Fran to hang around? And why did the idea of her departure produce a boulder of apprehension in her gut?

Nearby, someone's walkie crackled and Fran looked up and saw Chelsea. She left her tablemates and hurried to Chelsea's side.

"Hey, I'm so sorry." She offered Chelsea a bottle of water. "Let me walk you back to your trailer and I'll get you some lunch. There's carrot soup today, which smells great—"

"No."

Fran paused. "No trailer or no carrot soup?"

"Neither. Let's eat here. Get to know some people. I can sit with you and your friends if that's all right."

"Um, sure." Fran glanced back to where a few of her conversation partners had stood and were now lining up for food.

"Why don't I get you something to eat? Go back and sit down. I'll choose for you." Chelsea moved toward the end of the food line, and Fran trailed behind her.

"But…"

"What? You don't think I'm capable of getting you something you'll like?"

"That's my job. I'm sorry I wasn't there when they cut." She looked genuinely distressed.

"It's okay. I'm not upset." Chelsea reached out and grasped Fran's forearm, then pulled back at the shock of touching her, and the reminder of how it felt when she had tended to the scratches there. "I like this set. Why hide away in my trailer when I can be part of the gang?"

"You're sure?"

"Very."

"Okay, but I'll get my own food." She seemed to relax and took a step forward as the line inched along. "Who knows what I'd end up with on my plate if you chose for me? Probably a lot of kale. Did you know I don't like kale?"

Chelsea hadn't known that. "What did kale ever do to you? It's delicious."

"That's exactly what a rabbit would say, not a person. I don't understand when kale went from being a garnish to being an unavoidable celebrity vegetable. Kale is overexposed, an attention hog, and a little slutty. Kale would go to the opening of an envelope. Kale, how can we miss you if you don't go away?" She grinned at Chelsea.

"Okay, got it. No slutty kale for you." Something else she liked about Fran. Such a goof sometimes.

"What is the holdup?" Fran stood on tiptoes and tried to see over the heads in front of her. "You know you could jump the line."

Chelsea nodded. It was common practice for main cast to be served first. It cost money to delay the production because an actor was the last one to be fed. Still, Chelsea hated to use that particular perk. *Except when you're in the parking lot of In-N-Out and starving.* "We haven't been waiting that long."

"This role was a good choice for you. It's a great ensemble. And the script! What I really love about it is how it's a pretty heavy subject, but it's infused with these dazzling moments of funny. It's a hard balance to pull off."

"Don't you write comedic scripts?"

Fran whipped her head around and gazed at her. "I did, yes."

"Why don't you ever talk about them?"

"What's there to say?" Fran looked away. "I wrote some stuff. Nothing ever got close to production. I'm clearly talentless, so I gave it up."

"Do not say that." Chelsea was vehement. "Talent has almost nothing to do with getting a picture made. It's mostly connections and luck. I'm sure your screenplays are brilliant."

Fran stared at her; her cheeks flushed pink. "That may be so, but talent is the reason for the luck and connections. Nobody's interested otherwise."

"Not true. I got my first role out of sheer luck."

"Thus proving my point about talent being part of the equation. Your gift was apparent even in that tampon commercial you did way back when."

Jesus. That was the first acting job Chelsea had ever booked. Fran had seen it?

"It's on YouTube," Fran said, as if she could read her mind. "You can't get lucky without talent," she added. "Where is this coming from, anyway? Why do you suddenly want to talk about my screenplays?"

Chelsea stepped forward. The line was moving again. "Will you let me read one?"

"No, I don't think so." Fran shuffled along next to her, her eyes cast downward.

"Why not? You have a connection now, and you don't want to use it? You are in the unique position of having someone with a little bit of pull in the industry asking to read your work. Do you know how rare that is?"

"Yes, but I'm not going to use you like that. Besides, I'm not a writer anymore. Haven't you noticed? I'm an assistant. And not a very good one, apparently, if my boss won't let me get her lunch. If you were for real about getting mine, I'll have the carrot soup." She turned and walked back to the table she had just vacated and sat with the crew.

❖

Fran watched as Chelsea beguiled the craft services team with her wide smile and extravagant compliments. There was no one better at turning on the charm. Even if makeup did a hell of a job making her look like she was coming off a three-day bender, she was still lovely—inside and out.

Their conversation had Fran rattled. Why was Chelsea so interested in her writing? And why now? Truthfully, Fran had been rattled ever since the previous weekend when she and Carmina Piranha had clashed in the coffee shop in Van Nuys. She hadn't heard a peep from him since then, but each day that passed without telling Chelsea about her gossip gig produced an exponential number of worries.

Her phone buzzed with a text and she was super glad of the distraction. It was Lorraine.

Fran, are you going to stop by soon? Need to talk to you. Can't do it over text. Should we meet elsewhere?

Crap. She had forgotten all about that. *Can come tonight, but it's a shooting day for C. Might be late.*

Lorraine replied right away. *That's fine. I'm here until 12AM.*

Well, that settled the question of whether she would tell Chelsea today. It would have to be tomorrow. And she had just made her long day even longer.

❖

Fran pushed through the crowd at the bar where Lorraine cranked out veggie burgers in the back. It was after nine o'clock, and it was Friday, something she only realized while sitting in traffic after picking up her car at Chelsea's.

She was tired, and she had another early day tomorrow since Chelsea was on set again.

There was a line about six deep for burgers, and Fran remembered her last visit with Trina. She and Trina had been like ships passing lately.

At the order window, she called out to Lorraine, who had her back turned at the flat top, flipping patties. Lorraine held up a *give me a minute* finger. Fran stepped aside and entertained, then discarded, the idea of ordering a drink. Fatigue would make the drive home difficult enough.

Ten minutes later, Lorraine stuck her head out the order window and motioned her through the tiny kitchen and out the back door. They stood in a parking lot, and the sound of insects buzzing around the one streetlamp was a nice contrast to the muted music and conversation inside the bar.

"Word must be getting around about your spectacular burgers. Wish I had time for one tonight," Fran said.

"Yeah, I guess. Thanks for coming." Lorraine's smile was brief. "It is busy, so I only have a few minutes."

"Sure. Did you finally want to own up to telling the paps about Chelsea's schedule?" Fran still didn't know what the story was there, but she was inclined to believe it wasn't Lorraine. So why did she even say that?

"No!" Lorraine looked as if she wanted to tear Fran's head off.

Because she was an asshole. "Sorry. My bad. It's just doing my head in that I can't figure it out." Fran raised her hands in a gesture of peace. "What's up?"

Lorraine gave her a cautious look. "I'm in touch with Petal. Through Insta DMs."

"Yeah, she mentioned that once."

"She's a really lonely girl. And she needs someone to talk to sometimes, so we chat occasionally. Chelsea doesn't know. For a while Petal did a lot of complaining about you."

Fran nodded grimly. "She doesn't like me. I think I've already told you you're a tough act to follow—at least where Petal is concerned."

"I took it with a grain of salt. There's always an adjustment period. But she told me something and then asked me what she should do about it." Another considering glance at Fran.

"What did she say?"

"That you're a writer for a gossip website. Intravenousgossip.com."

It felt like all the blood in Fran's body froze in its veins.

"Now, she told me she read an email on your laptop, and she knows that was a real violation of your privacy, but considering what the email said, I thought I should confirm this with you before giving her any advice. Is it true?"

Fran took a deep breath through her nose. Lorraine was studying her, probably willing to give her the benefit of the doubt if she said Petal was wrong. But right now what Fran most wanted was to unburden herself, confess everything. It would be such a relief to tell someone. "Yes, it's true."

Lorraine's mouth fell open. "I totally thought she was lying."

"But you have to understand. I quit in order to take the assistant job with Chelsea." Not strictly true, but close enough. "I haven't contributed to the site since before I began working for her, but my boss wouldn't accept my resignation. That's the email Petal saw. He was asking me to come back."

"Chelsea hired you even though you wrote for intravenousgossip? She really hates that website." Lorraine's voice dripped with disbelief.

"I omitted it from my résumé."

She shook her head. "Fran, this is terrible. What am I supposed to tell Petal? She's been bugging me for a week about this."

"Look. I know it looks bad, but I would never do anything to hurt Chelsea. Just the thought of it…" Fran shook her head. How was she going to resolve this? "All I want to do is protect her, and I still don't know how the photographers are getting their info. They still show up sometimes as if there's a signal fire they can all see somehow."

Lorraine was about to say something, but then her mouth closed at Fran's words. She looked at the ground.

"What? I know you know something. Please tell me so I can put a stop to it."

"No." Lorraine gave her head a resolute shake. "I accepted responsibility for it. I tried to make it stop. I'll try again."

Fran studied her face. What the hell did that mean? Was Lorraine in touch with whoever was doing this? *Wait…* "Holy shit." The culprit finally dawned on Fran. "It's Petal, isn't it?"

Lorraine pressed her fingertips to her forehead. "Oh God."

"How is she doing it? Why is she doing it?"

"It's my fault!" Lorraine cried. "She was with me on a coffee run when I was approached by this sketchy dude—"

"Why was she with you? That's not your job."

"We were close. Chelsea let her accompany me on errands every once in a while. Sometimes it was easier to say yes to her than to deal with her when she's unhappy."

"I get that." Fran nodded. "Sorry to interrupt. Go on."

"This guy came up to us at the Coffee Bean and said I could make a lot of money just by calling him with information about where Chelsea was going to be. He would inform a bunch of photographers and I would get a cut of the money. And Petal was right there. He had to know who she was. This was when Chelsea and Beau first separated and their lives were batshit. He said people wanted to see Chelsea and Beau together. They'd pay good money for it."

"Oh no."

"Yeah, and that messed Petal up even more than the separation did. I told the guy to fuck off, but on our way out of the coffee place, I was juggling the coffees and the phone, and I admit I was distracted. Petal said she dropped her barrette, so I let her go back inside for a minute."

"And that's when she—"

"He gave her his number and she texted him whenever she overheard her mom's plans, especially if she was going to see Beau. Petal didn't want any money from him. She was convinced her mom and dad would get back together because that's what all the gossip sites were saying."

"There's a special place in hell for a guy like that."

"But is it any different than you profiting off of celebrities for that website?"

That brought Fran up short. "I—"

"I'm sorry. That was rude. And I don't have a leg to stand on. I put Chelsea's child in danger. I truly felt responsible, and that's why I did what I did." Lorraine put a hand to her forehead. "When you told me it was still happening, it felt like a punch in the gut."

"What do you mean?" Fran frowned.

"I thought it was over. I made Petal delete his number from her phone, and I watched her do it. She lied to me." Lorraine shook her head. "I DMed her to ask if she was still doing it, and she said yes."

Wow. Lorraine got Petal to admit it? Twice? "You have to know what I'm going to ask—why didn't you tell Chelsea?"

"Before the shit hit the fan, I truly thought Petal had stopped. I thought she didn't have access to that creeper anymore. Why put Chelsea and Petal through all that drama? Their relationship was already hanging by a thread because of the divorce. It was only going to make everything worse. And it was really my fault for not keeping a good enough eye on her in the first place."

"I'm sorry Petal did you dirty like that. I don't know if I would have protected her like you did."

"Don't be an idiot like me." Lorraine grasped Fran's shoulder. "Tell Chelsea about your job."

"I will. You have my word. I've been meaning to, but she's going to fire my ass so fast."

Lorraine nodded sadly. "I think you're right."

"Petal and I need to have a long conversation. She and Forge are at their dad's this weekend." Should Fran include Chelsea in all this? Yes. There was no getting around it. Everything needed to come out, and she would lay it all out there when the kids came back from Beau's. Let the chips fall where they may. "Can you give me the weekend? I promise I'll have this all sorted out by then."

Lorraine nodded. "Even though I don't work for them anymore, I still care about them. I want them all to be happy."

Fran wanted that too, but nowhere in the mix could she see where there was happiness for herself as well.

CHAPTER SIXTEEN

Chelsea was exhausted and there were still probably about three shooting hours left in the day. This was one of the most grueling scenes in *Tolstoy Was Right,* and what had started strong was slowly devolving into dysfunction. She and her castmates had sat in the cramped kitchen set all day, cameras and lights and bodies surrounding them, up close and way too personal. Someone's farts smelled like rotten eggs, and it was making Chelsea feel sick. They had to be due a break soon, right?

There were four actors in the scene, and they sat around the table like the cardinal points on a compass, which meant a ton of coverage and multiple takes for each set-up. Her character's brother had just picked her up from the drunk tank on Thanksgiving morning, and this was when the actors cast as her siblings used the situation for a little unplanned intervention.

She was playing the scene defiant, insensitive, messy—and still a little drunk. Her hair was styled to look lank and greasy, with some crusty fake vomit gumming up a couple of hanks near her ear. All evidence of good health had been leached from her face, her makeup artist going heavy on a sallow yellow foundation with prominent cheekbones and dark shadows under her eyes.

Her character was a couple of inches from rock bottom. She knew what that looked like far too well. As each take began, Chelsea let defensiveness radiate off of her in waves. All her character wanted was for her family to get off her back, but each of the actors she was playing against had opposing motivations. If they did it right, it could be a powerhouse scene, but they were not doing it right at the moment.

It was a little unbelievable that Jeremy was still flubbing lines at this point. They had run through the scene repeatedly through three set-ups already, and they were doing Chelsea's close-ups now. She hadn't half-assed her performance during their close-ups and deserved the same courtesy.

Jeremy got the line wrong again and Grace Commerford's flat voice called cut over the walkie. Everyone paused, waiting for instructions, and then the first AD said, "Take five, everyone."

Fran stood just behind the gaggle of camera department members, waving her over, appearing more agitated than Chelsea had ever seen her. She darted around the crew, and Fran handed Chelsea her phone. "Forge just texted you on Beau's phone."

"What the…?" She moved out of the way of the bodies streaming from the small space and gazed at her phone.

Mama its Forge. Daddy is sleping in the bathrom and I cant wake him up.

She texted *Where's Colleen? Where's Petal?* After waiting about an eternity for him to reply, she Facetimed Beau's phone. "Honey? Are you okay?" His little face was so serious, it made Chelsea's heart seize in her chest.

"Yeah. Dad sent Colleen home. Petal is upstairs. She said not to bother her."

"Is Jerry there?" Beau's assistant was always around.

"I don't know where Jerry is."

"Go get Petal and put her on the phone, please." The screen showed the ceiling as Forge made his way upstairs. Chelsea bit her thumbnail while she waited. Fran stood in front of her to shield her from the questioning eyes of the crew.

Forge kept talking. "Daddy was kind of weird today. Like he was before he left."

"I'm so sorry, Forgey. I'm going to come get you and Petal." When Chelsea said that, Fran signaled that she was going to get the car. Chelsea nodded and watched her dash off.

"Here's Petal."

"What?" Petal sounded annoyed, as usual.

"Petal, are you okay?" Chelsea found a corner where she had a modicum of privacy. Still, she lowered her voice as much as she could.

"Yeah, why wouldn't I be?"

"Has Dad been drinking?"

Petal hesitated before answering. "Yeah, but he always drinks."

She put a hand on her forehead, trying to contain the rage that threatened to melt the top of her skull. *No, get angry later.* "Here's what I want you to do. Go to your Dad—"

"He said he was going to take a nap."

"In the bathroom?" Chelsea tried to keep the hysteria out of her voice.

"No. He was—"

"Forge said he's sleeping in the bathroom."

"He is? Do you want me to try and wake him up?"

"No, honey. I need you to show me how he's positioned, okay? Please do it now, Petal."

Petal must have heard the urgency in her voice because for once she didn't argue. "Okay."

Chelsea could hear Petal telling Forge what they had to do, then there was silence on the line. She kept the phone outstretched while she frantically searched for her director.

"Mom?"

She stopped short. "I'm here. Show me."

Petal had the phone trained on Beau. "Can you see him? He's lying on his side. It smells bad in here."

His body was curled around the toilet, his head resting on his outstretched arm. And he was still fully clothed, thank God. He didn't look like he was in danger of choking. "Okay. Hang on just a second." She looked up and miraculously saw the one person she needed—Grace Commerford stood huddled with the first AD and a producer, and she almost ran into them in her haste. "Grace," she blurted.

"Hey, Chelsea. You've been so on it today. It must be so frustrating to—" Grace's brows lowered with concern. "What's wrong?"

"I'm sorry. I have to go. My kids—" She pointed at her phone, too upset to form words.

Her director immediately said, "Go to them. We were talking about calling it a day anyway what with Jeremy and his case of the yips." She spoke into her walkie, requesting a golf cart to take Chelsea off the set. "I hope everything is okay."

"Thank you! See you tomorrow." She pulled off her body mic and shoved it in Grace's hands, and then shouted into the phone, "Sit tight, guys. I'm on my way."

❖

Fran sped the entire way to Brentwood, where Beau lived. Between repeated calls to Petal, Chelsea used some napkins in Fran's bag to remove as much of the stage makeup as she could. Ever since Chelsea had practically thrown her costume at one of the wardrobe assistants and jumped into the workout wear Fran had ready for her, she had been tense and angry, but also quiet in a dangerous kind of way. Fran did not want to be on her bad side right now.

A mass of photographers swarmed as they approached the gate. No, Petal wouldn't. Jesus Christ, had she alerted her contact? Her mother was coming to her ex-husband's rescue. Of course, there would have to be pictures. She wanted to kill Petal.

"Oh no…" Chelsea moaned and gripped the dashboard. She raised the hood of her sweatshirt.

"Do you want to slide down in the seat?" Fran flipped up the collar on her jacket.

"What's the point? They'll still see me. It'll only be worse if they think I'm hiding from them."

Chelsea was right. Fran began to honk the horn as photographers surrounded the Defender. As she lowered her window to punch in the code Chelsea gave her, she yelled, "Fuck off, all of you! The cops have already been called." She would do that as soon as she stopped driving.

"Don't call the cops," Chelsea said quickly.

Beau's house was not that far off the street, and what was worse, the gate was constructed of iron bars that were easy to take pictures through. Fran figured it was a rental. The security at Chelsea's house was so beefed up, no pictures could be taken from street level. She swerved the car around the drive so the passenger side aligned with the front door. As soon as she braked, Chelsea ran out and into the house. Fran searched in her bag for her black Mets cap for added protection but couldn't find it. She found a hat of Chelsea's in the glove box and tugged it low over her face. Then she followed her inside.

Petal, Forge, and Chelsea were seated on an enormous sectional sofa in a vast living room, and Chelsea had her arms around both of them. She was kissing their heads and murmuring to them, but Fran couldn't hear what she said and began investigating the main floor. As she passed through the kitchen, she saw an empty handle of scotch at the top of a bin filled with beer cans, and another bottle three-quarters full on the counter among the takeout containers from what was probably the kids' dinner.

Beau was in a bathroom off the kitchen, lying on the floor. The room smelled of vomit. His shirt was wet at the shoulders and down the front. Fran knelt beside him and felt his neck for a pulse. Relief flooded her when her fingers found a steady beat. She called his name several times. No response. She shook his arm. Nothing. Patting his cheek made his eyelashes flutter but nothing more than that—and his skin was cold.

She kept saying his name, louder and louder, and shook him harder. She grabbed some toilet paper, wet it in the sink, and pressed it to his face. He groaned and tried to roll onto his back.

Fran braced her arms against his shoulder. "No, bro. Stay on your side."

Chelsea appeared next to her. "Is he conscious?"

"Not quite."

Chelsea pinched him on the arm—hard. "Beau!"

"Leave me alone." His eyes stayed shut and his words were slurred but understandable.

"That's close enough to conscious," she said to Fran. "Beau! Where's Jerry?"

"Jerry left. He and Daddy had a fight." Petal stood in the doorway, her hands wrapped around her waist. "He said he quit."

Chelsea's shoulders slumped. "Petal, honey, can you go check on your brother?"

"Forge is fine—"

"Just do what I asked you to do." Chelsea's voice was tight and came through gritted teeth.

Petal turned and disappeared from sight.

"Should we call 9-1-1?" Fran had her phone in her hand.

"He would absolutely kill me." Chelsea sounded utterly weary. "This is not supposed to be my problem anymore."

Fran quickly googled *What to do when someone is passed out from alcohol.* "If he's responding, which talking I guess is a response, he probably just needs to sleep it off."

"Yeah. This is not a new occurrence." Chelsea wiped her nose, and her eyes were glassy with tears.

"What can I do to help?"

Chelsea put a hand on hers. "I'm glad you're here. Would you get some water? Let's see if we can hydrate him a little."

When Fran returned, Chelsea had pulled herself together a bit and had made progress with Beau. She had him sitting against the tile wall. His eyes were open but he still seemed pretty out of it. They got him to take a few sips of water.

"Call Jerry," Chelsea said. "Ask him to come back. He knows how to take care of him. Also, call Joyce. She'll have to manage Beau out of this. Then call Colleen and Bernice. Make sure one of them knows to come to my house by four a.m.—before we leave for the set. As soon as someone shows up for Beau, we're leaving."

❖

In the end, both Jerry and Joyce arrived to support Beau. It was after midnight by the time Fran herded Chelsea and the kids back into the car and headed back to Pacific Palisades. She glanced in the mirror at Petal as they inched through the crowd of photographers, all shouting at Chelsea, asking her what was happening. Petal's eyes were round with shock, and when she saw Fran watching, her gaze darted away. Maybe there was some guilt in her expression. Fran certainly hoped so.

She followed the three of them upstairs. Chelsea had her arm around Forge as she led him into his bedroom, and Petal went into hers and shut the door.

Fran opened it. "I want to talk to you."

"Knock much?" Petal gave her a baleful look. "Get out. I'm tired. I want to sleep."

"Did you call your sleazy connect to bring the paps running? Do you know how much that hurts your mom?"

Petal opened her mouth but no words came out.

"What about your dad? Do you think he wants photographers witnessing what happened tonight? What if an ambulance had to come and there were pics of him being brought out on a stretcher? Hmm?" Yeah, it was harsh, but someone had to get through to her.

"Wait. Didn't it used to be your job to tell stories about my parents?" Petal seemed to rebound a bit from Fran's attack. "I'm going to tell my mom."

"Don't bother. I'll tell her myself. I'm serious, Petal. You need to stop doing this. Telling this guy where your mom is going to be all the time—it's not going to do what you want it to. It only makes her less safe."

"Fran." Chelsea's voice was like a whip crack. She stood at the threshold of Petal's room. "What in God's name are you talking about?"

Fran stood back and gave Petal a look. *Tell her*, she tried to say with her eyes.

Petal sat cross-legged on the bed, her spine straight in defiance. She glowered at Fran but didn't say anything. The silence was heavy and hot.

Fran exhaled. "There's something you need to know—"

"Fran works for a celebrity website. Intravenousgossip.com!" Petal cried.

Chelsea's gaze went from Petal to Fran, and the bewilderment slid from her expression, and something impenetrable replaced it.

"I don't." Fran hated that she sounded so defensive. "Not anymore."

"Intravenousgossip?" Chelsea frowned like she either had trouble understanding or she understood and didn't know how to proceed. "You're a journalist? You post things on that vile website?"

"It was my job before I started working for you. I haven't posted anything since then."

"But…" She seemed to struggle getting the words out. "You did?"

"I was going to tell you. I didn't want you to find out this way—"

"What way?" Chelsea's eyes were hard.

"See, Mom?" Petal gloated. "I kept telling you she was awful, and you didn't believe me."

"Quiet, Petal. Whatever Fran was saying when I came in, it was about you. We'll get to that. Fran, come with me."

She followed her to the kitchen, where Chelsea stood in front of the refrigerator with the door open.

"I would kill for a glass of wine right now," she muttered.

Fran slouched in the doorway. "So have a glass of wine. You deserve it." Maybe a drink would blunt the edge of Chelsea's anger.

"Do I deserve to be lied to by someone I trusted?" Chelsea asked. "Don't tell me what I fucking deserve." She grabbed a sparkling water and slammed the fridge door shut. "There's no alcohol in this house. There hasn't been for a long time."

Understanding rolled over Fran. She realized the only time she'd seen Chelsea drink was when they were out. The occasional white wine at a business lunch, a glass of champagne at the premiere. The slam of the cabinet door jolted her back to the here and now.

Chelsea set a glass tumbler on the counter with a heavy thud and filled it with water. "Why did I say that? It's just one more bit of information that you're going to use when you return to your real job, carrying all my secrets behind you."

"That's not fair. I wouldn't do that to you—"

"Don't forget about your NDA." Chelsea's voice was hard as diamonds. "I'll sue your ass off."

"Chelsea, please. I'm done writing gossip. I—I'm actually glad you know. I couldn't figure out how to tell you."

"Have you written any posts about me? About Beau? You must have. That website posts about Beau and me all the time. It's the one that continues to harp on the idea that I'm still in love with Beau. Did you write about that? Did you keep that inane garbage alive? The writers all have weird names on that website."

"Pseudonyms."

"Yeah. What's yours? I'm going to look you up and see how you've profited off my private life."

"I don't think—"

Chelsea smashed her glass down. Water arced out of it and toward the ceiling. "What is it?" she roared.

"F. Ulysses."

She nodded. She was so angry Fran was surprised the water in her glass didn't turn into vapor as it got close to her lips.

"Just so you know, I never wrote about you. I didn't know much about you until I started working for you. And I apologize, Chelsea. You don't know how sorry I am."

"Look me in the eye and tell me you didn't plan on using this job to write shit about me."

Fran couldn't do it. She stuck her hands in her back pockets and kept her eyes trained at the floor.

"Yeah, that's what I thought."

"I can't tell you that." Fran had to give her truth. "I wanted a higher word rate and I thought working for you would get that for me. But I never posted anything. First of all, you kept me too busy, and second, it felt disloyal. From those first days as your assistant, I was on your side."

"I would never have hired you if I'd known you worked for that website. It couldn't have been on your résumé."

"It wasn't," Fran admitted. "You have every right to be angry with me for omitting it from my résumé. But I would never do anything to hurt you."

Her response was a snort, as if she wasn't going to waste any more words on Fran.

That's when Fran knew she was in real trouble. She was fighting for her life here. What could she say to make Chelsea see? "Once I knew you, I wanted to be your fiercest ally. I want all the good things for you. You're beyond talented, and you work so hard, and if there's anyone who deserves success and happiness, it's you. I know I lied to you, but if you give me another chance, I will never lie again. Please don't let this end. I want to help you conquer this town. Make it kneel at your feet."

"You don't get it. As pretty as this picture you're painting is, you've soured it forever." It looked like Chelsea was going to say something else, but she shut her mouth with a click. "Leave the phone on the counter. As soon as you drive through the gate, the code will be changed."

"Wait. What do you want me to do about the contracts for—"

"That's not your problem anymore."

"But you have a meeting with—"

"How do you not understand? You're fired."

Fran stopped talking. Despite knowing full well what her fate would be, she was still caught by surprise. Yes, the end of her employment was a certainty. The surprise was how ashamed she felt, and the mortification of Chelsea having a low opinion of her. She blinked a few times to head off humiliating tears before they had a chance to fall. But she could have cried oceans and Chelsea wouldn't have noticed because she wasn't looking at her. She leaned against the counter with her arms crossed, and her expression was hard and blank.

Fran was still for a moment, working to master her feelings. After the lump in her throat subsided, she pulled the orange phone from her pocket and placed it on the counter. She turned to go, then stopped. "Petal is the one contacting the paparazzi. If she won't 'fess up, Lorraine will explain. She fell on her sword for your daughter. You seem to be making a habit of firing people who put you and your family before themselves."

Chelsea didn't move or acknowledge her in any way.

This was it. Whatever Fran said now would be the last impression she made on Chelsea—her last opportunity to tell her how she had reignited Fran's love of Hollywood, and of film. How good acting, and Chelsea's incredible talent, created a connection, how it soothed the soul, and how she should never stop. It was her moment to tell Chelsea how much Fran had changed by putting someone else's needs before her own, how her perspective had been altered forever.

But there was no way she could put all that into words that Chelsea would hear right now, so she said, "Goodbye, Chelsea. It was nice knowing you."

CHAPTER SEVENTEEN

"You and Beau are really making me earn my cut." Joyce sat on a stool at the island in Chelsea's kitchen. "Do you have anything to drink?"

Chelsea swallowed the fit of pique that threatened to escape, and forced herself to calmly pour Joyce some orange juice. "Are you saying that finding me a new assistant is the same level of difficulty as organizing Beau's rehab, withdrawing him from his commitments for the next six months, and fabricating a sudden new project to explain it all?"

Joyce took a sip and then grimaced. "Orange juice at ten o'clock at night just doesn't taste right." She put it down. "Good assistants are as rare as hen's teeth. You ought to know that by now."

She did. And despite the overwhelming outrage that coursed through her every time she thought of Fran's treachery, she could still acknowledge that Fran had been excellent at the job. Better than Lorraine. And she'd only had the position for less than six months. But knowing that didn't make her icy resentment any less valid.

She felt so intensely stupid! Angry—bitter—deceived. All those feelings just sat in her gut, an ever-present, unholy stew that made her an absolute bitch to be around. But was it her fault that she had been the subject of a betrayal so devastating she'd found it difficult to get out of bed in the morning? When that alarm went off at four, and she remembered what Fran had done, it took every single one of the thirty minutes before her car arrived for her to convince herself to get up and face the day.

And to think...no. She wasn't going to let herself go there.

Making a full examination of how Fran had made her feel was not going to happen. It would be a long while before she could kick over that particular log and inspect the chunks of trust and affection that were now rotten with the knowledge of Fran's deception.

Anger was getting her through the day. Anger at Fran, at Beau, at Petal, and most of all, herself. Who was ultimately to blame, when Chelsea was the one who opened the door to all this pain in her own life?

Thank God she had *Tolstoy Was Right* to distract her, something she could pour all her fractious, furious energy into. It was the one thing that was going right at the moment. Truth be told, she was using Fran's duplicity and Beau's irresponsible retreat into his disease as fuel for her character, and Grace Commerford had been generous in her praise. Eleven more days of shooting were a blessing right now. At least she had the work.

And Forge. Things were fine with him, as they always seemed to be. He was her stalwart little boulder, embedded in a raging river. Solid and steady as life's woes washed over him. She knew all this turmoil had to be wearing away at him, eroding his sunny disposition, but she didn't think she had to worry about him right now. Petal, on the other hand…

Chelsea hadn't confronted Petal with the information Fran had disclosed on her way out the door. But that same night, as she prowled the house, sleepless with rage, she snuck into Petal's room and took her phone. Not only was it a safety measure—Petal couldn't contact the press if she was without a phone, but it would also serve as a stopgap consequence until Chelsea could get to the bottom of the situation.

She needed to address it. It had to be settled. A week had gone by since the night at Beau's, and she and Petal had circled each other like a couple of Bengal cats ever since. Petal hadn't even mentioned the disappearance of her phone, which validated Fran's accusation. Chelsea didn't want it to be true. She didn't want to believe her little girl could do something as dangerous and foolhardy as this, so she had to go to the one person who could corroborate Fran's claim.

"Did you manage to get in touch with Lorraine?"

Joyce looked up from her phone. "Yes, but I have to tell you, I think it's a mistake. Why the hell would you want to even speak to her? What she did was just as bad as what Fran did."

"Have you arranged a meeting?"

"She's busy nights, so she won't be able to meet after your shooting day. I've organized a visitor pass for her to come to the set tomorrow."

"Good. Thanks."

"What do you want to do about a new assistant?"

"I can manage with the PA the production gave me for now. He's not too bad." Chelsea picked up Joyce's empty glass.

"Are you still thinking about the talk show deal? I can't put them off forever."

"I need more time."

Joyce nodded. "And Helen Cho's email? What do you want to do since Fran was the point person for that?"

"What are you talking about?" Chelsea halted on her way to the sink.

"Oh. Did you not know about that?"

"About what, Joyce?" She tried to keep the edge out of her voice.

"Fran reached out to Helen. She said you wanted a meeting. And Helen replied."

"She wants to meet? What did Fran say?"

"It was all about developing your own projects and contemplating a trajectory into producing quality entertainment for an underserved segment of the market. I thought it was a good idea, but I also thought it was yours. Who knows where else the bitch has overstepped? I'll forward it to you." She took out her phone and moved her thumbs over the screen. "At any rate, we don't have to do anything for the moment. Let's put it off until you wrap on *Tolstoy Was Right*." Joyce stood. "I'm gonna go. You need your sleep. Another early morning tomorrow."

"Joyce." Chelsea didn't want to think about how Fran had imposed herself on her career right now. She grasped the edge of the marble countertop hard. This was the first time she felt she could ask. "How's he doing?"

Joyce pressed her lips together and paused before answering. "Beau knows he fucked up. He's scared you're going to take the kids away."

He should be scared. She'd already called her personal attorney to discuss what this meant in terms of their custody agreement.

"But he seems to really want to change," Joyce continued. "It's only been three days, and it will be at least fourteen before he can talk to anyone outside. If you ask me, it looks like he has the right attitude this time."

Chelsea had heard this before.

"Last time, I think he was doing it for you. Maybe this time, he's doing it for himself."

"We'll see, I guess."

She saw Joyce to the door and watched as she drove through the gate, and then waited until the gate was completely shut before going upstairs. With her long days on set, she had barely seen her children this week. She checked on Forge, who was out like a light, Cheeto a round, ginger poof wedged against him. She put her ear to Petal's door but didn't go in. She wasn't prepared for a confrontation if Petal was still awake.

Restless in bed, she grabbed her phone. She didn't have the strength to read the email Fran sent to Helen, or its reply. Instead, almost against her will, she opened a browser and typed the address for intravenousgossip.com. She had been working her way through F. Ulysses's posts one by one for the past several nights. Fran's contributions were popular, garnering hundreds of thousands of views, and she seemed to have a following that enjoyed them just for the writing. And she had disappeared from the site about six months ago, so Fran had been truthful about that.

The posts mostly recycled information that had come from celebrities' press releases, stuff that was important to the celebrity and maybe a handful of their fans, but she did it with a sly wink, a nod to the absurd, and a large dose of wit that Chelsea could admit was amusing and a bit addictive. She had yet to read anything about herself or Beau under Fran's byline. It was mostly harmless fluff, and altogether different than other posters on the site, especially the mean-spiritedness of a person called Carmina Piranha, who seemed to relish the celebrity takedown.

Tonight, however, the gossip website wouldn't load. It just hung and hung, until Google produced a message that said *HTTP Error 404 (Not Found)*. Just as well. Chelsea tossed her phone on the empty side of the bed. Just as it landed, it lit up with a text alert. It was from a number that wasn't stored in her contacts.

Hi. It's Fran. I know I shouldn't be contacting you.

Chelsea gritted her teeth. Now Fran had violated her privacy in another way. She waited for the gray ellipsis to turn into text.

I had your number memorized in case I ever lost the orange phone.

While the ellipsis appeared again, Chelsea quickly typed: *Don't make me get a new number. I'm deleting yours. Don't contact me again.*

Fran's next words came through as she hit send. *Just wanted to tell you that working for you was the best job I ever had that paid me a salary, and I'm sorry I don't get to do it anymore.*

Chelsea stared at the message. What did it even mean? What job didn't pay a salary? She threw her phone down and listened for any more alerts, but none came.

At multiple times over the next few days, Chelsea's finger swiped across Fran's text to reveal the trash can button, but she never could make herself press it.

❖

Fran opened her eyes when she heard keys in the front door. She had an inkling that it was late afternoon, but the slanted light coming in the front window could just as easily have been early morning, if she could only remember which direction was east.

"Your back is going to hate you if you keep sleeping in that chair." Trina's voice, which had been positive and upbeat for the first few days after her banishment from Chelsea-land, had gotten progressively more flat as time wore on.

"A broken body is nothing compared to a broken heart."

"Jeez. Dramatic much? That's not real life talking. Have you started writing again?"

"No."

"Movie quote?"

"I don't think so." Fran sat upright and watched as her roommate pulled a four pack of snack-size containers of Jell-O from the center pocket of her hoodie and dropped it in Fran's lap.

"Here. Don't say I never gave you anything."

Fran tore one open. "Yum. Orange. My fave. Craft services?"

"Nope. Ralph's. I went to the supermarket for you. If that ain't love…" Trina got a beer for herself and a spoon for Fran. Beer meant it must be afternoon. Entitled Prick must be back on day shoots. "What is this broken heart business? This languishing for days on end isn't like you. You've been fired before. What haven't you told me about you and Chelsea?"

"Nothing. I liked her a lot, probably too much to be appropriate for an assistant. But it was mostly one-sided. All in my head."

Trina gazed at her. "What do you mean *mostly?*"

"We kissed—once." Fran didn't know how to describe what happened between them in Forge's bathroom, but no actual kissing had occurred then.

Silence. Fran looked at Trina whose mouth was wide open.

"Holy schnikes! You kissed Chelsea Hotness Cartwright?"

"I wasn't aware that was her middle name." Fran didn't want to smile, but she did—a little. "Yes, I kissed her, and then I got fired."

"You're my hero." Trina recovered from the news almost instantly. "But, Franny. You broke rule number one."

"I know." Was it normal to have had these kinds of feelings when you worked so closely with someone? "Have you ever crossed that line with someone you've worked with?"

"Like my boss? Even if he had a vagina and the most perfect tits on the planet, I wouldn't touch him with a ten-foot toilet brush. And that's why we've worked so well this long."

Fran wasn't sure she'd define Trina's relationship with her boss as working well.

"Answer me this—should I be worried about you?" Trina took a long pull from her bottle.

"Nah. I'm just going to wallow a little bit longer before pulling myself up by my sneakerstraps."

"How long are we talking? Are you going to be able to make rent this month?"

"Not that long, and yes." One thing about working for Chelsea, she had more stashed in her bank account than she'd had in a long while. "I just have to figure out what I'm going to do, and that seems like a really big question right now."

"Start with something small. You don't have to do it forever." Trina nudged Fran's leg with her toe. "And maybe cut out the Chelsea Cartwright-athon. That ain't helping."

They both looked at the TV, and at a freeze-framed image of

Sabrina Butler, riding her crappy mountain bike with a determined look on her face on *Landon's Way*. Trina pointed the remote at young Chelsea, and she disappeared.

Fran didn't even have the will to be embarrassed by this.

"Do you want me to ask around for assistant jobs for you? You got the hang of it really quick, and you liked it, right?"

She liked Chelsea, not being an assistant. "How am I going to get another assistant gig without a reference?"

"How did you get the first one?"

"That is a story you are well aware of. Through deception and omission."

"A time-honored method, though not very honorable."

Fran took a moment to consider. Assisting wasn't that difficult. It was all about organization and attention to detail. But what if she had to work for someone like Entitled Prick? That wouldn't end well. It wouldn't even start well. She had to respect whoever she was working for. "I think I should do something else."

"Do you want to go back to celebrity gossip?"

"Absolutely not. Never again." The day after she was fired, Fran had plugged her old cellphone in to charge and about fifty texts and emails from Carmina Piranha lit up the screen like she'd won a jackpot nobody would want to collect. With all the images taken that night, he had of course recognized Fran behind the wheel driving Chelsea to Beau's house. He insisted she tell him why she and Chelsea were there.

He was becoming a nuisance, and Fran didn't want to have to keep appeasing him in order to protect herself or Chelsea and her family. She'd have to check in with Patty and see if she was able to dig up anything else on Carmina Piranha besides what Fran had already found. A little more leverage might get him to back off completely.

"What about your screenwriting? Anything brewing with that?"

"Nope." Fran had never gone this long without some kind of kernel of an idea pinging around her brain, waiting to pop. Maybe the muse was gone for good? She had a feeling if she dwelled on that depressing notion too long, she might cry.

"If you want something casual to get you out of the house, my friend at Warner Props is looking for people."

"Props?"

"Yeah. For movies and TV. They make them, store them, rent them. You want her number?"

"Sure." It wasn't her dream of selling her screenplay to a movie studio that would then make an award-winning blockbuster out of it, but it was still on the fringes of the movie business. It could be something. And as much fun as wallowing in front of Chelsea's oeuvre was, she needed to get over herself. "I think I left my lucky hat at Chelsea's," she said, apropos of absolutely nothing.

"Aw, you sound so sad." Trina reached over and patted Fran's knee. "Don't worry, lil' slugger. We'll get you a new one."

❖

About halfway through the second set up, Chelsea noticed Lorraine behind the crowd of technicians. When they broke for lunch, Chelsea went to greet her.

"Hi, Lorraine. Thanks for coming."

"Hey, Chelsea. You were great! This looks like it's going to be a fantastic movie."

"You're very kind to say so." Chelsea's temporary PA stood close by, waiting to do her bidding. "Dante, will you please bring two plates to my trailer?" She ushered Lorraine away. "Hungry?"

"Sure. It's been a while, Chelsea. I was happy to hear from you." There was no denying the caution in her expression. She opened her bag to reveal a large plastic container. "I made some of those lemon cookies Forge likes so much."

"Thank you. He'll be thrilled." Chelsea gestured her inside the trailer. "Let me just clear the air a little bit. Fran no longer works for me. I believe you two are acquainted. She mentioned a few things that I'd like to talk to you about."

Lorraine didn't seem surprised by this news. "I'm sorry. I only met her twice, but I liked her." She sat on the sofa.

"How did you two meet?"

"She tracked me down at my new gig somehow. I'm not sure how she did it."

Now knowing she worked in celebrity media, Chelsea didn't think it would be that difficult for Fran to locate Lorraine. It was strange, to have to incorporate the idea of Fran-as-scheming-journalist into her image of Fran as her competent, compliant, captivating helper. She tried to ignore the cognitive dissonance. "Before her exit, she implied you were wrongfully terminated. If I made a mistake, I want to know."

Lorraine took a deep breath. "I guess you want to talk about Petal."

"I haven't asked Petal about this yet. I wanted to hear from you first. Why don't you tell me what you told Fran?" She sat on the other end of the small sofa and tried to project an aura of calm. She sat and listened to Lorraine's story. Their only interruption was Dante bringing their lunch.

"So even though I never spoke to that creep..." Lorraine finished up her story. "I still felt responsible enough to take the blame."

"I really wish you had told me. Do you have any idea how it feels to know after the fact that your child was repeatedly putting herself in danger every time she contacted this man?"

"I felt so awful when I figured out what she was doing. It was my fault she was able to work out some kind of scheme with that man. In retrospect, I really should have gone directly to you with my suspicion instead of confronting Petal. But she begged me and begged me not to tell. I felt so bad for her."

"I'm her parent. I needed to know."

"I'm so sorry. I truly believed she wouldn't do it anymore. I made her delete the guy's number, but she tricked me. I don't know whose number she deleted, but it wasn't his. She knew I lost my job because of what she was doing. We talked about it both before I left and again just recently—we're still in touch sometimes through Instagram."

Chelsea was speechless. How could Petal do this? Did she not have any scruples at all? "All I can do is apologize to you on Petal's behalf. Now that I'm aware of her behavior, I certainly won't be taking it lightly."

Lorraine nodded. "I'm glad you know now. My intention was to save your family from any more of the turmoil Petal's actions created. You had all been through so much. If Petal had only stopped like I believed she was going to, your firing me would have been worth it."

"You're a remarkable person, Lorraine. I don't know anyone as selfless as you are." A weight pressed down on Chelsea—hard and heavy guilt for accusing Lorraine, for firing her, and for Petal's shabby treatment of her. Still, the fact that she and Petal had been communicating without Chelsea's knowledge or permission rankled. "I'm thinking you're better off without me or my family making your life hell. And I appreciate your concern for Petal, but I don't think a private friendship between the two of you is good for Petal, or my relationship with her. I'm asking you to stop messaging with her."

"Of course. I totally understand." Lorraine took her phone from her bag. "I'll block her right now."

"Thank you." She watched Lorraine do it. "You said you had a new job. What are you doing?"

"I'm making a go in the food industry." Lorraine's brow smoothed at the change in topic. "I'm cooking vegan food, and I'm currently in negotiations to make my pop-up a real restaurant. I do plant-based burgers now, but I'm planning a more expanded menu."

Chelsea remembered the excitement Lorraine had for most good things that came her way, but she seemed beyond delighted to report this news. Chelsea was happy for her, but there was a tiny part of her that wished they could go back to what they had before. Clearly, that was no longer an option. "That's fantastic. I'm really proud of you. You were a terrific assistant, but always destined for bigger things."

"Thanks, Chelsea. That means so much, coming from you." Her smile was tentative. "Is that guy who brought lunch your new assistant?"

"For the moment, yes."

"He seems nice. I have to tell you, I didn't know what to think of Fran when I first met her. She was like a bulldog, so protective of you. And so determined to get the paps off your back."

"So you told her about Petal, but you didn't tell me."

"No, she figured it out somehow. She's pretty smart, I guess—and loyal. I bet she'd be a great friend."

Chelsea pursed her lips. Friend? No way. Never. Had Lorraine always been this naive?

She must have noticed Chelsea's distaste. "Oh, sorry. I meant for me, not you. I know you probably don't think much of her right now, but she was really nice about my food. And remember, you used to not like me, and here we are chatting over Caesar salads—like friends."

"So we are, Lorraine." It would be nice to think she and Lorraine could be friends, but Chelsea didn't have friends, she had employees.

Lorraine looked a bit wistful as she pushed a few leaves of romaine around her plate. "Maybe Fran will come in for another burger. I wouldn't mind that at all."

"You could form a club—The League of Chelsea Cartwright's Ex-assistants."

Lorraine laughed. "We'd drink a toast to you at our monthly meetings."

The best Chelsea could muster was a weak smile. What did it say about her that she couldn't hold on to the people she entrusted her career with? She couldn't remember when she had felt more lonely.

❖

Chelsea retrieved Petal's phone from a waterproof bag inside the toilet tank in the guest bathroom—a good hiding place since Petal never went in there and had no idea how toilets worked anyway. Next, she searched for a hammer, which she found in the linen closet next to a stack of towels, weirdly. Then she went into the den where Petal, Forge, and Bernice were watching TV.

"Remember this, Petal?" She held up the phone. "Come with me. Bernice, you and Forge stay here, please." She stomped out of the room.

"Mom, what are you going to do?" Petal's voice was laced with unease.

"Better come find out," she called, and slid the glass door to the backyard open. The concrete countertop that bridged the pizza oven and the grill would be the perfect spot. She set Petal's phone down right in the center and then rested the business end of the hammer on top of it, taking aim.

"Mom!" Petal screeched. "Stop."

"I had lunch with Lorraine today." Chelsea's gaze didn't waver from the phone. She relished this moment. Not because she wanted to destroy Petal's phone, but because she wanted to destroy something. She had been holding all of it inside her—her anger, her frustration, her disillusionment, her anguish—and now she got to release it all with a hammer blow to this small, seemingly innocuous, piece of shit technology. "How could you, Petal?"

"What are you talking about?"

"Acting dumb is not the way to play this. You put your family in danger—multiple times. You put yourself in danger. You treated Lorraine without an ounce of common decency. I fired her because of something you did, and you *knew* that. Doesn't that make you feel anything at all?"

"But Mom—"

"I mean, I don't even know where to start. How did I fail you so badly?" The tears started to fall—ugly tears, and Chelsea didn't even bother to wipe them away. "I tried, Petal," she sobbed. "I tried so hard to be a good mom to you, and I know it's hard to grow up in a family like ours. We're not like a lot of other families. I honestly don't know what I did that made you make such terrible decisions. When I think of what might have happened with you contacting some horrible creepy guy who wants to profit off me and your dad"—Chelsea began to hyperventilate—"I don't know what I'd do if anything happened to you. Thinking about it makes me want to die—"

"Mom, no." Petal sounded horrified.

"What did I do? What did I do, Petal? I only want to keep you safe. And Forge. And you made yourself so not safe by doing that. Why? I need you to tell me why you did that—"

"The websites kept saying you'd get back together," Petal cried. "Everyone online said it. Every time there were pictures of you, or him, or the two of you, they said it! I just wanted you and Dad to be together again. So we could be a family again!"

Chelsea dropped the hammer and grabbed Petal, hugging her tightly while both of them cried.

"But Dad is sick. And you said he went away, but he didn't say goodbye. He always says goodbye." Petal's sobs tore Chelsea's heart in two. She stood there holding her daughter as sorrow and grief and loss poured out of both of them. After a while, they were both quiet.

"I'm sorry he didn't say goodbye." Chelsea wiped her nose with the back of her hand. "You're right. He is sick. He had to go away to try and get better." She pulled out two stools that were tucked beneath the counter and they settled onto them. "And I really hope your dad can get better. He'll have to work very hard. But you have to know something—your dad and I are never going to get back together."

Petal hung her head.

"That doesn't mean we're not still a family. You, Forge, your dad, and I will *always* be a family. There will always be love among all of us, but the love between your dad and me has changed. The love we have for you and Forge is as strong as ever, and it will always be there."

Petal gave her a morose nod.

"And this may sound strange, but I love you too much not to punish you for what you did to us—and to Lorraine."

"I'm sorry about that. She's so nice. I know she's busy, but she still takes the time to answer my DMs."

"She won't be anymore. I've asked her to stop communicating with you, and she agreed."

Petal's shoulders sagged.

Chelsea felt a pang at her obvious dejection, but remained strong. "I hope you feel rotten for what you did to her."

"I do. I know. I feel awful." Petal wiped a tear from her cheek.

"Good. You have to listen to that instinct and follow it. Don't ignore it." Chelsea was going to have to get help for Petal. She was going to have to process this with a professional.

"You're really going to hammer my phone?" She looked up at Chelsea from under her bangs.

"No." Chelsea handed her the hammer. "You are."

Petal exhaled dramatically but didn't argue. When she stood up, Chelsea stood too.

"Wait. Wear these." She handed Petal the sunglasses that were perched on her head, and then stepped back from the demolition site.

Petal took the hammer in both hands and gave it a halfhearted swing. A crack appeared in the phone's screen but nothing else.

"Harder. Like you mean it. Use some muscle."

Petal gave the phone another couple of whacks, but it was clear her heart wasn't in it. "Here, you do it. I know you want to."

"You're damn right I do." Chelsea spent the next ten minutes smashing that phone to bits. When there was nothing left but tiny pieces of plastic and metal, she dropped the hammer and put her arm around Petal's shoulder. "Come on. We'll clean it up later. We're going to Lorraine's restaurant, and you're going to apologize in person."

Petal's head tilted in confusion. "But you just said—"

"You won't be hearing from Lorraine on Instagram or any other app, but as long as I'm with you, we can eat her vegan burgers and talk *in real life*. Isn't that what you kids say?"

"Mom, don't even," Petal groaned. "Is Forge coming too?"

The world must be righting itself if Petal could still feel embarrassed by Chelsea's unhipness. "Do you want him to come?"

"We should all go together. As a family."

"That's my girl." As they walked back into the house, Chelsea couldn't believe how good she felt. If she had known how cathartic it was to crush a phone into a million pieces, she would have done it years ago.

CHAPTER EIGHTEEN

Ten Months Later

Chelsea looked up from the report Helen had given her to read. She had tried to make the upstairs study her office, but Forge and Petal often wandered in at various points while she was trying to work. Since returning from school, they had both taken up positions in the room with her, but this was ground zero for the launch of a new production company. They would have to scram before Helen and Joyce arrived. "Forge, did you finish your homework?"

"Yeah." He sat on the Persian carpet playing with Cheeto.

This was one room that wasn't in keeping with the Spanish mission décor of the rest of their home. It had the warm, cozy feel of a gentleman's library, with dark built-in bookcases and leather club chairs beside a wood-burning fireplace they had used for s'mores about two weeks ago. It was supposed to be a sanctuary for Beau, but he had never made much use of it. Neither had Chelsea until recently, but she found herself very comfortable in it. "Bernice is running you a bath. When you finish, you can come back here for a while before my meeting."

"Okay. Come on, Cheets."

"How about you, Petal?"

"I'm doing it now. Can I stay while you're working?" Petal sat behind the giant oak desk that dominated the room.

"Maybe. Let's talk when you've finished your homework." Chelsea was glad Petal seemed to be having an upbeat day and wanted to encourage it.

After Beau's incident, and after she had completed her work on *Tolstoy Was Right*, Chelsea had pulled out of all the commitments she could. Beau ended up extending his stay for ninety days, and the one time Chelsea took Petal and Forge to visit him, not that far away in Santa Barbara, they had been spooked by his pale appearance and shaggy beard. Now that he had finished inpatient treatment, he was trying to win back their trust, but limited his time with Petal and Forge to visits here in his former home while Chelsea was here as well. It was as if he didn't trust himself to be alone with them, and they didn't trust him either.

But things were starting to get better. Petal seemed to realize she could count on Chelsea in a way that she currently couldn't with Beau. Chelsea, Petal, and Forge had become very close over the past ten months.

She looked at the clock on her phone. Joyce had texted that she was on her way, but she hadn't heard from Helen.

Dante walked into the study. "I have the samples from the GD."

Chelsea frowned. "The what?"

"The graphic designer."

"Oh, good." Chelsea put her hand out for them. "Any word from Helen?"

The chime for the gate rang. "That must be her," Dante said. "BRB."

She tried to stifle the annoyance she felt when Dante spoke in acronyms. *Never mind. It's his quirk. We all have them.* He was dependable and quiet—usually. She could do worse. She sat back in her chair to continue reading.

She and Petal worked in silence until Helen and Dante came into the study, each with a tall stack of scripts in their arms.

"What are those?" Chelsea asked. She stood and lightened Helen's load. They piled the manuscripts on the coffee table.

"We'll get to that. I have some news." It didn't sound like good news.

Chelsea and Helen and Joyce had been meeting for many months now, inching toward announcing their production company. They wanted to publicize both their new company and their first project at the same time, and of the two candidates they were preparing, Chelsea was more excited about one in particular.

"Can I get anyone something to drink?" Dante asked.

"Yeah, D. I want apple juice," Forge said, zooming into the room with Bernice behind him.

"Diet Coke, please." Petal didn't look up from her algebra homework.

"If you two want something, go with Dante and get it yourselves. No juice, and no soda. You know that. Helen, you want anything?"

"What can we have, then?" Forge interrupted.

"Milk or water."

"Chocolate milk?" Forge asked, his eyes filled with hope.

"Fine."

Bernice said, "Come on, buddy. Let's go to the kitchen. Petal, you want some?"

"Nah, I'm good." Petal looked at Chelsea. "Can I stay, Mom?"

Helen nodded at the stacks on the coffee table. "She may be able to help us go through these."

Looking at new scripts wasn't on their agenda for tonight. Chelsea needed to know what was going on. "Pet, why don't you go with Dante and help him bring some sparkling water, okay? Then when your homework is done, you can stick around if it's not too boring for you."

"Okay."

After she and Dante left the room, Chelsea said, "I thought we were talking financing and budgets tonight."

Helen exhaled sharply through her nose. "We lost the women-only dystopia. A24 got it."

"Shit! I really wanted that one."

"If you were a screenwriter, would you go with a proven hitmaker or us?"

"Yeah, I get it. This is why we had our backup—the adoption drama." She wasn't as drawn to that script. Even if she was only producing, it seemed too similar to things she had done in the past. But it was well-written and was still a relatively under-the-radar property. Helen avoided her eyes. "Helen—what?"

"My boss saw the script in my bag. He thought I was going behind his back—"

"He was right."

"And he optioned it for Universal."

"No!"

"I'm sorry, Chels. That's where I work. A place where people on the same team don't hesitate to double-cross each other. Are you getting how much I want us to succeed now? So I can leave that place once and for all?"

Chelsea nodded. That's what she got for getting too invested too soon. She stepped to the window and allowed herself thirty seconds to feel bad about it. It was like shopping for a house, she told herself. The right one was sure to appear, hopefully sooner rather than later. "It's okay. It just wasn't meant to be." She nodded at the stacks of scripts. "What are those?"

"Stuff that got passed over by Universal. But I truly believe there has to be some gold in there. You know what our slate is like. Superheroes and special effects. It's the reason I want to do this with you. We will find the right project for us."

She and Helen were each engrossed in a manuscript when Petal came back with Joyce.

"Quiet in here," Joyce said, depositing a bottle of Perrier and some glasses on the desk.

"We're back at square one." Chelsea raised her eyes to Joyce's to make sure she caught her meaning.

"Damn. Well, it happens." Joyce sat in one of the other club chairs. "Toss me one, will you, Helen?"

"What does that mean?" Petal asked, settling in at the desk again.

"It means we're looking through the dross for a blockbuster, kid." Joyce took out her readers and turned the cover page over.

"Can I read one?"

"Sure, honey. When you're done with your homework." Chelsea didn't have much hope for the pile of castoffs, but it was a place to start. They had all settled down to read—and solve quadratic equations—when Forge burst in with his half full glass of chocolate milk.

"Hey, what's everybody doing?" He put the glass down on the pile of scripts and sat on the arm of Chelsea's chair, draping himself all over her.

"I'm done. Can I read one now?" Petal shoved her books into her schoolbag.

"Nice to see someone your age want to actually read something that's not on their phone," Joyce said.

"Thank you, Petal. You're doing us a favor." Helen smiled at her.

"Forge, pass Petal one of the scripts, please." Chelsea nudged him off the chair, and he went willingly. "Then you can bring a book in here and read, or you can have a half hour of screen time with Bernice."

"Can it be a comic book?" As he turned back to ask, his elbow brushed the glass of chocolate milk and sent it sprawling over the other stack of scripts. "Oops!"

Joyce rescued the glass before it could fall off the table, and grabbed some tissues from the desk.

Helen stood and picked up the script on the top of the pile with two fingers, now slightly soggy with brown streaks all across its cover page. "No worries, it's still readable." She tore the cover page off, crumpled it up, and tossed it in the fireplace. "Here's your first assignment, Petal." Helen handed her the script minus one page. "Read the first twenty pages and give us a report."

"Yuck," Petal griped. "It's wet."

"No, it's not. Don't be a weenie." Helen said it with such good cheer, Petal couldn't take offense. She helped Joyce wipe up the last remaining spots of liquid on the table.

"I'm sorry, Mama," Forge said.

"It's okay. Let's go find Bernice." Chelsea escorted him from the room.

When they passed by the laundry room, she saw Bernice in there folding clothes. Instead of interrupting her, she went with Forge to his room where they checked over his homework, played with Cheeto, and then sat on his bed while Forge read to her from the latest *Wimpy Kid* book he was currently plowing through. She didn't want her little boy to feel uncomfortable or afraid, and spending this time with him and ensuring he felt safe was the least she could do. Even though Forge had seemed unruffled through the worst of Beau's crisis, family therapy had revealed some abandonment anxiety in both Petal and Forge. Chelsea was doing all she could to heal her children.

Bernice returned, and Chelsea left the rest of Forge's bedtime routine to her. Before she reached the study, she could hear laughter coming from inside. Petal had moved to the center of the couch, and Helen and Joyce sat on either side of her as all three read from the pages on Petal's lap.

"Mom, this is so funny." Petal's eyes were shining.

"And it's sweet and charming," Joyce added.

"How do you feel about a rom-com? About two professional soccer players?" Helen said.

"Two *girl* soccer players." Petal pressed her finger to the pages. "I want to see this movie, Mom."

"A love story between women?" Chelsea's mind flashed to Fran. This couldn't possibly be her. "Nobody does rom-coms anymore." This wasn't anything like the projects they'd selected before.

"Which might be the exact reason to do one," Joyce mused.

Chelsea sat behind the desk. "What's it called? Who wrote it?"

"We don't know. It's the chocolate milk script." Helen went to the fireplace where she'd chucked the wet cover page, which was now crumpled into a wet ball of paper covered in old ashes. They all could see it was unreadable. "Well, that's no good. But I can track it down. All the scripts we get are recorded in a database with their log lines and representation details."

"It shows promise. But we don't know if this is a new script or if it's been sitting around for years. If we want to pursue it, I don't think we should do it the usual way." Joyce put her feet up on the coffee table.

"What do you mean?" Chelsea asked.

"We lost out on our first two picks already. I think we should be stealthy about this one. Act fast, but act quietly."

"Hang on. You haven't finished it, and I haven't even read it yet," Chelsea said. "And I'll be busy the next two days with the *Mademoiselle* photo shoot."

"You're not going to be here?" Petal's voice was low.

"It's in Century City, Pet. It'll be two long days, but I'll be home at night, and Colleen and Bernice are going to be here."

Petal only looked slightly relieved.

"Here's what we'll do. You hang on to it and read it tonight. I'll pick it up in the morning to make copies and get it to Helen. Meanwhile, Helen can figure out who we're dealing with and set something up for next week. Sound good?"

"Wait a minute. If it *has* been sitting around for years, isn't that a good indication that it's a stinker? If it's so great, why hasn't someone else picked it up? We should find that out first. And who wrote it. That too."

Joyce gave her a baffled look. "That may be so, but it does us no good to let it sit around. We've already lost two interesting prospects."

Chelsea hesitated. There was no way this was Fran's script. The odds were too high.

"So we're doing this? Putting the cart before the horse?" Helen asked.

Joyce stood. "It's not going to kill us to get the ball rolling. Because this time, if we're going after it, we have to persuade the writer to let us option it right away. That way we don't get snaked again."

Helen took out her phone and made some notes. "Just read it, Chelsea. Chances are someone's already optioned it. It's that good. If it's available, I'll set up a meeting, but if we decide we don't like it, we'll cancel. No downside."

Chelsea was unconvinced.

"I've been working on superhero movies for too long, Chelsea! I want to contribute to the queer lady canon, darling. There's already some quality stuff out there, but this would fill a burning need. Yes, everyone loves *Carol*, and I personally can't get enough of *Portrait of a Lady on Fire*, but don't we queer ladies deserve some laughter along with our love stories?" Helen shook her phone at Chelsea. "Don't you want to laugh?"

"I haven't laughed out loud from words on a page in a million years," Joyce said. "I'm not gay, but I'm excited. And after those other ones slipped through our fingers, we have to be proactive. You look constipated, Chelsea. What's the problem?"

Chelsea didn't want to say. She was being ridiculous, right? Because even after ten months, she hadn't been able to shake Fran. And there were about a roulette wheel's worth of emotions her ex-assistant produced—anger, hurt, indignation, but also wistfulness—and Chelsea never knew which one was going to come up a winner on any given day. The one thing she did know was that she didn't want to see Fran ever again. "There was someone we used to know who wrote rom-coms with women protagonists." She gave Joyce a meaningful look.

"Who?" Joyce clearly didn't remember, if she ever knew in the first place.

She was being ridiculous. "Never mind."

Joyce blinked at Chelsea a few times before taking her at her word. "All right, then. Does that sound like a plan?"

"Sounds like a plan." Helen held her hand up for Chelsea to high-five.

"Yeah, sounds like a plan, Mom." Petal giggled when Chelsea didn't slap her hand and instead gave Helen a dubious look.

"Just read it, Chels. You're going to like it." Helen pointed at her still-raised palm.

"Fine." Chelsea touched it with the tips of her unenthusiastic fingers. "I'll read it."

CHAPTER NINETEEN

Fran stood back and inspected her work. One thing about her job at Warner Props, she never had the same day twice. What had once been a garden-variety oak dining table was now hand distressed with sandpaper, hammer, and chains of several lengths and gauges. There were hundreds of tables to choose from in the warehouse, but the production designer needed specific measurements for a reason unknown to Fran. Her job was to make it so, and she had done that. One rickety, ancient-looking table for the ultra-violent western they were prepping.

She sat on the table and checked the task off on her day's agenda. Before attacking the pick list for the other items the production required, she considered taking lunch. It was still a little early, but once she ventured into the cavernous warehouse that held eighty years' worth of set dressing, it would be a while before she came out.

Gazing once again at her handiwork, she imagined the saloon, or brothel, or farmhouse set the table would sit in, and as usual, her mind conjured Chelsea, in a costume that aligned with her fantasy production. Fran decided it was a saloon, and Chelsea came striding through those double swinging batwing doors that all western saloons had. She stood just inside, letting her eyes adjust from the bright midday sunlight, and all the black-hatted dudes shifted uneasily as they spied the pair of pearl-handled pistols that hung low on her hips. Dusty, well-worn boots protruded from the bottom of tight, dark leather chaps that covered her endlessly long legs. Bullet-filled bandoliers crisscrossed a denim shirt that had several of its snaps undone, and a red kerchief, so faded by the sun it was a mottled pink, was loosely tied around her throat. Her brown Stetson was pulled low over her brow, but then she poked the brim with one finger to reveal a not-to-be-fucked-with face.

Was she smoking a hand-rolled cigarette? Or a cigarillo? Definitely not a cigar. No. Fran rejected tobacco of any kind for Cowboy Chelsea. Back to her face.

She was contemplating how Cowboy Chelsea's skin would be artfully smudged with dirt and her lips chapped by the sun when her phone buzzed in her pocket. The interruption was probably for the best. If left to wallow in her fantasies, Fran probably would've cast herself as the damsel in distress who had nothing to pay Chelsea with except sexual favors. Then this scenario would've really gotten out of hand.

Kevin, her former agent, was calling. She didn't know what he wanted, but the timing couldn't have been better. Much to her relief, the ideas had started coming again. Well, an idea, would be more accurate to say, with a strong, complex, layered lead woman character at the center of it. And during every free moment over the past six or seven months, she'd been sweating over it. "Hey, Kevin. Long time, no talk."

"Yeah, Fran. How are you?"

"You must have some kind of ESP or something. How did you know I was going to call you?"

"You were?"

"I have a script that's almost ready. I want you to read it. Guess what? It's not a rom-com between two women." She was super proud of it, having poured all of her longing for Chelsea into a script that would be equal to her talent. And now that she was in the polishing stage, her brain was percolating with lots of other ideas. As a screenwriter at least, she was back.

"I'm intrigued. Surprised, but intrigued. I didn't think you'd ever stray from your goal of making two women kiss on the big screen. But I have news. There's interest in one of your scripts."

"You're kidding. Which one?"

"*A Love As Big As Wembley.*"

She had written it a few years ago. In an effort to circumvent the change-one-of-the-character's-gender note, she'd written a sports story where the characters played against each other. Not yet possible for a man and a woman—in soccer, at least. It got absolutely no love at the time. "No shit?"

"Absolutely none. Propolis Pictures wants to meet."

"Propolis Pictures? Never heard of 'em."

"They're new. They're taking meetings, and they want to meet with you."

"Really?"

"No one's more surprised than me, honey, but that's what they said."

"Hey! I still stand behind that script. And they want a queer rom-com? They don't want to option it and then rewrite it to hell and back?"

"I don't know about that. I got a message that they want to meet, and I'm passing it along. What do you say? Are you interested?"

"Are you going to represent me?"

"Of course. You're a solid writer, Fran. Maybe the world wants to buy what you're selling now. You free tomorrow? Eleven a.m.?"

"I'll make myself free."

❖

Kevin was outside the address for their meeting, talking on the phone, when Fran pulled up a few minutes before eleven. This new production company's offices were in the same business park and the same building as Joyce Adler's management offices. It was the place she had met Chelsea for the first time. What were the odds?

"Come on, Fran. If you're not five minutes early, you're late. Hold that elevator, please." Kevin bustled her in but she couldn't see which floor's button he pressed. "Now listen, I know it's been a while since you've been in a meeting. They called us. That means they're interested. Let them talk first."

"I couldn't find anything on Propolis Pictures online. Who did you speak with over there?"

"Somebody who works for Universal, or used to. I'm not quite sure. She wasn't very clear about it." The elevator doors opened and Kevin grabbed her arm and pulled her out, leading her to the double glass doors that read Adler Talent Management.

Fran stopped short at the entrance. "Kevin, this isn't a production company. I think we're in the wrong place."

"I told you. They're new. This is where the meeting is. Tits up, sweetie!" And with that, Fran was whisked into a conference room she had been in before. There were several people sitting at the table, but she homed in on Chelsea Cartwright, mortifyingly beautiful in a casual gray sweater and all that gorgeous auburn hair framing her exquisite face.

The world shrank down to the five feet of space between them. One woman filled her entire horizon. Fran's heart stilled. "Chelsea?"

She looked up, the life in her grass green eyes dying at the sight of Fran.

Her heart became every instrument in a brass band, sending all the blood in her body clamoring to her head, making it nearly impossible to think.

Joyce Adler was around the table and at the doorway in a moment. "Fran, what are you…No. You're the writer?" She planted herself with her legs spread wide, preventing them from advancing into the room.

"I'm Kevin Sala, and this is my client, Fran Underhill. Have you two already met?"

"We have," Joyce said, eycing her as if she were a cockroach that had suddenly crawled out of her espresso martini. "Under unpleasant circumstances. You wrote *A Love As Big As Wembley*?"

"Yes, Joyce, I wrote it. Are you Propolis Pictures?" Fran was nearly dizzy with seeing Chelsea again, but she also had about thirty questions she wanted answers to as well. "Wait. Is Propolis Pictures Chelsea's company? Is she not doing the talk show?"

"Talk show? What the hell are you—oh, yeah. No, no talk show. There must be some confusion—"

Another woman crowded into the doorway where Fran, Kevin, and Joyce stood. "Hello, I'm Helen Cho. Awfully sorry I'm late. You must be the screenwriter. I never did manage to get your name from"— she pointed at Fran's agent—"Kevin, is it?"

"You're Helen Cho?" Fran couldn't help an idiotic grin. "I sent you an email. Is Propolis Pictures your company with Chelsea? Are you really doing it?"

"Fran."

Fran whipped her head around at Chelsea's voice. She stood across the room, her face expressionless.

"Since everyone is here now, and we have solved the mystery of who wrote *A Love As Big As Wembley*, why don't we sit down?" Chelsea took her seat and waited for everyone to follow her lead.

Fran sat, unable to tear her eyes from Chelsea's face. After believing she'd never see her again, it was nearly dumbfounding to be in her presence. It felt like an electric current might be arcing between them, even if Chelsea wouldn't meet her eyes. She hoped she sounded like a functioning human being when she asked, "How are you?"

Chelsea ignored her. "Helen?"

Maybe Fran had been wrong about that electric current.

Helen looked as if she was about to ask a question, then thought better of it and shuffled some papers in front of her before speaking. "Propolis Pictures is Chelsea, Joyce, and me. We're forming a production company that is dedicated to creating stories that center strong women of substance and reflect the concerns and interests of women over male-led narratives. We also want to produce projects that cater to underserved segments of the movie-going public, such as stories that feature LGBTQ+ characters and people of color. Some might call us a niche operation, but we believe within that niche are stories that hold universal appeal."

Fran nodded. Sounded awesome. Every word.

"Finding quality scripts that include what we're looking for has been harder than one might think, but we're happy to say that *A Love As Big As Wembley* delivers on every item on our wish list."

Fran took a moment to bask in that last phrase—*delivers on every item on our wish list*—before forcing herself back into the here and now. It all sounded a little too wonderful to be true, and she'd had producers blowing smoke up her ass once or twice before they dropped the hammer on what they didn't like. She gazed warily at Chelsea, who hadn't raised her eyes from the tabletop since Helen started speaking. "What did you think of it, Chelsea?"

"Joyce?" Chelsea didn't look up.

Joyce leaned in. "We're new. That means funding is stretched very thin. We were hoping your prior relationship with Chelsea might make you amenable to a sixty-day-no-remuneration-exclusivity agreement."

"How does she know Chelsea?" Helen asked.

At the same time, Chelsea said, "That's not what we talked—"

"Wait," Kevin broke in. "What is a sixty-day-no-remuneration-exclusivity agreement? In eleven years as an agent, I've never heard of it."

"That's because I just made it up. It'll be a contract—"

"And it doesn't sound like it would benefit my client. With due respect to Chelsea Cartwright, you all sound like a bunch of amateurs."

"Enough, Kevin." The elation Fran felt seconds ago had long since dissipated. "You say you want the script. Do you expect changes?"

"We really like it. We don't want to change much," Helen said, but she shifted in her seat.

Fran gazed at Chelsea, willing her to look her in the eye. "What do you want to change?" If they said they wanted to insert a male character love interest, Fran thought her heart might break.

"Locations," Chelsea said, and then miraculously, she did look up.

Fran felt like she was drowning in those hurt, closed-off eyes.

"We can't afford to shoot internationally, and certainly not in the UK at a location as expensive as Wembley Stadium. Would you be willing to set your story in one or two more affordable North American cities?" Chelsea held her gaze for as long as it took for the words to leave her mouth, then shifted in her chair so Fran wasn't in her line of sight anymore.

She sat back and considered. Of course Fran wanted this to work. Her dream was sitting right in front of her, waiting for her to say yes. And Chelsea back in her life was something Fran never thought would happen. But would this be it? Would Fran be able to handle it if Chelsea and her new company took her script and then closed the door forever? The silence lingered at the table while they waited for Fran to answer Chelsea's question.

"I'm open to discussing it, but first I need to talk to Chelsea—alone. May I have five minutes?"

Chelsea shook her head. "I don't think that's necessary. We've made an offer. A not very clear offer—that has to be said. But we'll put it in writing, and you can decide. Maybe it's best to continue through our reps."

Fran might never get this chance again. "Three minutes. That's all I need."

Joyce said, "No. This is not a negotiation."

Silence descended again. Chelsea glanced at her once more, and Fran detected a glimmer of curiosity. "Please, Chelsea."

Another beat, then Chelsea said, "Three minutes. Can we have the room?"

Fran shut her eyes for a second. "Thank you."

After everyone cleared out, Chelsea tapped her wrist. "Time's ticking."

Well, first off, I have to give you credit for reviving my creativity." Chelsea furrowed her brow.

"I've got a new sense of purpose. My head is filled with ideas. When I'm not at my day job, I'm writing, and that's because of you." She didn't say that Chelsea was the leading lady in everything she wrote. Imagining Chelsea in a hundred different scenarios, giving her sassy dialogue, stirring dialogue, erotic dialogue, in a hundred different time periods, was life sustaining at the moment.

"This is screenwriting? Not gossip writing?"

Fran nodded. Chelsea could've checked up on that if she cared to.

"And you're not writing some smarmy tell-all exposé about your experience as my assistant?"

"Absolutely not."

"That website you wrote for is gone. Did you have anything to do with that?"

Fran nodded again. "There's a story there, but I'm not going to tell it if I only have three minutes. Maybe some other time."

Chelsea gave her a *watch it* kind of look.

"Or not." She leaned forward. "Look, Chelsea, I'll apologize a million times, but that's not going to change anything. I have never exploited my relationship with you, and I never will. I care about you too much to do that."

She seemed to have Chelsea's attention.

"I'm happy for you. Starting this company, investing in your talent and experience, it feels right to me. I wish you every success."

"Well, you did get the ball rolling." It looked like it pained Chelsea to admit that.

"And now look at you. The Propolis potentate. You have the ability to make my dream come true." Fran shook her head in disbelief.

"You wrote something wonderful, Fran. I think we could do it justice. We'd take care of your baby."

Fran couldn't stop her smile. "You liked it?"

"Is something wrong with your hearing?" One side of her mouth raised in amusement. Perhaps it was involuntary because she frowned immediately after. "I just said it was wonderful."

"Honestly? I wish I could put it on a loop. It means a lot coming from someone I respect so much." Fran continued before Chelsea could bring up the time when Fran had disrespected her. "Who are you thinking to direct?"

"I'd like to show your script to Grace Commerford. We've talked about working together again. It would be great to lock her down before *Tolstoy Was Right* comes out later this year."

Fran felt a fizzy sort of excitement at the idea of Grace Commerford directing her script. "Smart. She'll be untouchable when the reviews start rolling in. There's already Oscar buzz." Chelsea was included in that buzz. The word was her performance was electrifying.

"Still keeping up with the business, I see. What's your day job?"

"Warner Props. I love it. A great job for a movie buff like me." There was something else Fran needed to say. "Hey. It was really big of you to give my script a chance knowing I wrote it. I'm surprised. You still seem so mad at me."

Chelsea's chuckle was drier than the Atacama Desert. "That's because I didn't know you were its author until you walked into this conference room." She didn't seem to want to dwell on that. "What do you think? Your three minutes have turned into six and counting."

Now that the opportunity lay before her, something had her hesitating to take it. If there was anyone she trusted to take care of her work, it was Chelsea, but the vagaries of the movie business made the completion of a motion picture far from a sure thing. Was she willing to pass her screenplay into Chelsea's arms, hoping for its safe and careful upbringing, or could she fight for her baby a little more?

"And Joyce went off script there with that sixty-day business. I don't know what she was on about. We will make you a fair offer and you will be compensated appropriately."

Fran made up her mind. Now she had to convince Chelsea to agree. "What if I want my compensation to be a little unorthodox?"

"What are you talking about?"

"Hear me out." Fran put her hands flat on the table. "I'll give you my script for nothing."

There was that furrowed brow again.

"At no cost. Gratis. Free," she elaborated.

"I understand the concept of free, Fran. Why would you do that?"

"Make me a producer."

Chelsea started shaking her head. "No. No way."

"I want to help develop it. I'll work so hard. This is a good deal for you. You already know I have a great work ethic, and why wouldn't I work my ass off for my own script?"

Chelsea leveled a long, considering gaze at her. "Why do you want to do this—really?"

Redemption. Fran didn't say that. She also didn't say being around Chelsea again was a huge part of it. Then there was that little voice in her head that was telling her that this would put her and Chelsea on the same level—she absolutely did not say that. They could be working on a project together where they were both invested in its success, and she would not be an underling. They would be equals. "You know it's my dream. Anyone who loves the business as much as I do would want to do this."

"I thought your dream was to have one of your screenplays made into a major motion picture. You never said anything about wanting to produce." Chelsea clearly wasn't buying it. Fran would have to expose herself a little here.

"And this is the closest I've ever come to sealing a deal where the interested party wants my characters as they are—no changing Paula to Paul. Is it strange to say I feel like I owe it to my characters to see them through?"

"I get that, but…" She flung her hand in a dismissive gesture. "It's highly unconventional."

"But not unheard of. There are plenty of writers who are also producers."

"When they have the clout to negotiate that for themselves. You, Fran, have no clout."

"I know, but that's where the free script comes in. It's a trade. You're getting the better end of the deal, and you know it."

"I do, huh?" Chelsea was playing her cards close to the vest. "I'll have to talk to my partners. Don't be surprised if this comes back a no." She stood, signaling the end of their little détente.

Fran talked faster. "And I don't mean a producer credit. I want to produce. Get down in the producing muck. Pull my producing weight. See how the producing-sausage gets made."

"We're a shoestring operation right now, mostly working out of my home. I don't know how this could work since you're not welcome there." She shouldered her bag and rounded the table, heading for the door.

Ouch. Fran got there first, and put her hand on the door handle. "So I guess asking you to dinner is out of the question."

Chelsea hugged her folders to her chest. "Yes."

Had Fran heard that right? "Yes to dinner?"

"Yes, it's out of the question." Then Chelsea's hand covered hers on the door handle and levered it open. "Goodbye, Fran."

❖

Chelsea didn't exactly run down the hallway to Joyce's office. Scurry was probably a better description, and she hated that Fran had forced her to scurry. At any rate, she didn't look behind her although she had a sneaking suspicion Fran was watching her. Joyce was behind her desk and Helen was sitting on the credenza when she charged into the office. "Where's the agent?"

"We dropped him off in the waiting area and said whatever happened in there with you two, we'd be in touch." Joyce fiddled with a pencil. "This was why you were so hesitant, wasn't it?"

Chelsea flopped onto the sofa. "I thought I was being paranoid."

"You knew she wrote a lesbian romantic comedy?" She put her pencil down.

"I didn't think she was the only one in Hollywood writing them. I thought it might be her, but you two were so hyped about it, I didn't want my suspicion to put a damper on things. I hoped I was wrong."

"Well, you weren't," Joyce said.

Helen still looked puzzled. "Is she some kind of unhinged fan or something? She seemed pretty psyched to see you, Chels."

Chelsea let out a long slow breath but didn't say anything.

"She's Chelsea's former assistant. It didn't end well." Joyce told her. "Too bad. She was pretty good at the job."

Helen gazed at Chelsea with concern in her eyes.

Despite the huge chunk of her job history that Fran had omitted, she had always been on the level with Chelsea—an oasis of support amidst all the ridiculous shit that was happening at the time. Now that Petal's behavior had been reined in, and the paparazzi nonsense had been resolved, and Beau seemed earnest in working the program,

Chelsea was on her way to making real change in her career. Fran had contributed to the relative tranquility of Chelsea's life right now, whether she wanted to admit it or not. Sure, life was far from normal, and she still stayed home probably more than was healthy, but things had definitely improved.

The gossip surrounding her and Beau was drastically less than it had been a year ago. The public and the tabloids seemed to have moved on. And Fran had kept her word. It was as if Fran's avatar, F. Ulysses, had never existed.

But Fran was a different story. As much as Chelsea wanted to eradicate Fran's existence from her memory, it hadn't happened. Every once in a while she woke up from a dream where she was kissing Fran. Getting any sleep after that was impossible. She was sure Fran's deep, dark eyes were going to make an appearance when she went to bed tonight. In her weaker moments, she could admit to herself that she had been half in love with Fran before she fired her. And that was just not acceptable. Not while the possibility of Fran reentering her life loomed.

"So are we dumping it?" Helen asked, the reluctance obvious in her voice.

Chelsea owed it to her partners to share Fran's offer. "She said she'll give it to us for free if we let her produce."

Nobody said anything. Chelsea looked up. Helen and Joyce seemed to be having a silent conversation with their eyes, but immediately stopped when they saw her watching.

Joyce tented her fingers. "It's an incredible deal. Free script and free labor?"

"No." Chelsea held up a hand. "She'll need to live. We'll have to pay her if she's a producer."

Helen nodded. "We would be hiring more help eventually anyway. You just said she's good at the job, right? Maybe we give her all the shitty, assistant-y things to do."

"Co-producer," Joyce said quickly. "No sense giving her more power than she deserves."

Chelsea gazed at them. Were they actually going to go into business with Fran? Despite her fears, she couldn't deny the ripple of excitement she felt at the thought of seeing Fran more regularly. It aggravated her to admit that Fran made life more exhilarating, more entertaining. More fun. More dangerous too. "Are we doing this?"

"Get any notes together for changes you want to see in her next draft. How long should we give her for that?" Joyce opened her calendar app.

"A month? Do you think she could do it faster?" Helen asked.

"Let's see what she says to two weeks. I'll call the lawyer and get started on the contract. Hels, you want to get back with the agent? Talk him through the offer?"

"You got it." She picked up her phone. "Chelsea, can you give me your script notes by Friday? And are you going to set up a meeting with Grace Commerford?"

Chelsea gave her a vague nod. It was as if the decision had already been made. A giant boulder named Fran was trundling down the hill at top speed, and Chelsea didn't know how she was going to get out of the way.

Chapter Twenty

For the first time in approximately forever, Fran cared about what she was going to wear. She stared into her closet and summoned her nonexistent fashion sense. What did a gainfully employed screenwriter slash co-producer wear to her first official meeting? She decided to go with a plain white T-shirt and jeans but with a navy blazer on top. A blazer equaled professional, right? There was nothing fancier than that in her closet anyway. She wished she had her lucky hat, not that she could wear it to her meeting.

The 101 was busy but not impossible, and as she drove, she thought about the draft she had handed in four days ago. She wanted to please her new collaborators, so she had gone against her storytelling instincts and tried to heed every note she was given, even if a couple of them contradicted each other. It was obvious that all three partners had given her notes. She'd done her best, but the new draft felt diluted and muted, more story-by-committee than from a singular voice. There was no telling what might befall her at this lunch, or who was even going to be there. She had been corresponding with Helen, occasionally Joyce, and their attorney once or twice. Never Chelsea.

The meeting was at a trendy vegan restaurant in West Hollywood, and it was bustling when Fran arrived at noon on the dot for her meeting. Still, the host led her to a four-top with only one vacant seat. Fran inhaled deeply when she saw Chelsea there, looking fresh and sunny in a sleeveless floral day dress. Grace Commerford, the director, sat next to her. She wore an outfit almost identical to Fran's except her blazer was black over a black Ramones T-shirt. On Chelsea's right was a guy Fran didn't recognize who stood when she approached. Nice manners.

"Hello, Fran," Chelsea said. "This is Grace Commerford, who has agreed to direct our film. And this is Dante, my assistant."

Fran knew Grace from *Tolstoy Was Right*. She had been competent and calm on that set—great qualities in a director. Dante deserved a closer inspection. So he was doing her job now, was he? He nodded politely but didn't say anything. She wondered if he knew she'd had his job before him. The server interrupted her musing by asking for her order, and she hurriedly chose the first thing she saw from the menu.

As soon as their server left, Grace jumped right in. "Fran, I've read your original script and the latest rewrite. I have to tell you, I love your characters. May I ask, what was the genesis for a story about women's soccer?"

"Well, a while ago, it was late at night, and I flipped the channel— it was so long ago it was when people still flipped through the channels instead of scrolling a streaming site— and I came across *Bend It Like Beckham*. Do you know it?"

Chelsea and Grace nodded. Dante was absorbed in the same orange phone that used to be fused to Fran's hand. It still had the ladybug sticker on it.

"Yeah, of course you do. It was a big hit. I guess I had seen it when it first came out, but it didn't make that much of an impression on me. When I watched it that night, I became really invested in the relationship between the two female characters, who were both trying to achieve their dream of making professional soccer their career. There was so much to like about that movie, but then there's this love triangle with the male coach that's shoehorned in there and the subplot of the parent's misunderstanding about their sexuality. It left a terrible taste in my mouth. I wanted to see those two strong, determined women get together." She laughed a little bit. "That usually happens when I see two appealing female characters onscreen."

Grace grinned and nodded. "I totally get that."

Fran eyed her. Was she family?

Chelsea cleared her throat.

She got back to her story. "A queer female soccer romance. The Women's World Cup, because the US Women's National Team is so awesome. Pitting characters from two different teams against each other—all that built-in conflict and drama was too tempting to not to take a swing at—or kick at." She gave a self-conscious chuckle. "The thing practically wrote itself."

"And then Chelsea and her crew gave you notes."

"Yes, about that," Chelsea said. "We feel that some of the magic has been lost in your new draft."

"Oh. Okay." Fran felt her stomach drop. It wasn't as if she didn't already know that.

"But that was probably our fault. We pulled you in too many directions." Chelsea's tone softened slightly. "We're new at this. We loved your script, but then in the interest of saving money, we made you take out everything that made it special."

Grace nodded. "What I liked about it was how I felt I really knew these characters. The American player was from Queens, right? And the British character was from Croyden, and I loved how we got to know her and her family in the original draft, but she loses a lot of luster in the rewrite. There was such a sense of place in both of their stories, but now we've lost that for one of them." Grace sat back while the server deposited their drinks. She directed her next statement to Chelsea. "I think Fran should come location scouting with us."

It looked like Chelsea nearly choked on her sparkling water. "You do?"

"Spoiler alert," Grace said to Fran. "We're keeping the Queens location. New York City's tax breaks will make that possible."

"That's terrific." Fran was thrilled they were keeping Queens.

"But we'll need to find somewhere else for your other character. We're considering Atlanta, Albuquerque, and Austin." She elbowed Fran in a friendly way. "The fact that they all start with A is just a coincidence."

What a dork. Fran giggled. She was beginning to like Grace Commerford.

Grace turned to Chelsea. "With Fran with us, she can use some of that local juju to make the story sparkle again once we've decided on our second location."

Fran glanced at Chelsea, but then noticed someone at an adjacent table who had his phone out, recording their lunch, and probably Chelsea specifically. Dante was still gazing at the orange phone. She nudged his leg under the table to get his attention and tilted her head in the phone recorder's direction.

He clocked the guy, and said, "SMH." Then he buried his nose in his screen again.

Chelsea must have noticed their antics because she turned her head and saw the guy with the camera. She adjusted her chair away from it.

Giving ol' Dante the hairy eyeball didn't persuade him to take care of the problem, so Fran got up.

"No, Fran. Just ignore him."

Fran barely heard Chelsea. She was angry with the guy recording, but she was angrier with Dante. "Hey." She moved quickly and stood right in front of the guy's camera phone lens. "Can you stop? We're trying to have lunch here."

"Mind your business." He moved his phone so that it was angled back at Fran's table. She sidestepped so that she was blocking the phone again, and the man scraped his chair back right into a passing server. The four glasses of red wine the server carried flew right at Fran's chest. The entire dining room grew quiet after the contents splashed her upper half and the glasses crashed to the floor. She stood there for a moment, and then swiped at her dripping chin, a bold red now saturating her T-shirt and soaking her blazer. The server apologized profusely and the asshole laughed, pointing his phone at her now.

Glass shards crunched beneath her feet as she mustered her dignity and walked toward the restrooms. First meeting as a screenwriter slash co-producer was a giant fail.

❖

Chelsea got up and followed Fran toward the bathrooms. She was just pulling one of the unisex stalls closed when Chelsea caught the door and entered the tiny room with her, locking it behind her.

"I'm sorry. Now there's even more attention on you. I didn't mean for that to happen, obviously." Fran braced her arms on the vanity, her head down.

"I know. It was kind of you to try. As you can see, Dante's not very proactive, but then he hasn't had to be. My paparazzi problem has all but disappeared."

"Very recent evidence to the contrary."

"He's not a paparazzo. He's just a jerk." Chelsea grabbed some paper towels and blotted Fran's face and hair, then pressed them against the shoulder and body of Fran's jacket. "And here you are all dressed to impress."

"Please don't make fun of me," Fran whispered.

Chelsea saw tears welling in Fran's eyes. She took hold of Fran's sleeve, damp with wine. "I wasn't. I swear. What's wrong?"

"I'm frustrated." The edge in her voice corroborated her words. "I wanted today to go well, and now look at me. This is about as far from well as the moon."

"It's nothing. You'll have to dry-clean your jacket and throw away the shirt. That's all. You haven't lost any ground with Grace. We'll simply pick up where we left off when you return to the table. And if it's any consolation, Grace seems pretty enamored of you."

Fran flashed uncomprehending eyes at her.

"You didn't notice?" Chelsea had definitely noticed.

"No." Her voice was sullen. She pulled a handful of paper towels from the dispenser.

"An up-and-coming director interested in you? I'd have thought that's what you'd want."

"It's not what I want," Fran muttered.

"Well, what do you want?"

Fran twisted a paper towel between her shapely, strong fingers, but didn't seem inclined to answer the question. Chelsea forced herself to look away while they stood in silence.

Finally, in a subdued voice, Fran said, "Are you ever going to forgive me?"

Chelsea didn't know what to say. Forgiveness? It had honestly never occurred to her. Fran had become like a tiny pebble rattling around in her shoe. Thoughts of her poked at Chelsea at irritating times, in unexpected ways, and even after nearly a year, she couldn't shake Fran out of her life.

She had made her peace with working with Fran on this project, but there was no way she was going to share that information with Fran. Knowing where her feelings had been headed before—well, before— she absolutely had to keep Fran at arm's length. She was drawn to Fran in a way that confounded her, pissed her off. Her resentment was as comfortable and durable as a ski parka, and she was going to stay wrapped up in it, thank you very much.

But Fran had just now demonstrated her loyalty, her protective nature—at least when it came to Chelsea. A loyalty Fran had shown over and over while employed by her.

Forgiveness.

It was something Chelsea wanted Fran to have, she realized. For herself, just as much as for Fran. What better way to begin healing the hurt she felt? Chelsea wanted to give that to Fran. But if she took off that ski parka of resentment, the result was complete exposure. Utter nakedness before another human being—something she hadn't allowed herself since Beau—and it petrified her. Keeping Fran at a distance was the saner course of action. She couldn't weaken.

She took a step, got so close to Fran she detected the scent of fermented grapes. Fran's expression didn't change, but her pupils dilated. She became so still it was if she'd forgotten to breathe. The desire to touch her became irresistible. Mentally, Chelsea was strong as an oak, no way would she weaken. But her body was a willow—not weak exactly, but willing to bend when faced with the force that was Fran.

Fran heaved a breath into her lungs, as if remembering it was a necessity for life. She retreated a few inches until her back was against the tile wall. Chelsea advanced, leaving a whisper of space between them. She wasn't strong enough to withstand her attraction to Fran. Her fingertips grazed Fran's cheek, and at their touch, Fran angled her face into them, seeming to crave a firmer hand. Her eyes were glued to Chelsea's, still seeking a response to her unanswered question.

She pressed her lips against Fran's in a kiss that instantly smoldered and threatened to ignite into something heavy with heat. The almost soundless whimper that escaped from Fran had arousal spiraling down into Chelsea's core, and despite wanting to burn in the ferocity of her desire for Fran, she retreated when Fran went to put her arms around her. If she forgave Fran, there would be nothing stopping those half-baked old feelings from blazing into something volcanic, which was something Chelsea was not ready for. "I want to forgive you, but I'm"—*Hesitant? Unsure? Terrified?*—"not there yet."

It took a moment for Fran to open her eyes, and when she did, they were filled with wonder and not a little disappointment.

They were in a no-man's-land of sorts, Chelsea supposed, both staring at each other, wondering what was going to happen next. She had told herself she couldn't stand Fran, but neither could she stop herself from wanting her. She should go—couldn't remember what had possessed her to follow Fran in the first place—but her feet were not doing what they were told.

She rolled her lips inward and tasted wine. "I think that was a Cabernet Sauvignon." Warmth burst in her chest at Fran's incredulous chuckle.

Fran cast her eyes down at herself as if suddenly remembering her saturated outfit. Catching sight of her soiled T-shirt in the mirror, she shrugged out of her jacket and laid it on the sink. Fran looked at Chelsea as her hands went to the hem of her T-shirt and Chelsea knew exactly what was coming next. Even though her body was humming with the need to see and touch more of Fran, that way lay madness and bad decisions. She put a restraining hand on Fran's forearm. "No. I've used up my daily allotment of questionable judgment. You and I in the bathroom, your shirt stained, we've been here already. We are not going down the same road as before."

Fran tucked her hands in her pockets instead, her reluctance clear. "Just for the record, I have absolutely no problem traveling down that road. We've barely gone any distance at all. You and I might have an excellent road trip if we followed it a little further."

"Don't get ahead of yourself. That's never going to happen, but if it did, our trip damn well wouldn't begin in a public restroom."

"Fair. Or with a passenger who's just had a wine shower." Fran grinned and rolled her eyes.

Fran's composure frustrated Chelsea no end. How was she joking and smiling while Chelsea could still feel her heart pounding? But here Fran was, allowing Chelsea to dictate the parameters of their encounter, as she always had.

Chelsea had been the one to initiate intimacy with Fran every time, and Chelsea was the one who always backed away. It must be confusing as all get-out to Fran. Lord knew it was confusing to Chelsea. But Fran always accepted the limits Chelsea imposed, with seemingly unending amounts of patience. For a split second Chelsea imagined where they would be if they did travel down that road, and was assaulted by sensory images of heavy breathing, strong fingers, and the feel of hot skin on skin. *No.* She stifled the overpowering urge to throw herself into Fran's arms—wine shower be damned. *Nope. Let that go. Pivot back to the reason why you're both here today.*

While Fran busied herself blotting her jacket with paper towels, Chelsea's voice came out formal and stiff when she said, "I'm sorry we gave you notes that were so unhelpful."

"It's nothing that can't be fixed." Fran straightened. "Look, I'm going to go. I could wear my T-shirt back to front and maybe look semi-presentable, but I'm not going to be that comfortable. Could you make my excuses to Grace?"

Chelsea felt intense anger toward the man with the camera phone, but relief quickly followed it. With Fran gone, Chelsea could get back to some semblance of equilibrium. She maintained an outward calm. "I'll have Dante send you the notes from our meeting today, and I'll talk to Helen and Joyce about you joining us for location scouting."

"I know Grace surprised you with that. It's okay if it doesn't happen."

Chelsea didn't want to admit how quickly she had warmed to the idea. Little dangerous thoughts began to germinate. She edged toward the door.

"Chelsea?"

She turned back.

Fran looked down at the mess of pink-stained paper towels on top of her blazer before gazing into her eyes. "Would you have dinner with me some time?"

She hesitated. "Are you asking because you want to discuss the project? Talk about character arcs or casting or production design?"

"If you like, we could do that, but I'm talking about you allowing me to take you out on a date. You know—dinner, a movie, or maybe some dancing. The specifics are negotiable, but it'd be a real, all caps date. Exclamation point. With all the romantic intention that implies. A traditional, honest-to-goodness, maybe a bit old-fashioned date."

Chelsea raised her eyebrows. "Like the kind you see in the movies?"

"Well, depends on the movie." Fran's expression turned wry. "Not like a date in a horror movie that ends with blood spattered all over a windshield. Think romantic comedy—after the meet-cute but before the montage set to a peppy pop song. Because rom-coms are my specialty."

"Thank you for clearing that up."

"You're welcome. So…"

Fran had really laid it all out there. There was no doubt about what she wanted. Had Chelsea ever been asked out on a date like this? Ever? She marveled at the gumption it must take, to be willing to have your heart smashed by a refusal, especially when Chelsea had so recently disappointed her with a no. But sometimes, a person had to be rewarded with a yes. It was the law of averages, right? Why was she thinking about this in the abstract? Because it let her delay in her reply. Because it let her drift in a multiverse where a date with Fran was a possibility. But what she wanted and what she would say yes to were two different things.

Chelsea thought that Fran just might be the bravest person she knew, that she had the courage to come out and say exactly what she wanted and the guts to listen to the answer without flinching.

But then Fran did flinch. "I'm going to take that as a no, but you're still trying to figure out how to turn me down with some kindness."

And Chelsea was the opposite of brave. Not brave enough to say yes. Not brave enough to forgive. She reached out and gripped Fran's hand for just a second before releasing it. "It is a no. I'm sorry." Like the coward she was, she left quickly before she could see that no reflected in Fran's face.

CHAPTER TWENTY-ONE

F ran sat in her cramped aisle seat watching for Chelsea. When Fran had boarded their red-eye to Atlanta with the rest of group three, she'd seen Grace and Helen sitting in First, but no Chelsea. She and the rest of her fellow coach passengers had completed their game of roller-bag Tetris and were now waiting.

From Trina's experiences when Entitled Prick had to fly commercial, Fran knew that Chelsea, as a VIP wishing to avoid attention, would board last. Fran felt a little shortchanged that she had worked for Chelsea during a time when she had limited her travel. Sick as it sounded, Fran would've relished arranging all those details for Chelsea.

And then, there she was, wearing a dark jacket with the collar turned up and Fran's black Mets cap. Fran's eyes went wide at the sight of it. Chelsea appeared at the top of the aisle for a second before sliding into the first row window seat. If Fran had blinked, she would have missed it. Dante followed her but continued to a window seat in coach a few rows in front of Fran. A flight attendant immediately closed the aircraft door and they were taxiing thirty seconds later.

Fran was just about to switch her phone to airplane mode when she got an incoming text.

Are you onboard?

It was from Chelsea. She hadn't deleted her number.

Fran grinned. What a little liar.

Yes. Nice hat.

Chelsea didn't respond to that. *Did you check a bag?*

With flying the way it is today? You've got to be kidding.
Chelsea instantly replied, *Is that a no?*
Yes, it's a no. Fran gave her the clarity she seemed to need.
Good. See you on the ground.

They landed in Atlanta as dawn was breaking, and when Fran was about to exit the plane, she was met by airline staff and escorted through a door on the jet bridge and down a set of stairs onto the tarmac, where an Escalade idled. A driver stowed her bag, and she got in to find the only empty seat was next to Chelsea. Grace sat in the front and Helen and Dante in the rear seats. "Thanks for the lift. I really hate trudging through the terminal with all the other normies."

"This'll save us time," Chelsea said to her. "Dante, our car is sorted?"

"Yes, Chelsea. This driver will take us right to it."

She rotated her finger in the air. "Let's locomote."

❖

Fran had to hand it to Chelsea. If a good producer was someone who rode herd over their loud and loose posse, then Chelsea was a good producer. They'd hit the ground running, and after they'd picked up their local location scout, poor Dante had to drive around the greater Atlanta environs while five women yammered their opinions with no regard to the volume of their voices. Chelsea kept them on schedule and on task, and vetoed Helen when she wanted to go thirteen miles out of their way for some famous fried chicken she'd heard about.

Soaking in the local color had been great fodder for Fran, who had been taking nonstop notes for herself with every location they visited. If the production chose Georgia, she knew she'd have a rich environment to play around in.

Fran had also been able to soak up Chelsea's presence. It had been two weeks since the disastrous lunch meeting, and their conversation and kiss in the bathroom had never been far from Fran's mind.

Other than their brief text conversation on the plane, Chelsea hadn't said boo to Fran, but Fran could've made a detailed report on every move Chelsea had made. It was different than when she had worked for Chelsea, when Fran had a million things to keep track of at once, and was constantly weeding through the requests for Chelsea's attention while maintaining her schedule and safety. Today, with only one job to do, she had plenty of time left over to luxuriate in Chelsea's nearness, covertly study things about her like her alertness when discussing logistics with Grace and her kindness to a teenage girl and her dog when they had stopped at the Botanical Garden. A few people had noticed Chelsea during their stops over the course of the day, but their interactions had all been low-key and respectful.

The tension that had usually radiated off Chelsea when she and Fran had been out in public was nonexistent now. Chelsea seemed relaxed and focused, and utterly unaware of Fran as she took hundreds of pics with her phone and wrote in her notebook. It was unspoken that Chelsea always got the seat behind the driver, and everyone else took whatever was available. With the addition of the location scout, the vehicle had been crowded, and twice Fran found herself in the middle seat, crushed up against Chelsea. She had been close enough to catch the scent of Chelsea's distinctive perfume, and it was all Fran could do to keep her breathing regular and not sniff at her like a hound dog. But Chelsea seemed unperturbed. After an entire day of this, Fran was the definition of perturbed.

The sun had long since set, and thank God they had reached the final stop of the day. The original script featured several soccer fields of varying levels of extravagance, from scrubby school pitches to the most lionized mecca of British football—Wembley Stadium—for which they were currently hunting a replacement.

They rolled up to Mercedes-Benz Stadium, home of the Atlanta Falcons, and piled out of the car. Helen held her phone's flashlight aloft as they walked through one of the darkened access tunnels toward the field. Grace found an entrance to the stands and climbed toward the top of the lower deck to gain some height. Chelsea went to greet their contact, who was approaching with Dante.

After a long day of stifling her physical responses to Chelsea and enduring the high volume of chatter, Fran needed some distance from everyone and headed toward the middle of the field. The stadium was an impressive structure, and its retractable roof was open, but the night sky was obscured as, section by section, it was flooded with artificial light.

Helen moseyed over and stood next to Fran. "New title—*A Love As Big As Mercedes-Benz Stadium*. Whaddya think?"

Fran gave her a grudging smile. "Rolls right off the tongue, but loses the symbolic significance."

"Come on. It's almost as big as Wembley. And the Brits would understand that reference, but I would argue that your so-called symbolic significance is mostly lost on the American movie-going public. Now, we aren't going to use this stadium's name in our title, but is it such a sacrifice to change locations if it means the difference between making this picture and scrapping it?"

"Well, when you put it that way, I love it."

"I knew you'd see reason." Helen had great, easygoing energy, and had sown the day's conversations with insightful comments—from both the creative side and business end of movie-making. They hadn't hired a production designer yet, but Helen seemed able to wear that hat as well as several others when it came to producing a film. Chelsea had found a valuable ally. Fran wondered if it would be disloyal to Chelsea if she asked Helen to mentor her.

Helen did a slow three-sixty and took in the entire stadium. "You're responsible for kick-starting Propolis Pictures, you know."

"I wouldn't go that far. I sent an email."

"I thought that email you sent was at Chelsea's behest. But that was your initiative. I only heard the whole story a few weeks ago."

Fran's eyes found Chelsea, fifty yards away and deep in conversation with the stadium contact. "Chelsea told you?" Chelsea discussed Fran with Helen? Thought about her when she wasn't around?

"No. She doesn't talk about you much."

Fran deflated at this.

"Joyce filled me in," Helen continued. "But you did Chelsea—and by extension me—a giant favor when you sent that email. I had forgotten how terrific it is to work with Chelsea when she's on fire with creative passion. So thanks for that."

"You're welcome. And thank *you*. I never thought that email would lead to me standing on a football field in Georgia, envisioning people who only existed in my head running around on it."

"Nothing's guaranteed in this business, but I have a good feeling about the team of people we're assembling for this project. And it's way too premature for me to even think this, but if it allows me to never have to think about another superhero, I'll be grateful."

"You think this could be the start of something?"

"I think the market is so fragmented right now, targeting an untapped niche and delivering them a quality product as cheaply as possible could be a route to viability."

"This is the kind of movie I've wanted to see since I was a teenager."

"The sporty competitiveness of *Rocky III*, the depth of feeling of *Love and Basketball*, and the old-fashioned, sparring wit of *Adam's Rib*. I can't think of anything quite like it. You wrote what you wanted to see."

Fran flushed with pride at the comparisons, particularly *Adam's Rib*, one of her grandmother's favorite movies. "There's plenty more where that came from."

"Interesting." Helen eyed her. "Maybe we could talk about a first-look deal with Propolis."

Fran turned to gaze at Chelsea across the field. If a deal like that would prolong her contact with Chelsea, it would be an automatic yes.

"You've got it bad, don't you?"

Fran felt like her face erupted in flames. "Is it that obvious?"

Helen waggled her head. "Not to everyone. I'm observant."

She smiled. "I've observed that about you." She squinted up toward the lights and tried to ignore her embarrassment. "I'm just one of thousands lining up to adore Chelsea Cartwright, aren't I?"

"Everyone loves Chelsea. She's magnetic, and a magnet's job is to attract objects to itself. It serves her well in her line of work, but..." Helen hesitated, and when Fran looked at her she saw an expression that was impossible to decipher. "A magnet can feel the pull as well."

What was Helen trying to say?

"You know that, right? That's just science. Like with a compass? No matter how much that needle swings around, the magnet points it north. That's what it's drawn to. Everyone deserves to have that, you know? Their true north?"

"Sure," Fran said, distracted by Chelsea, now headed toward them with her head down.

"Work with me here, Fran. Weren't you just ranting about symbolic significance?"

"Symbolic? Ranting? I was hardly ranting." She tried to make it seem like she and Helen were deep in conversation and she hadn't just been mooning over Chelsea.

"Whatever." Helen saw right through her. "Hey. We about done?" she said to Chelsea.

"Yeah, almost. Another few minutes while Grace checks out some of the facilities. What do you think?"

"I think it's great if Shakespeare here can overlook her delicate literary sensibilities."

They both turned to Fran. "I can work with this," she said. Seeing actual locations did a lot to stir the imagination, but she foresaw many hours overhauling the script in her future.

"There's that can-do spirit I like so much." Helen gave Fran a light punch in the arm and started walking back to the sidelines. "I'll be in the car. These dogs are barking. And there'd better be fried chicken on the menu wherever we're going for dinner. I have a hankering."

Now Fran and Chelsea were the only ones standing on the field. They were only about two feet apart, but Chelsea still behaved like Fran was invisible. It was just about impossible to not think about the last time Fran had seen her—in the bathroom at a vegan restaurant— and what had happened there. It had kept Fran in a near-constant state of low-key sexual frustration all day, and frankly, it was exhausting. But after two weeks of only her thoughts of Chelsea to sustain her, she vastly preferred the discomfort of being in her actual presence.

When Chelsea finally directed her attention to Fran, she said, "I can see your characters out here, ninety-three minutes in and running on fumes. I can hear the crowd. I can feel the heat. Being here really makes it come alive for me."

Fran pictured Chelsea charging up the wing, making a shot on goal. A thought struck her. "Nobody has talked about casting. Will you take a role?"

"You didn't think I'd be a lead, did you? I'm too old. Besides, I think I really like producing."

Fran didn't say that in her mind, Chelsea had a major role in every story she wrote. God, she was pathetic. Hang on… "You haven't given up acting, have you?"

"No, I'm just going to be a lot more choosy." She crossed her arms as if to ward off a chill, but it wasn't cold in Georgia. "I'd take a smaller role if it would help us secure more financing, and it probably would."

"The American coach. A great character part. A good fit for you." Fran gazed at her own Mets cap atop Chelsea's head.

Chelsea nodded. "That's what I thought too. That rousing speech in the locker room in the third act? I could rouse the shit out of those players."

"Agreed. It's a shame, though."

"What is?"

"The coach is covered up in long-sleeve athletic wear the whole time—at least that's how I pictured her. If you were a player we'd at least see your jacked upper arms. I couldn't take my eyes off them in *A Triceratops in Tarzana.*"

"Shut up. Jesus, that movie." Chelsea laughed. "Hey, are you objectifying me?"

Oops. Might as well own it. "Maybe a little?"

Chelsea didn't look insulted. If anything she looked pleased. "I've worked really hard on my arms. I feel like they deserve to be admired. Is that arrogant?"

Fran felt like she was put on this earth to admire Chelsea, and she was tired of hiding it, or maybe she just didn't want to hide it anymore. "No. I admire all of you. In my dreams, I chart the contours of your entire body—the graceful slope of your spine, the line of your thigh, the curve of your breast. I touch every part of you. I use my hands and my mouth and all that I am to build a mighty heat between us, and you're breathless, and quivering, and aching for me to quench it, to take its strength away. And I can't wait to go to sleep every night because I get to do it all over again."

Chelsea stared, her mouth a little bit slack.

The banks of lights began to turn off, in reverse order to how they were illuminated. The stadium dimmed and the shadows increased in length and number until they were standing alone in the dark, and still Chelsea didn't say anything. Fran considered pulling a Chelsea and planting a soulful kiss on her, but she couldn't do that. She needed Chelsea to accept her, to give her some kind of sign that she wasn't suffering from massive delusions, that there really was something between them. She'd said what she'd said. Now she had to wait for Chelsea to say something back.

But she didn't. She reached into her jacket pocket and turned on the flashlight on her phone. She flung her hand out in what Fran guessed was a gesture for her to walk with her. They were almost back at the car when Chelsea stopped and said, "We have everything we need here. We won't need to go to Albuquerque or Austin if you can use Atlanta in the next draft, and we can get the permits rolling."

Really? That's how Chelsea was going to respond? By not responding? By ignoring what Fran had said like it didn't matter in the slightest?

She didn't meet Fran's eyes, and turned when she heard footsteps on the gravel. Grace and the location scout were returning to the car and Chelsea waved at them. Was Fran imagining the relief that appeared over Chelsea's features?

They were not ever going to happen. Fran needed to reckon with that. It had been almost a year, and nothing was going to change. Chelsea was never going to allow her past her defenses again. "I get it," she said. "I'll give you what you want."

CHAPTER TWENTY-TWO

Chelsea walked across the lobby toward the restaurant and saw Helen sitting alone in the dark and moody cocktail bar. She veered from her path, Dante trailing behind her. "Hey, I thought we were meeting for dinner."

Helen took a sip from the amber lowball in front of her. "Grace just took off with the location scout. They said they were going to check out a few more places, but the air between them was thick with hook-up energy. I doubt they'll be back anytime soon."

Chelsea frowned. They were supposed to work through dinner. Dante had reserved them a private dining room for that very purpose. "So we aren't going to do the cost breakdown?"

"We've been at it all day, Chels. It's Miller time." Helen waggled her glass.

She pulled out the high, heavy chair beside Helen and sat. "Thanks, Dante. I guess we won't need you or the laptop. Can you manage dinner on your own?"

"Sure, Chelsea. TTYL."

Chelsea didn't think she'd ever seen him move so fast.

Helen watched him go. "What is it with that guy and the acronyms?"

She shrugged and ordered a drink. The bar wasn't very crowded, not that it ever saw a ton of action. Its high prices and location—tucked away off the lobby of an upscale hotel in Buckhead—guaranteed its exclusivity. The hotel had a reputation for good security, and well-heeled guests seemed more interested in their own comfort than in disturbing Chelsea's. Still, she had arranged to stay with Helen in a two-bedroom suite and avoided registering under her own name. "You were gone when I got out of the shower."

"I didn't want to yell through the door. I knew you'd catch up with me eventually, and here you are."

She looked at her watch. It was past the time they were supposed to meet. "Have you seen Fran?"

"Yeah, she found me right after I sat down here. She said she wasn't feeling well and was turning in for the night. Said she'd be ready for our transfer to the airport in the morning."

Chelsea picked up her drink but didn't take a sip. Her stomach flip-flopped at the thought of Fran. All day she'd been pleasantly aware of Fran's calm and careful presence, and even if they hadn't needed to talk much, Chelsea felt better able to focus with her there. Then that exchange at the stadium. Fran's intense eyes, not to mention what she had said. Chelsea had immediately tamped it down and had made every attempt to ignore it, but little snatches of what she had said were still doing laps around her brain. It had led to a steamy little scenario she'd imagined in the shower, the vestiges of which had yet to fully vacate her body. Maybe alcohol would help. She gulped at her whiskey sour. "She didn't seem ill to me."

"She's not ill," Helen said flatly. "She's depressed. Whatever you did before you got in the car completely crushed her."

"I didn't do anything," Chelsea denied, ignoring the twinge from her conscience. "I don't know what you're talking about."

"Right." Helen gave her a judgy side-eye. "You're playing games with her."

"And you don't know what you're talking about. You don't know what she did."

"Joyce told me."

"Okay, then you should understand. I can't let that go. Of all the assistants in all the towns in all the world, she had to become mine."

"Ugh. You just butchered that line. I don't know if I can let *that* go." Helen turned in her stool to face her. "You're looking at this whole situation in extreme close-up. Change the lens, Chels. Pull the camera back to get a little more mise-en-scène. A down-on-her-luck screenwriter, doing something she hates, decides to turn a situation to her advantage. Then she works for you for like, a day probably, and decides she can't use you for her own gain. For whatever reason, she can't do that to you. Maybe because you're such a kind and compassionate person." Her voice dripped with sarcasm. "So merciful."

"All right. You've made your point. It doesn't change the fact that she lied."

"Look, I know we've just gotten back into each other's lives, but I do know you've had a rough few years. Beau's a shit, and kids are hard. Happens to the best of us. Someday when I'm a lot drunker than I am right now, I'll tell you about how Monica exited stage left from the life I thought we had built together."

"Oh, Hels. I'm sorry. I did hear about that, but I was so wrapped up in my own stuff I never reached out. Can you forgive me?"

"I can, Chelsea. You know why?"

"Why?"

"Because forgiveness is easy." Helen lifted her glass in salute and then drained it. "Another?" She waved the bartender over.

Chelsea refused another drink. "It's not easy to me."

"Have you forgiven Beau?"

Chelsea drew in a breath and exhaled slowly. "Even though there are times when I hate him and his disease with every fiber of my being, yes. I forgave him. It's a disease."

"Everything he's put you through? You've forgiven him a hundred times—probably more. Did you forgive Petal for that bullshit with the paparazzi?"

"Of course. She's a child."

"But Fran doesn't get a pass?"

Chelsea was silent. Fran did not get a pass. Why didn't Fran get a pass?

"You know, I lied to her today." Helen turned on her stool to face her.

"You lied to Fran?"

"I told her you never talk about her, but that's a blatant lie, isn't it. Ever since the first meeting when we all found out she was the writer, you haven't shut up about her. You find ways to bring her up in conversation that are so damn contrived. I thought someone was paying you twenty bucks every time you said her name. *Oh, you need an envelope? Fran needed an envelope once.*"

"Shut up. I don't do that."

"*Girl.*"

"I don't." Chelsea thought about the six or so weeks since Fran had crashed back into her life. "Do I?"

"She's obviously on your mind. And her eyes follow you around like you're a delicious gazelle and she's a hungry lioness. Why don't you live a little? Have some fun with someone who most definitely wants to have fun with you."

Chelsea's doubts must have shown on her face.

"Are you kidding me right now? All you have to do is go find her and say *here I am, my bones are ready to be jumped!* and her ass will be two feet in the air."

"It's not that easy."

"Give me one good reason why it's not easy."

If Chelsea forgave Fran, she'd have to acknowledge the feelings she wasn't currently ready to confront. Even simply talking about it felt dangerous, but she probably wasn't going to get another ear as empathetic as Helen's to listen. "If I open the door…it may lead to something I'm not ready for."

"Like what?"

Like how she felt like she was only a foot or two away from falling for her. But she couldn't say that to Helen. "She already has me acting in ways that I don't recognize." She put her elbow on the bar and rested her head in her hand. "I mean, Hels, I warn myself that nothing can happen and then I go and kiss her!"

Helen's eyebrows disappeared into her bangs. "You kissed her?"

"Yes. Twice! She makes me lose control of myself."

"Back there at the stadium?"

"No. Once before I knew what she did, and once after, in the bathroom at our meeting with Grace."

"I knew I should have gone to that meeting." Helen took a glug from her new drink. "Interesting. As a purely academic exercise, answer this—how many times have you wanted to kiss her?"

Chelsea scoffed. "A hundred? A thousand? Every time I look at her?" Just admitting that felt weighty.

"So look at it this way—you've shown remarkable restraint. You only kissed her twice among the infinity times you've wanted to. That's a pretty good ratio."

Chelsea laughed at Helen's logic. "You're not helping, but I'm so glad I have you back."

"Chels and Hels—together again." She raised her glass once more. "And that's another thing to be grateful to Fran for. If I was having big swoopy feelings for someone, you can bet your bippy I'd be running straight toward them. You do realize how rare big feelings are, right? Why are you running away from them?"

"You know why. They're scary."

"You banished her for—what—six months?"

"Ten."

"You didn't even have to count on your fingers. I bet you know the exact amount of time down to the minute." Helen giggled. "Ten months, six days, fourteen hours and—"

She slapped Helen's arm. "Stop it."

"Here's what I want you to do—envision a world where you don't see her for another ten months. Or better yet, a world where you never see Fran again. How's that for scary?"

Chelsea stared down into her drink. She refused to really think about it. "My life would be a helluva lot easier."

"And you call yourself an actor," Helen chided. "If you don't believe that, how do you expect me to?"

"Believe what you want." Chelsea got up to go.

"Hey, what about that fried chicken?"

"I've lost my appetite."

CHAPTER TWENTY-THREE

Fran heard a knock on the door. "Just a second." She tapped the space bar, got out of bed, and tightened the hotel's white robe. She swung the door wide, expecting room service.

It wasn't. It was Chelsea.

Her eyes roamed over Fran in her robe for a second before she looked at the floor. "Sorry. I'll come back later after you've dressed."

What now? "My day is done. This is as dressed as I'm going to get." Fran shifted her weight to her other foot. "I thought you were my dinner. Did you need something?"

The rattling wheels of a cart became audible, and Chelsea stepped aside as a uniformed woman hefted a tray from the cart to her shoulder. "Room service?"

"Right in here." Fran waved the attendant forward. "Um…do you want to come in?" she asked Chelsea.

She stood to the side while Fran signed for her meal and escorted the server out. "I was just having a drink downstairs with Helen. She said you weren't feeling well."

"Just tired. I'm okay."

Chelsea surveyed the room—the laptop on the bed, some handwritten notes and her phone on the table next to the room service tray. "I hope I'm not interrupting anything." She didn't show any signs of getting to the point of why she was there.

Fran made up her mind to be pleasant. "I'm relaxing for a bit. After I eat, I'll jump right in, transcribe my notes and stuff. You haven't given me a deadline for the next draft but I know you're not going to wait forever. I'm working the day after tomorrow and the next five days after that, so I have to be organized about my time."

"Working?"

"Yes, the prop house? I think I told you."

"You're a co-producer now and you're still working your day job?"

Fran crossed her arms. "Don't worry. I'll give my notice before things really get rolling. I'm grateful for the job with Propolis Pictures. You'll get your money's worth, I promise."

"That's not what I meant."

Fran tried to hold on to the remnants of her patience. Chelsea seemed to want everything to be strictly business between them, and Fran was doing her best to comply. Hadn't Chelsea had enough today? Did she have to invade Fran's room while she was trying to lick her wounds? "I must have misunderstood, then. What can I do for you? Is it something we can take care of quickly before my food gets cold?"

"Oh, go ahead and eat. I'm so sorry. Our working dinner didn't end up happening. Whatever you ordered smells delicious." Chelsea stepped away from the table where a metal cloche covered the food.

Fran sighed. She couldn't eat in front of a hungry Chelsea.

She seemed distracted. "I'm a little annoyed. Why couldn't we work through dinner? All of Propolis is together right now—except Joyce. Why not use the time?"

"Because unlike you, people need a break. I got no sleep on the plane, and we've been going balls-out since we landed at six a.m." Fran was dead on her feet. She sat at the foot of the bed and watched Chelsea, who seemed wired with nervous energy, prowl around the room.

"I'll tell Dante to upgrade you for tomorrow's flight. I don't know why you weren't."

"It's fine. You don't need to do that."

"I'm just really pumped about this whole thing. I kind of feel like I've got all this power—to shape, to mold, to make something excellent—you know?"

At this specific moment, Fran wasn't interested in knowing.

"For once, I'm the one who gets to make the important decisions. Well, Grace and me. And Helen." She darted a look at Fran. "And you."

"Chelsea, why are you here?" *And how can I get you out of my room so I can finally have a little peace today?*

She wandered close to the bed and gazed at the laptop. "Are you watching a movie? Another oldie?"

Fran leaned over and shut her laptop. "Does it matter? Look—"

"What you said earlier..." The words burst out of Chelsea, and she faced Fran but didn't say anything else. She looked like she was hunting for her next line, but needed a prompter to tell her what that was.

Fran let her off the hook. "It's okay. I'm sorry for saying it."

Chelsea looked her in the eye. "You are? Why?"

"Well, obviously, you didn't like it. I should have kept my mouth shut."

"Did you mean it?"

Here was her opportunity to take it back. They could probably get back on an even keel if Fran swept all she had said under this bed she was sitting on. She couldn't do that. "Every word."

"Then we have a problem." Chelsea sagged down onto the bed next to Fran, so close that her knee pressed into Fran's thigh.

If Fran's heart rate had picked up to a trot when she saw Chelsea at the door, it had now accelerated into a canter.

"What you said made me feel...things." Chelsea rested one finger on the hem of Fran's terry cloth robe. "You don't even want to know how I got through my shower earlier."

Fran was desperate to know—was hoping Chelsea would tell her every minute detail, and then write it down, publish it, and adapt it for the screen.

"I know things between us aren't great. They're not even good. If you forced me, I would say a medium distance away from good-ish— or thereabouts." She shut her eyes like she couldn't believe what she was saying.

Was Chelsea babbling? Was she nervous? "I'm really not forcing you." Fran gave a dry laugh. "Maybe we don't have to calculate exactly where we stand this second." She gazed at where Chelsea's finger still lay on her robe. If there were an option, she would much prefer to discuss why Chelsea felt compelled to touch her.

"Maybe we don't, but there are a few things I need to say." Chelsea looked away. "What you did—it really hurt me."

"I know. I'm sorry." Fran reached for her hand, and Chelsea allowed her to hold it.

"I need you to understand why it hurt so much." She turned Fran's hand over and stroked her fingers—almost unconsciously. "From the very beginning, you did more than just assist. I was suspicious, and fearful, and detached—and you managed to sneak in anyway."

Sneak in where, Fran wondered.

"You made me feel safe. For the first time since my divorce, I felt like someone had my back. It was such a relief. Finally, I was getting my life back on track, and you were partly responsible for that. You were there whenever I needed you, doing the exact thing I needed from you..." Chelsea stopped. It seemed like she was struggling to put her thoughts into words. "Do you know that story of the frog in a pot of slowly boiling water?"

Fran nodded.

"That's you and me. I feel like that frog."

She tried to understand. "You're the frog that can't tell the water's getting too hot? And what am I? Am I the water?"

"Yes, you're the water."

"I'm the danger? The thing that kills you?" Fran didn't do a very good job of hiding the alarm in her voice.

"Yes—no. The thing is, you didn't *feel* dangerous."

"I think that's the point," Fran said glumly.

"No frogs are dying in this story, okay?" Chelsea seemed to go into babble-mode again. "The water is hot, not boiling, not like two hundred twelve degrees. It's comfortable. Like a hot tub or something." She was silent for a moment. "Anyway, the point is—you're not dangerous, not really. I mean, don't get me wrong. What you did felt like a betrayal. It's taken a long time for me to get past it. But with time and a bit of perspective, I now realize you never—in actual fact— betrayed me. Leaving pertinent information off your résumé doesn't rise to the level of betrayal, but it is dishonest. I really wish you had been honest with me from the very beginning."

That didn't sound good. Fran had been veering toward hope, but now she was no longer sure.

"But if you had, we wouldn't be here right now."

Which is where, exactly?

"I think what that water really represents is change," Chelsea said. "You came into my life, and my feelings for you came on so slowly, so gradually, I didn't realize how thoroughly immersed I was in you. And then when I found out about your former job, it was as if I was scooped out of the hot water and dumped into an ice bath. Life preserving, maybe, but all I wanted was the sweet comfort of that hot water." She looked right into Fran's eyes. "I still do."

"You do?"

"Yeah, you and me. Frog soup. Weird, right?" Her smile seemed delicate somehow. "But this time with the awareness of it. And...I forgive you, Franny."

Fran felt such intense relief, she imagined her bones had turned to water.

"I shouldn't have been so stingy with my forgiveness. It was pointed out to me that I was able to forgive far worse sins than yours but couldn't offer you that same grace."

"Can I ask why?"

"I think it's because you make me feel things I haven't felt in a long time. Big, scary things. And if I was able to keep you at a distance by putting you in an untouchable category, you couldn't hurt me a second time."

"I'm sorry I hurt you. I never want to do it again."

"I believe that." Chelsea nodded with an air of closing the case. "And I'm sorry too. For not hearing you out that night. For letting my anger rule me for so long. And most of all, for not responding to those brave and beautiful words you said on the football field today. I can assure you, I did react. I just didn't say anything."

"What would you say to me now?" Her heart pumped at a gallop.

Chelsea paused, lost in thought. "I can't make promises right now. My heart can forgive, but my head is still all over the map. All I know is that I want to be with you tonight, but I'm not sure what we're going to look like tomorrow. Can you be okay with that?"

Tomorrow was a word that had no meaning. It wasn't even a word. It was gibberish. Maybe it was foolish, but all Fran cared about was right now. She moved closer and was intoxicated by that unknowable scent of Chelsea's that was hers alone. Her hands rested on the knot of the sash that held her robe closed. "I'm okay with that."

Chelsea's eyes were on her hands. "I can't remember the exact words you used out there on the field. All I know is you said the word *quivering* and it's been imprinted right here ever since." She pointed to a spot over her breastbone. "What was it you said?"

Intent on showing her instead, Fran put her hand over the place Chelsea pointed to and kissed her. This was not going to be a quick kiss like the others had been. They were going to sink into it like she hadn't had the chance to before. No one was going to pull away if she had anything to do with it.

Somehow Chelsea received that message. Her lips moved slowly but surely over Fran's, her hands gripping the lapels of Fran's robe. There was a tentativeness, and also a tenderness to the way Chelsea kissed her at first, but then it was as if a switch flipped, and it deepened into something forceful and demanding.

Fran surrendered to the onslaught as Chelsea took control with every move she made. She drew Fran against her and she somehow found herself splayed halfway across Chelsea's lap. She snaked her arms around Chelsea's shoulders, holding on as she twisted their bodies and dipped her head toward her again. Chelsea's kiss was a wave that Fran was happy to crash against, and she felt blissfully battered by a fury of tongue, teeth, and lips.

Chelsea drew back for a moment, panting, her eyes wild with desire. "Is this okay?"

"Okay? You're magnificent." Fran needed more. She slid from Chelsea's lap and stood. Her robe had failed at keeping her covered up. It now sagged open, the sash nearly completely undone. Chelsea stretched and made a grab, but Fran stepped back, just beyond Chelsea's reach. She undid the sash and gave a playful shimmy so the robe slipped from her shoulders. She held it so it just covered her breasts.

Chelsea put her hands on the bed and became still. "Come here." Her voice was low and Fran felt it deep in her chest. She obeyed instantly, standing between Chelsea's spread legs.

"So close now," Chelsea murmured, sneaking a hand up Fran's thigh, under the robe, to grip Fran's waist. "Do you know how many times you've appeared in my dreams, claw marks on your beautiful chest? I'd wake up thinking I was the one who had clawed you."

Fran felt her clit pulse. "You dream about me too?"

"Yes. Take off the robe."

Fran dropped it to the floor.

Chelsea's expression didn't change as her eyes roamed over Fran's skin, but the fingers at Fran's waist tightened and she stood as well. "If I had known you were in your room with nothing on except a hotel robe

I would have been here a lot sooner." She clutched at Fran's hips with both hands while she gazed at Fran's breasts.

"You're here now." Fran began to unbutton Chelsea's blouse. "This is okay, right?"

"Oh, yeah." Chelsea kicked off her shoes. "Take everything off me."

Fran pushed the shirt from her shoulders and undid Chelsea's fly.

Chelsea put her hands on Fran's shoulders, now in her hair, cupping her face. She dropped kisses on Fran's forehead, and brushed her fingers over her eyebrows. "I was turned on by your eyebrows first, you know."

"I did not know." Fran giggled and pushed Chelsea's trousers down her hips. "I'm learning so much right now."

Chelsea smoothed her lips over first Fran's right and then her left eyebrow. "So sleek. With a perfect arch. And to me, it seemed like your eyes saw right through me when you got in that elevator on the first day we met, but your eyebrows were much nicer and sort of had sympathy for me? Oh my God, I don't know what I'm saying. Just ignore me. Can this night live in a cone of silence?"

"Yes." Fran was touched by Chelsea's blathering. Emotion welled up in her, and she leaned in and kissed Chelsea's neck to cover it.

"I'll never live this down." Chelsea stepped out of the pool of fabric at her feet.

Fran wanted to say there was nothing for Chelsea to live down. Whatever happened tomorrow, this night was going to be a cherished memory for Fran. Even if they stopped this second, it was probably going to be one of the most important nights of her life. But that was too much for Chelsea to know. Not being able to tell her that wasn't ideal, but it only meant that Fran had to express herself through her actions instead. She slid her hands beneath Chelsea's panties and pushed them down her legs. Chelsea shivered when Fran dragged her fingers up the backs of her thighs. "You feel incredible."

Chelsea reached behind and unhooked her bra, letting it drop on the floor. "Now, come here. I want all of you." She wrapped her arms around Fran's waist and pressed them together so as much as their skin as possible was touching. Fran wrapped her hands around Chelsea's forearms, then slid them upward and finally got to feel Chelsea's upper arms, and then squeezed the muscles in her shoulders.

Chelsea bent her head and kissed her way down Fran's neck from her jaw to her collarbone, and then took the skin there between her teeth.

Fran hissed at the sharp sting. "Are you biting me?" It was more pleasurable than painful.

Chelsea ran her tongue over where her teeth had been, soothing the red marks she'd left. "Maybe," she breathed. "I can't get enough of you."

"My God, talk about a lesbian vampire fantasy."

Chelsea cradled Fran in her arms, and her breasts pushed against Fran's. Fran could feel her erect nipples on her skin. She let her head drop back and Chelsea planted her mouth right over the hollow intersection where Fran's throat, clavicles, and sternum met.

"I need to feel you under me." Chelsea pivoted and propelled them onto the bed. She landed on top of Fran and quickly straddled her. She looked like a goddess—eyes hooded, sitting upright, surveying Fran beneath her.

"Wait."

"What?" Chelsea's fingertips drew designs on Fran's stomach for a moment, like it was a map and she was planning the route for a successful campaign.

Fran was usually the one who took charge during sex, and having Chelsea on top, poised to start making Fran feel really good, was not typical for her. But why would she want to stop her? "Nothing." She grinned, and the smile that Chelsea returned was a few degrees shy of feral.

It was going to be so glorious to be conquered by Chelsea.

She bent over Fran's breasts and lashed her tongue over one nipple and then the other. Her lips and tongue were everywhere on Fran's chest, licking and sucking, and Fran couldn't do much more than hang on, her whole body shuddering as need pooled in the deepest part of her. Her hips strained against Chelsea in an involuntary rhythm she had no control over, and when Chelsea recognized it, she sat up and looked into Fran's eyes, her auburn hair a wild mane. "You're ready for me, aren't you."

"Yes." Fran reached up and pulled Chelsea down to her, her tongue surging into Chelsea's mouth as she tried to tell her without words what she desperately needed. "Please."

She kept her eyes on Fran as she reached down between her thighs with one hand and caressed her. Her breath seemed to leave her with a barely audible *oh* when her hand felt Fran's searing wet heat. Fran lifted her hips. She needed more. Chelsea was now content to explore, using her fingers to probe over Fran's center, still staring into Fran's eyes and noting her minutest reactions. When Fran's eyes fluttered shut, Chelsea retreated. When she bit her lip in anticipation, Chelsea backed away. Teasing, forever teasing. It was as if she was saving each erogenous spot left unsatisfied until later.

A half second after Fran registered how absolutely enmeshed in Chelsea's thrall she was, a thin thread of anxiety entered her consciousness. She tried to beat it back through force of will. *No, just stop. You're going to make it crawl back up.* She opened her eyes. This wasn't happening right now.

Chelsea caught her gaze. "What just happened?"

"No, nothing." Fran took a deep breath and tried to relax.

"It's like"—she stilled, then lowered her torso so it rested against Fran's—"every single one of your muscles just seized up." Her fingers reached up to brush strands of hair from Fran's forehead.

"I know," Fran groaned. "I'm sorry. Let me do something for you." She tried to sit up.

"Wait." Chelsea gently urged her back down against the mattress. "Was it me? Something I did?"

"No. God, no. You're doing everything right." Fran silently prayed for Chelsea to ignore her weirdness and not abandon this, not abandon her.

Chelsea studied her, and then something in her eyes changed—softened. "Focus on me, on what I'm doing," she said as she pressed a kiss on both cheeks and then lingered on her mouth. Then her chin. Her neck. The dominating zeal she seemed to feel from plucking Fran's strings like a concert harpist became more obliging, more sweet and yielding—but no less potent.

One by one, every part of Fran's body received loving attention from Chelsea's lips. Her shoulders and biceps and wrists, her belly button, and Fran concentrated on the light touch of each of Chelsea's fingertips, how her breath heated Fran's skin just before her mouth made contact, the way her tongue created a world of sensation as it swirled over each of Fran's nipples. And then she was back in the moment with Chelsea, barely able to breathe as desire rose in her.

And Chelsea somehow knew exactly when that happened. "There you are." She raised her head from Fran's breasts, her hands replacing her mouth, stroking and grasping Fran's now powerfully sensitive skin. But it was her eyes, gazing into the depths of her, that drew all Fran was feeling closer to the surface, closer to release.

Chelsea moved down the bed. She positioned herself like a supplicant between Fran's legs. She parted Fran's thighs and inched closer to her core. Fran wasn't normally so open to her partner, especially not during the first time, but she trusted Chelsea so completely it seemed the most natural thing in the world. She was now nearly beside herself with anticipation, but Chelsea seemed so far away. Fran put a hand on her head, forging a connection with Chelsea.

When Chelsea's fingers entered her, Fran felt it like a lightning bolt. Then Chelsea's tongue, flat and hot, right there where her finger was, and upward—a thousand lightning bolts. She slowly explored, taking her time, until she reached Fran's clit.

She cried out, unable to stop herself. It was right there, just beneath the surface, and Chelsea's tongue was coaxing it to the light. There was no way it was going to crawl back up, or fade, or disappear into the ether. It was nearly here, and it felt unstoppable. Chelsea's hand slid from where it gripped her hip to right between her breasts, and Fran could feel its weight on her wildly beating heart. Chelsea whispered, "Let go."

And Fran did.

It was light released, shining and brilliant and vivid, and it exploded out of her in waves of feeling that slowly receded in intensity. When she became aware of herself again, she found her hands cradling Chelsea's head, and Chelsea watching her with an expression Fran couldn't have interpreted even if her brain were entirely working.

Chelsea moved to lie beside her. She turned her body into Fran's chest, burying her head so Fran couldn't see her face. Fran wrapped her in her arms, basking in wonder that her life was so perfect right now.

❖

Up until about five seconds ago, there had been a tiny cynical part of Chelsea that told her she just needed to get Fran out of her system. But now, swaddled in Fran's post-orgasmic embrace, Chelsea wondered how she was going to walk away from it, or if she even wanted to. The way Fran had put herself in Chelsea's hands, and how she had allowed herself to come apart like that. How had she forgotten how vital trust was to an intimate encounter like this? And Fran had trusted her completely. The invincibility that had coursed through Chelsea as she brought Fran to the heights of pleasure was quickly converted to awe.

"Chelsea, you're astounding. I want to touch you. Can I touch you?" Fran's exhilaration somehow made Chelsea feel proud.

They were now lying on their sides, facing each other, and even under artificial hotel lighting, Fran's skin glowed like something otherworldly. And her wide-open smile was alight with something that drew Chelsea like a bug to a flame. It almost hurt to look at her.

"Maybe we can dim the lights a bit?"

Fran gazed around the room as if seeing it for the first time. "Of course." She hopped out of bed and began turning off lights.

It gave Chelsea a moment to collect herself. In a protective move, she got under the covers. Why did she feel the need to protect herself? If that was what she was feeling, then she should get up out of this bed and leave. But that was not going to happen. Chelsea wanted Fran to make her come so fiercely she could practically taste it already. The self-protective instinct had nothing to do with achieving an orgasm.

A moment later, Fran had bounced back toward the bed, leaving one bedside lamp on. She crawled up Chelsea's body and straddled her over the covers. "I want to make you come."

Yes. Chelsea wanted that too. So much.

Fran braced her arms on either side of Chelsea's head and gave her a playful kiss. "I want you to be as blissed out and floaty as I am. And now, I'm going to say hello to my not-so-little friends!" She pulled the sheet down and exposed one of Chelsea's breasts, giving it a loving kiss. "Hello there," she said to it, and then exposed and kissed the other one. "And hello to you too." She raised the sheet so both breasts were tucked away again and waggled her eyebrows.

Chelsea burst out laughing. "Two words for you—Corn. Ball. And my breasts are not that big."

"Sorry." Fran didn't seem sorry in the least. She seemed gleeful. "They are fucking gorgeous. They're bounteous." She stared at Chelsea's chest like it was a present she couldn't wait to unwrap. Again.

Why did Chelsea feel she needed protecting from Fran, the merry cornball? Moments earlier, Fran's emotions had been as naked as everything else about her, and even now, her happiness and excitement and anticipation were shining out of her, as bright as sunrise.

Tendrils of apprehension snaked up Chelsea's throat. Her own feelings were sure to be just as visible. How could she allow Fran to see how much she felt for her? Chelsea was a good actress, but she'd never been called upon to act while she was having sex. Acting out a sex scene—yes. Acting as a way of concealing her own emotions during sex—no.

She pushed her misgivings away, determined to savor this moment with Fran. Sex should be lighthearted and fun, right? Why fight it? She needed the release. She wanted the release. And Fran was making it very easy to be here with her. She pushed the sheet down to her waist. "Come here."

Fran was already only inches away, but she wasted no time now that permission had been granted. Her hands cupped Chelsea's breasts reverently, and then seemingly mesmerized, she began to play. She palmed them, then rubbed her palms in circles. Her fingers pinched and plucked, and Chelsea's nipples became even more erect.

Under the covers, Chelsea scissored her legs in agitation. "Your mouth. Put your mouth on them."

As Fran's head lowered to her chest, taking her time, using her tongue and lips and teeth to tease out her arousal, Chelsea plunged her hands into Fran's hair, glorying in the feel of her silky strands. She wasn't going to be able to take much more of this, and she wanted something very specific. She gently tugged on Fran's hair, and she willingly raised her head.

"Can I tell you what I want?"

"Yes, please." Fran's eyes shone with eagerness. "I'm excellent at taking direction."

Chelsea hesitated. "I don't want to make you do anything you don't want to do."

Fran continued to grope Chelsea's breasts. "I want to do everything. Just tell me."

She couldn't believe she was going to say it, but she wanted it so much. "I want to ride your tongue."

The look Fran gave her was sizzling. She immediately acquiesced and rolled onto her back.

Chelsea swung a leg over Fran and maneuvered upward while Fran slid down a few inches so Chelsea was close to her face. Fran reached up to hold Chelsea's ass in her hands.

"Are you comfortable?" Fran asked.

Chelsea felt a whisper of heat against her wet pussy. "Yes," she breathed. "Are you?"

"Chelsea. It's my absolute favorite thing." She sounded like she couldn't wait to start. "Sit on my face now."

Chelsea brought herself still closer to Fran, and felt her lips kiss her thigh, then wander toward her center, dropping hot wet kisses over her pubis. Fran wriggled her body about an inch downward. For a second, Chelsea didn't feel anything. Then, breathing. Fran was simply breathing, taking air in through her nose and slowly exhaling through her mouth. It was probably the most erotic thing Chelsea had ever felt because it was proof Fran really did enjoy it, was reveling in her closeness to the most intimate part of Chelsea. And even if Fran was clearly in no hurry, her hot breath was making Chelsea's pussy even more damp with arousal, and it was all she could do to not take control, to not force Fran into action with her pelvis. But the anticipation was sublime—she made herself wait. Finally, finally she felt Fran's tongue, flat against her labia, then pointed and between them. She almost cried out in relief, but then sensation overtook everything else as Fran's tongue probed, explored—tentative at first, then surer and more certain.

"Yes," Chelsea hissed, reaching behind her and gripping Fran's thighs for support.

"Mm-hmm." Fran's murmur sent vibrations through her and it made Chelsea's legs quiver.

Chelsea panted, "It's good. You're so good." She couldn't help it. She canted her hips to where she wanted Fran's tongue, and Fran divined her desires. The intensity only increased when Fran's fingers dug into her ass cheeks, propelling Chelsea forward, even closer to Fran's mouth. She grabbed the top of the padded headboard and held on as Fran raised her head and mashed her face against Chelsea, as if she wanted to consume her. All of that sensation, it was almost too much, and then Fran's lips closed around her clit and sucked.

For a second, Chelsea couldn't feel her own skin. Everything was too sensitive, but Fran kept on, alternating between sucking and licking and kissing and Chelsea made a noise—a desperate keening wail—that didn't sound at all like her. She didn't know whether it was a second orgasm or the first one that just kept recoiling from her clit through her body and back again. It became sensory overload—too much. She pushed against the headboard and somehow was sitting on Fran's stomach, her back against Fran's thighs.

Fran sat up on her elbows and gave her an adorable wet grin. "I think we achieved quivering."

Chelsea gave a wheezy laugh. With a distinct lack of grace, she flopped to the side so she was lying next to Fran.

"That was just...wow. How was it for you? Was it okay?" Fran gazed at her with such concern and care, Chelsea wanted her to see that reflected back on her own features. What had she been afraid of? Fran only wanted to make her feel good, and Lord almighty had she succeeded.

"Much, much better than okay. That was"—she shook her head and tried to think of the right word, but they all seemed inadequate—"beyond description." Chelsea held her face in her hands. "That's really your favorite, huh?"

"Number one. Without a doubt." Fran grinned. "We seem pretty compatible."

Chelsea was about to say something when her stomach growled—loudly. "Well that's embarrassing."

"I know how we can remedy that." Fran stood and placed the room service tray in the middle of the bed.

Sharing a sex bed picnic with Fran was so far from where she thought this night was going. "You're willing to share your dinner with me?"

"Sure. I'm under no illusions that this will be a stellar culinary experience, but it will be edible. Cold, but edible." Fran removed the metal cloche to reveal a grilled cheese sandwich and fries—both probably ice cold.

The sandwich was nestled on a curly leaf of kale, made fancy with thick, golden brown slices of bread that trapped a generous amount of now congealed cheese between them. It still looked totally delicious.

Who ordered a humble grilled cheese at a five star hotel? It was so Fran. "Did they not have any Jell-O?"

"Nope. I asked. And all the man on the phone said was a simple no, but what I heard was *Don't push it. We're already making a damn grilled cheese for you and it ain't even on the menu.* And the kale is all yours if you want it." She found some glasses and poured sparkling water for both of them.

Chelsea grabbed the little pot of ketchup and poured out a puddle next to the fries. "I'm sorry I interrupted your dinner, and I'm sorry your food got cold, but I'm not sorry that I'm still here and that I get to eat it with you."

"I'm not sorry at all." Fran leaned in and gave her a kiss. Chelsea could taste herself on Fran's lips. It was so distracting she wondered if they could shove all this aside and go again, but Fran kept talking. "And anyway, you paid for it, or Propolis did. It's probably the most expensive grilled cheese I'll ever eat. I was bummed they didn't have any tomato soup." Fran stood back and surveyed the scene. "Naked grilled cheese with Chelsea Cartwright in Atlanta, Georgia. Nobody would believe me if I told them." She settled in beside Chelsea, and handed her half of the sandwich.

Chelsea held it in her hands. "Grilled cheese and tomato soup is for rainy days and Mondays, usually. I'm getting the sense that you needed some comfort."

Fran nodded, but took a bite of her half sandwich instead of answering.

"Because of me. You didn't want to see anymore of me today."

"I was tired, and I had a headache...and yeah, I was disappointed." She shrugged. "But I don't regret saying what I said. Look where it got us." She gestured between the two of them.

Chelsea placed a hand on Fran's ankle and gave it a loving squeeze. She took a bite of her sandwich. "My God, this must have been amazing when it was fresh."

"I bet there is, like, eight dollars of jarlsberg in there."

Chelsea grinned at her. "At least." She dipped a fry in ketchup and ate it.

"I have a few questions for you, since we're here together, breaking bread—and cheese."

"Uh-oh. This isn't an interview, is it?" Chelsea didn't know why she said that. Her caution was a perpetual habit she now wanted to break—at least where Fran was concerned.

"No. Just simple curiosity."

This could work both ways. "Let's do one for one. You ask, then I get to ask. Okay?"

Fran nodded. It looked like she was shuffling through scores of questions in her head. Finally, she said, "How's Petal?"

Chelsea was surprised this was what Fran chose to ask. She didn't believe there was any love lost between her daughter and Fran. "She's doing okay. Is there something in particular you want to know?"

"How did you handle the paparazzi thing? And I guess, has she come to terms with you and Beau?"

She looked down at the meal between them. Fran couldn't ask something easier? "I'm ashamed I didn't know how deeply our breakup affected her. We're in family therapy now. We're learning a lot about each other. What she did was still monumentally irresponsible, but I understand her better."

Fran nodded.

"I think I scared her when I finally confronted her about what she did. This was after I talked to Lorraine, like you told me to. I was trying to make her understand how frightened I was of the danger she put herself in and I broke down crying." Chelsea stopped talking. It was still hard to think about that moment. Fran put a reassuring hand on her back. "I'd always been the bad guy in her eyes, but when Beau left for rehab without telling her or Forge, I became all they had. And then there I was, broken and bawling. It shook Petal up. It made her grow up some, I think."

"I'm glad she's coming through it okay, but I hate to think of you broken and bawling."

"I'm better now too. The three of us are so much closer than we were. And now Beau is back, and it's like he has to earn their trust and love all over again. Sometimes I feel bad for him, but he made his bed."

"And Forge? He's okay?"

"Yeah, my Forgey. The pillar of our little family. He's good." Chelsea wiped her hand over her eyes. "My turn."

"Okay, shoot."

"How were you involved with the demise of intravenousgossip?"

"Ah. You were ready with that one." Fran sat back against the headboard.

"I've been wondering since you told me you had something to do with it."

"Well, my boss was almost subhuman. He went by the pseudonym Carmina Piranha."

"I recognize the name. He wrote for the website and he was your boss?"

Fran nodded. "He figured out who I was and when he saw me in photos with you, he tried to blackmail me into writing gossip again—about you."

"His posts were always vicious. It was like he wrote to inflict as much damage as he could. Not like your posts."

Fran lifted her eyebrows. "You read my posts?"

"A few." She felt her face get hot. "Anyway, it obviously didn't work."

"Nope. I did some research and found out a few things to use against him that were a matter of public record, but I also have a cop friend, and I asked her to take a look into him. Turns out, on top of all the messy personal crap he was guilty of, the website was a front for a money-laundering operation."

"You're joking."

"I'm not. He developed this thing called the VIP Lounge, where if you paid more money you'd have access to exclusive content and all that, but there was never any exclusive content. It was just a payment mechanism for Russian mobsters to dump money into the site and withdraw it somewhere far, far away."

"Holy shit." It almost sounded like a movie plot.

"Apparently, he couldn't pay back the money he borrowed from some dangerous guys, and this was the way he had to make them whole. My friend was really happy I tipped her off. Apparently, they were able to connect a bunch of dots on a major investigation."

"I can't even believe it. What are the odds?"

"Who knows? And now there's one less celebrity gossip website in the world."

"Thanks to you." Chelsea stood and removed the remains of their meal. When she returned, she snuggled up to Fran, grasping her around the waist and resting her head on her shoulder. She couldn't remember when she'd last felt so content. "I'm going to have to go soon."

Fran's arms stole around her. "You don't have to, you know."

This was a moment out of time for Chelsea. No matter how happy she was here in Fran's room, with the warmth of Fran's body against her, she didn't know how this bracingly new development could fit into her life. "I don't want to leave, but Helen would have too many questions if I don't come back to the room." It was a weak excuse. Chelsea could easily handle Helen, who would probably give Chelsea a round of applause if she knew. But she hoped Fran would accept it. This was new and big and good and scary. She needed a little bit of space to acclimate.

"Do we have time for one more question?" Fran asked.

"Sure."

"When was the last time you were with a woman?"

Chelsea tensed. "Why? Was it bad for you?"

Fran sat up, and Chelsea fell back among the pillows. "That's not why I asked. You were right here with me. You have to know it wasn't bad. It was the furthest possible thing from bad, and if you didn't know that, then it's my fault for failing to convey how not bad it was. Okay?"

"Okay."

Fran loomed over her now.

Chelsea resisted pulling her closer. "Why are you asking, then?"

Fran blew a breath upward. "I didn't think I would have to qualify my question. It's pretty personal." She looked away. "But I stupidly asked, so you deserve to know."

"Do you want to retract it?" Chelsea was curious now, but would abide by Fran's decision.

"I don't really need to know. It was more a way of figuring out my own response to you."

"What do you mean?"

"Well…I've had a couple of girlfriends, and a couple of purely sexual partners, and the sex has sometimes been…"

Chelsea held her breath. She couldn't imagine what the next word from Fran's mouth was going to be.

"Unfulfilling? Satisfaction not guaranteed? For me." Fran averted her gaze.

"You didn't have orgasms with your previous partners?"

"Sometimes. But it took a lot of effort. I don't need to climax every time. Mostly I focused on making sure my partner was satisfied."

"And they didn't do the same for you?"

"I get all in my head. You saw. Once that happens, I can usually wave goodbye to an orgasm. But you saw me tense up. Nobody's ever noticed that before. You knew exactly what to do, and you took command and I felt so good and—" Fran's eyes were locked on Chelsea's now. "It's never been like that for me. You just bowled me over."

Chelsea reached up and caressed Fran's cheek. "Oh, Franny." One thing Chelsea knew about Fran: She was a giver. It stood to reason she'd put other's needs before her own in the bedroom. But had there been no one who made sure her needs were met too? "I can't help but pay attention to you. I notice every sound, every movement, when you relax, and when you become tense. I wanted to make it good for you."

Fran nodded and tucked her head between Chelsea's arm and her chest. "I'm embarrassed now."

"Don't be." Chelsea raked her fingers through Fran's hair.

Fran lifted her head. Her eyes were doleful, but they stared into Chelsea's with an intensity that made movement a necessity. In a moment, Fran lay with her back among the pillows and Chelsea had mounted her.

"To answer your question…" Chelsea dragged her fingers over her breasts. "It's been a long time since I've been with anyone, man or woman. I haven't wanted to. But it's different with you. I've wanted to be with you for a lot longer than I care to admit."

Fran gripped Chelsea's hips. "I've wanted you for a long time too. And I want you right now. I want to do everything to you."

"And you're going to, but not until I've made you come again." Just before Chelsea descended for a kiss, she saw a smile of utter delight on Fran's lips, and it made something in her chest break open.

❖

Fran waited in the lobby for the rest of the Propolis gang to show up for their ride to the airport. She had awoken to the sound of her phone's alarm and an empty bed. Even though Chelsea had told her that's what she would do, it still left Fran feeling bereft.

Two black SUVs pulled up to the curb. Dante appeared, rolling two carry-on suitcases out on to the sidewalk. He handed off the bags and chatted with both drivers for a moment. Fran caught him when he came back inside. "Hey, Dante. Why two cars today when we all squeezed in together yesterday?"

"Chelsea and I are going to the private terminal. The rest of you aren't. STBY." He gave her a tiny grin. "Oh, she asked me to upgrade you. You're on the list, but it's probably not going to happen."

Chelsea breezed toward them, all laid-back glamour in a long gray duster with the collar turned up, dark sunglasses, and the black Mets cap. "Are we ready, Dante?"

"Yes, Chelsea. All set."

"Great. I'll be there in a minute." She watched him get in the car before turning her attention to Fran. "Good morning." The soft, seductive timbre of Chelsea's voice made Fran weak in the knees.

She wanted to reach out and grab Chelsea's hand, or step closer, or do anything that would show Chelsea how irresistible it felt to be near her. She wished Chelsea would take off her sunglasses, but Fran got what she needed from Chelsea's smile. It was wide, indulgent, and seemed genuinely happy to see Fran.

She picked imaginary lint from Fran's shoulder, her hand resting there a moment longer than necessary. "We've designated Helen to give you notes. She'll probably have something written up for you by the end of the flight. Do you think you can turn around a new draft in thirty days?"

Fran nodded.

"She'll be down in a minute. You two can talk about it in the car." Chelsea took off her sunglasses. There were dark smudges under her eyes.

Fran couldn't stop her feet from taking a step closer. "You look—"

"Don't say it," Chelsea interrupted. "You know why I look tired. You got just as little sleep as me, and here you are looking fresh as a daisy."

"Make no mistake. You wore me out, Ms. Cartwright. It's probably the absolute jolt of joy I felt when I looked across the lobby and saw—" Chelsea gave her a warning look, but Fran smiled and said, "My lucky hat."

Her mouth curled in amusement. "You mean *my* lucky hat?"

"No—"

"Would you look at the time? Gotta go." Chelsea grinned at her and donned her sunglasses before turning toward the door.

Fran touched her forearm with two fingers. "Would you have dinner with me sometime?" She wished she had asked before Chelsea had put her sunglasses back on.

"Chelsea Cartwright!"

It was a woman about Fran's age and her daughter, who looked about six. They were maybe ten feet away and coming in hot.

"I'm so sorry to bother you," the woman said. "I just wanted to tell you how much I love you! Every time I watch *Frankie's Fortune* I just cry and cry."

"How kind of you. Thanks so much." Chelsea took off her sunglasses. Fran recognized her smile as the one she turned on for the public.

"Would you take a picture with me and my daughter?" At Chelsea's nod, the woman held her phone out to Fran. "Do you mind?"

Fran took the picture and watched Chelsea give them a little piece of herself. What a way to make a living. A few people had noticed the exchange, and Chelsea noticed them noticing.

"I've got to go, Fran. I'll see you in a month." She backed up a step or two, and then turned away.

Fran didn't know if Chelsea had forgotten her question or if she was avoiding it. "Do you want me to stop asking?" she called after her.

Chelsea stood stock still for a moment, and then came back, standing close enough to put a hand on Fran's sleeve. "No." Then she was gone.

CHAPTER TWENTY-FOUR

Fran sat in her recliner and stared at her laptop. Atlanta was two weeks behind her, and she had come home from work and pored over the original script for *A Love as Big as Wembley*. She examined every scene and searched for a way to make the story stronger, better, while still adhering to the notes Helen had given her. For the first time in her writing experience, she was second-guessing herself left and right. The pressure of delivering something of quality, something that pleased her producers, was leading to a major absence of inspiration.

When her phone buzzed, she was grateful for the distraction.

Hi. It's Chelsea.

Fran was very aware. Her former boss and most recent sexual partner needed no introduction. *Hey.*

I'm in the general vicinity of your neighborhood, Chelsea texted. *Weiler's in Canoga Park. Do you know it?*

Fran had driven past Weiler's many times but had never eaten there. It seemed like a run-of-the-mill greasy spoon. What the hell was Chelsea doing there? *Yes. It's not far from me.*

Can you meet me?

Fran jumped out of her chair. *Be there in ten.*

Probably closer to fifteen minutes later, Fran pushed through the glass door and scanned Weiler's small dining room for Chelsea. At a table in the back, she spied her black Mets hat.

"Fancy meeting you here." Fran slid into the booth across from Chelsea. It must have been a shooting day, and Chelsea must have been in a hurry to get out of there. Remnants of makeup streaked her hairline and the side of her face. She looked tired, but also pleased to see Fran. "Long day?"

"The longest." Chelsea reached out a hand and Fran took it. "Thanks for coming."

Instead of fixating on her hand in Chelsea's on the tabletop, which was something Fran could've stared at for approximately thirty minutes, she gazed around the restaurant. "Where's Dante?"

"I let him go around six. I imagine he's getting a disco nap in before hitting some WeHo club."

"You haven't been here since six, have you? It's after nine. And how will you get home?" Fran frowned. Was Chelsea here by herself? What if something happened? What if a fan had gotten obnoxious and Chelsea had no one to run interference?

Chelsea withdrew her hand, reached in her pocket, and pulled out a car key fob. "I'm driving again."

Fran's mouth dropped open. "You are?"

Chelsea nodded. "Not all the time, but tonight I wanted to. I made Dante get an Uber from Ventura Beach."

"That's where you were filming today? That's pretty far after a long day."

Chelsea didn't seem to hear that. "And I saw the turnoff for where I used to live when I first arrived in LA and got off the 101." Her smile had a wistful quality to it. "Did a little tour of my old haunts and ended up here."

"Warm that up for you, Chelsea?" An older woman stopped by their table, a coffee pot in each hand. She darted a look at Fran. "Coffee?"

Chelsea sat back. "Thanks, Doris."

Fran flipped her mug over while Doris filled Chelsea's cup with the orange-handled pot. "You want anything else?"

"There's something you've got to try," Chelsea said to Fran, and then turned to Doris. "A tuna melt and an extra plate, please."

"Anything for you?" Doris asked Fran.

She thought for a moment. "Do you have any Jell-O?"

Doris's expression told her even if they had it, Fran didn't want the Jell-O.

"Nobody orders it. It's probably been sitting in the back of the reach-in for a year," Chelsea said. "Is there any chocolate babka left, Doris?"

"I'm sure we can rustle some up." Doris gave Chelsea a doting smile.

"Two slices? Ask Pete to slather them with butter and grill them on the flat top for me?"

"You got it." Doris walked away.

"Sorry about the Jell-O, but you'll love the babka. It's the best way to have it." Chelsea opened a tiny tub of creamer and added it to her mug.

"She's nice," Fran said. Chelsea seemed awfully familiar with this place.

"She is. I worked here way back when—my first job in Los Angeles. She trained this hick farm girl to wait tables like a pro."

Fran nodded. Now things made a bit more sense. "I don't think I've had babka since I left New York. Yum. And God only knows how long it's been since I've had a tuna melt."

"You shared your favorite sandwich with me, now I'll share my favorite with you. They do a great one here. It's closed-faced, not open-faced like a typical tuna melt." Her enthusiasm was adorable.

"Who knew you were such a student of the tuna melt?" Fran tried to hide her amusement. "And I never said my favorite was grilled cheese."

Chelsea's eyes danced. "I was talking about your cute little brown-bag turkey on wheat."

"Well, then. Guilty as charged." Fran grabbed one of those giant glass sugar dispensers and poured some into her mug. "And a tuna melt is just about the last thing I'd guess as your favorite."

Chelsea exhaled. "You can take the girl out of upstate, but you can't take upstate out of the girl."

Upstate New York, Fran remembered. "Whereabouts exactly?"

"Way up. A tiny little town named Schuyler Falls, outside of Plattsburgh. Speaking of..." She reached in her bag and produced a ball cap. "A new lucky hat for you."

Fran took it from Chelsea. It was black canvas with an embroidered logo above the bill. In golden yellow thread, a stylized honeybee sat within a hexagon with *Propolis Pictures* beneath it. "Thank you. I absolutely love it. The logo is fantastic."

"Thanks." Chelsea couldn't have looked prouder.

"Would you explain it to me? Why a bee?"

Chelsea looked over Fran's shoulder and paused while Doris served their tuna melt. "Thanks, Doris. It looks delicious." She took half and pushed the plate toward Fran. "I'm going to steal a couple of those fries."

Fran put her new hat on the windowsill so it wouldn't get dirty, and then took a bite. The humble tuna melt had become something mouth-meltingly delicious. "Wow. That. Is. Good."

"You can judge a place on the quality of its tuna melt. The diner in Schuyler Falls had an excellent one." Chelsea grinned with her mouth full. "I hated growing up on my dad's farm. I lived for the day when I could escape to Hollywood and become a big-time actress. It's actually pretty miraculous that I was able to make it happen."

"Not so miraculous. Remember? Talent." Fran pointed at Chelsea.

"I've worked hard, and I've been lucky." Chelsea put her sandwich down. "The one farm chore I liked was taking care of the beehives. They weren't a big part of the business, but they're important for pollination, and we had a sideline in selling honey and wax. Did you know that beehives are ninety percent female?"

Fran considered. "I knew that worker bees were female, and the queen obviously, but I didn't know there were so few boy bees."

"Worker bees do pretty much everything in the hive and outside of it. They produce compounds like honey and wax, but they also produce something called propolis. It's made of wax and resin, maybe a little bee spit, and it works like bee glue. They use it to build and maintain their hives."

Fran began nodding. "I'm getting it."

"Yeah. A hive is a female-led super organism, and it's held together by propolis. A pretty neat metaphor for what I want my company to be."

"I'm honored that I get to be a part of it." Fran sat back. "Seriously, I am so proud of you, and proud that you've chosen my story."

"How about an update?"

"On the script?" Fran scratched her chin. "It's...coming along."

"What's the matter?"

"Nothing, nothing."

"Tell me."

"I'm having a sort of…paralysis."

"A block?"

Fran winced. "Don't use that word. It's a jinx. No, I'm writing, but I don't love it. I want to love it."

Chelsea's brows lowered. "Is it a particular note that's hanging you up?"

"No, no," Fran said. It wasn't, really. She didn't know what the problem was.

"How about this? Why don't you just talk about it, and I'll listen. Ramble away. Say anything you want. Maybe something will come of it. I want to help."

"Chelsea, it's late. I'm sure you need to get home. This is not the best use of your time."

"I get to sit here, eat a damn good tuna melt, drink a bottomless cup of decaf, and hang with you. There's nowhere I'd rather be." Chelsea looked out the window for a second, and then back at Fran. "And I might've planned all this days ahead of time because I really wanted to see you."

"You did?" Fran couldn't stop her smile.

"I couldn't wait an entire month." Chelsea's voice became sultry and low. "I wanted to knock on the door of your little apartment in Reseda and push you down onto that ugly pleather recliner and slowly drive you crazy using only my tongue. But I couldn't remember exactly where you live, so I came here instead."

Fran's mouth was instantly dry. She felt Chelsea's leg brush against hers and looked down to see Chelsea's left sneaker, and then her right one, wedge against the ancient, vinyl-covered bench and bracket her thighs, trapping Fran right where she sat. This was the audacious, assertive Chelsea from the Atlanta hotel room, and Fran was instantly turned on. She rested her hands on Chelsea's ankles. "Those are some bold words right there."

Her sensual smile faltered. "Too bold?"

"No. That limit does not exist." She tightened her grip on Chelsea's ankles. "We can go back to my place right now if you want. Trina is in Vancouver with Entitled Prick."

Chelsea looked blank for a moment, then she nodded grimly. "Is that what she calls him? What do the two of you call me?"

Fran reddened, realizing her blunder. *Idiot! Chelsea's flirting with you and that's what you say?* "She doesn't call him that. I do, because that's what he is. I've never called you anything but Chelsea. You were a good boss. Always. Trina was jealous when I worked for you. I got to spend all my time in heaven while she was stuck in hell."

"Okay, you don't have to lay it on quite so thick." Chelsea gave her a tiny smile and started to move her feet, but Fran held on and kept them in place.

"So what do you say?"

"We can't go back to your place, Fran. You have to love what you write, and you can't do that until you're relieved of this"—she leaned in and whispered—"block."

"Maybe if you relieve me in a different way, it will lead to an outpouring of creative energy." Fran ran her hands from Chelsea's ankles upwards, sneaking under her pant legs, and gripped her calves. Chelsea didn't reply, and her eyes were locked on Fran until they flicked upward. She sat up straight and put her feet back on the floor.

"Babka time, Doris?"

"Wanted to bring it out fresh and hot." She set it down and filled up their coffee cups again. "Enjoy, ladies."

"Okay, that was a mistake," Chelsea said when Doris was out of earshot.

"What was?"

"Letting you touch me." Chelsea picked up a slice of the babka and then put it down again. "I'm a little flustered right now." She shook her hands out a few times and took a couple of mindful breaths. "Let's focus. Start talking, Franny. Give me the lowdown on what you've done over the past two weeks—with the script."

Fran couldn't be more charmed right now. As much as she wanted to get up and slide in next to Chelsea, be closer to her, she stopped herself. Instead, she talked. She spoke about the overarching changes she'd made to incorporate a new setting, the research she had done for the revised character and her backstory, the hundred or so YouTube soccer videos she'd watched, and how she had expanded the American coach character so she was now featured in every scene.

"You did not." Chelsea laughed. It was now about thirty minutes later and nothing was left except one stray fry, a few smears of ketchup, and a smattering of babka crumbs.

"No, I didn't, but she's become my favorite character now that I see her as you."

"It sounds like you have it all mapped out. I'm not sure what's causing your anxiety."

"I need a spark." Fran put her napkin on the table. "Yes, the characters meet and there's instant conflict, but what is that thing that makes it impossible for them to love anyone else?"

Chelsea stared at her for a moment before averting her eyes to somewhere across the restaurant. "That's the eternal question, isn't it?" Her eyes returned to Fran. "Something I do when I'm having trouble nailing down a character is to write about her life before that first scene."

"A backstory, you mean?"

She waggled her head. "Yeah, no, not really. Not an overview. More like a day in the life—a week, a month, two years, ten years— pick a random day—before the audience meets the character. What fills their hours? What's on their mind? Who or what is important to them at that particular moment?"

Fran nodded. "I'll try it." When Chelsea pulled her wallet out of her bag, Fran reached in her pocket.

"No, Fran. I've got this."

"But—" Fran took out her credit card.

Chelsea held up a hand. "Please. I'm going to leave a tip so enormous I hope it doesn't give Doris a heart attack. It was nice to come back here, and lovely to spend some time with you, but this was a meeting. Propolis will pay. We worked, didn't we?" Chelsea left a tall stack of hundred dollar bills under her coffee mug. She saw Fran eyeing the money. "Told you I thought about all of this in advance. I never normally carry that much cash with me."

Fran felt herself deflate as she put her credit card away. It was the first time she had felt off balance with Chelsea tonight. She had thought they were getting closer, but when Chelsea took such obvious pains to draw a circle of professionalism around their time here, it left her wondering. She took a moment to adjust the Propolis hat and fitted it on her head. There was an edge of formality to her voice as she said, "Thank you for the work session, the tuna melt, the babka-licious babka, my new lucky hat, and your company."

Chelsea studied her for a second. "Let's get out of here before Doris comes back."

They strolled out of the restaurant and through the parking lot to Chelsea's big black car. Fran noticed Chelsea scan the parking lot, probably for photographers, but there were only one or two cars besides hers and Chelsea's, and neither were occupied. Canoga Park was a long way from the typical celebrity haunts.

"Thanks for meeting me." Chelsea faced her. "I'm going to tell Dante to put a meeting on the calendar for the twenty-seventh, which is when your thirty days are up. Do you think you'll be able to meet that deadline?"

"Yes. It'll be done. Without a doubt."

Chelsea made a note on her phone. "Oh, but that's a Saturday. Will that be a problem?"

"No, it's better. I won't have to switch around my work schedule."

"Still at the prop warehouse?"

Fran put her hands in her pockets. "Still there."

Chelsea paused. She seemed to be waiting for something. Was Fran supposed to initiate a kiss? After Chelsea just said this was a work thing? Fran had no idea what to do. She scratched the back of her neck and debated a little too long because Chelsea pulled out her keys and said, "All right, I'd better go."

Fran stood next to the car while Chelsea got in and started it. She made a motion for Chelsea to open the window. She gripped the door and leaned in. "I know work meetings don't usually end with the participants kissing each other, but could we make an exception this one time?"

The unmistakable relief in Chelsea's eyes quickly turned to desire. "Oh, hell, yes." She pulled Fran by the shoulders farther into the car and kissed her slowly and thoroughly.

It felt like a cool, revitalizing rain shower after wandering the desert for the two weeks they'd been apart. Fran relaxed into it, happy to stand in a scrubby parking lot for the rest of her days if it meant she'd be kissing Chelsea while she did it. When they finally came up for air, Chelsea said, "You're just as good a kisser as I remember. Better." She looked at Fran like she wanted to devour her. "New policy for just you and me. All meetings end with kisses. Hell, we should start meetings with them too."

"Agreed. Bye, Chelsea. See you on the twenty-seventh." Fran

backed away from the car and watched as Chelsea left the parking lot. It was only as Chelsea's taillights disappeared from view that Fran realized she had forgotten to ask Chelsea out to dinner. Was that what Chelsea had been waiting for? And would she have said yes this time?

CHAPTER TWENTY-FIVE

"Hey, Mom, look at this piece." Forge held out a blue plastic brick in the shape of a C. "Like your name."

Chelsea looked up from her laptop. "Nice, Forgey."

A tiny bit of order had emerged from the chaos of the incomplete Lego train set spilled all over the kitchen table.

"We almost have the passenger car done." Beau was Forge's picker and slid over the pieces he would need for the next bit of construction. "I'm going to start on the tracks while you finish this. Okay, buddy?" He gestured at Petal to take her AirPods out. "Petal, you want in on this? The engine is next."

She put her phone down. "You want my help?" she asked Forge, who nodded. "You usually don't."

"Yeah, but as soon as we put it together, we'll get to play with it."

"I wanted to go swimming. We could do Marco Polo with Dad."

"I'll go swimming," sweet, agreeable Forge said immediately. "Dad, can we do this later? Do you want to swim?"

"You bet. Chels? Want to join us?"

"I have to finish this before my meeting tonight, but go ahead. Your suits are in the pool house. There's probably a few of yours still in there too, Beau." She bent her head toward the screen again.

The kids scraped their chairs back in unison and headed for the sliding glass door. Forge turned back and said, "C'mon, Dad."

"Be there in a second. Start without me." Beau remained in his seat. "Who has meetings on a Saturday night?"

"I do."

"Who with?"

"Our screenwriter."

"For the lesbian-lady soccer movie?"

"Not it's working title, but yes." Chelsea had restricted herself to only contacting Fran through a Slack channel the Propolis women now used to update each other. Fran had work and her deadline, and Chelsea had her non-Propolis commitments that kept them both busy, but she'd be lying if she said she didn't think about Fran—a lot.

The twenty-seventh had finally arrived. The new draft had appeared in her inbox yesterday, and Chelsea was prepping for her meeting with Fran. She didn't think it was possible to want something as much as she currently wanted to see Fran.

"In the history of the world, no one has ever looked as excited about a script meeting as you do right now. What's going on?"

"Nothing." Chelsea shifted in her chair and kept her eyes trained on her screen.

There was a teasing smile in Beau's voice. "Right. The only reason for scheduling a meeting on the weekend is if you want it to turn extracurricular after." The thought seemed to bring Beau up short. "Wait. Do you?"

Chelsea tried to appear blank. "What? I'm busy here."

"You do." Beau seemed incredulous. "You like this woman."

She looked at him over her laptop but didn't say anything. Was it too much to ask not to get into this with Beau right now?

"You forget that I know you about as well as anyone in the world." Beau leaned in and put his elbows on the table. "Your silence is speaking volumes."

"Okay." She threw her hands up. "I like her." Under her breath she added, "A lot."

"Huh." He gazed at her as if he was seeing her again after a long time away. "Is it in a sit-on-my-face kind of way? Or is it more?"

She reddened, thinking about their night together. "Don't be crass." It was more. To Chelsea at least.

She was exhausted by the mental gymnastics her brain constantly engaged in. Whatever she was supposed to be doing, her mind would become preoccupied with thoughts of Fran. And as much as she tried to force herself not to imagine them building some happy life straight out of Fran's screenplay, that's where she always ended up. Then she'd have to drag her brain back to whatever mundane task was supposed to be occupying her attention. Everything seemed mundane compared to thinking about Fran. The only thing that made thinking about Fran mundane was actually being with her.

"By declining to answer, you've told me all I need to know."

"I was still thinking about it!" *Her.*

"By taking so long to think about it, you've told me all I need to know." Beau's smile faded, and he sat in silence. He watched Forge jump in the pool while Petal skimmed its surface for fallen leaves. Chelsea didn't think he saw any of it. This was the first time Beau had to confront her interest in anyone post-divorce. She was under no illusions that it was going to be easy for him. Change never was. The last thing she wanted was to upset his nascent sobriety.

A range of emotions flitted across his face, and he clenched his jaw in what was probably the effort of suppressing them. Finally he looked at her. "I knew this day would come. Knowing you like I do, you would never allow this to come up in conversation if it wasn't serious. Still, I'm surprised at how blindsided I feel."

Chelsea kept quiet.

It looked like Beau was endeavoring to tuck his feelings away as he fiddled with an empty Diet Coke can in front of him. "You're making a sports movie now, so I'm going to reference one of those. You know how in every boxing movie ever made, there's the boxer's hardnosed, unsentimental old coach? He looks all gnarly and grizzled, like he's lived his life inside a gym sock, but he's loyal and devoted, standing behind the boxer between rounds as he spits out a mouthful of blood along with three teeth. And with a few wise words and all the belief in the world, the coach stands him up, turns him around, and sends him back out there with the determination to go on for at least three more minutes."

"I think I've seen one or two of those movies." She waited for the other shoe to drop.

"That was you for me, Chelsea."

"I knew you were going to say that. Did you have to go so hard with the *gnarled* and the *gym socks* and all that?"

Beau didn't seem to hear her. "You kept me going for so long, babe. I can't believe you carried me for as long as you did. And I will never have a bigger regret than losing you."

Chelsea felt moisture gather in her eyes.

"What you deserve more than anything is to have that boxing coach for yourself. Someone who is going to be in your corner and put you before them always. When it gets to that point, make sure she'll be that for you."

She had thought that was Fran before, when she was being paid to be in Chelsea's corner. Now? She wanted to be in Fran's corner for a change. She'd seen Fran's uncertainty at the deli, and knew she was the cause of it. Chelsea was so out of practice here. The only thing she knew was that these strong feelings were telling her that Fran was someone Chelsea needed in her life. "You've met her, you know."

"Who? Your screenwriter?"

"About a year ago in Marchetti's. She drove me away from the paparazzi on the back of a pizza scooter. She was my assistant back then."

Beau looked like he was trying to place her. "I don't remember. She went from assistant to screenwriter?"

"Yeah, and she's a good one. If she's got anymore screenplays like the one we're doing, pretty soon I'll be trying to hitch a ride on her coattails around this town."

"I doubt that very much, Ms. Mogul."

"But what you said before about her being in my corner always. Maybe that's where we went wrong, you and me. We should have shared that job—equally trading off being in each other's corner."

"I'm sorry I always made you be the coach and not the boxer."

"Okay, I think we've taken the whole boxer-coach thing as far as it can go." Although putting up her dukes and hoping not to get punched in the face did sound an awful lot like love. But it didn't feel that way with Fran. Chelsea's feelings, once so angry and aggrieved, were now all admiration and affection.

"Heard." He slapped his hands on his knees and stood. "I know I'm not at the point of unsupervised visits yet, but I'll be happy to take the kids when you're ready for some private time with your screen-writer."

"Thank you. That means a lot." Before he opened the door to the backyard, she said, "Hey. I'm proud of you, you know. You're doing so well."

"I have to be honest. If there was ever a conversation that could drive me back to the bottle, it was that one. I'm going to go swim."

❖

A wave of nostalgia rolled over Fran when she pulled up to the gate at Chelsea's house. It had been almost a year since she was last here, and much had changed over the course of that year, but not enough to have a major impact on her life. Yet. Hope sprang eternal, both in terms of her career and her love life. Her usual spot next to the garage was free, so she parked there. She honestly didn't know how this meeting was going to go. Helen was the only one to respond to her email with the new draft attached, and that was just a *received, thanks*. Today would be the reckoning.

Fran was confident she had done all she could do to keep the heart of the story intact while changing some of the circumstances and setting according to the parameters set by Propolis. Her late night meeting of the minds with Chelsea two weeks prior had done the trick. The manuscript was solid, and maybe even a little stronger with the changes. Trina had stayed up too late reading it last night and proclaimed it the best movie of next year.

No, her faith in her writing ability was not the issue here. It was something else that was a cause for anxiety—how would Chelsea receive her? Would she get closed-off, face-like-a-brick-wall Chelsea from the pitch meeting? Open, passionate, uninhibited Chelsea from Atlanta? Mixed-signals Chelsea from the diner? Or maybe an entirely new version Fran had yet to encounter? She'd dressed a little better and stuffed a toothbrush and a change of clothes in her work bag, hoping for Atlanta Chelsea, but she had to be ready for any of them. Maybe it was presumptuous of Fran to think Chelsea would ask her to stay behind after their meeting broke up. Still, she wanted to at least smell nice should the opportunity arise.

Before Fran could touch the doorbell, the door flew open and Chelsea was there. Fran froze right there on the porch and beheld her. Only Chelsea could make a baggy cardigan sweater, jeans with a hole in the knee, and bare feet look like it should be on a magazine cover.

Her expression was unreadable, but the way she backed Fran into a post was downright predatory.

"Meetings now begin with kisses, right?" she said before she planted a forceful kiss on her.

Fran had just started to relax into it when Chelsea pulled back. "Hi. I just wanted to do that real quick before anyone else comes to see who's at the door."

"Anyone else?" Fran smiled. "Do I need to kiss them too?"

Chelsea gave her a look. "You do not."

"Mom, who's here?" Forge's voice. A moment later he appeared. "Oh. It's you."

"Hi, Forge. You're taller." Fran held out her fist for a bump.

Forge obliged and said, "You're the same. Do you work for my mom again?"

"No." Chelsea stood back and waved her inside. "Fran and I are collaborating on a project. She works *with* me. We'll be in the study. You can have an hour of screen time and then it's bed for you."

"Forge, can you do me a favor?" Fran took a small tin foil-wrapped package from her bag. "Can you stick this in the fridge for me?"

"What is it? Is it dessert?"

"No, it's something for your mom. I don't think you'll like it but feel free to have a look. Have some if you want."

He lifted a corner of the foil. "Uh...I have no idea what this is. Looks weird."

Chelsea reached for it, but Fran stopped her. "It doesn't concern you right now. Shall we?" She moved farther into the house, and Chelsea led her upstairs. She set her bag down on the desk in the empty study. "Where is everyone? Am I the first to arrive?"

Spots of pink appeared on Chelsea's cheeks. "This is an unofficial pre-meeting—just you and me. Everyone else will be there when we meet on Monday. Did I forget to mention that?" She locked the door and leaned against it.

"You did." Fran was beginning to think she'd been snookered and didn't feel the least bit bad about it. But hang on...Chelsea wasn't giving her a lot to go on here. "Is this because there's a problem with the new draft?"

"No." Chelsea approached, gazing at Fran with what looked like indecision before grabbing her belt and pulling her closer. "Did you wear that shirt on purpose? You are impossible to resist." She smoothed her hands over Fran's hips. "I'm going to kiss you now."

"Yes, please," Fran muttered.

Chelsea's lips moved over hers in a way that felt possessive and dominating, and Fran surrendered completely. Entirely too soon, Chelsea placed her hands on Fran's chest and pushed her back, ending a kiss that had felt like the rumbling that happens before seismic activity. It took Fran a moment to realize it was over.

When she recovered the power of speech, she said, "Did you ask me here on false pretenses? Not that I mind. These are awesome pretenses, whether they're true or false. And what did you mean about my shirt? It's new. You've never seen it before." Fran looked down at her shirt. It was a simple gray button-down.

"It has buttons," Chelsea said, as if that explained it.

"Yeah, and? Many shirts do."

"They were mocking me."

"The buttons on my shirt were mocking you?"

"It was as if they were saying *don't you want to undo us?*" Chelsea shook her head. "I'm losing it. Let's just get to work."

Whatever this mood Chelsea was in right now, Fran was loving it. She turned around and opened her workbag. "Oh, so true pretenses? We're going to work?"

Chelsea's hands were on Fran's hips again, and then she squeezed Fran's butt. "You bet your infinitely grippable ass we are."

Fran backed it up and ground herself into Chelsea. "Infinitely grippable?" She laughed. "I think I should put that on my résumé."

Chelsea groaned and clutched at her for a moment before pushing her away "Good God, you're tempting. Work first."

"That suggests something else will come second?"

Chelsea ignored that. "Wine?" She picked up a bottle of red from the coffee table. A small but elaborate cheese board and two glasses sat beside it. "I'm breaking my no alcohol in the house rule. This was a gift, and it's too good not to drink. Also, Beau never comes up here."

Fran picked up the glasses while Chelsea opened the bottle. "Will sexual innuendo and alcohol be a part of all Propolis meetings? That's something I can get *behind.*" She waited for Chelsea to acknowledge the joke.

"A pun? Really? If I hadn't already read your new draft, I would be afraid."

"Now that you've brought it up, don't keep me in suspense—what did you think?" She held her breath.

Chelsea took one of the now filled glasses from Fran and clinked it with hers. "Franny, you nailed it. I love it. You haven't lost one iota of drama or tension by switching it to Division I and the NCAA tournament, and the high school soccer camp prologue deepens the love story so much."

Fran thought she might blow Chelsea over with the strength of air leaving her lungs. She was so relieved. "That's good news." She took a gulp of her wine. "The prologue was a result of the writing exercise you mentioned. A very productive suggestion."

"I'm glad. I really love it." Chelsea bit her lip. "But I do have a few notes."

"Okay. Let's work, but you sit over there." She pointed to a leather chair next to the fireplace. "I'll take the desk. That way we won't be distracted by—you know—buttons or butts or what-have-you. I noticed you locked the door, Cartwright."

Chelsea opened her mouth in faux shock. "What are you accusing me of, *Underhill*? I told you we had to work. I did that so the kids won't interrupt us. You have no idea how smart I am to do that." She proceeded to tell Fran how Forge spilled his drink all over her script and the confusion it had caused.

"I think if I ever hit the big time, I'm going to buy Forge something nice, like a leather jacket or an amusement park."

"Actually, it was Petal who read it first, chocolate milk stains and all. She was your biggest supporter. Granted, she didn't know she was supporting you."

"Huh." That really surprised Fran. "Make that two amusement parks. One for each of them. I don't think I'd be sitting here if you had seen my name on that script that day."

"Things must have turned out this way for a reason. God knows what it is." Chelsea refused to look at her and busied herself pressing buttons on her computer.

"I changed my mind. I think we should be a little closer while we work. How about I come over there and sit in your lap?"

Chelsea put a hand up. "Don't you dare. The sooner we do this, the sooner we can do…that. Now open up your laptop and go to page sixteen."

Even though it was third or fourth on the list of activities she wanted to do right now, Fran booted up the old laptop.

❖

After an hour or two, Chelsea quietly got up and left the room. Fran didn't notice. Chelsea had made a suggestion to insert a short scene in the second act and Fran had immediately seen the benefit of it. Now she seemed to be in another world altogether as she typed like her life depended on it.

Chelsea checked on Forge, now asleep, and Petal, awake but deeply absorbed in a book. She didn't look up when Chelsea wished her good night. Bernice was downstairs watching television, available for the children while Chelsea had evening meetings scheduled, but it was Saturday night. Chelsea told her she could go. She watched Bernice's car leave and the gate close behind her, as was her habit, before returning upstairs. She discreetly locked the door again behind her.

Fran had moved the cheese plate to the desk and looked up from transferring a wedge of cheese onto a slice of baguette. "Hey. Whatever this is, it's da bomb."

"It's a triple cream from a dairy in Marin County. Women-owned." She moved to the desk and fixed herself some cheese on a slice of green apple. It was luscious—buttery and soft—the most decadent cheese she knew. "A special treat for both of us."

"The best I've ever eaten, I think," Fran said with her mouth full. After she swallowed, she said, "I'm just about done. I just want to look it over before I let you read it."

"Take your time." She stood next to Fran and plucked a deep red grape from the plate. "Grape?" She offered it to Fran, and her fingers lingered over Fran's lips as she took it between her teeth. Chelsea loved the fleeting softness of Fran's lips. She grabbed another grape. The second time, Fran was ready and captured both the grape and Chelsea's finger in her mouth, her tongue gliding over it and sending a dart of lust straight to Chelsea's core.

Fran sounded a little breathless when she said, "Do you want me to finish this?"

"Sorry." She moved behind the desk chair, beyond the range of temptation, or so she thought. She rested her arms on the back of the chair, but before she even knew what she was doing, her hands were on Fran's shoulders. She caressed and squeezed, relishing the feel of Fran's trapezius and deltoid muscles. It felt almost like a capitulation when Fran took her hands from the keyboard and sat back. Chelsea thought she heard a sigh. It was all the invitation she needed.

Her hands eased over the fabric of Fran's shirt, down toward her breasts. She cupped them quickly and then retreated. Over and over she soothed Fran's chest, swiping her hands down and up, lingering longer each time over her soft curved flesh. When she couldn't take it anymore, she finally undid those enticing buttons, registering the quick rise and fall of Fran's breathing. And there, like a gift from heaven, she looked down Fran's body at the easy, obliging front clasp of her bra. She pressed kisses into Fran's hair and temple as she undid it and separated the fabric that had been the barrier to her goal.

Fran wrapped her hands around Chelsea's upper arms, keeping her right there, but Chelsea was damned if she was going to move one inch from where she stood. Fran's skin was warm, her nipples already stiff and pointed, and she arched her back when Chelsea brought her thumbs over them. Her mouth watered as she imagined Fran's breasts in her mouth. Her shirt flapping open, Fran let go of Chelsea's arms and pulled away. She snapped her laptop shut and moved it to the extreme edge of the desk. Then she put the cheese plate on top of it. She stood and kicked the chair out of the way. "I know I should be violently sweeping everything off the desk like people do in the movies, but that cheese is too good to waste."

Laughter died in Chelsea's throat as Fran turned her around and pressed her against the desk. In a moment she had Chelsea's sweater and T-shirt off and her breasts in her mouth.

Fran looked up, her grin wicked. "My turn to be the boss."

Good God, yes. Chelsea looped her arms around Fran's neck as she made quick work of her jeans and underwear, adding them to the pile. And all of a sudden Chelsea was naked in front of Fran. How had that happened? Were they really going to do this here? "Oh my God. I want you so much right now. But we have to be quiet. The kids are—"

"You're the one who'll have to be quiet. My mouth will be busy doing other things, but it will absolutely be trying to make you scream." Fran's eyes were black with desire as she nudged Chelsea onto the desk.

Fran's words were a challenge that Chelsea was dying to accept. She wrapped her legs around Fran, trying to bring her as close as possible, and Fran's hands were everywhere, wandering over her back, kneading her thighs, pulling at her hips. And as promised, her mouth stayed busy, nuzzling Chelsea's neck and placing hot, wet kisses from her clavicle up to her ear. Chelsea grasped her face and took her lips, pushing her tongue past her teeth. Fran's tongue swirled against hers, and it was the kind of deep kissing that made Chelsea hold on for dear life. When Fran's fingers found her nipples, it was all Chelsea could do to not cry out.

Fran stuck a leg out and hooked the chair with her foot, bringing it back to where they stood. She sat down in front of Chelsea and leaned back. Her eyes were sly, and the smile that played over her lips already seemed bruised from overuse. "I'm very comfortable right now."

They stared at each other, both of them breathing heavily. It was like a break in the battle. She had no idea where Fran was going with this, and it thrilled her.

She inched closer and lifted Chelsea's left leg onto the chair's armrest, then did the same with her right leg. Chelsea couldn't be any more open to Fran, and her heart slammed against her ribs as she anticipated what was going to come next.

"Are you comfortable?" Fran asked her. "Because we're going to be here awhile. We're not leaving this room until I've satisfied you in every way I can think of, and any other way you'd like to add to the list."

Chelsea looked into Fran's eyes. There was desire there, yes, but also melting tenderness and absolute honesty, and she knew now that there was nothing in her life she couldn't trust Fran with. This wasn't just about sex. Fran cared for her, wanted to please her, and Chelsea wanted with all her heart to do the same for Fran. She leaned back and gripped the front edge of the desk. She hoped Fran could see the trust and devotion in her eyes. "We can stay here all night. Just know I'll be spending twice as much time making you feel good."

Fran's grin was all excitement and eagerness. She scooted an inch closer and leaned in, beginning a trail of kisses high up on Chelsea's inner thigh that slowly wound its way toward her mound. Instead of directing her attention there, Fran retreated to forge another path along Chelsea's other thigh. Chelsea was beginning to learn that Fran was excellent at drawing out the anticipation. When her arms reached around and anchored Chelsea in place, it was as if she were saying, *It's about to get wild now.* And she was right, because Chelsea couldn't remain still as Fran plundered every inch of her pussy with her tongue. She gripped the desk hard and lifted her hips, trying to put Fran's mouth where she wanted it, but Fran stayed maddeningly one step ahead, never lingering long enough for Chelsea to achieve release. For a moment it seemed like they were never going to sync up, and then, they locked into place—together—Fran's lips encircling her clit, and Chelsea finally finding some comfort.

But it wasn't enough. She stopped moving, and Fran raised her head. "Are you okay?" Her words were slurred, like she was drunk on sex with Chelsea.

"I need you here with me. And inside me. Please, Fran."

She immediately stood, and Chelsea held her face and kissed her. This is what she wanted, to be connected with Fran as she brought her to the heights of sensation. She put her hands on Fran's shoulders and gazed into her eyes. They glowed with a light that made Chelsea think she could see right into her heart. And then Fran entered her with two confident fingers and Chelsea couldn't believe how good it felt. Fran filled her up, physically and emotionally.

Then Fran withdrew almost completely, and Chelsea almost sobbed with frustration. But Fran's fingertips remained just inside, teasing her opening, and it felt like all the nerve endings there were begging to be satisfied. Slowly, with a hand bracing Chelsea on her lower back, Fran pushed into her again, and withdrew again, and established a rhythm that gathered in speed and urgency. Then the world swelled and burst. Chelsea clasped Fran's hand, holding her deep within her, and was carried along on undulating currents of feeling.

When the tide of emotion subsided, she let go of Fran. She gazed into eyes that were turbulent and fretful. Fran quickly unbuckled her belt and undid her fly, and said, "You're the most...I can't wait. I have to..." She pushed the same hand that had been inside Chelsea into her pants.

"No, let me, baby." Chelsea slid off the desk and shoved Fran's jeans and underwear halfway down her thighs. She cupped Fran's warm, wet heat and just savored her for a moment. "You're so ready."

"I feel like I've been ready all my life for you." Fran's whisper was edged with desperation.

Chelsea had to give her relief. She moved her fingers over Fran's pussy, between her folds, trapping her clit between them. Over and over, her fingers stroked. She took Fran's turgid nipple between her thumb and forefinger and squeezed. It didn't take long before Fran was grinding against her hand and tremors overtook her body. Chelsea held her until she was quiet. She gave her a long, lingering kiss. "How do you feel?"

A burst of breath escaped Fran as she smiled wide. "Like I can do anything."

"Before you do anything, we're going to my bedroom so I can do you again. You were so fast. I feel shortchanged."

"That doesn't usually happen." Fran gave her a bashful look. "In fact, I think that's the first time that's happened. You are pretty goddamned inspiring." Fran pulled her pants up and zipped her fly.

Chelsea watched her. Even after coming not even five minutes ago, desire rose up in her again. "I'm amazed we were able to be so quiet. My room is farther away from the kids' rooms so we'll be able to let loose a little more."

Fran's eyes went a little unfocused. "A little more? I think this is the best night of my life."

Chelsea felt absolutely ferocious. "You ain't seen nothing yet."

❖

Fran was awakened by sunlight streaming through unfamiliar windows. She turned over to behold one of the most splendid sights known to humankind. Chelsea Cartwright, her eyes closed, mouth open, and drool staining the pillow.

They had stayed up very late, taking turns architecting the other's pleasure. Both giving and receiving had left her almost giddy. She had never shared an experience as intimate and fulfilling with anyone else, ever. Was it normal to have such incredible sex so soon? The emotions brought out by their night together made Fran feel like she was living inside one of her screenplays—the actions that inspired those emotions would require an altogether different rating from the MPAA.

After writing about it time and again, Fran knew she finally felt it. It might be too soon, but she couldn't deny the way it kept forcing itself to the front of her thoughts. It made her want to do every good thing for Chelsea, and it brought her so much happiness to contemplate how she might be able to express this feeling someday.

She was totally awake. Should she leave? Chelsea had disappeared from her hotel room back in Atlanta. Maybe Chelsea wouldn't want her here when she woke up. They had been so wrapped up in each other they hadn't discussed what would happen after. Despite the urge to simply lie there and gaze at a sleeping Chelsea, Fran left yesterday's clothes on the floor where Chelsea had stripped them from her and put on the T-shirt and shorts she had thrown into her bag—just in case. She headed downstairs, thinking she could at least do something nice for Chelsea before she left.

The kitchen was quiet. She collected an armful of veggies and the roasted sweet potato she asked Forge to put in the fridge yesterday. She chopped everything up and dumped the ingredients into the blender and flipped the switch. After the ingredients were sufficiently pulverized, she turned the blender off and got the fright of her life.

"What are you doing here?" Petal stood right behind her, her voice accusing.

"Damn, Petal, you scared me half to death."

"Where's Dante? Did my mom hire you again?"

Fran waited for her heartbeat to get close to normal before she answered. "No. We're working on a project together. It got late so she said I could stay the night." It wasn't Fran's job to explain who she was to Chelsea. She wasn't even sure herself.

"I don't believe you."

"Your house has world class security. There's no way I got in here without your mom knowing about it."

"You were fired. Nobody comes back after that." She took a step closer.

"That's usually true." Petal had pretty much cornered Fran. There was no escape from the inquisition unless she pushed Petal away. *Calm. Don't let the kid get under your skin and DO NOT put your hands on her*. Fran reached for a tall glass and poured Chelsea's smoothie into it. "You want some? I made extra."

Petal's suspicion shifted to the blender. "What's in it?"

"You know your mom only likes healthy things. But it's my special recipe—no, actually it's Lorraine's special recipe."

The magic fucking words. "I'll try it."

"All righty." She considered it a win and poured a few inches of smoothie in two smaller cups. Fran was never going to be as chummy with Petal as Lorraine, but maybe she could smooth things over between them a little, especially if Fran was potentially going to be around her more in the future. "Could we talk for a minute?" She brought the two cups to the kitchen table and sat.

"What about?" Petal took the chair across from her and cautiously sipped. Then she sipped again. It was a good sign.

"I want to thank you."

❖

Chelsea woke to an empty bed. She sat up quickly. Oh no. What time was it? Had Fran left? She had meant to wake her and ask her—nicely—to go before Petal and Forge got up.

No. Her clothes were still on the floor. Maybe she was getting ready for a shower. Chelsea threw the covers aside.

No Fran in the bathroom.

Holy shit, was she wandering around the house naked? Chelsea threw on some clothes and burst from her room. *Please, please let the kids still be asleep.* Then she heard the blender.

Okay, it was sweet of Fran to make her a smoothie, but so help her, if she was doing it in the nude, Chelsea was going to kill her. She hurried back into her room for a T-shirt and sweats for Fran to put on and went downstairs.

That was Petal's voice. She couldn't make out the words, but she didn't sound happy. Shit shit shit. What if Fran was standing there with only a dish towel or a pot holder to cover herself up?

Chelsea stopped on the bottom step and listened.

"I want to thank you." Fran sounded normal and not particularly naked.

"Thank me? Why?"

Chelsea's heart twisted at Petal's guardedness, her mistrust. That was some of Chelsea's worldview rubbing off on her daughter, she was sure.

"There are a bunch of things I want to thank you for, but I guess the first thing would be—thanks for telling your mom about my old job."

"Your—But I told on you."

"Yeah, you did."

Chelsea heard the confusion in her daughter and the smile in Fran's voice. She sat down on the step and settled in to listen.

"I had been struggling a lot with how to tell your mom about my gossip-writing job. I knew I had to tell her, but I also knew she was going to be really upset with me, and I didn't want her to be upset. I wanted her to think only good things about me, and we both know that job was really not good. So you did me a favor, kind of. I didn't like the way you did it, but at least it was out there, and it wasn't a secret anymore."

Cheeto brushed against Chelsea's arm. She reached for him and pulled him onto her lap.

"I read your email." Petal's voice was low. Chelsea had to strain to hear it.

"I know." Fran's voice was forbearing.

"But I didn't tell anyone—only Lorraine. She told me to let you handle it. Then the night Daddy got sick, it just came out because I knew I was going to get in so much trouble. I wanted you to get in trouble first so Mom wouldn't have a chance to get mad about what I did."

"And that worked. I got in big trouble with your mom, and I got fired. I deserved to get fired."

"You did?"

"A lie of omission is still a lie. Do you know what I mean?"

Petal paused before saying, "Not really."

"I didn't tell your mom about my old job. Not telling her is the same thing as lying." There was another pause, and then Fran said, "You taught me something really important—how necessary it is to be honest with the people you care about. Now that I'm working with your mom again, I tell her everything I think she should know."

"I think my dad lied by omission a lot."

"You do?"

"Yeah. And I guess that's what I did whenever I texted Mr. J."

"Mr. J? That's the man you…What ever happened with him?"

"Mom and I met with the police, but they said he didn't do anything illegal. I've never seen her so mad. She yelled at them *a lot*."

"I can see her doing that. She'd do anything to protect you."

"I know." Both were quiet. Then Petal said, "Out of all of us, Mom is the only one who didn't lie. And Forge too. I can't believe what I did to them. My friend Laken said her therapist would call me self-sabotaging. My therapist never says that, though."

Silence descended again. Chelsea fought the urge to reveal herself.

"I don't know your friend or either of those therapists, but I do know you, Petal. You're a good person. You know how I know that? Because we're not as bad as the bad things we've done. And the people we love usually forgive us. And we learn from our mistakes and try to be better."

"My mom and I are cool now."

"I'm glad," Fran said. "I'm not sure what temperature your mom and I are right now, maybe lukewarm."

Chelsea almost snorted. She supposed if Fran took the moments when they were burning up the sheets together and the times Chelsea had been cold and business-like to her, the average temperature between them would be lukewarm.

"But things are getting better, I think." The hopeful tone of Fran's voice made Chelsea wince. Then Fran said, "There's something else I wanted to thank you for. Do you remember the script you read about the two soccer players? The one you liked?"

Petal's voice sounded lighter. "Yeah. It's going to be a movie. My mom is producing it."

"Guess who wrote it?"

Silence.

"Really? You did?" Petal sounded shocked.

"If you hadn't shown your mom that story, if you hadn't convinced her it was worth reading, I would not be here right now." There was glee in Fran's voice. "My dream is coming true because of you."

Chelsea heard footsteps behind her and turned. "Good morning, Forge."

After he let out a huge yawn, he said, "What are you and Cheeto doing on the stairs?"

She pulled him close and Cheeto leapt off her lap. "I love you, you know. I love Petal. I love…" Oh God, she'd almost said it.

"Cheeto?"

"Yes, Cheeto. I love you all so much." She pecked his head with kisses and he started to giggle.

"Who's out there?" Petal called from the kitchen.

"Who do you think?" Chelsea called back. "I'm making pancakes!"

❖

Fran stayed for breakfast, and even helped load the dishwasher. Then she snuck upstairs to gather her things. Chelsea was waiting for her when she came back down.

"I'm going to go. Thanks for the pancakes…and everything else. Sorry if I made things awkward by being here this morning."

"It was fine. I think Petal has some newfound respect for you."

"Maybe." Fran scrabbled for something to say. "We had a pretty good chat before breakfast. I think we reached an understanding."

Chelsea frowned. "I'll walk you out."

What had Fran said? How had she overstepped? Did Chelsea not want Fran talking to Petal? Was she annoyed that Fran had disrupted family time? Fran didn't know. She waited for Chelsea to start talking about work. It was what she did when things threatened to get too personal between them. They stopped not far from where Fran had parked. "I guess I'll see you tomorrow at Joyce's office—for the official meeting."

"Right. The official one." Chelsea gave her a distracted smile. "I thought our unofficial meeting was pretty productive."

"In more ways than one," Fran cracked. She couldn't help it. Chelsea had teed it up, and she couldn't help but take a whack at it.

Chelsea rolled her eyes, but she looked amused. "I knew you were going to say that."

"Have a good rest of your Sunday, Chelsea." She considered giving her a kiss, but then thought better of it, and backed up a few steps in the direction of her car.

"Wait."

Fran stopped.

"I heard your conversation with Petal."

"Oh. I'm sorry. I only wanted to clear the air with her—"

Chelsea stepped closer. "Don't apologize. What you said was lovely. You're making me feel awful."

"I am?" She didn't think she could hide her confusion if she tried. "I'm sor—"

Chelsea came even closer and put her fingertips over Fran's mouth. "Don't say it," she said. "I feel like I've been lying by omission too. I woke up and when I saw your clothes on the floor, I thought you were traipsing naked through the house. Of course you wouldn't do that. You're totally familiar with my life, and you're a decent, respectful human being who observes boundaries—maybe too well."

"I don't understand."

Chelsea put her hands on Fran's shoulders. "Since the day I met you, you've been honest with me in every way except one. Let me be honest with you now. The amount of time I spend thinking about you when you're not around is—well, let's just say I'm getting a lot less work done lately." She reached up and smoothed Fran's eyebrow with her thumb. "And even though I really like thinking about you, it scares me. Terrifies me, pretty much. But I can't lie by omission anymore. You need to know."

"Know that you think about me all the time?" Fran could hardly believe what she was hearing.

"Yes."

"This thinking you're doing about me—is it in relation to the movie or the script?" Fran didn't want to misunderstand.

"Sometimes." Chelsea diverted her gaze to somewhere over Fran's shoulder, but then exhaled and looked her in the eye. "There I go—lying again. No, I hardly ever think about you in terms of the script. I'm not worried about that. It's only you. And me. And things we've done together or may do together in the future. But not just sexual." Her whole face was turning red. "Please tell me to shut up."

"Not on your life. Do go on." Fran was starting to enjoy this a lot.

"No, I think I've said enough." Chelsea's sheepish expression was so freaking cute.

"Thank you for telling me." She took a deep breath. Should she say exactly what was in her heart right now? Nope. She was a big chicken. "I think about you a lot too."

"You do?"

"Of course I do." Only just about every minute of every day. She put her arms around Chelsea's waist. "Is this okay? The kids might come out and see."

Chelsea was thoughtful. "Maybe they should. What are you doing today? Do you need to go home? Can you stay awhile? Hang around with me and Petal and Forge on a do-nothing Sunday?"

"Sounds like a really good time. I wouldn't be intruding?"

"No, Franny. I want you here." Chelsea squeezed her shoulder muscles. "It's not like you have a deadline or anything."

"True. Okay, I'm in." Fran felt a little light-headed. Was this her life right now?

"Good. Oh. Before we go back inside, I have a question for you."

"Sure, what—" Oh wait. What was she...

"Will you go on a date with me?" Chelsea asked quickly, as if she wanted to beat Fran to the punch.

"Hey, that's usually my question for you."

"I know, but you didn't ask last time, so—"

"That's because you grabbed me off the street from your car and kissed me to death."

"Did not. Not to death. I'll always leave you a little bit alive." Chelsea didn't take her eyes from Fran's. "Will you?"

Was she nervous that Fran was going to turn her down? There was no way that was going to happen. "I will. I'd be delighted. Thrilled. Overjoyed, even."

The smile that came over Chelsea's face was like the sun coming out after stormy weather, and it made Fran warm all over. "How's a week from Wednesday?"

"You mean, like, ten days from now?" That seemed so far away. Chelsea didn't want to go out sooner than that?

"Yeah, and can it be a daytime thing?"

"You already have this planned out?"

"Kind of. I know it's still a ways off, but I think it'll be worth it. What about your job? Can you get the day off?"

Nothing was going to stop Fran from attending this daytime Wednesday date with Chelsea. "I absolutely can."

"Good. I'm glad that's sorted." Chelsea looped her arm around Fran's and led her back inside. "How do you feel about Marco Polo?"

CHAPTER TWENTY-SIX

A t eleven a.m. on a hot Wednesday morning, Fran waited on the sidewalk and tried not to pace. Chelsea was due in a few minutes, and even though Fran had spent a lot of time with her over the past ten days, she hadn't given away any details about their date.

Chelsea had said to dress nice, so Fran had removed the dry-cleaning plastic from her blue blazer and matched it with her best jeans and a collared shirt. She was about to go back upstairs and ask Trina if she had anything nicer she could borrow when a black limousine turned onto her block.

When it pulled up, the passenger window came down, and Chelsea appeared. "Hey there, going my way?"

Fran did an awkward pose right there on the sidewalk. "Do I look okay?"

Chelsea lowered her sunglasses and gave her a smoldering look. "Good enough to eat. Get in here."

Fran stowed the overnight bag Chelsea told her to pack in the trunk and settled in beside her. She had a daytime sophisticated lady look going on in a narrow skirt and matching jacket. The color was the exact shade of a box from Tiffany, and it suited Chelsea right down to her nude pumps. "You're gorgeous. That outfit looks like it was tailor-made for your body."

Chelsea preened. "Thank you. Since it's a special occasion, I busted out the Chanel. I wanted you to like it."

"Thank you, Coco, for giving my eyes this legit treat to look at all day." Fran gazed heavenward for a moment before giving Chelsea another head-to-toe inspection. It was unbelievable to Fran that Chelsea had dressed with her in mind. She couldn't stop staring. "If I forget to tell you later, I had a really good time today."

She laughed and pulled Fran in for a lingering kiss. "You always know exactly what to say. I missed you."

"I left at midnight last night." Fran had spent a lot of time at Chelsea's house ever since their script meeting a week and a half ago. The household seemed to have taken it in stride. Forge didn't seem to mind and even Petal was tolerating her presence. Although sometimes Fran felt she was straddling the line between wanting to be with Chelsea always and forever and not wearing out her welcome.

"That was about a million hours ago." Chelsea's hands found Fran's and held on to them.

But Fran never doubted Chelsea's affection. It had only become more open and obvious with each passing day. "Will you tell me where we're going?"

"I'll only say that the first part of what I have planned is a bit unconventional for a first date, but I'm hoping you'll enjoy it. After that, we'll veer back into more ordinary first date territory."

"Nothing is ordinary when I'm with you."

"A girl could get used to compliments like that."

"Well, I'm not going anywhere." Fran put her arm around Chelsea. "Stick with me. I'll give you more than just compliments."

"Like what? Flowers? Poetry? A new lucky hat?"

"No." Was this the moment to tell her? "Well, I can do those too, but…I wrote something. A script. If I ever got you to say yes to going out with me, I had this very elaborate plan for our date and part of it was presenting you with this script I wrote. I actually have a bunch of things on the go that I put aside for revisions to *A Love As Big As Wembley*, but this one is finished. It's called *Steadfast*. And I think it's really good. Totally outside my usual wheelhouse of putting women in situations where they have to kiss."

Chelsea sat up and faced her. "Wait. I need more information about everything you just said. But is it bad that I want to know what you planned for our date before you tell me about the script? What were you going to do?"

"I knew that going out to a restaurant was probably not going to be comfortable for you, and my place is…not suitable."

"It would have been fine. Where were we going?"

"To my job. The Prop house."

"Really?" Chelsea sounded intrigued.

"I earmarked all the stuff I was going to borrow. Everything was going to be from our inventory. We'd eat at a table that was used in *Divine Secrets of the Ya-Ya Sisterhood.*"

"Why? Does that movie have special meaning to you?"

"No, it's just a really nice table."

"Got it." Chelsea laughed. "And what would we be eating on this really nice table?"

"I went through about a hundred drafts of the menu, but my latest idea was tuna melts and champagne."

"Yum. And for dessert?"

"Not sure. Maybe some nice Jell-O. And I was going to give you a little tour, and show you some of the cool things I'd found, and then I'd show you the shovel."

"A shovel, huh?" Chelsea's expression was quizzical.

"No. *The* shovel. Used by Paul Newman in *Cool Hand Luke.* Because that's how I see this script—*Steadfast.* For ten months I sweated over it. Honestly, I poured everything I was feeling at the time into it." Fran suddenly couldn't meet Chelsea's eyes. "All the regret, and the sadness, and anger at myself—it all fueled the story."

"Aw, Fran." Chelsea lifted Fran's chin, forcing her to look at her.

It made Fran want to tell her more. "This character, she could be your Cool Hand Luke. She's tough and she's fragile, sort of mean yet noble, restless and unsatisfied and outraged. And she's a mom. She's about as multifaceted as a person can be, and utterly, utterly human. And you're the only one who can do her justice. I just know—the way you'll play her—she's going to live forever. I want to give you something as meaty—as worthy of you—as *Cool Hand Luke.*"

Chelsea pressed a kiss into Fran's neck. "You had me at Jell-O." She made Jell-O rhyme with hello.

Fran laughed, feeling something close to exhilaration. She hoped she and Chelsea could crack each other up for a long time to come. "What are you gonna do? I like Jell-O."

"So I've heard. Now I'm dying to read it. Do not show it to anyone else, please."

"It's only for you. It's a gift. Do with it what you will."

"We're going to have to talk about your business sense. You can't keep giving your work away." Chelsea kissed her again. "Can we still go on that date?"

"Now that I've told you all the surprises? You still want to have a meal with me in a dusty warehouse?" She hadn't told Chelsea all the surprises. She hadn't mentioned the view from the roof of the main warehouse, and how she would have saved that for the end, probably needing the entire date to work up the guts to say the one thing that was becoming more and more impossible to keep silent about.

"Yes, I do. It sounds magical."

"We'll have to arrange something soon. I gave my notice yesterday."

"You did?"

"I'm going all in on screenwriting and my new job as co-producer. Two is enough, don't you think?"

"As long as you still have time for me." Chelsea snuggled against Fran's chest, pulling her arm more securely around her.

"Always." Fran didn't notice the slowdown on the 405 or anything much at all for the next little while, but she did notice when they hit downtown. They passed LACMA and then made a turn onto Fairfax, and Fran's Spidey-sense began to tingle. "Are we going to the Academy Museum? I've never been."

Chelsea nodded. "You guessed it."

"I've been wanting to go. This is an awesome first date."

"Hang on, it won't be a typical visit. Just wait. We're almost there."

The limo drove by the museum's glass and concrete sphere—the city's newest architectural wonder—and joined a queue of cars depositing passengers at the entrance to its adjacent structure, the art-deco Saban Building. They entered and moved with the tide of people, all women, into a waiting elevator.

As they were whisked to the fifth floor, Chelsea caught the eye of one of their very recognizable elevator companions. "Tessa, I'm hearing great things about your project with Gina. Can't wait to see it."

A flash of a movie star smile. "Thank you, Chelsea. Can you even hear yourself with all the buzz surrounding your performance in *Tolstoy Was Right*?"

"You're sweet. Let's find each other later. I want you to meet Fran." She put her hand on Fran's shoulder.

"Hi, Fran," Tessa said. "See you out there." She sauntered out of the elevator.

"Holy shit, I can't believe she just said hi to me." Fran turned to Chelsea. "We're not going to the museum, are we?"

"No, this is the Academy Women's Luncheon, and you're my plus one." She gestured Fran out of the elevator and pulled her to the side. "I thought I could introduce you around, help you start making a few connections. I'm in your corner now, Franny. I want to be the one backing you up on your way to success—professional, personal, and everything in between." She paused, the sureness in her expression devolving to uncertainty. "But if this wasn't what you had in mind for our date, we can do something else. It's up to you."

Fran didn't think her tiny heart could hold all the feelings packed inside it right now. "You are amazingly thoughtful. I want to kiss you so bad right now, but I—"

Chelsea pressed her lips against Fran's—fierce and quick and tender. "Kiss me anytime you want. You're a part of my life now, and I kind of want to shout that out to the world."

"I love you so much." It came out on a sigh, and Fran couldn't believe she had said it, here, next to the elevators with a bunch of strangers wandering past. She squeezed her eyes shut for a second before opening them to Chelsea's reaction.

Her expression was soft, her mouth curved into a tender smile. "You look like you wish you could rewind the last five seconds."

"I do, but not for the reason you think." Fran grabbed her hand and pulled her away from all these annoying people, searching for anywhere with a bit of privacy. She saw a door marked *Cloak Room* and stuck her head in. No cloaks, no coats, and no people. She ushered Chelsea in and closed the door behind them, and then gazed at their uniformly drab surroundings. "I've written this scene with fictional characters so many times, and there's a reason I never once set it in an empty coat check. But here I am, doing it for real, and—oh boy, catch your breath, Fran."

Chelsea took Fran's hand and placed it on her chest, right over her rapidly beating heart, as if to say *I'm right here with you.*

"When I imagined telling someone I love them, I thought it would happen in some beautiful place—with sweeping vistas and a warm breeze, in sunlight or in moon glow, with a bottle of champagne chilling within arm's reach."

"Reality can't be stage managed like that."

"No, it can't. Instead of beautiful surroundings, I have beautiful you. And you are all I need. I love you, Chelsea. I've loved you for so long. No matter what happens after this moment, I'm glad I was able to say it, and mean it, with all the love in my heart."

Chelsea pulled her closer. "Do you know what I planned for after this?"

"Tell me."

"I reserved a suite at the Four Seasons, with a view and a private dinner and the champagne chilling nearby, and I was going to say the same thing."

"You were?"

"Yes. My love for you is undeniable. I'm done denying it. In the end, not anger, not fear, not even pure bullheadedness could stop me from loving you." Chelsea stepped back and looked deeply into her eyes. "I love you, Fran."

"Can we just hang out in here for a while? I want to let that sink in."

"As long as you like."

"And are we still going to the Four Seasons after this?"

"Damn right we are. Petal and Forge are both at sleepovers. You're not going to escape my evil clutches until tomorrow morning."

Fran brought both of Chelsea's hands to her lips, kissing the knuckles of one and then the other. "I see no evil clutches. Just really nice, well-manicured ones. Hey, have you ever thought of playing a villain? I bet you would tear the scenery from the walls, you'd be so good."

"Nobody's ever seen me that way, but I bet I could."

"Yeah, you could. You can do anything. I see you in all the ways, and I'm going to write a screenplay for each and every one."

"Am I your muse?" Chelsea's smile was indulgent.

"Practically since day one." Fran thought of how far they had come since those early days—how different life was now. But then a thought occurred to her. "Were you serious about shouting it to the world?"

"Absolutely. You make me so happy."

"But…"

Chelsea frowned. "But what? Tell me what's wrong."

Fran shot a look at the door. "It's not lost on me that once we walk out that door, we are coming out of a literal closet. If we go public, it will stir the entertainment press into a frenzy. Chelsea Cartwright in a relationship with a woman? Every outlet will be after you. The paparazzi will hound you again. I refuse to put your comfort and your safety at risk."

"And I refuse to live my life according to what anyone else thinks. I did that once, and I will never do it again. No one dictates who I love."

"You say that now, but think about it. Think of those times when you were surrounded by a horde of photographers. I would hate for that to happen again because of me."

"Make no mistake, Fran. It's not because of you. It's because of me. You need to think about it too. Are you willing to lose a ton of your privacy and freedom because you love me?"

"I had a front row seat to what that looks like, and I can absolutely say that if I have you, it'll be worth it. I love you, and we'll make it work. We'll figure it out." She stepped back and put a hand out. "Are you in?"

"I'm so in." Chelsea put her hand in Fran's and it felt like providence locking into place. She eyed the door. "Are you ready to go out there? With me?"

She squeezed Chelsea's hand. "There's no one else I'm doing this with. Only you." Fran took a deep breath. "We're going to crush this luncheon."

"Make it kneel at our feet." Chelsea repeated what Fran had once said to her. "And after that, we'll take this whole town by storm."

"Together? We're going to take the whole world." Fran kissed her once more before they opened the door to their future.

EPILOGUE

Two Years Later

"It's snowing again," Fran said after she heard the door open and close and the *zhuzh* of an unzipping parka. She didn't turn from the window. After so many years in Los Angeles, watching the snowfall was mesmerizing, especially with a stunning view of Park City and the Wasatch Mountains as a backdrop.

Two hands slipped under Fran's sweater from behind. Two *freezing* cold hands. "I know," Chelsea murmured. "I've been out in it."

"Holy shit," Fran yelped. "Your fingers are honest-to-God popsicles." She grasped Chelsea's hands and held them against her stomach to warm them.

"I forgot my gloves." Chelsea nuzzled her cold nose against Fran's neck. "Missed you."

"It's only been a couple of hours." Fran turned and kissed Chelsea's cheeks, pink with exposure to the cold. "How did the meeting with that director go?"

"Helen and I gave her our spiel. She was pretty tepid in response."

"Not everyone is as smart as Grace Commerford, jumping on the Propolis bandwagon the first chance she got."

"We'll see what happens." Chelsea's eyes reflected disappointment. "Her film was our second favorite here, after ours. But she's busy fielding offers for distribution. She wasn't trying to hear about what comes next just yet."

"I think it's smart to try and get the jump, though. Spread the word about the Propolis brand."

"Yeah, but everyone's waiting to see how *Woman of the Match* does."

Fran still felt a frisson of excitement when anyone said *Woman of the Match* out loud—the movie formerly known as *A Love as Big as Wembley*. "We were lucky enough to secure our distribution at TIFF. So technically, the only reason we're here is to generate buzz, and we're definitely doing that. The Sundance crowd is loving it just as much as Toronto. When I was in the coffee shop earlier, I overheard some people say they voted for it for the audience award."

Chelsea grinned. "Did that give you a tingle?"

"Multiple tingles. Massive tingles. There's plenty of other stuff in Propolis's pipeline. I know you're impatient, but you will eventually be where you want to be." She pulled Chelsea's shirt out of from the waistband of her jeans and plunged her hands down the back of her pants, simultaneously gripping her ass and pulling her closer. "And standing at the back of the Eccles Auditorium and watching people react to something I wrote—laughing, cheering, clapping"—Fran shook her head in disbelief—"it gave me every single one of the feels."

"Yeah, I'm feeling something too." Chelsea leaned in, but then withdrew. "You know you have a good chance at the screenwriting award."

"No. We're not talking about that." Fran refused to think about that as a possibility. It felt like a jinx. It was never going to happen, anyway.

"But the awards are this afternoon. Don't you want to prepare a speech—"

Fran stopped her words with a kiss. Chelsea's hands crept around her neck as she melted against her. Before it got too hot and heavy, she said, "You're the award winner of this duo. Two Oscars, and a third in the bag when people see you in *Steadfast*." The script Fran wrote for Chelsea was going into production in May, and Fran was beyond excited to see what Chelsea would do with the role. "I don't want to think about later. What I want right now is to have a little time with you before we have to go out in public again."

"That can most definitely be arranged." Chelsea pulled her toward the bed.

❖

"You ready?" Chelsea asked, shoving her gloves in her pocket after donning her parka and boots. She put on her yellow *Woman of the Match* beanie. There were never too many opportunities to publicize their movie.

Fran wore her yellow hat as well. "Let's get this parade started." They exited the room and headed toward the elevator. Their accommodation was within walking distance to the Ray Theater, the site of the awards ceremony.

Chelsea had attended the Sundance Film Festival once, early in her career, but it seemed to have changed from the relaxed, sleepy little event she had known. It was now extremely sceney, and appreciating independent film seemed to be a much lower priority than wheeling and dealing and self-promotion. It made her a little wistful for how it had changed, but as a producer, she was here to wheel and deal as well.

There were probably just as many entertainment news outlets reporting from Sundance as the bigger festivals like Cannes and Toronto, and whether Chelsea liked it or not, she needed the media now. Or rather, her business did. The success of Propolis's first release, *Woman of the Match*, partly depended on having the press on their side.

Chelsea and Fran had been riding a wave of goodwill from the public and the press ever since the Academy Awards a year ago, when Chelsea used that event's red carpet hoopla to introduce Fran publicly as her partner. And just as Fran predicted, the whole world seemed to want a piece of them. With all the attention surrounding her second Oscar for *Tolstoy Was Right*, people were curious about the woman at her side. They did one interview as a couple, but as always, Chelsea kept tight control over her appearances, so their presence at Sundance was a rare opportunity for the public to see Chelsea and Fran together. The media attention had been unrelenting, but she was willing to remain the focus of it for their movie's sake. It didn't mean she wasn't very weary of it.

"Just think," Fran said as she pressed the call button for the lobby. "This time tomorrow, Forge and Petal will be here, and we'll leave Park City and this media circus behind."

Chelsea blew a breath upward. "It can't come soon enough. You've been really good at handling it all. But then you always are." She slipped her hand in Fran's and squeezed. Fran was always outwardly calm and composed in the face of press attention, and that calmed Chelsea. Fran had become Chelsea's rock.

"What's the name of the place we're going next?" Fran asked as they stepped into the elevator. Of course, Fran knew where they were going—she was distracting Chelsea from the paparazzi scrum they would encounter in about forty-five seconds.

"Solitude Mountain Resort. We chose it because of its name."

"That's right. Now I remember. You know I've never been skiing in my life, right?"

Chelsea couldn't help her grin. "So you've said once or twice." More like a hundred times.

"I've only lived in Queens and Los Angeles—neither of which are known for their winter snow sports."

"But you're going to try, right?" The elevator doors opened onto a crowded lobby. "I'm going to teach you. You and me on the bunny slopes. Pizza for stop. French Fry for go. It's going to be so fun."

"I have no idea what any of that means. I think I'm going to meet a grisly death on Solitude Mountain."

"Don't be so dramatic. I taught Petal and Forge, and I can teach you. And Utah snow is so much fluffier and easier to land on than New York snow." Chelsea didn't let go of Fran's hand as they moved toward Helen, Grace, and Trina standing by the door.

"You mean you're going to let me fall down?" Fran's eyebrows had almost reached her hairline. "Trina, you hear this? Chelsea's going to make me fall down in the snow when she teaches me to ski. I'm definitely going to break a leg."

"As long as Chelsea doesn't break a leg." Trina didn't look up from the orange phone. "She's doing Kimmel the day after you get back."

"Nice to know where your loyalties lie, friend."

"Hey, ever since I started working for Chelsea, you've been relegated to the back seat. She's the one paying my bills, not you." Trina gave Fran a good-natured poke in the ribs. She had been on the job four months and was excellent at it.

Fran had suggested it after the last time Trina had been fired. Chelsea found Dante a place with Joyce's management company. And everyone was happy. Except maybe Fran right now as she dwelled on skiing accidents, but Chelsea knew it was a ploy to soothe her on their way to the theater. Fran was handling her, and she didn't mind at all. She barely noticed how everyone casually flanked her as they stepped out onto Main Street to a barrage of camera flashes going off.

Fran looped her arm around Chelsea's. "Now, I need to know exactly how pizza and french fries figure into ski instruction. And don't skimp on the details. Forewarned is forearmed." She ignored the pack of photographers that moved backward down the sidewalk in front of them. "Oh, are you going to carry one of those tiny barrels of brandy strapped around your neck like the Saint Bernards do in case I need medicinal assistance?"

Chelsea threw back her head and laughed. "For you, yes. I will assist you in any way you need." One thing was certain—Chelsea was going to have a smile on her face in the entertainment press tomorrow morning.

❖

Fran released her nervous energy through her right leg, which had been jiggling since the awards presentation started. Fortunately, Sundance's ceremony was a casual come-as-you-are affair, so Fran didn't have to worry about sweating through formalwear. According to her program, the screenwriting award was coming up. Yes, she had told Chelsea she wasn't bothered, told herself that awards were not a reliable marker of talent, but she didn't believe that to be entirely true.

Thankfully, Chelsea seemed to know that. She had held on to Fran's clammy hand throughout the whole ceremony so far, distracted her with tidbits of industry information and gossip, and was a general all-around calming presence. Chelsea was handling her, the same way Fran did for her sometimes. And at that very moment, Fran couldn't love her more for doing it.

"Everyone gets nervous," Chelsea whispered in her ear. At the Academy Awards last year, Chelsea hadn't seemed to need calming, had been a picture of poise and composure. But her nerves were betrayed by her viselike grip on Fran's thigh when her category was called.

But thinking about that didn't make Fran any less anxious right now. She slapped her program with the back of her hand. "I mean, the award is named after Waldo Salt. He was a genius. *Midnight Cowboy*. I'm nowhere near his league."

"Hey." Chelsea turned in her seat and looked Fran in the eye. "Do you remember when we met at Weiler's and ate tuna melts and babka?" she murmured. "Way back when?"

Fran lost every bit of her agitation. Her focus was solely on Chelsea and the memory of that night. "Yes, you gave me my lucky hat that night."

"We were talking through the script. And you said something that has stayed with me."

"I did?"

Chelsea nodded and kept her voice low. "You were struggling with the characters, and you said *what is that thing that makes it impossible for them to love anyone else.*" Chelsea leaned in. "That was the moment I stopped fighting my feelings for you. When you were thinking so hard about how to make two fictional people happy."

"It was important to know." She took Chelsea's hand. "For the story."

"I agree. And for us, too." Chelsea laced their fingers together. "I think about it sometimes. What is that thing that makes it impossible for me to love anyone but you?"

"And? What's the answer?" Fran held her breath.

Chelsea's smile turned devilish. "Damned if I know. Lucky for me, I have the rest of my life to figure it out." Her eyes flicked toward the stage.

"—*goes to Fran Underhill for* Woman of the Match!"

Fran gaped at Chelsea. "Did they just say my name?" The sound of applause seemed deafening.

"They did!" Chelsea kissed her, and it felt like Fran's entire life was wrapped up in that kiss. "Now go up there and accept your award."

About the Author

Nan Campbell's debut novel, *The Rules of Forever*, is a Lambda Literary Award winner. She grew up on the Jersey Shore, where she first discovered her love of romance novels as a kid, spending her summers at the beach reading stories that were wholly inappropriate for her age. She was, and continues to be, a sucker for a happy ending. Nan lives in New York City.

Books Available From Bold Strokes Books

Coasting and Crashing by Ana Hartnett. Life comes easy to Emma Wilson until Lake Palmer shows up at Alder University and derails her every plan. (978-1-63679-511-9)

Every Beat of Her Heart by KC Richardson. Piper and Gillian have their own fears about falling in love, but will they be able to overcome those feelings once they learn each other's secrets? (978-1-63679-515-7)

Fire in the Sky by Radclyffe and Julie Cannon. Two women from different worlds have nothing in common and every reason to wish they'd never met—except for the attraction neither can deny. (978-1-63679-561-4)

Grave Consequences by Sandra Barret. A decade after necromancy became licensed and legalized, can Tamar and Maddy overcome the lingering prejudice against their kind and their growing attraction to each other to uncover a plot that threatens both their lives? (978-1-63679-467-9)

Haunted by Myth by Barbara Ann Wright. When ghost-hunter Chloe seeks an answer to the current spectral epidemic, all clues point to one very famous face: Helen of Troy, whose motives are more complicated than history suggests and whose charms few can resist. (978-1-63679-461-7)

Invisible by Anna Larner. When medical school dropout Phoebe Frink falls for the shy costume shop assistant Violet Unwin, everything about their love feels certain, but can the same be said about their future? (978-1-63679-469-3)

Like They Do in the Movies by Nan Campbell. Celebrity gossip writer Fran Underhill becomes Chelsea Cartwright's personal assistant with the aim of taking the popular actress down, but neither of them anticipates the clash of their attraction. (978-1-63679-525-6)

Limelight by Gun Brooke. Liberty Bell and Palmer Elliston loathe each other. They clash every week on the hottest new TV show, until Liberty starts to sing and the impossible happens. (978-1-63679-192-0)

Playing with Matches by Georgia Beers. To help save Cori's store and help Liz survive her ex's wedding, they strike a deal: a fake relationship, but just for one week. There's no way this will turn into the real deal. (978-1-63679-507-2)

The Memories of Marlie Rose by Morgan Lee Miller. Broadway legend Marlie Rose undergoes a procedure to erase all of her unwanted memories, but as she starts regretting her decision, she discovers that the only person who could help is the love she's trying to forget. (978-1-63679-347-4)

The Murders at Sugar Mill Farm by Ronica Black. A serial killer is on the loose in southern Louisiana, and it's up to three women to solve the case while carefully dancing around feelings for each other. (978-1-63679-455-6)

A Talent Ignited by Suzanne Lenoir. When Evelyne is abducted and Annika believes she has been abandoned, they must risk everything to find each other again. (978-1-63679-483-9)

All Things Beautiful by Alaina Erdell. Casey Norford only planned to learn to paint like her mentor, Leighton Vaughn, not sleep with her. (978-1-63679-479-2)

An Atlas to Forever by Krystina Rivers. Can Atlas, a difficult dog Ellie inherits after the death of her best friend, help the busy hopeless romantic find forever love with commitment-phobic animal behaviorist Hayden Brandt? (978-1-63679-451-8)

Bait and Witch by Clifford Mae Henderson. When Zeddi gets an unexpected inheritance from her client Mags, she discovers that Mags served as high priestess to a dwindling coven of old witches—who are positive that Mags was murdered. Zeddi owes it to her to uncover the truth. (978-1-63679-535-5)

Buried Secrets by Sheri Lewis Wohl. Tuesday and Addie, along with Tuesday's dog, Tripper, struggle to solve a twenty-five-year-old mystery while searching for love and redemption along the way. (978-1-63679-396-2)

Come Find Me in the Midnight Sun by Bailey Bridgewater. In Alaska, disappearing is the easy part. When two men go missing, state trooper Louisa Linebach must solve the case, and when she thinks she's coming close, she's wrong. (978-1-63679-566-9)

Death on the Water by CJ Birch. The Ocean Summit's authorities have ruled a death on board its inaugural cruise as a suicide, but Claire suspects murder, and with the help of Assistant Cruise Director Moira, Claire conducts her own investigation. (978-1-63679-497-6)